NOTHING SHORT OF DEATH

The men and women who hated and feared Andrew Durant had done their work well. His marriage was ruined. His career was wrecked. His name had become a thing of contempt. His body had been brutally beaten, even his mind bore the scars of merciless pressure.

Andrew Durant was a fugitive now, alone in a world where every hand was against him, and where the least miscalculation could be fatal.

But Andrew Durant's enemies had made one mistake: they had not taken his life. And now Andrew Durant was ready to strike back . . . in a titanic struggle that would bring the modern temples of the mighty crashing down . . . and bring himself a revenge stranger and more terrible than anyone could dream . . .

Also by Taylor Caldwell from Jove

THE BALANCE WHEEL
DYNASTY OF DEATH
THE EAGLES GATHER
THE EARTH IS THE LORD'S
LET LOVE COME LAST
MELISSA
THE STRONG CITY
THERE WAS A TIME
TIME NO LONGER
THE TURNBULLS
THE WIDE HOUSE

TAYLOR CALDWELL

THE DEVIL'S ADVOCATE

A JOVE BOOK

This Jove book contains the complete
text of the original hardcover edition.
It has been completely reset in a typeface
designed for easy reading, and was printed
from new film.

THE DEVIL'S ADVOCATE

A Jove Book / published by arrangement with
Crown Publishers, Inc.

PRINTING HISTORY
Nine previous editions
Jove edition / September 1979
Third printing / June 1984

ISBN: 0-515-07864-6

Jove books are published by The Berkley Publishing Group,
200 Madison Avenue, New York, N.Y. 10016.

PRINTED IN THE UNITED STATES OF AMERICA

THE DEVIL'S ADVOCATE

FOREWORD

MY FATHER ONCE TOLD ME AN OLD SCOTTISH LEGEND which forms the basis for the name of this book: THE DEVIL'S ADVOCATE.

We Scots have long been known as a race which produces the most meticulous, eloquent and canny lawyers, and, in fact, we are sometimes designated by the English as "a race of advocates." After theology, the Scots love law, and even a Highlander however remotely situated on his mountains is an authority on local or national statutes, and can and will argue them with passionate and exhaustive interest.

A people so devoted by nature to law have many legends about it. It seems that centuries ago the Devil was incarcerated in the gaol of an obscure Highland village, charged with various crimes against humanity. No "advocate" would at first defend him, but a scrupulous judge finally appointed a lawyer for the defense. The entire hamlet was determined that the Devil be condemned, including the advocate who was a very religious man of great probity. He spent many nights in desperate prayer. How could he, while maintaining his integrity as the appointed defender of the Devil, so present the case to the jury that the Devil would be condemned?

While "defending" the Devil he must also awaken the people to the presence of evil, and its horrors, which the Devil represented. He finally hit upon a solution.

He would reveal the Devil in all his power and his terribleness and his infamy while ostensibly defending him! He would gain the admiration of his just neighbors by an open defense, and their respect when he "lost" the case. Moreover, they would learn to recognize evil forevermore when it was exposed before all eyes.

So, in court, he conducted the defense brilliantly. He subtly revealed to the judge and the jury and the assembled people all the potency and frightfulness of the Devil, by questioning the Devil and having him condemn himself by his own words. He adroitly brought out the fact to the people that the Devil would not be in their midst without their own guilt and the secret envies, sins and errors in their own hearts. He was able to lead the Devil to admit that his plot against mankind had no limits, and, at intervals, the advocate would exhort the people to "admire" such vast intelligence and wickedness. Stimulated by the advocate's eloquence and apparent defense of him, the Devil became even more excessive in his expressed hatred for the world and all in it.

The people listened with dread and guilt and fear. They remembered their sufferings under the influence of evil, and how they had contributed to the power of that evil, by way of their stupidity and their jealousy of their neighbors, and their avarice and lack of compassion.

Then the judge charged the jury. He said: "Evil is among us because we have invited that evil. We have suffered much, but we brought upon our own sufferings. The Devil would have had no power over us except that we gave him the power. We became bondsmen because we willed it; we are in despair because we brought despair to our neighbors. We died because we acquiesced in death. We were silent when we should have spoken in behalf of our brothers. For a moment's security we looked away when our neighbor was robbed. In behalf of a false peace we postponed a war with evil when we should not have been moved from our places. At every step we compromised, when we knew there is no compromise with hell. If the Devil is guilty, we are not guiltless. In his condemnation, we are included. In a judgment against him we are also judged. May God have mercy on our souls."

The Devil was condemned to eternal banishment from the hamlet. However, the "advocate," in his zeal to expose the devil, had not reckoned with the obtuseness and stupidity of his fellow citizens. They had not understood his plan at all. On the day the Devil was banished the "advocate" was hanged.

TAYLOR CALDWELL

February, 1952

THERE WAS NO SOUND OF TRAFFIC IN THE ROOM, the prisoner's exhausted mind told him. The Guards who held him let him stand a moment on the threshold, so that the brilliant lights that shattered into his bloodied eyes could further daze him. But he had no thoughts left at all, except one grim one: they can kill me, and it's all they can do. It was a thought firm and unbroken in spite of two hours of torture, that remained far back in his consciousness. The only other thought that came to him consciously was that because there was no sound of traffic from Forty-second Street outside this great and blazing room must be underground.

Then this thought, this vague and semi-conscious one, went away as he looked about him. The Guards held him roughly. His right arm had been smashed by a club; it wasn't hurting much as yet though he knew the pain would soon come. Blood was clotted on his cheek and forehead; one of his eyes had swollen shut. His legs had been beaten, and he sagged on them. He could hear his own breath, ragged and loud, in the silence of this terrible room, from which no one had ever returned alive.

Andrew Durant's head rang from the blows he had just recently received. One of his ears was deafened, and he felt a trickle of blood running down his neck. The fingers of his left hand had been cunningly burned; the agony in them was worse than the original fire. But, as he looked about the room, feeling the horrible nausea in the pit of his stomach, he was not afraid. They could do little more to him in their efforts to force him to betray his friends. He would just keep on fainting until he died, and that would be the end.

The immense room was furnished lavishly in the manner of a prince's office, like, thought Andrew Durant, Mussolini's office far back in the nineteen-thirties when that monstrous dictator had ruled Italy. His old grandfather had told him. Joseph Durant had actually seen that room after the tyrant had been murdered. He had described it to Andrew. It must have looked like this—rich carpets on the floor, magnificent paintings on the walls, glittering chandeliers dripping prisms and blades of light from the high ceiling, soft red leather couches arranged comfortably behind that enormous mahogany desk, red and green leather chairs, deep and inviting, scattered about, vases of fresh flowers on big tables, several bookcases filled with fine leather-backed books, and a white marble fireplace in which a low fire burned to keep out the damp of the spring night. Tyrants, thought Andrew Durant grimly, always arrange things for their comfort. They love ease and pleasure, the smell of fires and flowers and leather, while they urge austerity, devotion and sacrifice upon their multitudes of victims.

The room came clearer and clearer into focus. Now Andrew saw the big Guards at the door, murderous Neanderthal men in dark-green uniforms decorated with red loops of braid at the shoulders: the Picked Guards, the élite police of The Democracy, the special and pampered pets of The Democracy. Their organization had been founded by the Chief Magistrate of Section 7, Arthur Carlson, and it was under his entire control, not affiliated with the Military, superior to the Military, and contemptuous of the Military, and accountable to no one but the Magistrate. Not even the dread Federal Bureau of Home Security was so feared by the people as the Picked Guards, who were all chosen for their intelligence, their ruthlessness, and their ability to act in a crisis on their own initiative. Carefully recruited, they were given a two years' course at Government expense in order to cultivate their natural gifts of wit and cunning and intellect. Andrew looked at the Guards in this room and hated them with fresh strength. The Picked Guards, the many tens of thousands of them, were the denial to the sentiment that men of mind would eventually save America.

Then Durant no longer looked at the Guards. He saw that the room had several occupants. One was his friend, James Christian, bloody and broken as he was bloody and broken. James was sitting on the edge of a chair, his white shirt torn and red, his face almost a pulp. But James was not sagging. He was looking fixedly at the man who sat behind the desk in his dark-green uniform of the Guards. Now Durant looked at him also, and though he knew who this man was he had never seen him before. He had seen his photograph in secret, furtive places, by the spurt of a match, the glow of a flashlight, the burning of a dim lamp. This was Arthur Carlson, the Chief Magistrate of Section 7, a man whose death was endlessly plotted, a man who would one day, perhaps, die by a bullet fired by a Minute Man.

Arthur Carlson was a tall thin man in his middle fifties, aristocratic, quiet, soft-spoken and invariably courteous even to those he tortured, prosecuted or arrested. His family had been a wealthy New York one, until the third, or perhaps the fourth, World War. He had once been an editor of the New York *Tribune* and *Gazette*, and he had, from the first, written very brilliant essays deriding the Constitution of the United States as an "anachronistic document, unsuited to modern times." He had taken the Articles one by one and had disposed of them by irony, by contempt, by suave invective, by devastating derision. He had upheld The Democracy with fanaticism and fire, as opposed to the outmoded "ideal" of democratic government. Within four years he had been called to Washington and appointed Assistant Secretary of State. After the assassination, under very mysterious auspices, of the old and confused Secretary, Mr. Albert Cunningham, Arthur Carlson had been made Secretary in his stead. He had held this position for five years, and then the President, who was no longer elected by the people but elected by a captive Senate for life, had sent him to New York as the Chief Magistrate, with absolute power over the lives of fifteen million people.

He had returned to a New York which was ominously restive and muttering, with demented gangs murdering each other on the streets, with assassinations of minor officials proceeding by night and day, with crowds of maddened women screaming in the subways, with hordes surging up and down the island, armed and desperate, applying fire to public buildings and then melting away like ghosts. He had returned to New York just as one of the larger docks had been blown up, and the thunder of it had reached his ears. The city, riotous and uncontrollable, was not the place for a weak or nervous man. Arthur Carlson was neither. Within two months he had restored complete order. Except for the faceless Minute Men whom he had been empowered to destroy, the Minute Men who were springing up all over the nation, armed, swift, terrible, and without mercy, New York had been subjugated.

So, thought Durant, swaying a little in the grip of his Guards, this was Arthur Carlson, this calm and serious gentleman sitting behind his desk in his perfectly tailored dark-green uniform with the red shoulder stripes. If he was a frightful man, it was not evident. He had a long and thoughtful face, like a scholar's, with slender and well-cut features. His eyes, a deep and piercing blue, were almost gentle. His mouth, broad and thin, was stern but contemplative. He had thin blond-gray hair, so fine and so neat that it appeared painted on his skull. He had the hands of a scholar, tapering and white. He was smoking a cigaret in a gold holder, but he sat upright like a soldier, his broad flat shoulders erect and unbending. Near him sat two men in uniform, but Durant dismissed them after one glance. They were not important. Only Arthur Carlson, whom the Minute Men were sworn to assassinate, was important. The others were only officers in the Army of The Democracy, professional soldiers both stupid and nameless. Arthur Carlson changed these, these generals and these lackeys, every two months, and sent them off to conduct what was now confusedly only called the War, and replaced them with other generals. For there was always a War. There was always an Enemy, somewhere in the world, which must be crushed. That was the fixed pattern of the times.

So intent was Andrew Durant upon Arthur Carlson that he forgot even his friend, James Christian, for it had been evident, after the first glance, that Christian had not been broken. If he had, he would not have been here in this room.

The Chief Magistrate spoke, and his voice was grave and even gracious: "Andrew Durant?"

The Guards thrust Andrew farther into the room and flung him into a chair near James Christian. Andrew hardly was aware of him, so fascinated was he by this frightful man who, among all the frightful men who had enslaved America, was surely the worst. Here he was, and he, Andrew, who had taken the oath to kill him when and if he could, was unarmed, torn by torture and fire, probably doomed to die within a very few minutes.

A Guard slapped him viciously across the face. "Answer His Honor, the Chief Magistrate!" he shouted.

Andrew felt James Christian turn to him convulsively, but he did not glance at him. He just stared savagely at Arthur Carlson and did not answer.

The Magistrate shrugged, and smiled slightly. "Never mind," he said. He took up a paper on his gleaming desk, and read aloud, musingly: "Andrew Durant, Attorney. Address: 340 East Fifty-seventh Street. Educated at the American State University in Washington. Admitted to the bar. Age: thirty. Member of the Soldiers of America, in good standing. Superior intelligence. Wife, Maria, and two children, aged four and five. Recommended by the Capitol Authority as a faithful reliable citizen. Record clean of all disloyalty. Mother died resisting arrest. Father, Joseph, wanted for incitement to riot and revolution. Family of Catholic origin. No education in religion, as forbidden by The Democracy. Under the auspices of the Soldiers of America, is prospering very well, and has been recommended for a judgeship."

The Magistrate put down the paper and smiled again. "An excellent record. Only one mar: a report that Andrew Durant belongs to the Minute Men, a dangerous, subversive, traitorous organization which has sworn to overthrow the majesty of The Democracy."

He looked at Durant. "Well?" he asked gently. "I understand that you have not denied this, when presented with the facts this morning. This report states that you were not surprised when you, and nine others of your revolutionary and criminal organization, were arrested last night."

Andrew tried to speak. But he had received a blow in the mouth which had removed three of his teeth, only an hour ago, and his mouth was filled with blood. He coughed, and a dark fluid ran from his mouth. Then he could speak. "I deny nothing," he said. He turned to James Christian with bitter apprehension, but Christian gave him a smile from his broken lips. Andrew sighed, straightened a little in his chair.

"But eight of the others talked quite freely," said the Magistrate, almost with reproach. "Only you, and this other criminal, have refused to reveal the names of your other friends. The Guards are out searching for many of them now, and will doubtless find them."

"No," said Andrew. "We have a system of warnings. You won't find them."

The Guard beside him lifted his fist, but the Magistrate said, with fine disgust: "No. You'll only knock him insensible, and we wish him to remain conscious. For, Durant, you will talk. It is only a matter of time. We have your wife and children in custody."

From the very beginning Andrew had known this would happen some day. He had been warned, and had been given his opportunity to withdraw from the Minute Men. He had consulted his wife, his beloved, black-haired Maria, and she had upbraided him for his hesitation. "You have been trained for this all your life, Andy, and you dare not betray your country and your God, not even for me or the children." Yes, he had known. During the torture he had thought of his little boys and his wife, and he had prayed that his friends might take them and hide them. But the murderers had been quicker than his friends. Andrew's black eyes flickered; he bent his head and a few matted and bloody strands of his dark hair fell over his forehead. He clenched his left fist. His right was numb, but threads of pure anguish were creeping up his arm. Andrew, his head hanging, prayed for Maria and the boys, and if it was with despair it was not with weakening. What were their lives, and his, if America could be saved eventually? If he spoke, now, he might rescue them from horrible death, but America would be the lesser for his betrayal.

He turned his head and looked at James Christian, who also had a wife and three children. They had not been able to make Christian speak. Christian's eyes were shining at his friend with resolution and a mute appeal for courage.

Andrew lifted his head and spoke hoarsely: "It doesn't matter. Kill them, if you want to. Kill me, too. But I'll never speak, and you know it."

The Magistrate's face darkened, but he said nothing. Instead, he watched Andrew. He saw the hatred in the younger man's eyes, and the strength. He began to tap the table thoughtfully. At last he sighed.

"Very stupid of you, Durant. You have intelligence and fortitude. You could be a valuable member of our organization, rich, and with considerable power. I admire men like you. Devoted and loyal, even if loyal to a traitorous rabble of ignorant criminals and revolutionaries. Perhaps, during your schooling, at the expense of The Democracy, you were corrupted by some teacher of subversive inclinations, who turned you from your country and indoctrinated you with lies. We are prepared to deal very lightly with you, and your friend, Christian, here, if you'll both only come to your senses and understand what you have done to your country, and how you have betrayed her. A period of some discipline, perhaps, in a State prison, where you'll be reeducated and confirmed in devotion and loyalty to America. And then, who knows? a time of trial, and then whatever you wish."

Quiet and peace and comparative safety with Maria and the boys. A post of distinction, somewhere, where he'd be as merciful, and as careful, as possible. A house in the country. Maria hated the city. Perhaps even a vineyard, and some cows and flowers and the laughter of his children. Andrew became rigid. The laughter of his children! What children laughed these days, anywhere in America? His children would never laugh, so long as The Democracy was in power. It was for their laughter that he was prepared to die, their future laughter when America would be free. If, in his dying, they died also, it was not too terrible. They would all meet again, somewhere, somehow, out of the reach of The Democracy. And, if they did not, and there was no God, as The Democracy asserted, better endless darkness and endless sleep than no laughter, and only fear and hatred and despair.

"No," said Andrew Durant. His voice was stronger now. "I don't want my children to live under The Democracy. I prefer them to die." He added, with profound bitterness: "They ought not to have been born. But I hoped that when they were still young, all of you, all you murderers and torturers and liars and tyrants, would have been killed. If the time hasn't come yet, then I, my wife and children, prefer to die when you order it, than to live."

Again the Magistrate regarded him with a long silence. Then he stood up, and the Guards came to attention, and the bloated-faced generals, who rose with him. He went to the windows, and imperatively motioned Andrew and Christian to come forward. Andrew tried to stand up, but his legs refused to help him. The Guards dragged him to his feet, and wrenched Christian up from his chair.

The Magistrate pulled aside the rich blue draperies, and the Guards thrust Durant and Christian to the big windows. There was a small courtyard outside, lit by the moon and blinding floodlights. Eight men, sagging, half-conscious, had been bound to stakes, eight men who had spoken under torture, eight men who were Minute Men, and Andrew's friends. Twelve feet from them stood eight Guards in khaki, with upraised guns. An officer stood near by. The room was not underground at all, but soundproof.

Andrew looked once, and then turned to Christian, and received again that strong smile of courage. Then Andrew turned to the window again. The officer raised his hand, the guns roared, and the men roped to the stakes died. Clouds of smoke spiralled up to the very windows. Andrew sickened, but his swollen lips came together tightly. He prayed for the souls of those who had been weak. He felt no anger against them. It was just that some men had a threshold beyond which fortitude could not rise, no matter what their resolution. Every man had his price, and it was not necessarily money or bribes or offers of mercy. Sometimes too much sensitiveness, too much tiredness, too much hopelessness, made them betray. The hideousness of living, itself, could break a man's spirit where even torture could not. The curtains dropped with a silken heaviness and shut out the sight of the courtyard.

The Magistrate sat down without comment. The Guards threw Christian and Durant into their chairs again. The Magistrate rested his chin in his palm and looked at the two prisoners seriously. His eyes seemed to pierce them, study them, weigh them. After a long time he seemed satisfied. He smoothed his painted hair delicately.

"James Christian, professor of history, student of philosophy. You are a quiet man, Christian, and a young man. As I told you before, we have your wife and children in custody, too. You have said that it does not matter, and that you are willing to die. Durant: I warn you and your friend that neither of you shall die as easily as this. You know that, don't you? Before you die, you'll see your wives and children die, also, and it won't be quickly. You are prepared for all this?"

"Yes," said Durant, in a low voice.

"Yes," said Christian, a little louder.

The Magistrate turned to the Guards. "Clean them up at once. We don't want them to die before we make them talk. Give them fresh clothes, and some food and some whisky or coffee. Have them ready for me in half an hour."

It was ten o'clock, and a warmth and sweetness hung in the damp air, even here in this great city, for a wind blew in from the sea. But New York, at ten o'clock, had become quite silent, for it was against the law for private vehicles to be on the streets after that hour, not only for the ostensible purpose of "preserving our national resources of oil, gasoline and rubber," but for the real purpose of keeping any "subversives" from gathering together in secret places. Public vehicles were permitted to run once an hour on the main thoroughfares, such as Fifth Avenue, Broadway and the Avenue of President Roosevelt, once known as Sixth Avenue and then the Avenue of the Americas. (It was a misdemeanor to call the street by either of its two former names, particularly the Avenue of the Americas, for Washington, at that very hour, was solemnly attempting to decide which South American country would be the next Enemy, in the fifth World War.) However, even the few public vehicles permitted to run had a uniformed Country Guard on board to intimidate, by scowl or by the tentative swinging of a club, any bold soul who might be tempted to strike up a conversation with his neighbor. Casual conversations might be ambiguous, and loaded with treachery. For this reason, too, no conversations even between husband and wife were permitted in a foreign language which the Guard could not understand. So it was that public transportation was conducted in a muffled silence, even in the subways.

A long black automobile, its glass bubble-roof shrouded in black curtains, waited at the door of the large and darkened building on Forty-second Street. It was almost invisible there, for, to "conserve power in the present emergency," few street lamps were permitted to burn precious electricity. Far down the street, Fifth Avenue was only a pallid sprinkling of lights, misty in the spring atmosphere.

Andrew Durant and James Christian had been repaired physically, and each had been given a clean shirt. But no attempt had been made to splint Andrew's arm, and he understood that this was not necessary. This was his last night of life. However, one of the Guards did, and roughly, lift the hand of the broken arm and thrust it into Andrew's pocket. During this, Andrew almost fainted again. He was pushed into a chair and he was given a glass of some peculiar but very clear red liquid, which looked like wine. He drank it, numbly, and discovered it was not wine at all. It had a curious but not unpleasant taste, and it pricked on his swollen tongue. He decided it was not alcohol, even though he almost immediately felt a strong warmth spreading from his stomach to every nerve in his body. He looked up to see James Christian also drinking a glass of this fluid. Poison? Probably not, thought Andrew, somberly wishing it were.

When the two young men were brought back into the enormous warm office of the Magistrate, they found Arthur Carlson there alone except for his two Picked Guards. He nodded at the prisoners, as if satisfied. He glanced at one of the Guards and said, briefly: "Dickson and Tyre have been called?" When assured by one of the saluting Guards that the men mentioned were waiting in the hall outside, the Magistrate nodded again. Then he looked at Durant and Christian.

"This is your final opportunity," he said, in his kind and indifferent voice. "Has either of you changed your mind?"

They did not answer him, but they stared at him with hatred. The liquid they had drunk had given them some strange courage and assurance.

"Well, then," remarked the Magistrate, as if with regret, "I must take you away. The windows of my car are not covered. Look your last at the city, for, I am afraid, neither of you shall ever see it again."

Christian spoke, then: "We don't want to see it again, so long as you, The Democracy, are in power. You, all of you, have made this country so foul and bestial, and have so degraded it almost beyond hope, that it is impossible for a decent man to live in it. We know the suicide figures, Arthur Carlson. We know that at least eight thousand American people kill themselves monthly, not in prisons, and not under actual threat of your State Police and Guards, but quietly, in their own homes, because your kind has made the whole world, and not only America, too horrible to bear."

The Magistrate was amused. "Yes, weaklings," he said. "Not fit for the brave new life we have established, where each has according to his needs, and each must work for his country." He added, sternly: "If I hadn't known you for a traitor before, Christian, I'd know it now. Your revolutionary Minute Men would destroy our war effort overnight and make us defenseless against our enemies."

"What 'enemies'?" asked Durant, with passionate contempt. "We conquered Russia in the third World War, and even if she's smashed and has retreated behind her ruined cities, and even if she's still malignant—like you—she's no threat to us any longer. We can't, any longer, build up Germany and Britain so we can fight them again, as we did in the fourth World War. They haven't the strength for it now. Who's next, on the list of 'enemies'? Brazil, Argentina, Chile? How long do you think it will take until we have armed them so that we can fight them? Yes, we always have a 'war effort'! Tyrants are perpetuated by war. I understand politics and economics, too."

"And how long," asked Christian wearily, "are the American people going to be able to arm and then fight 'enemies'? How long can they stand this?"

"For a long time, I believe," said the Magistrate, smiling. "How long do you think, for instance?"

Neither of the prisoners answered him, so he replied to his own question, musingly: "They've stood it for fifty-three years, without any particular complaint. There was some slight agitation about ten years ago when we annexed Canada and Mexico, but that died down within a month. With our assistance. No, the American people have never complained about war, for the very simple reason that they, like all other peoples, enjoy it, even if it has deprived them of what they used to call their 'liberties.' Give a nation war and she'll be only too happy to surrender the sentimentality of freedom. You know your history, don't you?"

The two huge Guards at the door listened impassively, gazing straight ahead as though of iron and not of flesh and blood.

History, thought Christian. The history of the tyrants is always more vivid than the history of the saints and the heroes and the men of good will. The tale of a soldier is always more interesting than the tale of a martyr. Men prefer to read of the crimes of a murderer rather than the deeds of a virtuous man. Was there something fatally wrong, fatally evil, at the very center of the human soul, something so monstrous that it can never be torn out or prayed away? Who heard the name of Christ these days? Was this, and all the agony and despair and torment in the world of today, the result of that awful flaw in the human spirit?

A sick hopelessness came to James Christian, then.

"I see you're thinking," said Magistrate Carlson. "I like intelligent men, even if they are enemies of America, and traitors to their people. If you'd not become corrupted and twisted in your thinking you could have gone far with us, Christian."

"Far into hell," said Andrew Durant.

Christian glanced at him quickly, and smiled. Only a few left in America. But those few could become mighty. How could he have forgotten all those thousands of men and women all over America, who, in thousands of hidden places, were speaking nightly to the confused and desperate and lost and enslaved? They were very often found, these dedicated people, and murdered, but where one fell ten more sprang up as if from the ground itself! He and Durant would die, probably within an hour, just as the other eight had died. But eighty would take their places. And eighty times eighty, tens of thousands of times over, until America was free again.

"I think my car is waiting," said the Magistrate courteously. He pointed to the door, and one of the Guards opened it. Durant and Christian, exhausted and silent, passed through it. There was a long white hall outside, barren and cold, and at every ten feet a Guard stood, wooden and sightless, with a gun in his hand. There were two other men, also, not in uniform, but armed. The prisoners looked at them dully. They appeared to be of the Magistrate's kind, urbane, quiet and aristocratic. They were aware of the prisoners, but in the manner of gentlemen aware of mongrels. But they smiled and bowed as Arthur Carlson stepped into the hall, and they moved into place beside Durant and Christian with an air of distaste.

They all marched down the hall. Durant's broken arm had become one long anguish of fire. He clenched his teeth. He had withstood the torture in the cells of this building. It would be ironic if he should suddenly begin to scream about his arm. Christian's shoulder brushed his left shoulder comfortingly, and all at once the pain was easier to bear.

In silence, they emerged into the street, where six Picked Guards were on duty near the door. The warm wet air struck the faces of the prisoners, and suddenly everything that had taken place was less dreadful than this scent of freedom. Men who are about to die, thought Durant, should never be allowed to see the sun or feel the air or look at a moon like this. It makes their suffering the more intense.

A Guard opened the door of the long black car, and one of the strangers who had waited for the Magistrate entered. Christian and Durant followed. A seat was pulled down and the other stranger sat in it. They held their guns in their hands. In the front seat sat a stiff, uniformed driver, and a Guard. The Magistrate was seated between them. The car rolled down Forty-second Street to Fifth Avenue in the silence of the muted city.

The two Picked Guards stood alone in the office of the Magistrate. They heard doors closing, and they knew they were alone. It would be midnight before they were relieved. The larger of the two shifted a foot restlessly. He did not know the other Guard even by name, but his movement caught the other's eyes. He fixed it upon his fellow, just slightly turning his head.

The first Guard moved his gun, as if it had grown somewhat heavy. The other watched him alertly. The first man moved his gun to his left arm, and sighed, glancing hopefully at the gilt clock on the fireplace. Then, very casually, with the index finger of his right hand he scratched his right ear. The other man continued to watch him, and now his eyes sharpened.

The first Guard yawned elaborately, studied the clock for another moment, muttered: "Only a minute." He paused, then went on: "You just watch the clock and it moves only a minute!" The second Guard smiled briefly. He, too, shifted his gun to his left arm. He scratched his ear as the other had done. He scrutinized his finger thoughtfully. The first Guard watched him as he had been watched by the other. "Only a minute," said the second Guard, and he lifted his right finger up and out.

"But time runs out, minute by minute," said the first Guard. "We'll be relieved at midnight."

They looked at each other and smiled. They shifted their guns to the prescribed position and stared before them, not speaking again. But they were not Neanderthal men, now.

Because of the wars, there had never been enough money during the past twenty years to repair the streets, or to erect new buildings except Government ones. Consequently, Fifth Avenue was a pock-marked mass of large and small craters, filled, now, with water from the recent rain. These black mirrors reflected the wan and feeble light of the occasional street lamps and shattered fragments of the moon. The proud shops and theatres of two decades ago had degenerated into formless heaps of decay, for there were no luxury goods any longer and few people, even those most overcome with despair, would attend The Democracy theatres which droned endless indoctrination on the stages in the guise of "plays." (Government employees, and they were multitudinous, were "encouraged" to attend regularly, but even these could not support a depraved theatre.) The great moving picture houses displayed a few pale lights, but Hollywood had long ago become part of the Department of New Education, and the products offered to the people were so devoid of all laughter, all artistry, all human interest, that they squealed and shouted and blazed the prescribed sentimentalities to empty seats.

The Empire State Building, the Chrysler Building, Radio City, and many other magnificent buildings of New York had been converted to Government use. All other buildings looked blindly at the moon like huge, dead monuments, so that the Government towers among them resembled spires of light. Behind their windows the thousands of evil ants plotted and toiled sleeplessly, their faces fixed and fanatical, their hands busy with files and telephones and mountainous heaps of paper. From their countless offices gushed new "directives," new restrictions, new oppressions and new cruelties, hour after hour, like some sinister and poisonous stream.

The Magistrate's car rolled very carefully up Fifth Avenue, for the treacherous, water-filled craters could easily destroy a hasty tire or wheel or break even the best of springs. Only an occasional bus could be seen, dimly lighted, with the cowering passengers huddled in their seats. There was a soundlessness in this city which had been full of sound. It had been silenced as if by a marauding plague. There were some people moving on the sidewalks, but they, too, were almost speechless. Their footsteps shuffled on the broken walks and echoed like a hopeless army in retreat. The dark windows which they passed reflected their silence masses as ghosts might have been reflected, featureless and amorphous and unreal.

Andrew Durant, watching them grimly through the windows of the car, saw that, as the clotted groups passed under any revealing light however pale, each man or woman was careful to bend his head and compose his features into the proper expression of these days: docility and submission. Some of the people moistened lips and set them into obedient patterns. Some of them appeared to be shrinking into their shabby clothing, as if to escape censorious eyes. They trudged on, no one exchanging a word with his neighbor, carefully stepping over broken curbs, hurrying, here and there, like animals looking for shelter.

Perhaps it was his knowledge that he was soon to die that made Andrew look at the people so sharply and with such sudden detestation. Those older men and women, those men and women of fifty and over: what had made them betray America when they were young? In the days when America had still been a free nation, their parents must have taught them the long traditions of freedom and pride in their country. Their teachers must have taught them, and their ministers, their rabbis, their priests. The flag must have meant something to them, once. The Constitution of the United States, the Declaration of Independence: surely there were some among them who remembered! Why had they, then, allowed the Constitution to become outlawed? Why had they averted their eyes when its Articles, one by one, had been eaten away by the rats? Had there not been a single hour when they had revolted like men in their hearts, and had raised their voices in protest? Had there not been one brave soul among them, one virile soul, one American soul?

Dazed by pain and grief and anger, Andrew tried to remember what his father had told him. He tried to remember what he had been taught, by his father and his priest, of the long iniquity of Washington. There was 1945, when Russia had been hailed by Presidents and Generals as "our noble Ally." That was after the second World War, was it not? Yes. And immediately after those days of war Washington had lent many millions of dollars to Russia, had "leased" her fleets of ships, had sent her millions of tons of food. Then there had been some sort of a Plan, which had sent countless billions of the American people's money to Europe, for rehabilitation. The American people had been taxed into misery for this Plan, which had been used, to a great extent by the recipients, to arm Russia. The many other "noble" allies of America had done a fine and roaring business with Russia, especially those with Socialist governments. The atomic bomb had been presented to Russia by American spies who had had access to American secrets. All this had been done with full knowledge of its significance. Yes, with full knowledge of its significance!

Then, when the hour had come, Russia struck, not at her friends who had armed her with the money of the American people, but at America, herself. And in that hour, the "noble allies" had frantically declared themselves neutral, in spite of the United Nations.

But long before that time, Andrew's father had told him, the degeneration of the American character had begun. All the violence of wars, all the cynical crimes committed against America, had been only the visible flowering of the innate disease which had long before devoured the strength of the American people. The car rolled on, in utter silence, and Andrew tried to remember. He was not only unconscious of James Christian beside him in the car, but of the Magistrate, the car itself, the people on the streets outside.

Yes, he remembered now. America had given up her freedom, which had made her strong and powerful and great, even before the second World War. She had watched that freedom erode, from the early thirties on, and she had done nothing. It had begun so casually, so easily, and with so many grandiloquent words. It had begun with a loathsome use of the word "security." And in the name of that fantasy, that dream-filled myth, American pride, responsibility, grandeur and strength, had been systematically murdered.

What manner of men had lived in those days, far back in the thirties, who had so eagerly surrendered their sovereignty for a lie and a delusion? Why had they been so anxious to believe that any government could solve problems for them which had been pridefully solved, many times over, by their fathers? Had their characters become so weak and debased, so craven and so emasculated, that offers of government dole had become more important than their liberty and their humanity? Had they not known that power delegated to government becomes the club of tyrants? They must have known. They had their own history to remember, and the history of five thousand years. Yet, they had willingly and knowingly, with all this knowledge, declared themselves unfit to manage their own affairs and had placed their lives, which belonged to God only, in the hands of sinister men who had long plotted to enslave them, by wars, by "directives," by "emergencies." In the name of the American people, the American people had been made captive.

It was not the many wars, then, thought Andrew Durant, and the exigencies of those wars, which had made America captive. The wars grew out of the weakness of the people themselves, out of their disease and their fantasies. If they had not been mad in the very beginning there would have been no wars, for there would have been no tyrants raised up and supported with their own money and their own work. They would not have lent all their energies, their lives and their hopes, into the creation and then the demolishing of "enemies," into the searching for new enemies after the last had been subjugated. They would not, finally, have become the slaves of an all-powerful government in Washington, slaves of a monster they had fabricated in their demented dreams.

Even when the Republican Party had been outlawed and declared "subversive," the people had refused to see what there was to be seen. Even when the American Communist Party had suddenly joined forces with the party in power in Washington, and had supported it with shouts of joy, the people would not see. But it was too late, then. The disease had shown itself with all its fatal symptoms. The men with brave voices had been silenced, had been imprisoned, had been driven into exile, had been tormented to death.

But the disease which had stricken down the American people had stricken down Europe, also. The whole world was diseased, except for the South American nations. And they had made their continent an armed camp, their eyes watching America with mingled disgust, fear, and resolution. They knew that some of them were, even at this hour, being weighed and measured in Washington as potential "enemies." America might be prostrate, hungry, desperate, filled with terror and despair. But she had always the strength for a new and maniacal war which would perpetuate her tyrants and prevent her people from revolting. All unions had been outlawed, many years ago. The people worked, staggering with exhaustion, in war factories, on the farms, for twelve hours a day, seven days a week, to maintain the gigantic war machine which the oppressors had created. They worked in numbness and in silence, like beasts.

Andrew looked at the speechless crowds on the sidewalks, and hated them. He thought of the Minute Men, who had dedicated their lives, and the lives of their families, to these hundreds of millions of animals who had lost, not only their minds, but their spirits. The Minute Men were like a few sane souls in one vast prison of madmen. They believed that sanity could be restored to this continent of murderers, bureaucrats, slaves, soldiers and robots. They believed that America could again be free.

But America was not worth the Minute Men, thought Andrew. She was not worth the life of a single one of them!

The Magistrate in the front of the car turned his head graciously, and asked: "Did you speak, Durant?"

I have only to say one word, thought Andrew, sweating and aching, and they'll let me go. They'll release Maria and the boys, and I could work for The Democracy. One word, a single word. What was this debased people that he should die for them, and his wife and children, also? Somewhere, he might find an island of peace, a refuge.

James Christian turned his head and looked at Andrew, and Andrew saw his face, calm, gentle and comforting, in the light of a dimmed street lamp. Andrew saw his eyes, strong and eloquent. Christian was a young man, too, and he, too, had a wife and children. He had looked at these faceless masses on the street, and he had not hated them. He had pitied them. He was prepared to die for them.

"Did you speak, Durant?" repeated the Magistrate, in an interested voice.

Andrew looked at the passing people. Now, here and there, he saw a head that was not bent, a face that did not move itself into an expression of submissiveness. A young face, a tired but thinking face, a brooding face. Only a few, but they were there.

"No, I didn't speak," said Durant. James Christian, beside him, sighed, and his shoulder touched his in understanding and consolation.

The black car crept up Fifth Avenue, weaving from side to side to avoid the holes in the pavement. Just ahead, Durant knew, were the ragged and unkempt fringes of Central Park, where, during the day, starved children listlessly played, desolated women crouched on broken benches, and derelicts of all sorts skulked, ate, and slept at night. Decades ago it had been a place of beauty and refreshment. Now it was little more than a refuse-filled jungle, dangerous by day and desperate from the first moment of darkness, its paths overgrown with weeds, hundreds of its trees dead, its ponds choked with old papers, broken branches and garbage.

At some signal which the prisoners did not catch, black curtains suddenly rolled across the car windows. Durant was startled from his somber revery by this. Why should their destination be hidden from him, and Christian, when within an hour or so they would both be dead? Involuntarily, he spoke: "Why did you do that?"

The Magistrate replied, tranquilly: "For obvious reasons."

Durant, in astonishment, tried to see Christian's face, but the meager light filtering in from the front showed him nothing. However, he had also felt Christian's start of surprise. Durant leaned back, more and more confused. His arm pulsed and flamed with pain, but he almost forgot it. Once more, he tried to see Christian's face. The car began to turn, drove on for a space, turned again, then seemed to be doubling back. The driver muttered: "No one." The Magistrate nodded.

Then the car stopped. The doors were opened, and Durant saw the uniforms of the Picked Guards. The street outside was very dark and empty, though Picked Guards strolled, armed and alert, along the deserted sidewalks. Only a vague street light here and there showed the glint of guns; it was so silent that the footsteps of the Guards echoed back from the blank fronts of buildings. Durant and Christian tried to guess where they were, but it was an unfamiliar neighborhood. The big hands of the Guards reached in for them, and to Durant's further confusion, the hands did not seize him roughly. The Magistrate said, in a low voice: "Careful. He has a broken arm." Durant was then helped from the car with gingerly consideration. Christian was already on the walk, and now Durant could see his face, and his blank amazement. They both looked at the gloomy house before them, which was very closely guarded, and the sightless windows. A Guard held Durant's uninjured arm, and helped him across the broken walk. Durant glanced at the Magistrate and the three strange men who had accompanied them, and they were smiling slightly. Then, the Magistrate leading, they went up the broken steps of the house, quickly and silently. A broad door opened, and Durant saw the Guards again, and the wide, high hall of what had once been a mansion. A dim blue light flickered from the plastered ceiling. Stumbling a little, and bemused, Durant saw the door shut swiftly behind them. A Guard opened an inner door, and the two prisoners were pushed, almost gently, into the sudden white blaze of what appeared to be a small operating room.

Two men, in the white uniforms of physicians, stood up at once. Dazed, the prisoners looked about them. They heard the door open again, and shut, and they were alone with the white-clad men, one of whom was elderly, and two Guards. An operating table stood in the center of the immaculate room, and there was a tank of anesthesia and the usual paraphernalia of a surgical clinic behind glass doors.

The doctors smiled at the prisoners, not professionally, but with friendliness. The younger lifted a chromium bottle and poured its yellow and sparkling contents into two glasses. Bewildered, the prisoners took them. "Drink it," said the older doctor, nodding his head. "It'll refresh you."

Durant stared at the operating table. Diabolical means of torture? That did not matter, either. There was a limit to human capacity. The two prisoners drank the liquid; it was strong and almost hot on their tongues and in their throats. Instantly, a sense of invigoration came to them.

"Sit down, please," said the older doctor, all briskness. He picked up a pair of scissors, and while Durant watched him, stupefied, he gently cut away the clothing from the broken arm. Now it was exposed, in all its swollen and purple injury. The doctor frowned, shook his head. He nodded to the Guards, who lifted Durant to the operating table, and then forced him into a lying position. The younger doctor was examining Christian's wounds very carefully.

The older doctor motioned to a Guard, who instantly clapped a mask over Durant's face. He struggled against it, pushing it aside with his left hand. His hand was caught. For one moment he stared up at the face of the doctor. "What?" he cried. The doctor said reasonably: "How are we going to set that arm without an anesthetic? Or would you rather I do it the hard way?" The mask was firmly placed over Durant's face again, and he was at once choked by the fumes of some rapid gas. His senses floated off into warm darkness, in which sparkled one brilliant star of disembodied pain.

He began to dream. He dreamt that Maria was standing over him, kissing him and weeping; he dreamt that he heard the voices of his children. He felt the touch of Maria's hand on his cheek, the warmth of her hair on his face. Then, abruptly, she and the children were gone, and loud sounds battered against his ears, confused sounds as of great voices. They subsided to a murmur, and he opened his eyes.

He was still lying on the operating table, but the pain in his arm had gone. Through a mist, he saw that it had been splinted and bound. There was a prick in the flesh of his left arm, and the mists melted away, and he felt a surge of well-being and strength. He looked for Christian, who was well patched, and sitting near by. A Guard helped Durant to a sitting position, and he saw the smiling faces of the doctors and the Guards.

"Feeling better now?" asked the older doctor. Durant could not reply. He was helped off the operating table, and to his greater astonishment, he discovered that the anesthetic had left no effect on him. A Guard was opening a rear door, and he motioned to the prisoners with his head. More and more astounded, Durant hesitated, put his hand to his face. It was wet, and then he remembered his dream. Trembling, he followed Christian into the next room, which was white and bare, and contained only a table and some chairs. On that table was set a tureen of steaming soup, coffee, bread and butter, and some cold slices of meat. The Guard said: "You have half an hour."

The prisoners fumbled for chairs, and, stupefied, looked at each other. The Guard repeated, patiently: "Half an hour. And no talking, please." Durant turned to him abruptly. The Guard's face was large and quiet and noncommittal. Durant then looked at the table. Christian was ladling soup into a bowl for him, and the other man awkwardly picked up a spoon with his left hand. All at once they both discovered that they were extremely hungry, and they began to eat with ravenous haste.

The Guard watched them eat, thoughtfully. He saw the two men exchanging eloquent and bewildered glances. He hooked his fingers in his belt and moved restlessly. He asked: "How is the arm? Better?"

Durant turned to him again, and asked rapidly: "Why was it set? Why are we being fed?"

The Guard smiled. "You have ten minutes more," he said. For the first time Durant noticed his voice, strong and interested, and even sympathetic. The Guard came to the table and lifted the heavy pot of coffee and carefully poured the hot brown liquid into the mugs. "Five dollars a pound," he said, reflectively. "When did you last drink real coffee?"

In his stupefaction, Durant could find nothing to say. Then it came to him that this was the part of the plot. He was to be reassured, he and Christian, and led into some trap. He frowned at his friend, and shook his head warningly, and lifted the mug to his lips. The taste was delightful to him, recalling childish memories of his father's house, and his mother's kitchen. His father, who had probably been murdered, his mother who had died of grief! He put down the mug, and for the first time tears came into his eyes. He saw Christian regarding him sadly.

"Time's up," said the Guard briskly. He opened a door and the prisoners saw the hall again, outside. They followed the Guard into the hall, and then to its rear. The Guard flung open a door, and there before the two men was what had originally been the drawing room of the mansion, lofty, high-ceilinged, intensely lighted and warm. But all windows had been removed, and instead there was a whisper of warmed fresh air circulating through ducts.

There was a dais like a speaker's stand at the end of the room, and below it a long table and a number of chairs. Behind the dais stood two great flags.

"Look!" cried Durant, stopping suddenly on the threshold and pointing with an agitated hand. Christian cried out, also, and then, they stood, staring, unable to believe. For one of the flags was the old lost flag of the United States of America, rippling in all its ancient splendor of red and white bars and shining stars, the old flag which had been abolished twenty years ago in favor of the debased rag of The Democracy of America, bloody of background and having on it only one bloated white star. At a little lower level, gently fluttering, stood the flag of the Minute Men, white background, blue shield on which was imposed a snowy crescent moon above two crossed rifles.

The two prisoners, after their first exclamations, stood petrified and unbearably agitated. The Guard passed them and drew out two chairs from the table. "Sit down," he suggested. Stumbling, their eyes still fixed on the flags, the prisoners went to the seats. Then the Guard moved to the single door and stood there, looking at the flags also.

A trap? Durant turned impetuously to Chrisitian and could not restrain his voice: "The flags! What are they doing here? Where are we? What is all this?"

Christian said thoughtfully: "I think I am beginning to see. But why did they kill our eight friends?"

Durant moved his splinted arm a little. "Why did they set this? Yes, why did they kill all those—" He shook his head over and over. "It must be a trap."

"For whom?" asked Christian. "Not for us, surely. They knew we'd never speak."

"They think we will," said Durant grimly, "with this masquerade." He again fixed his eyes on the flags and all at once something broke in him with unbearable pain. The flag of the United States of America, destroyed as completely as the Constitution had been destroyed and defamed and befouled! It fluttered in a fresh blow of air from the ducts, and seemed to lift itself proudly, a thing which lived, a thing which had not been killed after all, in spite of the edict which had made it a grave criminal offense to have even a photograph of it in one's possession. How many children knew there had once been such a flag over a free nation? How many tens of thousands, yes, millions, of young men had died under the monstrous flag of The Democracy of America, and had never known these bars, these wonderful stars, this flow of shining color and majesty? Durant's head dropped on his chest, and his black eyes became blinded with tears.

He heard the door open and several men, headed by the Magistrate, entered the room silently, and without a glance at the prisoners. Durant heard their quiet footsteps but did not raise his head. Then he heard Christian exclaim in a muffled voice: "Look! It isn't possible."

Durant blinked. The Magistrate was on the dais, the flags moving behind him. Then men who had accompanied him were seating themselves at the table, all about the prisoners, and facing the Magistrate. Durant looked at them, and it was like gazing at the dead, for he had believed them dead. There was his father, younger and stronger than he had been in Durant's memory, and there was Father Vincent Martin, who had allegedly been executed for insisting upon teaching children their ancient religion, and there was Professor Alan Williamson, who, three days before his "death," had dared to read the proscribed Constitution of the United States to his graduating class at Columbia University, and there was Dr. Herbert Vogelsang who had been taken into custody at Yeshiva College for reciting the Declaration of Independence in full to his students.

"Papa! Father Martin!" whispered Durant hoarsely. But they did not speak to him, though he half started from his seat. They only regarded the Magistrate intently and waited for his first words.

Christian, too, had recognized old friends and relatives among those twelve men, men whom he had believed dead. He said nothing, but tears began to roll down his cheeks, and then he sobbed aloud. He touched Durant's shoulder, and pointed. All the men wore the insignia of the Minute Men on their sober black coats, a small gleaming flag in blue and white enamel. And then Christian pointed to the Magistrate, who also wore the insignia.

The Magistrate looked down at them all gravely, slightly smiling. He included Durant and Christian in that long, slow glance, and then he finally looked only at them. He was Arthur Carlson, the murderous officer of the tyrants who had captured America, but he was also Arthur Carlson with the blue and white flag of the Minute Men pinned like a heroic medal on his chest.

"Durant, Christian," he said, and his voice was strong and firm. "We who are about to die salute you, who are also about to die. Perhaps we shall not die tonight, or tomorrow, or next week, or next month, or even next year. But we shall die. There is not a man here in this room who is not a brave man, an American, but he shall die. For America. You two have shown yourselves worthy to be in this company. Had you not been worthy, you would have been shot with those eight friends of yours, who did not have the final fortitude to face death without betraying comrades. They were good men, honest men, American men. But they were not, at the last, Minute Men."

Durant and Christian could only regard him with amazement, though Christian nodded once or twice as if confirming something to himself.

The Magistrate turned, then approached the Stars and Stripes. He knelt and reverently kissed the flag. He got to his feet, stood before the flag of the Minute Men of America. Every man stood up with one movement, and Christian helped Durant to rise. The Magistrate saluted the blue and white flag, and each man saluted also, even the Guard at the door, in his uniform. Then the Magistrate approached the edge of the dais again, and all sat down, still watching him in silence. There he stood, his hateful uniform redeemed by the insignia on his coat, and his face became hard and brilliant under the strong light above it.

"We are desperate men in a desperate cause," he said. "There can be no squeamishness or terror or selfishness in us. That is why we kill the weak, who would betray us and our enslaved country, and why we sift out the heroic men and bring them to us. We dare not do otherwise, for we have only one goal—the saving of America. We are, each and every one of us, the Devil's Advocates, for each one of us must wear the uniform of the murderers and in their name oppress, oppress and oppress, until the people can no longer endure us and must kill us and remove their chains. There is no hope for us, either from our enemies or our friends. There is no promise of life for us, for we shall be killed by enemy or friend. We have only our knowledge that America shall be free, and we shall die in the freeing of her."

It seemed to Durant that there was only one voice in the world, and that was the voice of Arthur Carlson. He could hear himself panting, and he swallowed painfully.

"You, Durant, and you, Christian, shall have other names from this night henceforth, and you shall forget your old names and your families, and these men who are with us tonight. Neither of you shall see each other again, except by accident, and you must not recognize each other. Not one man in this room knows what the other man is doing. and he shall not know. You two will be given your orders tonight, but you will not know where the other is sent. I offer you nothing but your duty. Hope for nothing but your country. Live and die for nothing but your country."

His eyes sparkled like blue fire as he watched the two men sternly. "The uniform of The Democracy is the uniform you will wear to the day of your death. You will die in it. You will be buried in it, either by The Democracy, or by your friends. There will be no honor for you in life, and no honor for you in your graves. For we, the very heart of the Minute Men, must forget you as you will forget us. America, when she is free, will remember you with loathing and hatred, and that will be good. For in the remembering of all of us she will, perhaps, never again permit herself to be chained.

"I know where each of you is, and where you will be, but no other knows except one man in Washington, who is my father and the best friend of the President. Prepare, then, for your death. For there is no escape for any of us."

Durant stood up, and Christian stood beside him. The men about the table did not turn to look at them, but the Magistrate waited, and for an instant, only an instant, his eyes were compassionate.

"Our children. Our wives," said Durant.

"They are safe. They have already been taken to safety," said the Magistrate. "Within a few days they will be thousands of miles away from this city, and will have other names. You must forget them."

Durant thought of his dream. It had not been a dream at all! Maria had been with him for a brief moment. She knew he was not dead. He turned dumbly to Christian, and Christian smiled and nodded. "Yes," said Christian.

Durant looked at his father, at his old friends, but he saw only their grave profiles. They were with him in this room; they could not speak to him and he knew he could not speak to them. He and Christian sat down again, and waited.

"From this night on you are the trusted servants, officers and magistrates of The Democracy," said Arthur Carlson. "Wherever you are sent, you will have your orders to oppress and suppress, to torment and to destroy. Exceed your orders, out of excess of zeal! Drive the people over whom you will have authority to distraction and complete despair. Have no mercy, because upon your mercilessness depends the freedom of America. When the people finally arise, out of new courage or new wretchedness, your work will be done, and you shall die."

The Magistrate stopped speaking, and the silence in the room became intense. He stood on the very edge of the platform, and now it was as if he gathered up and into himself every personality and fused it into one single purpose, one dedication. Each man looked at him as at a hypnotist. There was no vivid color about him, except for his eyes, full of blue power and profound and steady concentration. Yet, there was nothing of the fanatic about him, no trace of the evil which is in fanaticism, and which had reduced almost all the earth to slavery. Durant and Christian knew that here was a man who had no future, and had given his life without question or doubt to his country. They were aware that he had renounced marriage and children for himself. They now understood that he had done this for faith, as the saints had renounced the world for their faith, also.

I have done what I could, thought Durant, but what I've done is nothing to what he has done all the years of his life. I've had some comfort and love but he has had nothing. No, I am wrong. He has had, and has, everything. He is like a priest, who has turned away from the world for a greater love and a greater dedication. How many men are there like him, in America? If there are only a hundred, it might be enough! He has chosen us to help him, because he believes in us. He's called us to his faith, and we dare not be less than what he trusts us to be. He hasn't a single doubt that America can be saved, even in this desperate hour, even in this prison. Yet I doubted. I'm not fit to be one of those who serve him.

Durant looked at that pale and aristocratic face, at those eyes, at that quiet intensity of mouth and shoulders and body, and felt humble and worthless.

Arthur Carlson spoke again, and now only to Durant and Christian.

"You never knew what freedom was and can be," he said. "You were born when America had already lost a great part of her freedom. You were born into the age of tyrants, and what you know of liberty and justice and all the old American virtues is only hearsay, from your parents and from a few teachers. But I was sixteen, before the first terror manifested itself in America, for I was born in 1917. So I had almost sixteen years of experience in a free, responsible and glorious climate. Peace had not been banished as a way of life, and man had dignity. I breathed the air of freedom, and so I am much richer than you."

He gazed down at them with compassion and sadness. "You do not know what that means, for you were born into slavery, and have lived in slavery. Perhaps, in many ways, you are better than I. For, in slavery, and never having known liberty, you still dreamed of it, worked for it, and pledged your lives for it. Yes, you are better than I, better than your relatives and your friends who sit about you tonight. We are working for a world we once knew; you are working for a world you hope to create. We draw upon the past; you draw upon the future. We feel humble before you, for we've had what we have had, and you have had nothing. Your courage and faith, then, are founded in a great dream, and dreams are the very substance of life.

"Your teachers have told you much about America, of her freedom, and then her slavery. You will hear no more of it, for you shall be alone after this night. So I must tell you what I know of America as she was before 1933, and what she became. I hope it will sustain you. I know it will.

"Before 1933 America had lived by the code of freedom of the individual, the dignity of the individual, the self-responsibility of the individual. She became, by this code, powerful, rich and strong. Consequently, she aroused the hatred, not only of the rest of the half-free and half-slave world, but of the men in America, herself, who wished to dominate the country. It is not possible to dominate and destroy a nation while she has strength and self-respect, and is at peace. It was necessary, then to destroy these things. More than in the outside world, itself, there were men in America who saw they must do this if they were to succeed as despots.

"It was done with Machiavellian villainy and intellect. In 1932 a war-fearing people elected a man to the Presidency who, a few years later, earnestly assured them there would be no further war. Before this event, there was no body of the people who believed themselves to be 'common men' or underprivileged. Every man believed, and he had full reason to believe, that by his own efforts, courage and hope and work, he might succeed in raising himself to a higher position. But in 1933 he was defamed, and became despicable, for he accepted the shameful name of the Common Man, and lent himself to its cult.

"The Common Man was defined as all those who are unskilled, semi-skilled and skilled 'labor.' Thus, for the first time, a huge and artificial class was created as an instrument of the potential despots. They watched the walls rise about them, and they called them 'security.' They listened to labor leaders, who were part of the plot against them, and they became arrogant, hating, envious and demanding. The free men beyond the walls were anathema to them, and following their masters like stampeding animals, they set out to destroy. It was necessary to destroy these men—the middle-class—because their very existence was a danger to the tyrants. So the middle-class, over two decades, were systematically hounded, badgered, threatened, and finally taxed out of existence. They were called 'traitors' and 'subversives,' for, to the last, they refused to become slaves."

Durant and Christian listened with absorption. They had heard this story before, but when the Magistrate spoke of it again it was with such quiet and bitter vehemence and eloquence that it seemed a new and dreadful tale.

"You know, you young men, what finally happened to the middle-class. The press, already enslaved and degraded to the position of mouthpiece for the murderers, demanded that the remnants of the proud and stubborn middle-class be 'punished' as traitors for daring to raise up their voices against the endless wars, the punitive taxation, the constant violating of the Constitution.

"But long before this final act of murder was done, America was already slave. After the first two deliberate wars of this century, which had not completely ruined the world, a plot was laid for the ultimate tragedy. Communist Russia had been exhausted by the second World War, and upon her all the hopes of despots and tyrants had been laid. So American Presidents lent her billions of the American peoples' money, directly and indirectly, fed her, armed her, encouraged her, until she was strong enough to 'fight,' and thus create another World War. The tryants of Russia and America well knew what they were doing. So began a calculated era of declared and undeclared wars, of complete confusion, of plotted ruin. In the name of 'liberty' and 'security' America was deprived of all liberty and security, her best died on a multitude of battlefields. It was no accident that the strongest, the youngest, the most intelligent, the better-bred, the best-educated, were forced into monster armies. Their murder had been cleverly arranged, so that there would remain in America only the stupid, the weak, the eager-to-be-slaves, the inferior, the old, the tired, the hopeless, and the debased, who would give no trouble and who had either lost the dream of liberty or had never heard of it.

"However, the superior obstinately insisted upon being born. It was necessary, then, to arrange to destroy them in every generation, or even every few years. So, we raised up potential enemies, armed them and encouraged them, and then fought them. This you, young as you are, know."

The Magistrate's voice remained level and quiet, yet in some mysterious way it was also passionate, filled with hatred and contempt and rage.

"But still the superior are born, here and there. Not very many, and in diminishing quantities. On them we must set our faith. We must have teachers for them; we must seek them out; we must encourage them. We must discipline them and threaten them, until all traces of fear are gone from them and they are willing, themselves, to teach and fight. You, Durant, and you, Christian, are only two of these."

Am I? thought Durant, remembering his thoughts while being driven up Fifth Avenue. Do I deserve to have him believe this of me?

He looked at the Magistrate, and the Magistrate smiled at him kindly. "Yes, Durant," he said. "You are one of us."

He waited a few minutes and then resumed: "The extremely wealthy were not persecuted or eliminated by Washington, for the despots knew that these hated liberty for all as much as they did. They were lightly taxed, if at all, for their help was needed in the universal conspiracy. Neither in Russia nor America was any hand lifted against them, but their assistance was sought, and it was given.

"Now we come to another privileged segment of all populations: the rich farmers.

"I was twenty-nine when I visited prostrated Europe in 1946, after the second World War. In every country I was told the same foul story. The people of the cities, especially the middle-class, were starving. The peasant, who has been known all through history for his avarice and greed and suspicion and mercilessness, had not suffered notably from wars. In fact, he had become rich, by deliberately withholding his produce and then charging enormous prices for it. The desperate poured from the cities to the countryside, carrying in their hands and upon their backs their few last treasures. They even withdrew the gold from their teeth, and women gave up their wedding rings. They bartered all this for bread, for a little meat, for milk for their starving children. A loaf of black bread for a diamond; a jug of milk for a set of silver; the organs of farm animals for a treasured ring; strips of leather for a priceless masterpiece. Yes, the European peasants grew fat and rich and strong through their greed.

"The potential tyrants of America saw this and understood it. Therefore began a shameless campaign to coddle and pamper the American farmer. The farmer, then, lent himself enthusiastically to the enslavement of the whole country, accepting bounties from the purse of the American people, and devotedly voting for the tyrants who had been his benefactors. The independence and pride of the American rustic had once been the sturdy backbone of America. But he willingly surrendered these for the sake of bribery, in the evil days of the twentieth century, and he joined with his masters in the oppression of the rest of the people. He is, today, extremely potent, because upon his production depends the existence of the military power which now rules America.

"We have a third privileged class in America: the managerial and supervisory technicians, some of whom were formerly the guiding geniuses of industry and commerce. Three decades or so ago, many of these men recognized the advancing menace of governmental control, which called itself 'the Welfare State' and other euphemistic names, such as various 'Deals.' They attempted to warn the people in the public press, at their own expense, but the people scoffed, or did not read. Later, these heroic men were liquidated for their refusal to cooperate in the plan for the industrial slavery of the workers, but those who cynically did cooperate kept considerable of their wealth and their privileges. They are, as you know, operating in the Department of MASTS, that is, the Managerial and Supervisory Technicians, who are responsible only to the Military for their programs. The MASTS are also in full control of all inventions and patents.

"The Government sedulously caters to these three privileged classes, and rewards them extravagantly. They escape regimentation and oppression, for if they were oppressed and deprived, they would revolt and the tyrants would be threatened."

The Chief Magistrate became paler and more haggard, and yet more resolute. His voice rose stronger in the room, ringing with authority.

"Good men and men of public conscience will revolt if their principles are threatened, and today this small minority is still a threat to our present tyrants. A small threat, and one constantly intimidated, constantly watched, for out of them can rise, and is rising, a passionate determination to overthrow authoritarianism. They are men of learning, of understanding, and they have not forgotten what this country once was, and what it might yet become again. The State is not unmindful that these men could form the nucleus of restored liberty. That is why this handful is sought out unremittingly, and persecuted and destroyed and declared 'traitorous.' No, there is no hope for us in the masses. The middle-class has virtually disappeared. Who, then, could overthrow the tyrants? The bureaucrats, the farmers and the MASTS. We must use them. We must begin to oppress them, defame them, persecute and regiment them, in the name of the State. We must be zealots, fervent and fanatical. When they howl, we must howl louder and call them traitors!

"We will, in short, use the same methods as the tyrants, in the name of the tyrants, to create a terrible revolution, out of which will be born a new liberty and a new dignity."

Now the Magistrate fixed his eyes upon Christian. "You wish to ask a question?"

"Yes. Will Washington support us in this? Or will we be murdered to shut us up?"

"A number of us will be slyly shot, certainly," said Arthur Carlson. "But we'll be so fervent in our devotion to The Democracy, and our voices will be so loud and fanatical, and we'll draw so much attention, that we'll not only embarrass The Democracy but will, quite possibly, make it afraid of us. We'll be advised to be quiet, but we'll only scream the louder, in the name of the Government, and be very much enraged." He smiled.

"You know what is already happening. The teachers of America, as a class, are very docile, and always eager to serve the most powerful master. You know how their so-called 'liberalism' helped to enslave the people several decades ago. When America became completely regimented, the teachers followed every instruction. For a while they were a privileged class, also, with every honor paid them, and every consideration.

"But three years ago I picked a number of Minute Men to oppress the teachers and professors of America, who had so willingly lent themselves to her betrayal. Their salaries were cut, for the sake of 'national economy.' Their comfortable houses were confiscated for the Military and the bureaucrats. They began to be badgered, inspected, bullied. What they would not do for man in general, they began to do for themselves. They became restive, and then when the press began to denounce them as potential traitors, they were terrified. They rediscovered 'liberty.' Most of them were dishonest and frightened self-seekers, but out of the mass of them slowly emerged men suddenly sobered and honest. They realized what they had done, and they were angered against themselves and against the Government. So we have, now, many teachers and professors subtly and artfully teaching our children and our youth of the lost brave past of America. Some, who become too bold, are imprisoned or executed. But the others are cleverer, and they will live and continue to breed restlessness.

"When the time comes they will join the bureaucrats, the farmers and the MASTS in fomenting a violent revolution."

The Magistrate pointed to Durant. "The farmers of a certain section of the country are your victims, Andrew. A very rich and fatted section. And you, Christian: the MASTS are yours." He laughed a little. "I will support you. There will be many nameless men who will support you. I am the most powerful Magistrate in America, and my father is the President's only trusted friend. The day of liberation is not too far away."

He stepped back on the platform. "But we must hurry. We have no time to waste. You two men may pick only one of these, your older friends and relatives, for a moment's private talk. You must ask them no questions, however. They will comfort and sustain you, and will assure you of their affection. But that is all. Which do you choose?"

The profiles of the other men did not move in the direction of the two young men. They only waited. Durant looked at his father, and then at his priest. It was a distressing choice. He said, in a low voice: "Father Martin."

The priest immediately rose. Durant glanced imploringly at his father, who did not turn to him, but he saw the older man's shriveled lips curve in a gentle smile.

The Magistrate said: "Your choice, Christian? Ah, your brother. Durant and Christian: say good-bye to each other. You will probably never meet again, and your new names will be unknown to each other, even after the Liberation."

The two young men shook hands, tried to speak, and could not. The Guard opened the door for Durant, who went out with the priest. They crossed a hall and entered a small white bedroom. There was only a narrow bed in the room, a washbasin and a chair. Durant sat on the bed, careful of his broken arm, after the priest had seated himself. "Father," said the young man. But the priest turned the television set on and answered gently: "Listen." Suddenly, there was projected on the screen the face of the President of The Democracy, a little meager man with a small, crafty face, a man who had been Chief Executive for over fifteen years, and who would serve for life. Durant, with loathing, looked into these wizened eyes, saw the cunning and sanctimonious mouth with its cruel smile, the distrustful sly glances, the pinched nose with its sharp and quivering point. The President of The Democracy was the appalling archetype of that dehumanized creature, the "Common Man," created in the twentieth century and extolled by "idealists." Imaged by this century, dreamed into being by drab and soulless men, he could have lived in none of the lusty and robust eras of the past. He had been created by enfeebled imaginings, so that he had no color and no vitality but only meanness and greed, a two-dimensioned little monster in gray and white, a puppet with the spirit of a rat.

He was screeching now: "We must have unity! In this hour of our dread emergency all freedom-loving peoples must stand together as one, with no subversive or traitorous voice raised in protest! The Enemy is about to attack us and to destroy our liberty! All the traditions of a proud and righteous America are at stake tonight, and we must all put forth our strongest and most vigorous effort to defeat him. I call upon my people to sacrifice and to resist the forces of disaster, to bend themselves to every effort in order that our glorious nation shall not perish from the earth! I, your leader, call upon you again, knowing that in this dangerous age no man should think of his own safety, his own comfort, his own life, but only of The Democracy and her very existence! America has not refused to heed the call to duty in every menacing hour of our past. She will not refuse it now!"

The priest turned off the television set, and President Slocum's face disappeared.

"Who? Who is the Enemy now?" cried Durant, aghast.

"Always the same Enemy," replied the priest sadly. "Man, himself."

But Durant muttered: "Again and again and again! World without end."

"Oh, no," said the priest. "The world is not yet completely insane. But we must not waste any time."

Argentina, Chile, Peru—all of South America tonight? Europe was a complete ruin, and Asia was a wilderness. It could only be South America. Durant groaned desperately. He knelt down with painful difficulty on the bare floor, remembering how many years had passed since his last confession. He said humbly: "Bless me, Father, for I save sinned."

Later, the priest gave him comfort and fortitude. "In your dedication, Andy, there must be no doubt and no fear. However, I need not tell you this. A world of men depends upon you, a whole world of slavery and fear and despair. The Cross is yours, and death is yours, too. What you do tomorrow, and in every tomorrow left to you, will help or hinder humanity. You know that the Church has been proscribed, and every other religion. You not only are to fight for man but for God, also."

Durant said: "I never before believed in a personal and universal Evil. I never before believed in Satan. I do now."

"This Evil always existed," answered the priest sadly. "It will always exist. Its greatest triumph was when it persuaded men that it had no reality. Men must understand again that Evil is a definite and infinite force in all the universe, and that, forever and forever, they must struggle against it, and fight it, with prayer and resolution and faith."

A little later the Magistrate entered, and the priest, giving a final blessing to Durant, left the room. The Magistrate said: "Let me help you remove your clothes. You will be awakened in six hours, ready for your duties."

When Andrew, exhausted, lay on his bed, the Magistrate gave him a sheaf of papers. "From this time on, Durant, you are Major Andrew Curtiss of the Army of The Democracy of America. You will be taken to a section of the country which you once knew as the State of Pennsylvania. Your orders are here, and your credentials, and your uniform will be ready for you in the morning."

Andrew said: "Shall I ever see you again?"

"Perhaps. Perhaps not. Does it matter? You are Major Andrew Curtiss, a man without a wife or a family, without parents, without any loyalty except to us. Trust no one, not even the men who will be closest to you. You won't know if they are friends or enemies, not even at the end, nor do they know about you. You will be in a compartment, where you will work alone. Ask no man any question, nor try to discover what he is. This is not only to protect you and to save your life as long as possible, but to protect all of us. Good night, now, and God bless you."

It was hardly dawn when Durant was awakened by a Guard. He was astounded by his feeling of refreshment, and by the fact that for the first time in years he had slept the deep sleep of one who is not apprehensive, desperate or afraid. Then he understood that it was because he had felt safe! All his life had been shadowed, clouded and blackened by the universal fear. He would continued to be in awful danger. Yet he felt safe and confident and at peace, and these were so unfamiliar to him that he became exultant. There was no fear in him any longer.

His breakfast was brought to him in his room by a Guard. He glanced at the impassive face of the man, and, as ordered, asked no questions. He was departmentalized; he would work in a lonely cell, perhaps hearing the movements of fellow-bees in the cells all about him but he would never see them. He accepted this. He even kept his face from expressing any emotion when his uniform as a major in the Army of The Democracy of America was brought to him, the right sleeve carefully slit to allow for his broken arm. The doctor visited him once, with impersonal friendliness, examined the splint, gave him another glass of that strange, pungent fluid, and a box of tablets. But this was his only visitor.

The Guard assisted him in dressing, in complete silence. He placed his papers in a leather case brought to him by the Guard. The Guard had also shaved him. Neither of them spoke. When they went through the hall of the house there was no one about, no voice, no movement, only the stolid Guards who looked at him indifferently, and saluted. Where was Christian? But he no longer knew Christian, his new name, or where he was going, or if they would ever meet again. He, Durant, was Major Andrew Curtiss, and he was to forget what he had been, and remember only his duty.

A handsome black car was awaiting him. He regarded the two occupants of it with brief scrutiny. They got out of the car as he came down the crumbling brown steps of the house, and briskly saluted. One wore the uniform of a first lieutenant and the other, a sergeant. "Lieutenant George Grandon, sir, and Sergeant Howard Keiser, at your service," said the lieutenant. He was a tall young man with lively brown eyes and yellow hair and an intelligent, quick face. The sergeant was short and stout, with brutal but expressive features, and as dark in coloring as Durant, himself, and of the same Latin features. Durant speculated, for a moment, on whether or not these were actually the names of these men, if they were Minute Men like himself or genuine soldiers of the State. Probably he would never know. He returned their salute by touching his cap with his left hand, awkwardly, and was assisted into the rear seat with immense politeness and respect. The car rolled off in the early morning mist which poured over the city from the sea. The sergeant drove carefully, avoiding the larger craters. The first sun struck the decayed towers of the mighty buildings, the sifting mortar, the blank windows. There was a deep silence in the city, though the streets, even at this hour, swarmed with mobs going to or coming from their endless jobs in the "war effort." Only the mutter and shuffle of their feet could be heard, for there was no conversation, and little movement of traffic except that "authorized" and "essential," such as a few shabby buses and the glittering cars of supervisors and bureaucrats. These, like Durant's car, wove in and out the holes in the pavement.

The sky overhead was the tenderest blue, serene and gentle, over this desolated city. Pigeons blew against it, and, in the heavy silence, could be heard to cry and squeal. Now the morning light filtered on the pale and ghastly faces of the multitudes, and Durant thought of the dead. For a moment he was compassionate, and then again he was bitter. How easily they had surrendered to the tyrants! With what original fervor had they accepted the American brand of Communism! How indifferently, or with zeal, they had watched their last safeguard, the Constitution of the United States, go down under the muddy heels of their oppressors; Andrew knew they had been warned, by reasonable or by shouting voices, decades ago, and they had either shrugged their shoulders, laughed, denied, jeered, cursed or turned aside. Step by step, they had watched their freedom taken away, openly and cynically, and they had not cared, preferring to look with delight at their larger pay envelopes and enthusiastically assenting to wars which would increase, they believed, their "security" and their money. In the end they had lost everything, their freedom as men, their rights as men, their dignity as men, and had become nothing else but slaves of an omnipotent State, working endlessly, half-starved, half-clothed, half-sheltered in ruined buildings, endlessly spied upon, supervised, commanded by the Military and treated like dogs.

The Chief Magistrate had been right. There was no hope in the masses of the people. They would listen to no last brave voice. They would not revolt, until others led the revolt. The workers of America had betrayed America, as they had betrayed Germany and Britain. Always, the workers are the prey of tyrants, out of ignorance or greed or envy.

Durant thought of the State schools, where history was perverted and where new slaves were trained to docility, obedience and devotion to their masters. The children of mere workers were allowed to learn to read and write, and to memorize a few basic lies. Beyond this, there was no opportunity for learning for them. The children of the devouring bureaucrats, the farmers, the MASTS, and the higher military officers, were educated in higher schools, and the more brilliant were chosen to replace those who died or disappeared or became too old to carry on the oppression.

The car passed St. Patrick's Cathedral. But the Cross no longer soared against the blue sky of the morning. The State, ordaining its own crafty "ministers," had confiscated all the old churches, and, four times a month, on a Thursday, permitted a sterile religion to be taught. But it was the religion of the State, and God was mentioned only as a "force," probably blind and unaware, and quite indifferent to the misery and anguish of the people. The "ministers" were third-rate scientists and psychiatrists, who indoctrinated the crippled spirits of the congregations in weird and merciless theories, all destitute of spiritual values, and all designed to destroy hope and any last remnants of a "medieval superstition."

A few labor leaders, so many years ago, had exhorted, warned and cried out—they had been killed and silenced and imprisoned. They had been "subversive," and their liquidation had proceeded in lethal quiet.

"Would you like a newspaper, sir?" asked the lieutenant. Durant started. He saw that the lieutenant was watching him with furtive curiosity. Durant cursed himself; he must control his Latin expressiveness of feature. It had led him into trouble before. He answered, yawning: "Yes." The lieutenant smiled faintly, and spoke to the sergeant. The car stopped at a corner, teetering on the edge of a crater, and the sergeant went into a shabby shop for a paper. Durant, making his face still as possible, continued to watch the shuffling throngs. He saw them notice the conspicuous State car in which he sat, and he saw their meek and humble glances. Damn you, he thought, as he had thought last night. The lieutenant hummed some ribald song under his breath. Durant did not glance at him; he knew the officer was looking at his splinted arm. "An accident, sir?" asked Grandon, with respectful interest. Durant said: "Yes." He forced a smile. "Too much to drink, at a dinner." The lieutenant laughed. It was a gay and youthful laugh, and jarred on Durant's nerves. It was such a terrible contrast with the moving faces outside. In spite of himself, Durant wondered if the lieutenant's laughter was knowing and understanding, or just simply careless mirth.

The sergeant came back with the paper. There it was, in thick black headlines: "The Democracy Attacked by South American Alliance. Congress Meets for Declaration of War!"

Durant read impassively, the paper on his knees. "Attacked!" Always the battle-cry of a nation gone mad, a world gone mad.

The "Alliance" appeared to be Chile, Argentina, Brazil and Uruguay. Warships of these four nations, it was alleged, had fired on the coast of Florida, and had closed the Panama Canal. The Democracy of America was being "immediately mobilized." The people must "sacrifice." There would be new controls, new shortages, new war plants, new "essential" materials, new priorities. All the hateful terminology of despotism! All the new despair, hopelessness, cruelty, military oppression, bureaucratic regimentation! Durant glanced again at the multitudes. They must know of this fresh calamity. Yet not one face showed any alarm or disgust or dread or indignation or hatred. They accepted, as they had always accepted. Damn them, thought Durant, with renewed bitterness.

The car rolled on and approached the Holland Tunnel. Durant continued to read. Now his eyes, just awakened, began to notice certain smaller headlines which had not impinged on his consciousness in the months past. "Three colonels, five majors and a number of lesser officers" had been shot for "subversive" acts and opinions, in Chicago. Durant had read of these things before, and had dismissed them indifferently, for there was always rivalry and jealousy among soldiers. Now he began to wonder if the Minute Men were not responsible for the occasional oppression of the Military. He would never know, of course, but he suddenly smiled.

There was a photograph in the newspaper of a burly farmer and his three sons, all grinning joyously before the background of their large white home: "We are ready!" said the caption over the photograph. And underneath: "John Lincoln, of Tauton, Section 7, and his three sons, Harry, Merle and Bob, pledge themselves to do their part for the war effort. Mr. Lincoln owns one of the largest farms in Section 7, two thousand acres, and is a veteran of World War Three. During World War Four his farm produced almost twice as much as any other similar farm in the Section. He has received three Government prizes for his wheat, and one for his cattle, which are famous. Harry and Merle are married, and each has two children and a home of his own on the farm, while Bob, the youngest, is his father's right arm. Bob is a veteran of Warld War Four, and has developed a new hybrid corn. Not shown is Mr. Lincoln's pretty daughter, Grace, who was a member of the Women's Combat League in the last war, having held the rank of sergeant, and later, lieutenant. Typically American, they were chosen by the President as the Family of the Year. 'This family reveals all the traits which have made The Democracy the greatest and most independent and prosperous country in the world,' the President said, when the Lincoln family paid a visit to the White House."

"Nice piece of white meat, Gracie," said Lieutenant Grandon, who had been reading the paper over Durant's shoulder.

"You know them?" Something began to stir in Durant's mind.

"I sure do. They live about twenty miles out of Philadelphia, sir. Wonderful house, a mansion I suppose you'd call it. Everything at fat as butter on that farm, the old man and his sons and his wife. Except Gracie." The lieutenant smacked his lips and rolled his lively eyes. "Twenty-two years old, and not married yet; old man's darling."

"As fat as butter." Durant looked through the car window again, and saw the shuffling, pallid swarms, their pinched faces, their haggard eyes. He thought of the millions of pounds of meat and butter and the tons of wheat and sugar which were destroyed every year by order of the Government, in order to maintain "shortages," rationing and regimentation, and in order to keep the farmers rich and satisfied. He glanced again at the shining white house, which was "a mansion," the massive trees sheltering it lovingly, the rolling lawns which were almost parklike. And he thought of the tumbling tenements of the cities, the foul choked alleys, the broken windows, the heatless rooms, the filth, the rationed electricity, the stench, the starveling children, the scraps of mildewed food on tens of millions of plates, the milkless, meatless, wheatless, breadless, sugarless days. Such a rage filled him then that his throat closed and he choked.

"Something wrong, sir?" asked the lieutenant, with concern.

Durant strangled for a moment or two, and turned scarlet. Then he said in a stifled voice: "Swallowed the wrong way." He coughed hoarsely.

Not on the farmers had the Military been afflicted. But the homes in the city had been used by officers and men as their "quarters." The farmer shut his strong door, and his fat and ruddy family were safe, come war, come peace, come "emergency" or "sacrifice." Let the farmers revolt—

Durant said abruptly: "That hotel, in Philadelphia. I've changed my mind. I've taken a liking to that farmhouse. We'll move in on them."

The lieutenant uttered an exclamation, but his eyes danced. "Isn't that against the law, sir?" he asked.

"The Chief Magistrate of New York is also the Magistrate of Section 7," replied Durant. "I'm sure he'd want his military staff to be well housed, and I prefer the country anyway. I'll call him when we are settled there."

"There are four of us on your staff, Major—me, the sergeant here, and two captains."

"Good. I think we'd all like the best—fresh country milk, the fresh eggs and the meat, instead of the city rations. Not to speak of Gracie."

Now the lieutenant whistled, involuntarily, and the sergeant grinned. Durant said tolerantly: "I'm sure the great patriot, our friend Mr. Lincoln, will be happy to have us. What do you think?"

The lieutenant burst out laughing, and slapped his knee. "The old boy would have us out to dinner when the other major was in Philadelphia, but not too often. Have to coddle the damned famers, you know, sir. Government orders. Old Johnny would watch his little pet lamb, too, and wouldn't let us put a paw on her, or have just a little feel. He won't like us crowding him in his big house. He's got big friends in the Government, and he might make trouble."

"The other major." What had happened to him? But Durant could not ask. He said, with a wink: "Well, I have even bigger friends in the government, so perhaps you'll have even more than a 'little feel,' Lieutenant."

The young lieutenant roared with delight. The warm spring sun poured into the car. Durant sat back and pretended to doze. But he was thinking furiously. He had been directed to a certain hotel in Philadelphia, and he began to question his new decision. However, Arthur Carlson had told him: "What you think should be done, do. Move boldly, but carefully. Time is closing in on us, and you must improvise as fast as you can, according to the situations. I depend upon your intelligence, and, if in doubt, communicate with me immediately. However, I'm certain you'll have little reason to do that very often, if at all."

"Desperate men in a desperate cause," the Magistrate had said last night. This was a time for desperate moves. Durant decided not to call the Magistrate, but to write him after he had installed himself in Lincoln's house. He thought: if there was just someone I could trust! But there was no one. During his life as a lawyer and his few years as a Minute Man, he had had some friends. He had had companions in the secret places where they had all gathered. Now he was completely alone.

All that had once been New York, New Jersey and Pennsylvania was no Section 7, under the jurisdiction of the Chief Magistrate, Arthur Carlson. All at once Durant felt completely confident, and he smiled grimly to himself. When other military staffs heard what he was doing they would descend like rats upon the fatted countryside, and this time the farmers would feel the lash of oppression, themselves. The President was Commander in Chief of the Armed Forces, and so far they had been his bulwark, and he had pampered them. He was also mortally afraid of them. Move quickly! Boldly. But not too boldly at first, for if he, Durant, were killed he would have gained nothing. However, if the Armed Forces swarmed upon the country, as he intended to swarm now, the President would not dare oppose them. The Military, even more than the President and his Cabinet, ruled America, and they served him because he served them, and they were more powerful than the farmers.

Now Durant firmly believed that the Chief Magistrate had known what he would do, and again he smiled grimly.

The streets of the cities might be pock-marked with craters, but the monster highways were kept in perfect condition "for defense." The great fleets of private cars, which, twenty years ago, had rolled like masses of beetles on the highways, had almost disappeared. There had been little, if any, steel for private cars during the last two decades, and even the few cars were invariably marked for the Military, farmers, officials, and bureaucrats. Only occasionally did one see an ancient, twenty-year-old car, staggering along the roads, wrapped in a cloud of burning oil, but quite often sleek new vehicles owned by the privileged classes raced along like silver, black and golden bullets. A few contained the rich farmers, rotund and red-faced, and their families, equally rotund and rosy; more, however, were occupied by military officers and their men. Durant noted with satisfaction that farmers were careful to give their friends, the Armed Forces, the right of way. At first he did not respond to their jocular salutes, for he was too full of hatred. Later, he saluted smilingly, remembering his new role.

The car rolled along the glorious spring countryside. Farm after farm passed the windows in the green haze of newly leafed trees and brilliantly green fields. Golden bushes blazed briefly as the car went on, and herds of rounded cattle stood mildly in the sunshine. Here was no starvation, no misery, no hopelessness, no fear! Joyous children ran along the road to school, plump children with bright eyes and good shoes, and arrogant young voices. Durant thought of the tattered white-faced children in Central Park, and his rage returned. Wait! he thought savagely. There was no pity in him when he looked upon these farmers' offspring, and he tried to keep down another surge of hatred. The children were not at fault, he told himself. But these, too, were being trained as oppressors. He must remember that, as he must also remember not to hate, where hatred would do no good.

Each farmhouse he passed appeared more comfortable and brighter than the last. The red silos glowed in the sun; the barns were heaped up with food which would inevitably find its way to Government storehouses, there to be rationed meagerly to the cities, the rest to be destroyed or to be sent to current allies. There would be fresh gold in the farmers' pockets, for the farmers had, fifteen years ago, demanded to be paid in gold and not in the frightfully depreciated paper currency. The farmers deposited their gains in the Grange Banks, where it would be safe, and not in Government institutions.

"The farmers live well, don't they, Grandon?" asked Durant idly.

"They certainly do, Major Curtiss," replied the lieutenant. "Better than we do, especially better than those of us who are in the cities." A curious flicker, like the flash of a bared knife, passed over the young man's face, and Durant looked more closely at him. Durant felt, rather than saw, the sergeant's shoulders jerk. "Sometimes," continued the lieutenant reflectively, "I hate the goddamn farmers."

Durant kept himself very still. He pursed his lips. "Oh, I wouldn't say that. What would the country be without them?"

"Yes," said the officer very softly, as if to himself, "what would the country be without them?"

Again, the sensation of complete isolation came to Durant. He had been warned not to approach anyone, not to speak thoughtlessly to anyone, not to trust anyone, not even the men in his command. If there were Minute Men among them, he was not to know, just as they would know nothing about him. Grandon might be a friend, or an enemy.

What had Grandon been told about him? That he was simply a new major, replacing the old? He could not ask. His loneliness, his isolation, began to impress themselves forcibly upon him.

He said: "As we are not stopping in Philadelphia, after all, we'd better avoid it. When we get to the Lincoln farm you must call the other officers and have them join us in the country."

Grandon smiled broadly, and again slapped his knee. Durant closed his eyes, and thought about his wife and children who had been sent to an unknown section of the country. Maria, too, had been given her orders. She would have her own private problems in teaching the children to respond to new names, and in obliterating the memory of him from their minds. She, too, would be desperately lonely, and would live in fear for him.

In spite of what the Chief Magistrate had told him, that he was inevitably doomed to die, he found himself resolutely determined that some day he would find his family, and that he would live. He had only to trust no one, to be careful, always to be alert, always to watch. He was willing to sacrifice his life for America, but if there came on opportunity to save himself he would do so, honorably and boldly.

He must have dozed, for all at once he heard the lieutenant say in what seemed a very loud voice: "We're about there, Major." He opened his eyes at once. The car was slowing down, approaching two gray stone pillars at the left. "Entrance to the Lincoln farm, sir." The car turned in on a smooth gravel driveway, and in the distance, atop a proud rise, was the big white house of the photograph, shimmering in the sun behind its trees. Quiet purplish mountains had appeared, and the land was rolling and gentle, almost unnaturally green in its fertility.

"How did Lincoln get those two thousand acres?" asked Durant.

The lieutenant grinned, and shrugged. "Why, sir, don't you know how the 'subversive' farmers were liquidated, when they wouldn't come to heel a long time ago? And don't you know how their farms were turned over to—men like Lincoln?"

"Yes. But I had forgotten," replied Durant, angered at his own stupidity. The young officer gave him a sidelong glance. "You city officers have too much else on your minds," he suggested.

Durant only nodded. He concentrated on the house. Two yellow collies came racing and barking toward them, their coats sleek in the sun. The trees fell back, and Durant could see the polished windows of the farmhouse and the red chimneys. "City officers." Durant could not restrain himself. "You've lived in the country, Grandon?"

The young officer's face closed, became blank of all expression. "Yes, in Section 18," he replied. "Out west." He stared ahead at the farmhouse, and Durant did not ask him any other questions, nor did he notice, a moment later, a white line about Grandon's mouth.

There was a circular driveway in front of the house, and the car stopped before the closed door. The sergeant jumped out to open the car door for Durant, and for an instant Durant stared at that brutal but intelligently Latin face. Italian, French, Spanish, blood? The sergeant looked back at him in silence.

Grandon ran up the white steps of the house and knocked loudly and gayly upon the door. Durant and Sergeant Keiser followed him. There was an annoyed grunt inside the house, and the door opened. John Lincoln, himself, in fine gray country tweeds, a pipe in his hand, stood there, scowling. When he saw the military men, he instantly smiled, but there was no servility about him.

"The new major of the district, Mr. Lincoln," said Grandon, with a quick salute. "Major Curtiss."

"How do you do, how do you do!" exclaimed Lincoln heartily. "Come in! Glad to see you, Major. How's Major Burnes?"

"Very well, I believe," replied Durant, taking the big beefy hand offered him.

"We miss him," said Lincoln. "Nice old feller. Sent to another Section?"

Grandon replied: "Yes, indeed. He's a colonel now." Again that knifelike flash passed swiftly over his face, but he smiled easily.

They entered a pleasant hall with paneled walls of carved mahogany, and a fine bare wood floor of darkly polished wood. The hall was large and square, and in its exact center was an exquisite Oriental rug flowing with blue and rose and gold. Excellent antique chairs stood about a beautifully turned chest. Durant's mouth tightened, especially at the sight of a wonderful landscape in oils which hung on one wall. Here were the treasures which had been drained from the starving city for a little bread, a little meat, a little milk. He stood and examined the landscape minutely, and wondered what the genius who had painted it had received for his magnificent work.

Lincoln, on the threshold of the living room, saw that Durant had stopped. He smiled, pleased. "Nice, eh?" he asked. Durant deliberately let his eyes rove over the chairs, the chest, the rug, the walls. Lincoln chuckled contentedly.

Durant said absently: "When I was a child, I spent two summers in a farmhouse. It was a very good place, but it wasn't like this."

Lincoln chuckled again. "I bet not! But we farmers have come into our own, now."

"Congratulations," murmured Durant. He turned to look for his companions. Grandon was humming indifferently, but Sergeant Keiser had narrowed his black eyes intently on the major, though the rest of his face remained impassive.

The vast living room, radiant with sunshine, was no less lavishly furnished than the hall. Cloisonné, marble, silks, Oriental rugs, eighteenth century love-seats, lace, pictures, ornaments—all the loveliness of aristocratic families reduced to beggary, or worse, was here, exchanged for a few days' extra survival. Lincoln beamed about the room, his large fat face ruddy and complacent, his little hazel eyes proud, his pipe in his big thick mouth. "Got most of it for a song," he confided. "There was a rich subversive family in Philadelphia, who wouldn't be reconstructed. Feller's business taken away from him. Government invited farmers to the auction, and kept the money. I got the best part; in with Washington, you know." And he winked at Durant.

Durant laughed pleasantly. "What would we do without the farmers!" he exclaimed. "Most influential class in The Democracy, second only to the bureaucrats and third only to the Military. Good. Good."

His voice had been genial, but Lincoln, who was no fool, thought that there was something disagreeable in the intonation. Like all the members of the great Farm Bloc, he was afraid of the Military, who were the absolute rulers of the country. Even the President truckled to them, for without the vast Armed Forces of The Democracy he would be nothing. The Grange would be nothing, in spite of the millions of farmers. The Military, if it so desired, could oust the President in less than an hour, and it could subdue and take over the farmers in less than a week. It had the guns, the officers and the men. Everything lived by sufferance of the Military, or died at its word.

Lincoln, after a moment's uneasy reflection, boomed happily: "Sit down, sit down, Major! And you, Lieutenant." He drew out his best chairs, opened boxes of precious cigarets, cigarets which had almost disappeared in the cities. He glanced at the sergeant, and hesitated. It was customary for sergeants and lesser of the Military to find their way into the big kitchens of farmhouses. Durant knew this, so he said: "Thanks. And you, Sergeant, find yourself a seat, too." Sergeant Keiser smiled surlily, and sat down. Again, a finger of uneasiness ran down Lincoln's padded spine.

Smiling broadly, he produced several bottles of whisky from a delicate and beautiful cabinet, and brought out four crystal glasses touched with gold. Then he banged on a large silver bell, chased with gilt. "Ice? Soda?" he asked. A moment later a middle-aged man in a white coat entered. Durant glanced idly at the servant, and then his heart lurched. He had never known this man personally, but up to five years ago he had been famous all over The Democracy for his literature and his poetry. Then he had written a passionate exhortation to his countrymen to restore their long-lost freedom, to oust their tyrants, "to be men again, as men were once men, and no longer the driven cattle of despots." He had been seized, his property confiscated, his books openly burned, his wife and three daughters conscripted for the hardest manual labor in the war plants, their identities wiped out, his son assassinated in the streets. No one had known what had happened to the teacher and poet, Dr. William Dodge; it had been taken for granted that he, too, had been murdered. All pictures of him had been obliterated from the public files. However, Durant remembered that tall thin figure, that dark and ascetic face, those large deep eyes, from prints and news reels and other photographs.

The face had not changed, but the manner had. It was a dull and shuffling robot who looked expectantly at Lincoln, and who bent its head in a humble and servile manner. There was no glow in the eyes, no remembrance. Along one cheek was a twisted scar, which pulled his mouth aside.

"Ice. Soda. And be quick about it," said Lincoln, with a rough gesture. "No fumbling this time, Bill."

Durant, shocked and sickened, fixed his eyes on the cloisonné vases on the mantelpiece. He appeared to be staring at the comfortable fire on the marble hearth. He told himself, over and over: I must control myself. He made himself breathe very slowly, and then turned to his host. "Many conscripted workers on your farm, Mr. Lincoln?"

"Two hundred," answered the farmer, with satisfaction. "Can't see their barracks from these windows, but they're out behind the woods. Fifty girls." He gave his rich chuckle again. "Need 'em all. Thinking of applying for twenty-five more. Nearly a hundred of 'em were farmers, themselves, but disloyal." He made his face express indignation and contempt. "Others are city folks. Took a lot of hard work to train 'em, but we did it! Hardened up their soft hands! Twenty of the girls and women were schoolteachers, but the country needed 'em for essential work on the farms, and here they are!"

All labor, all the professions, including the medical, had been conscripted nearly fifteen years. Durant had known that. However, in the cities it had not seemed so frightful, for even tyranny could become anonymous in vast anonymity. Here, on the golden land, it was more imminent, more terrible, more significant, more personal. Dr. William Dodge! A forced servant to this bulky and flabby brute who wore fine tweeds and exulted in his serfs and his influence under The Democracy!

"I'd like to know something about my district," said Durant. "I know Philadelphia, which is part of it, but the countryside is a little hazy in my mind. How many farmers do I—control?"

Lincoln studied him, and a little of his ruddy color left his face. Control! He didn't like the word. But he answered cautiously: "Well, now, there are about twenty of us big farmers in your district, Major, all about like me." (Control! Nobody had dared use that word before when referring to the farmers. Nobody but this feller in his army suit!)

Lincoln's scrutiny became more alert. He saw before him a slender young man, not very tall, with a dark complexion, dark and penetrating eyes, a large aquiline nose, a mobile mouth with three teeth missing, and a thick mop of black curling hair. Lincoln noticed that his right arm was in a sling. He cleared his throat, for that nameless uneasiness in him was increasing.

"Had an accident, Major?"

"Yes. A party. Too much to drink last night. And just when I had been detailed to take over Major Burnes' post. I wanted to wait a few days, to visit my dentist, and get over the party, but orders are orders, you know. The Chief Magistrate can be all military, you know, and besides, I suppose he thought I needed discipline."

Dr. Dodge brought in a silvery tray holding ice and soda. Lincoln, as he deftly filled the glasses, laughed. "Oh, I know the Chief Magistrate! That is, I've met him. All patriotism. All for the country. When he looks at you he scares the hell out of you, don't he?"

Grandon said demurely: "He certainly does. I overstayed my leave one time by just forty minutes, and I was in the guardhouse a month."

Durant sipped at his glass of excellent whisky. "I have the highest regard for the Chief Magistrate. But perhaps that's because he's given me absolute power over this district, more than Major Burnes ever had, and so I suppose I'm flattered. Told me to make all my own decisions, and he'd uphold them, whatever they are." He smiled blandly at his host.

Lincoln was alerted. "Then you could get my twenty-five extra farm workers for me, Major?" He leaned forward in his chair, eagerly, forgetting his uneasiness.

"I certainly could," Durant said, with an amiable nod. "Suppose we go out over your farm, later?" He added: "After we've all had dinner, of course."

Lincoln had had a meeting scheduled in Philadelphia with his fellow farmers. There was a Government check in his pocket, for which he would receive gold that afternoon to be deposited in the Philadelphia Grange. He had looked forward to the merry meeting at one o'clock with his friends. However, he said, as if with immense pleasure: "Wonderful, wonderful! I'll show you all around, Major." He didn't like Durant, for he had an animal's sensitivity for danger, and he had been especially alarmed by Durant's easy information about his absolute power. However, he had as much as promised twenty-five new laborers, and Lincoln was prepared to be the most sedulous and happy host. Nothing was too good for the Military.

Two women entered the room, one about fifty years old, the other practically a young girl. The men got to their feet, and Durant glanced over them quickly. The older woman was evidently Mrs. Lincoln. She was big and stout and perspiring, even though the spring day was not too warm, and her skin was smooth and red like her husband's. She wore a fine dress of dark silk, which strained over the balloons which were her breasts and the bellows which were her hips. She had legs like inverted pyramids, and her thighs were like logs, and her hands were meaty. She had a great porcine face, tiny gray eyes, a mass of gray hair tortured into many curls, a loose mouth, and an arrogant and overbearing manner.

The girl with her was charming, not over twenty-two, small and slender and dainty, with long chestnut hair and pretty blue eyes. Her mouth was red and full and smiling, and the parted lips showed two rows of fine white teeth. Her blue dress matched her eyes, and she was artlessly pleased with her diamond rings. The farmer's daughter of ancient story had become the oppressor's daughter of the new world, flirtatious and gay and captivating, and girlishly petulant.

"Mazie! Gracie!" boomed Lincoln, with expansive pride. "Our new administrator, Major Curtiss! Major, my girls!"

Mrs. Lincoln's choleric eyes brightened as she looked at Durant, grew cold again as she glanced at Grandon, became filmed as if with outrage when she detected the presence of the sergeant. Then she turned again to Durant and extended her warm thick hand and beamed. "Major!" she cried, hoarsely and loudly. "Major Curtiss! Welcome to our home! Such a young man, too!" She flicked her eyes at her daughter speculatively. However, Grace Lincoln was evidently very happy at seeing Grandon again, and had no time for Durant. Grandon was smiling at the girl, and holding her hand tightly. "Gracie!" shouted Mrs. Lincoln. "Major Curtiss!"

Grace hurriedly gave her attention to Durant, and examined him. She held out her hand and he took it with his left. A natural flirt, she decided he was very attractive, but "peculiar." Curtiss was a good American name, but he looked Jewish or Italian or something. "Major Curtiss," she said tentatively, and her charming eyes were shrewd.

"An old family name," answered Durant gravely. "Far back as the Revolution."

"Uh?" said Grace, puzzled.

Lincoln roared with laughter. "He means the American Revolution—old 1775 or something, Gracie. Don't you remember?"

The girl became pettish. "Daddy, you know they don't teach those things in school any more. They haven't for years." Her tone deprecated his age. Lincoln scratched his chin thoughtfully. "Yeh, remember. Teach kids more interestin' things in school, these past twenty years. Social studies, and such. Besides," he chuckled, "couldn't bring in the American Revolution without mentioning the Declaration of Independence and the Constitution, could they? And that's subversive." He winked broadly at Durant who, with dismay, cursed himself for his own slip. He forced himself to laugh.

"We're taught Americanism and Democracy in the schools and colleges," Grace informed her father severely. "Not what a lot of revolutionary foreigners did two hundred years ago."

"Yes, foreigners," agreed Durant.

Grace smiled at him. It was an empty but pretty smile, and she moved her hips in a slight wriggle. The sergeant devoured her brutally with his eyes.

"In another twenty-five years all the old people who remember what they had been taught will be dead," said Grandon enthusiastically. "And history will be confined to the present, and will be changing constantly as we are taught new concepts of it."

"Hum," said Lincoln, who evidently shared his wife's suspicions and dislike of the young lieutenant.

"Don't you agree?" asked Grandon, with an odd pouncing note in his boyish voice.

"Yes, yes," answered Lincoln hastily. "Of course, of course! Whatever the Military says is exactly right! Who quarrels with the Military? They've got the best minds, haven't they? They know what they're talking about, don't they?" He hurriedly asked his wife if she wished some sherry. She shook her mountainous head.

"Our friends are staying to dinner," Lincoln informed her.

Durant caught her sudden consternation. She was looking at her husband, and Durant saw only her profile. Her lips moved in a single monosyllable, but very distinctly. Bob? Was it "Bob?"

Lincoln became very genial indeed, but crinkles of worry appeared around his eyes. "I've decided not to go to the Grange meeting, Mazie. And the major ought to meet the boys." He hesitated. "That is, the two older ones. Bob was in the Army a while ago, Major, and sometimes he don't feel so good. Maybe, Mazie, Bob could eat in his room, uh?"

But Durant said: "I'd like to meet all your sons, Mrs. Lincoln. I've heard that your Bob is your right arm. Tell him I want to meet him more than I do your other sons."

Mrs. Lincoln had lost some of her high color, and her eyelids trembled. Grace said, with annoyance: "Oh, Major, you won't like Bob! He's so sullen. He isn't always responsible for what he says. He was hurt in the war, too, and we've got to take care of him. Sometimes—sometimes he loses his temper and we're always afraid—"

"Still," said Durant kindly, "I'd like to meet him. I'm an old Army man, myself. I was first a sergeant and then a lieutenant, and served for nearly four years. Your other sons weren't in the Armed Forces, Mr. Lincoln?"

The farmer shook his head helplessly. "Bob didn't have to go. But he wanted to. Said he ought to go, and find out what it was all about. He hasn't been the same since—"

"It was kind of stupid for Bob to go," said Mrs. Lincoln, with affront. "No farmer's boys ever have to go into the Army. Farms are essential. The farm boys got priority; needed at home, for the war efforts. And it wasn't that Bob was patriotic—"

Lincoln interposed almost with panic. "He was very patriotic! Thought he ought to do his share. Said I had two other boys, and he wasn't needed. Mazie! It's dinnertime!"

"You'll like Bob," Grandon informed Durant. "He has a mind of his own. That's all right for farmers, unless they let their minds run away with them." He grinned. "But you don't have to worry, Mr. Lincoln. Not when you have such a lovely young lady like Miss Lincoln, here."

Durant smiled inwardly. This was becoming very interesting. Lincoln said: "Dinnertime, Mazie!"

She nodded; her fear was rising. She motioned to her daughter, who was again engrossed with Grandon. "Gracie, let's go."

"I hope three unexpected guests won't inconvenience you," said Durant, approaching his hostess.

The little gray eyes turned toward the lieutenant and the sergeant. "Two extra at the table's all right," she said.

"Three," corrected Durant, gently. "I, the lieutenant, and the sergeant."

There was a sudden abrupt silence in the room. Mrs. Lincoln opened and shut her mouth without a sound. Grace stared. Lincoln's red face turned faintly purplish. Grandon smiled happily, and the sergeant grinned and straightened his shoulders. "Three," repeated Durant, in that same gentle tone. "Nothing is too good for the Army, you said, Mr. Lincoln."

"Yes, yes, of course!" exclaimed Lincoln. His wife was rooted on the threshold. He seized her arm, and they lumbered ahead, unevenly.

While in the vast parlor of this farmhouse, Durant had been conscious of an incongruity between everything which was supremely tasteful and yet was without taste. It had been a very subtle difference, and now he understood intuitively that objects, themselves perfect and exquisite, could acquire a dullness and lack of sparkle of life when in the presence of innate coarseness and insensitivity.

The dining room, with its wonderful carved and mosaic-work furniture, held that same uneasiness of inanimate yet peculiarly conscious things. Everything was overlain with the dulled patina of grossness which was a part of the Lincolns. Durant thought, with a smile at his own fancifulness, that everything in the room resented its owners and refused to give up its ultimate charm for them. The magnificent silver, highly polished, gave off a plated and tarnished gleam; the brocaded curtains lacked a certain grandeur of fold. The painting of fruits over the buffet was the crude work of a child. Durant strolled over to study it, excited over his own imaginings. Then he saw that it was a Van Gogh; he had seen this very painting reproduced, long ago, in magazines.

The light struck the painting fully, and so it ought to have revealed itself in all its brilliance of color and captured light. But it did not. It had blurred itself, hidden itself as if in a revolted shadow.

"Picked that up in Washington for three hams," said Lincoln, with proud complacency. "Like it, Major? Maybe I was cheated, uh?"

"Yes," said Durant, reflectively. "You were."

"I told you so!" said Mrs. Lincoln, angrily. "That old thing! It don't look like fruit, anyways."

Durant thought, looking at the Van Gogh: You're mine. Wait.

Grace giggled, "Daddy always wants his money's worth. And he gets cheated. Three hams for that awful thing."

Before they seated themselves, a young man entered, a big young man with rough dark hair and a sun-darkened face, and sullen, intelligent eyes. He had Mrs. Lincoln's heavy features, but his had a quickened quality which eliminated the coarseness. His mouth was tight and hard, and he had put a coat over his farmer's overalls. His hands, though clean, showed evidences of hard work in the thickened knuckles, ingrained soil about the fingernails, and calluses. It was evident that he had known nothing about the three military guests, for, when he saw them, he stopped sharply on the threshold and a look of intense and open hatred stood on his face.

Mrs. Lincoln and her husband greeted him effusively, as if they had not seen him for weeks. Mrs. Lincoln waddled to him and linked his arm with hers, and said loudly: "The new major, Bob! And you know Lieutenant Grandon, and—and—" Her bellicose but frightened eye touched Sergeant Keiser, then fell away, affronted.

"Yes, yes!" said John Lincoln, and in his voice was a pleading and desperate note. "Son, the new major of the district!"

Bob Lincoln did not even glance at the lesser officers. His eyes fixed themselves on Durant, and his hatred was naked and without fear. He said nothing; he did not move, yet he seemed to be resisting his mother's desperate tug on his arm.

Lincoln laughed heartily, as he waved the officers to places at the lavishly set table. "Bob doesn't talk much," he explained. "Kind of shy with strangers, like all us farmers. Major, right there beside Mrs. Lincoln. Lieutenant, er, beside Gracie, in your usual place, of course. Sergeant—" He paused. He was, in his way, looking for a seat "below the salt." Sergeant Keiser stared at him. "All right, Sergeant, right here near me." He sat down, without waiting for his wife and daughter. "Yes, Bob's shy. Don't like to talk, do you, Bob?" There was warning in every word.

"Please, honey, please," Mrs. Lincoln whispered to Bob, who still stood rigidly on the threshold. She pulled at his arm, and, his eyes still fixed on Durant, he allowed himself to be drawn to the table. He ignored the place next to Durant, and sat down at the far end of the table near Sergeant Keiser. And then he settled weightily in his chair, his back bent, his eyes riveted on his plate. Durant felt his immense hostility and loathing, and there was a quickening interest in him. Here was no placating of the omnipresent, the omnipotent Military, but a powerful repudiation.

Every silver serving-dish was loaded with ham, chicken, lamb and beef, and the best of vegetables, the most tempting of gravies, the whitest of bread. White bread! Durant had not eaten white bread for years. He had never seen so prodigal a meal in his life. There was enough food on the table to feed thirty people—thirty starving people in the cities! The scent of good cooking, hearty and lavish cooking, rose in a steam of plenty over the lace tablecloth. Pitchers of rich yellow milk stood near every plate. The dinnerware was white with a wide border of fading gold, and the silver was heavy in Durant's hand, and delicately chased. He saw an initial on each piece: "M," enscrolled and shaded. Who was "M"? Was the family dead long ago, or in exile, or starving in some war-plant barracks, or in some rat-ridden tenement? Anything was possible. Durant surveyed the table again, the heaps of food, the lace, the plates, the pitchers of milk, and the violence of his own hatred almost choked him. Involuntarily, he looked at Bob Lincoln, and the hatred was there, too, for him, stronger and wilder than before.

For an instant the two young men regarded each other, their eyes locked together. Then a strange thing happened. Bob appeared startled and taken aback and uncertain. He picked up a piece of silver and his big hand shook.

Dr. Dodge entered silently, carrying a tray of coffee cups, beautiful pieces of eggshell steaming with fragrant liquid. Grace was babbling to Grandon, Lincoln and his wife were talking loudly and genially along the length of the table, Sergeant Keiser was already stuffing himself ravenously. There was a dreamlike and disembodied air about the illustrious doctor, as if he did not know where he was but was moving in a trance. Out of the corner of his eye Durant saw Bob suddenly watching the old man, and the young man's expression was inscrutable.

Durant, as a lawyer in the service of the State, had been allowed slightly better rations for his family and himself in New York. But he had forgotten that such food as this ever existed. He found himself extremely hungry. Yet, after a mouthful or two, he could no longer eat. The food sickened him. When Dr. Dodge tried to serve him some gravy, he shook his head. It was then that Dr. Dodge paused and stood immobile, the silver gravy-boat in his hand, his white-sleeved arm almost touching Durant's shoulder. He gazed into space, like a dreamer vaguely disturbed, and the corners of his mouth quivered. Then he moved almost imperceptibly, and his wrist lightly pressed itself against Durant's arm, as if something had dimly stirred in him, and was blindly reaching and exploring.

Struck to the heart with his compassion and sorrow though he was, Durant knew that he dared not betray his sensations for an instant. The old man had sensed him, had subconsciously known, if only for an instant. That instant, if prolonged, could become dangerous. He moved his left arm with an expression of annoyance. Lincoln saw this. He roared furiously: "Bill! Have you gone to sleep? Come over here. I want that gravy, if the major doesn't want any." He turned to Lieutenant Grandon. "Sometimes we have trouble with old Bill, and I'm thinking of sending him back to the city."

Grandon laughed blithely. "That'll be the end of him, then. Be big-hearted, Johnny, be big-hearted! The old goat does know how to serve, doesn't he?" His quick eyes touched Dr. Dodge with humor. "He couldn't work in any war plant, could he? He'd just 'disappear' in town. Just keep him in pasture." He was highly amused at what he apparently considered his wit, for he laughed delightedly, and Grace joined him.

But Mrs. Lincoln was pettish. "Even though we don't pay him anything, and just keep him in the barracks with the others, he's getting to be a nuisance. Like—like hypnotized, or something, Bill!" she said sharply. "Miss Grace needs more coffee."

Dr. Dodge moved away in his trance, his head bowed. Durant studiously avoided looking at him. Then he became aware that

Bob was not eating at all. Durant said: "How many years were you in the Army, Bob?"

The young man seemed not to hear for a second or two, then he said, huskily, without glancing at Durant: "What's it to you? Nearly three years, if you want to know." Then, abruptly, he looked at Durant and the hatred was vivid on his face. "I was a captain. I was wounded twice. And I had radiation sickness for a year." He continued to glare at Durant. "What happened to old Major Burnes? Was he murdered?"

"Oh, Bob!" Mrs. Lincoln screamed in absolute terror. "Why do you talk like that? You don't know what you're saying! The major—"

But Bob repeated, as if his mother had not spoken at all: "Was he murdered?"

Grandon was laughing gleefully. "What a thing to say, Bob!" And he shook his head as if delighted.

"Was he?" asked Bob of Durant, and his fists clenched.

"Don't be ridiculous," replied Andrew coldly. "He's a colonel, now. In—in Chicago."

Lincoln was frightfully alarmed, both at his son's attack and Durant's tone. He tried to speak, but could only wet his lips fearfully, his eyes darting from one young man to another. Grandon was highly amused, and grinning. Sergeant Keiser, momentarily diverted from his food, moved his bull-like neck from side to side as he watched Durant and Bob Lincoln acutely.

"In Chicago," said Bob, as if bitterly reflecting. "You wouldn't have his address, would you, Major? You must have known him, didn't you, Major? You'd know where he is, and what he's doing, wouldn't you, Major?"

Durant shrugged. "Suppose you write to the Chief Magistrate, Bob."

"The Chief Magistrate," repeated Bob absently. "Yes. The Chief Magistrate." Then he turned fully to the major. "This new war: good for the Military, isn't it? When did you make up your minds whom to fight next?"

"Bob!" moaned Mrs. Lincoln, desperately trying to catch her husband's attention.

Mr. Lincoln said ponderously, and his face had turned gray: "Bob, it's your old war injuries botherin' you. Why do you always—I mean, why do you say such things? Here's our new major, a young feller like you—Major Curtiss. He's here to help us, specially now we got another war. We'll need at least twenty-five more people, for the war effort, raising food. Maybe fifty more, and the major promised—"

" 'The war effort,' " said Bob, without the slightest inflection in his voice. "Yes, yes, 'the war effort.' I'm always forgetting there's always a new 'war effort.' " Then, without warning, he burst out laughing, and the sound was terrible. He stood up, spilling his cup of coffee, unaware of his mother's faint scream, his sister's dim dismay, his father's terror. Then, without a word or a look, he stumbled from the room, still laughing maniacally. They could hear that laughter retreating, diminishing. Yet, it seemed as if the echo remained in the warm and pleasant dining room like an ominous presence.

Durant drank his coffee thoughtfully, listening to the heavy silence. He said, with kindness: "Some of these young veterans suffer a long time from their injuries. Well, he won't have to go for this new war. He's essential. He shouldn't have gone in the first place."

Lincoln exhaled, released from his terror. He said effusively: "You're right, Major! Exactly right! We tried to stop him—needed him right here on the farm. But he went away and enlisted under another name. We didn't know where he was for nearly three years. It was awful, wasn't it, Mazie?"

"Yes," said the woman, whimpering. She had not liked Durant at first. Now she regarded him with docile pleading and relief. He hadn't been offended; he hadn't taken offense at Bob. He had understood. He was a veteran himself, a soldier. And the Military needed the farmers. Why, if the farmers refused to produce, the Military would starve! The farmers were everything in The Democracy. Hadn't the President himself said so? She felt quite warm, and reassured. No, she hadn't liked Durant at first. She and her husband had "managed" the old major. He had been a friend of the family. Perhaps this young officer could be managed. Why, he was even nice-looking, and a major, too! She moistened her lips: "Major, are your wife and children living in Philadelphia?"

"Oh, I'm not married," said Durant, smiling easily.

Mrs. Lincoln's little eyes flashed to her daughter. Now, a major in the family! He seemed very important. Hadn't her husband whispered to her that Major Curtiss had been given much greater powers than old Major Burnes? Mrs. Lincoln trilled coquettishly: "We'll just have to find a wife for you, Major!"

Durant let his glance rove first to Grandon, who had stopped smiling so broadly, and then to Grace Lincoln, who was giving him a long blue stare. "Why, yes," said Durant gravely, "it might be a good idea."

Grandon was not smiling at all. His young face darkened. Grace Lincoln smiled and preened herself. Sergeant Keiser watched everybody.

Lincoln, having noticed Durant's apparent and admiring interest in his daughter, became expansive. A major, and a powerful one, would be excellent in this family. He, Lincoln, did not like Grandon, who was only a lieutenant, and "light-minded" and without "a grain of sense." With the small but tight suspiciousness of the countryman, Lincoln thought: Andrew Curtiss. A good old, a fine old, American name. This major did not "suit" the name, it was true, with that complexion and those eyes and that hair, but he spoke "American" and acted "American." Lincoln, glowing like the sun, brought out his best brandy, and to show his sophistication he poured it, himself, into large brandy glasses. He almost forgot the indignity of having a mere sergeant at his table, and his early uneasiness.

He eagerly assented to Durant's suggestion that the farm be inspected. So he and Durant, accompanied by a somewhat resentful Grandon and a silent Keiser, went on a tour of inspection. The mighty barns, bulging with farm products, attracted Durant, and Lincoln, intoxicated by praise, was only too glad to explain. He showed Durant the mountains of fat smoked hams, the granaries, the sides of bacon, the freeze-houses where hung endless rows of fine, fresh beef, and where stood countless jars of excellent butter. "We use all we want, ourselves, first," explained the farmer, smiling broadly. "Then we sell the rest to the Government. The Armed Forces get it, and the Government men, and our allies. I got to admit that I've some wonderful things, here, but there's millions like me, all over the country, some bigger than me, some smaller. The Government scientists sure have taught us the best way to raise things, and we produce twice what we did twenty years ago."

"Enough to feed everybody in The Democracy to the bursting point," suggested Durant, with a wise smile and wink.

Lincoln laughed with rich knowingness. "Yep, that's right. But you know the Government knows best! Feed the cities too much meat and white bread and butter and such, and first thing you know they'll get uppity and out of control, and that's be the end of our wonderful Government, and the rest of us." He poked Durant in the ribs with a comradely elbow. "Got to keep the rabble in the cities just fed enough so they can work but not enough to give 'em ideas."

Durant affected to find this very amusing. "Anyways, we farmers get our money, and big money, for it, from the Government. And now, with the new war effort, we'll have to raise more."

"And get more," said Durant, with friendly confidence.

"That's right. The Grange takes care of all negotiations with the Government. No paper money for the Grange! We got to protect ourselves. Like the Armed Forces."

"We don't get gold," said Durant, yawning to show his indifference. He turned around, suddenly, and caught Keiser's sudden black glower and the strange expression on Grandon's face. He held back his own conspirator's smile, and angrily warned himself. How did he know what these men were really thinking?

They wandered out to the fields, in the most confiding terms. They leaned casually on the well-kept fences. Before them, the broad valley rose and fell gently in green brilliance under the spring sun, and herds of fat cattle grazed placidly beneath trees filled with a green mist. Beyond the valley the mountains rose in blue clouds against a lighter blue sky, and birds, returned from the south, chattered and sang shrilly in the warm stillness. There was such an air of peace and plenty here, such a richness and fecund steadfastness and hope. Durant thought of the dark and ratty cities, the flaking buildings, the want and hunger. He thought of the hopelessness, the faceless multitudes, conscripted and hunted and watched and driven to motiveless work, if one wished to believe that the constant wars were motiveless. No, they were not motiveless, Durant remembered with sudden and smothering rage. They were motives in themselves, though the "Enemy" was never the same.

Durant leaned on the fence with his left arm, and studied the scores of men who were busy in the fields and around the farmyards. They appeared to be a little better fed than their fellows in the cities, though their clothing was ragged. They went about their work, heads bent, faces dull and expressionless, motions automatic. Some of them had distinguished features. Teachers and doctors, businessmen and artists, probably, before they had been conscripted for this labor because of "subversiveness." Durant examined them a little more closely, looking for one bitter or rebellious eye, one eye aflame with hate. But no man, or no woman, glanced up.

Well, thought Durant, with a sudden and somber hatred of his own, you had your chance. But so many of you were so enthusiastic about Socialism and Communism and "Government control of the means of production," and Statism, and all the other ancient horrors of oppression, not more than twenty years ago. You were young, then, and you were either too unrealistic, or greedy, or you were full of "idealism." I wonder, thought Durant, if those emotions aren't, in the final analysis, one and the same thing after all? At any rate, you men and you women out there, tending beasts or plowing or planting, are in a great part responsible for your own serfdom. You were used by your masters all the time, and perhaps your punishment is just.

Five middle-aged men, carrying spades and other farm equipment, passed near Durant and Lincoln, on the other side of the fence. They moved silently, as if in a trance. Durant raised his voice. "Your two-legged animals don't look as intelligent as your four-legged ones, Mr. Lincoln."

The farmer roared happily at this witticism, and slapped his broad thigh. The farm laborers shuffled on, apparently deaf. They were about ten feet beyond the farmer and the soldiers when two of them suddenly glanced back, and their thin browned faces were contorted with malignant hate and menace. Their eyes had come alive, and there was murder in them. Lincoln did not see this. He shouted angrily: "Go on there, you Jimmy and Tom. There's work to do. Don't lag behind."

Jimmy and Tom. Durant concentrated on these men with surprise and satisfaction. When the day came, Lincoln and his family would probably be very efficiently, if slowly, slaughtered. And I, too, probably, thought Durant, without much pleasure. Again, he was determined not only to fight for the restoration of the Republic and the Constitution, but to live for it. There must be a way. He was a young man, with a wife and family. The Chief Magistrate had dedicated his life to his country, and had no other interest. This was excellent, and without him nothing could be done. Steely fanatics were necessary if the Republic were to live again, but there must also be men to restock that Republic so that it would be strong and invulnerable. The masses in the cities were quite hopeless. They had eagerly delivered themselves to their crime-infiltered unions twenty-five or thirty years ago, had become the slaves of gangsters and exploiters, decades before the Republic had been crushed. So, there must be free and honorable men left alive to beget a finer and nobler race, to again establish liberty and justice for all.

Deeply, Durant inhaled the vividly fresh and fragrant air of the countryside. He would never again, he resolved, live in any city. His grandfather had once told him that when men go too far from the earth, become too engrossed in the artificial life of cosmopolitanism, they spiritually become exiles and homeless. How many men, in the cities, knew from what distant streams, what deep mountain wells and rivers, their water was derived, and from what smiling and silent acres they drew their sustenance?

Lincoln was now pointing out to Durant the chimneys and red roofs where his two older sons lived, and he was pridefully boasting of their families. "Kids as fat as butter, and porky, too," he was saying. "Not like those little white mice in the cities." His voice was full of the countryman's contempt for the city-dweller. "Got ten good bedrooms in my own house, with four baths; big enough for the whole three families. But my boys wanted their own houses, and now I think it's fine."

"Wonderful, to live here," Durant remarked.

"Yes, indeedy," said Lincoln, with complacence.

Durant leaned more comfortably on the fence, and nodded at the fields. "I'm a city man myself, I've decided I don't like it, Mr. Lincoln. And I think a lot of my men would prefer to be out here, too." He lifted himself from the fence, and smiled at the suddenly sober farmer, and his smile was disarming. "So, Mr. Lincoln, you've got yourself five new boarders. We're moving in on you, Mr. Lincoln. Tonight."

As at a signal, the lieutenant and the sergeant quickly stepped closer to Durant, and Lincoln, gray as ash, saw the three smiling and alert faces, and the three pairs of eyes which were, all at once, not friendly but cruelly amused. His big knees began to shake; his voice rumbled in his throat and he could hardly speak.

"Move in on me?" he stuttered, incredulous. "You—you can't, Major. That—that's against the law. We farmers got the law—We—"

"The Army makes the law, Lincoln," replied Durant curtly, but still smiling. "Remember? We make the law. The President just signs what we tell him to sign. Besides, the Army is your friend, isn't it? You aren't going to turn on the Army, are you, Lincoln?"

"My God, no!" cried Lincoln, with absolute terror. He clutched the fence-rail, and swallowed visibly. "But, Major! It—it ain't right. The other farmers—"

"I am going to issue a directive, tonight, that all the Military who want to may move in on the farmers—and enjoy the happy life, too. Of course, that is only for my district, but I think that the Military all over the country will follow the action of the Military in Section 7, very soon."

Wildly, Lincoln thought of the Grange. Why, the Grange wouldn't stand for this stupefying thing. The Grange was Everything! All the farmers had to do was to lie down on the job, and then see who was really the strongest, the Military or the farmers! Why, the President, threatened by a countryside strike of the farmers, especially now that he had created a new war, would soon know who was Boss in this country!

Durant, watching that jerking and that twitching face, understood exactly the thought behind it. He said casually: "I suppose the farmers won't like it, at first. Maybe some of them will go on strike, or shout that they won't produce. That'll be very bad for them, Lincoln. Because we'll just take over their farms and let their conscripted labor run them. Besides, thousands of the Military were once country boys, themselves, and with the help of Government agriculturists they'll manage very well." He paused, as if musing. "I've often wondered why it was necessary to have independent farmers at all! Why can't we have collectivized farms, the same as they have in Europe? Why hasn't somebody thought of that in Washington before this?"

Lincoln, completely desperate, blurted out: "Because we've been boss of this country for forty years, that's why! Every President for forty years has made us his special pet, with subsidies, in the beginning, and then with conscripted labor! No President would dare col—collectivize us. Why, us loyal farmers—all we had to do was report other farmers that was subversive and stuck up their noses and voted for the old Republican Party, and we got their farms away from them without any trouble. The President knew who was—" He stopped, appalled at what he had said.

Durant's face was nothing but attentive and quiet, though he was thinking of the brave and independent men who had been murdered in order that rascals like this one might have their property. It was hard for a man of Durant's nature to restrain fury and disgust, and not to betray his emotions. He succeeded, he decided, very well. At any rate, his voice was quiet and almost uninterested, as he said: "You're wrong, Lincoln, and you know it. The Military is 'Boss' in The Democracy. We've been very good to you farmers, and now it is time for you to be good to us. Your gold: well, from this time on, the farmers in Section 7 receive paper money, just like the Military. And in Section 7, the Military will decide how much your crops are worth to the country."

Lincoln was struck dumb. He blinked over and over at Durant. His staring eyes pleaded with Grandon and Keiser, who only smiled grimly. Then Lincoln thought again: The Grange! He'd telephone the local chairman at once.

"The Grange," said Durant thoughtfully. "When you talk to them will you please tell them I'd like to see your chairman tomorrow morning, in my office in Philadelphia? I'll give him a copy of the directive then."

Durant pretended to an outraged anger, and he struck the fence-rail with his left fist. "To think of the Military having to live in the city, eating what the farmers want to give them, sweltering in the summer, picking their way through the broken streets, having paper money, loitering in the ratty parks on their time off, breathing filthy air! And all this, out here, for millions and millions of acres, enjoyed by only a few! It's terrible. It's time something was done about it, and I'm making a start."

Lincoln was terrified at the rage on Durant's face. But still his stubborn mind came back, again and again, to the Grange, and all its power. He stuttered: "Why, Major, the Military's got the best hotels and such in the cities, and it gets good food, almost as good's the farmers. We got gold for our crops; we won't take paper money, no sir! Crops is gold. We've worked real close with the Military all the time; we've been loyal and patriotic. Nothing too good for the Military, in the cities." He was gasping, now, and his forehead purpled. "Why, there's a law about—about quartering the Military on the people—"

Durant lifted himself to as stiff a height as possible, and glared savagely at Lincoln. "What!" he cried. "What's this subversion? You're quoting the old—the old Constitution!" He paused, to let this awful fact enter Lincoln's floundering mind. "The Constitution! Lincoln, I could order your arrest right now, and within an hour you'd be in the military prison in Philadelphia, and within two days your farm would be confiscated, and given to a loyal man, and your wife and family would be in the war plants, working for the war effort. Don't you realize that you've practically branded yourself as a traitor by quoting," and here he let his face show horror at the obscenity, "the Constitution, a document which was abrogated years ago?"

He shook his fist under Lincoln's nose, which had become white and pinched. "This deserves a thorough investigation, my man. An investigation of all your activities. Perhaps we can show that you're really a Minute Man, betraying your country in secret, and preparing for a revolution."

"Oh God, God!" groaned Lincoln, his knees bending. "Major, you oughtn't to say that. I'm a good, loyal, patriotic American, Major. Why, way back when I was a young feller I never voted Republican. You can look at my records. Major, you don't mean what you say." His agonized eyes begged at Durant like a whipped dog's. Mazie and Gracie, in the city, in war plants! His girls, starving like the rest of the damned city! His boys in labor camps. Himself, tortured and finally murdered. His farm, his land, given to someone else, with all the nice things in the house which he'd got from the city rats! He squeezed his eyelids together, involuntarily, and a few tears, like drops of blood, appeared on his cheeks.

Durant contemplated him. Was this flabby and suddenly broken man a possible source of revolution? Would he resist? Under designed pressure, would he talk to his fellow farmers and incite them? No, he was too old, he was too greedy. There were his sons who were younger: could anything be done with them? It might be. The older men were hopeless.

"The Constitution!" said Durant, with loathing. "You old fellows remember that dangerous paper, don't you? You can't forget, can you? I suppose you've taught your sons about it eh, Lincoln?"

"No! No!" moaned the farmer. "I ain't, honestly, Major. Look, Major, you can move in right away. I got a nice room—"

Durant shook his head, smiling. "I want the best room, Lincoln. Yours and your wife's. I need privacy and space. And then there's Lieutenant Grandon, here. The next best room, and privacy. Sergeant Keiser will need a nice room. And there's my captains. They'll want very fine rooms, to themselves, of course. All rooms will use the bathrooms. On other thought, Lincoln, you'd better move your whole family downstairs, or in the attic. Your son, Bob, can move into the barracks. A good idea! He can keep his eye on the workers. You see, Lincoln, the Military needs absolute privacy. No one permitted on the second floor except for cleaning purposes."

The whole shining countryside revolved around Lincoln. Anguish and fear clutched at his heart, and he put a trembling hand on his big chest. "Why, Major," he almost sobbed, cringing, there ain't any bedrooms on the first floor, and only three attic bedrooms on the third."

Durant shrugged. "I'm afraid you and your wife and daughter

will have to arrange something on the first floor for yourselves, or sleep in the attic. Bill and the other two servants can sleep in the barracks. Or perhaps you'd rather your family did?"

"I think Gracie ought to have the best attic room," said the lieutenant, with the utmost gravity. "I like to think of Gracie right near us."

Lincoln's distended eyes swung wetly to Grandon, and then to Keiser. He moistened his lips. He saw the lewd and knowing expressions on the men's faces. He gasped. "Gracie—she'll sleep in the same room with me and my wife. I—I—" He could not speak and could only cling to the fence-rail.

Durant said: "Make the arrangements at once, Lincoln. I've got to run into the city for a few hours. We'll be back tonight, all five of us. Have things ready. If anything goes wrong," he added menacingly, "I'll remember what you've said here, Lincoln. But if you behave, I'll forget." He turned to his officers. "We'll forget, won't we, boys?"

He turned to Lincoln again. "And here's an order, to save time. Call the Grange offices in Philadelphia, at once, and let them know. That's an order."

A soft voice said near them: "Anything wrong, Dad?" They all swung about and saw Bob Lincoln standing near them. There was a dangerously gentle smile on his face. Durant eyed him with what he hoped was an intimidating glower.

"Nothing wrong," he said darkly. "I've just given your father some orders, Bob. He'll explain them to you."

"Orders?" repeated Bob mildly, raising his brows.

"Military orders," said Durant crisply. Openly, and with meaning, Grandon and Keiser put their hands on their guns. Bob saw the gesture. He smiled with contempt. Durant studied him. Yes, a good candidate for revolution. Durant went on: "Have you forgotten that the Military runs this country, Bob? When we give orders, they're absolute ones, and you know it. After all, you farmers helped to give us our power, didn't you? Well, then, obey."

"Don't say anything, don't say anything, Bob, in the name of God!" cried Lincoln, in panic. He clutched his son's arm, and then began to whimper. "Just don't say anything, Bob."

His son surveyed him in amazement. He jerked his arm as if to throw off his father's hand, then he stopped. Slowly he turned his head and stared piercingly at the officers. He thoughtfully bit his lip. He seemed very quiet, but his dark face became rigid.

"Your father has just been quoting the Constitution to us," said Durant, smilingly. "You haven't heard about the Constitution, have you, Bob?"

The young man's hands clenched into great fists. Lines sprang out around his mouth. But he was silent.

"That's a capital offense, in itself," Durant reminded him. "But I want to work peacefully with you farmers in my district. I'm not venegeful. Sometimes these old men forget—things—and remember what they learned in school. That can't be helped. So we're going to forget what your father said, provided none of you cause us any trouble."

Two big young men were now seen approaching them across the green field. Durant, after a glance at their faces, dismissed them with disappointment. It was easy to see that they were the other sons of Lincoln, but they had none of their younger brother's dark ferocity or intelligence, nor his secret thoughts. Bland, coarse of feature, avaricious of small eye, loose of mouth, like their mother, it was unlikely that they could be stirred to revolution. But still, they were young, and there was Bob.

Durant said: "I'd like you, Grandon, and you, Keiser, to go into the city with me for a few hours."

He glanced back over his shoulders, as he walked away. Lincoln was leaning in collapse against the fence. His two older sons were questioning him excitedly. But Bob stood apart, and he was looking after the new enemy. The sun struck full on the face, and it was the face of a murderer. Durant smiled.

On the way to Philadelphia, Durant tried to infer something of importance in the conversation of his sergeant and lieutenant. But the young men were only clearly jubilant over Lincoln's downfall. It was clear that they had contempt, envy and animosity for the farmers, and were delighted at the prospect of the military dictatorship subjugating the countrymen. They laughed and chuckled and shook their heads, and glanced admiringly and approvingly at Durant.

His loneliness was on him with stifling weight. Philadelphia did nothing to reduce his burden. Broad Street was a wilderness of craters and holes and crumbling and deserted buildings. It was as if the city had been bombarded by enemy planes, just as all other American cities had this appearance. But not a single enemy bomb had fallen anywhere upon America, throughout all the ghastly wars, though Europe had had this opportunity. Only America had used the atomic and the hydrogen and the nitrogen bomb. This was supposed, exultantly, to be the result of superior American technology and the fear which the rest of the world felt for The Democracy. Not even shattered Russia or Germany or Britain or Scandinavia, or any other nation, or coalition of nations, had attempted to strike at American cities, nor had Asia or Africa. Durant doubted the given reasons, and thinking of them now he was more embittered than ever. He looked at the streets and the buildings of Philadelphia, and he saw the same degradation and ruin and despair and meekness of the people's faces such as he had seen on the faces of the New York mobs. Even the mass bombings of American cities could not have produced more devastation than all this. He was a young man, and he had always been resolute. For the first time he was shaken and disheartened and without hope. He could only do what he was ordered to do. He had no real faith in the outcome. The people were lost.

But, in the final hours of national fall, no one should have comforts and privileges, he thought, with hatred. The farmers, the MASTS, the pampered and the safe, would, with his help, go down with the rest of The Democracy. Let the utter wilderness come! There would not be one left to gloat over his gold or his stores of food or his position and safety. There was no longer in him any faith in the revolt of the outraged few. His experience with Lincoln had convinced him of that. No, he no longer had faith; he wanted only vengeance. Death would come to everybody, or starvation, or complete barbarism. The hell with the whole, goddamned stinking world! he said to himself.

Soldiers, armed with guns and clubs, patrolled the almost silent streets. Over twelve years ago the Military had replaced the police, with directives or with violence. The police had resisted manfully for a time, for, in the main, they were simple and honest men, and had believed in what they had learned in their schools. However, "for reasons of security," their piteous attempts at independence had been crushed. "For reasons of security," reflected Durant. The jargon of the despots. The people had listened, and for some years they had had the strength and the power to revolt. They had not done so. The hell with them, thought Durant, and he looked at the passing multitudes with detestation and would not let himself try to discover if here and there there might be the face of a man.

The car began to wind its way up some very handsome streets, well kept and secure and prosperous. Here, as in some streets in New York, lived the extremely wealthy and invulnerable, the MASTS and the bureaucrats. Their rosy children played under the supervision of nurses in the heliotrope spring twilight. Shining cars lined the curbs. Windows shone in the last red sun, and pretty women walked up and down the scrubbed steps. The military police were much in evidence, very brisk and very wary, stopping only to smile at the nursemaids or to keep a sharp eye on the shrieking and leaping children. The Government had never had any difficulty in persuading some men of enormous wealth and industrial power to join it in the oppression of the people. Washington, shrewdly utilizing the experience of Russia and other Communist nations, had not even had to threaten, stupidly, the lives or property of many of the affluent and secure. It had needed only chuckling words behind official doors.

"Aren't we going out of our way?" Durant asked.

"Oh, we thought you might like to see some sections of the city," replied Grandon blandly. His quick, mischievous eyes stared without guile at Durant. "They have it nice here, don't they?"

"Perhaps we could move in on them, as we're going to do with the farmers," suggested Durant, with a smile.

Grandon shook his head, and laughed. "Can't be done. Not with these fellows. They know too much, and—they help too much. We've got to be on their side, and they have to be on ours."

Durant studied him, but Grandon's smile was boyish and amused. However, Keiser's face was clearly visible for an instant in the rearview mirror of the car, and it was black and scowling. Durant was alerted. Then Keiser's eyes, meeting his own in the mirror, became blank.

"Well, Major," said Grandon, "this city's all yours. All the Military. Everybody. The big fellows in these streets will be inviting you to dinners and parties, and you'll meet all their pretty wenches. You'll have a good time, when you're in town."

"I expect to have a very wonderful time," said Durant grimly.

The executive offices of the Military in Philadelphia were housed in the best hotel, and here, Durant was informed by Grandon, the major would have his own luxurious suite. He, Grandon, would call a doctor immediately to look over the broken arm, and tomorrow he would arrange for the best dentist in the city to take care of the teeth "injured in the accident." Durant nodded. The three young men entered the fine lobby of the hotel, and lesser officers came to curious attention and saluted. They took Durant's measure instantly, and decided that the "old Major's" indulgence and tolerance were not in this "new feller." He looked hard and bitter, even savage, and scarcely noticed the salutes. One of these strict military bastards, they decided among themselves with dismay and resentment .

In silence, the three officers were taken up in the gilded elevator, to the tenth floor. Two military policemen came to attention as Durant and Grandon and Keiser came out. Grandon, obviously pleased by his position as guide, led Durant to an excellent suite, lavishly furnished. Durant hardly having fallen into a velvet chair near the window and hardly having closed his eyes for an instant, was startled by Grandon's sudden laugh. The lieutenant had been glancing over a pile of notes on the large walnut desk in the middle of the living room. "Well, action's begun," he grinned. "Walter Morrow, head of Section 7's Grange, is already waiting for you, Major! Note here says it's important. Shall I tell Morrow to come back some other time?"

"No, said Durant, wincing at the pain in his arm when he sat up. "Send the—send him in. Might as well get started."

Highly delighted, Grandon went out and returned with two captains, who saluted Durant smartly. Durant scrutinized the new arrivals. Captains Bishop and Edwards were men in their thirties, with the rock-like and brutal faces of professional soldiers. If they had any intelligence at all, it was not visible. Durant sighed, spoke to them briefly. He did not notice, in his weariness, that Grandon was watching him. He told Bishop and Edwards that tomorrow they would join him in their new quarters on Lincoln's farm. They displayed no surprise. They had been trained from boyhood to obey and to have no thoughts of their own. Durant dismissed them from his mind as he would dismiss unthinking animals.

Then Walter Morrow of the Grange came in, a short portly man with bristling gray hair, restless brown eyes glittering with anger, and a violent mouth. He barely listened to Grandon's introduction, but stood, braced and belligerent, in the corner of the room, his fists knotted.

"So, you're the new major!" he said in a loud, rough voice, regarding Durant with mingled contempt and umbrage.

"I am. Sit down," said Durant courteously.

But Morrow did not sit down. He stood there and slowly and deliberately contemplated Durant, and every flick of his eyes was an insult. "What happened to the old major?" he asked abruptly.

"Why don't you ask the Chief Magistrate of Section 7, who sent me here?" asked Durant, in return.

"Dead, eh?" Morrow smiled with unpleasantness.

Durant shrugged. "Why don't you ask the Chief Magistrate?" he repeated.

Grandon and Keiser smirked. The other two officers merely stood like wooden replicas of themselves.

"Perhaps I will ask," said Morrow, after another contemplation of Durant.

"Did you want to see me about anything?" demanded Durant impatiently. "I've been in an accident, and I'm tired and need a doctor. If what you have to say isn't important—and these are not my business hours—please go, or make an appointment with Lieutenant Grandon here to see me in about four weeks' time. Grandon," and he glanced at the young lieutenant, "make an appointment four weeks from today for Mr. Morrow."

Grandon made a considerable frowning show of glancing through an appointment book. "I'm sorry, Major," he said, "but there is nothing open for six weeks. On a Thursday, perhaps, from one-thirty to one-forty-five P.M."

Morrow inhaled a deep breath and exhaled it like the snort of a bull. "No," he said. "Today. Now. I've just heard from Johnny Lincoln, Major, and I've come here to tell you that the Grange protects Lincoln, and all the other farmers—"

"From what?" asked Durant, with interest.

Morrow's face paled, but became stronger. "From you," he answered, with calm simplicity.

Durant affected to be galvanized with fury. "Are you insane?" he demanded. "Who are you, or any of the oafs you represent, to insult the Army like this?" He struck the arm of his chair with his fist. "Who rules this country, but the Army? Who gives out absolute directives, but the Army? Who lives or dies, except by permission of the Army? I think it's time that you and your followers learned this, Morrow. You'll begin to learn it as of now."

Morrow was silent. But he was not terrorized or cowed. He just stood and looked at Durant, still braced and belligerent.

"I was about to send out word that I wanted to see you tomorrow," Durant went on. "You've anticipated me, and I've been fool enough to let you burst in on me like this. Well, you've had your answer. You've heard from Lincoln, so you know that the Army's moving in on the farmers, and that the farmers in Section 7, hereafter, will be paid with paper money just like everyone else, and that the farmers are now subject to military law, and that they'll have to give up the gold in the Grange banks for regular legal tender. That is the new law—my law—approved by the Chief Magistrate."

"Your law," said Morrow thoughtfully. "But there is the law of The Democracy. Oh, I know you'll say that the President obeys the Military. He also obeys the Grange. If it comes to a contest, and with this new war on now, the President will listen first to the Grange. The country can't live without the farmers."

Durant smiled. "Well, that is something we'll try. Unless, of course, Morrow, you intend to organize your yokels in a revolutionary force? Are you implying that?"

Again, Morrow was not cowed. He narrowed his eyes at Durant. "I don't care what you're trying to infer," he answered. "What I imply is my own business. The country can't work or fight without the farmers. Oh, I know what you told Lincoln! The Army'll run the farms! Do you think the farmers are city sheep, Major?"

Durant pushed himself to his feet. "Morrow, what you're saying is treason. Or are you threatening us? The Army? Or, as I said before, are you insane? There've been thousands of insane men in this country who ended up in hospitals—and never came out, Morrow. Would you like that? Or would you prefer to be shot as a traitor?"

Morrow said nothing.

"We are faced with a desperate war," said Durant, watching him keenly. "Our very existence is at stake. Whether or not The Democracy survives depends upon the heroic American people. We must have Unity! We must stand together! There must be no division of interests, no selfish and private gains, no profits at the expense of the whole nation."

"I," said Morrow, "am fifty-two years old. I've heard that story many times. I know all the words by heart. I can repeat them backwards. I only want you to know that the farmers won't be collectivized or forced to harbor the Military without a fight. I intend to go to Washington tomorrow."

"Good," said Durant. "However, a word of advice: if you have a family say good-bye to them before you leave for Washington."

Morrow's features hardened. "No one ever threatened the farmers before, Major. Nobody is going to threaten them now. We're free men, and we intend to live as free men."

Durant laughed. " 'Free men'? You must be out of your mind, Morrow. This Democracy is ruled by the Army, and is at the mercy of the Army. You know that. You've known it for years. You've never said anything about it before, have you? Everything was wonderful so long as your yokels were safe and prosperous and collected their gold and had their big cars and their fat tables. When, before this, did you ever speak of 'free men,' Morrow? Don't you know that under a military dictatorship there are no free men, and that is only a matter of time until everything and everybody is under Army control?" He paused. "Yes, you've thought of that, I see. But you still thought that the farmers could remain a privileged class. Leaders of the old unions thought that, too. Now, you'll have to learn the lesson they learned."

Morrow watched him, and there was a strange expression in his eyes.

"No country is free where any single man or group is regimented or exploited," went on Durant. "The workingmen, twenty years ago, considered themselves very privileged and free when they permitted employers to be harassed and driven and threatened for their benefit. They didn't see that they were next on the list for regimentation; later, they tried to protest. You know what happened to them. It is about to happen to the farmers, Morrow. Make up your mind to that. As a beginning, I want you to give me a complete report of all gold held in the Grange banks. I want that report in two days. Our country is in terrible danger, and—"

"The people must unite, must stand together, if the country is to be saved," interrupted Morrow. "I told you, I know all the words."

"Excellent," said Durant. "You know the words: obey them." He sat down again, and regarded Morrow with amusement. "Yes, the words. Why didn't you farmers, twenty or more years ago, say them to the whole country? Were you so stupid? No, I suppose not. You were just greedy."

Again, Durant scrutinized the other man's face. Would Morrow be broken? Would he do nothing, for the sake of his own skin? If he spoke, would he be followed? He, Durant, could tell nothing from Morrow's expression, which had become shut and tight. However, here was a man who would at least struggle, if only briefly, before he was shot.

"Greedy," repeated Morrow. "Yes, I suppose we were. And this thing always happens to the greedy, doesn't it?"

"Yes, it does." Durant made his voice sonorous. "When any man puts his own advantage before the advantage of the country, he's not only greedy but traitorous. I don't know much about you farmers, Morrow, except that, probably, you're subversive."

Morrow smiled. "That's just a word, too, Major. You can't frighten me with it."

Durant said, reasonably: "See here, Morrow, I'm new here, and I'm a tolerant man. I'm here to administer, and I've given you the new directive. Let us work together. You must admit, as a sensible man, that the Army has the right to enjoy the advantages of the farmers. We'll give as little trouble as possible, but we demand our rights and are prepared for anything if you resist. This is war, Morrow."

The farmer looked from one watchful face to the other. Then he straightened his shoulders. He said: "Yes, it is war." He turned quickly and went from the room.

Durant sat down again, and sighed, shaking his head. "The farmers," he muttered, as if to himself. "Who the hell do they think they are? Do they think they're more important than the Military? If they do—we'll break them."

Bishop and Edwards said nothing. But Grandon said, with glee: "The old major was always scared half out of his pants by Morrow! All Morrow had to do was shout, and talk about Washington, and the old major curled up like burnt paper. But, there's a new day a-coming eh, Major?"

"Yes, a new day," said Durant, smiling. Or, he remarked to himself, I hope so.

He looked up as if impelled involuntarily. Keiser was regarding him closely and with intense interest. Bishop and Edwards stood at attention. Grandon smirked.

Two cars brought Durant, Grandon, Keiser and the two other officers, Bishop and Edwards, to Lincoln's farm that night. Durant was completely exhausted. It seemed incredible to him that so much had happened in twenty-four hours, and he was constantly afflicted with a sense of disorientation. Over and over, he had to repeat to himself the oath of the Minute Men: "We are at war with a totalitarian society, based on Communism and Fascism, and as soldiers, dedicated to the freedom and dignity of man and the Constitution of a vanquished United States of America, we swear solemnly that our lives, our freedom and sacred honor are now in the service of our country."

Durant remembered what Goethe once said: "When the masses fight they are respectable." But the masses had not fought, so they were no longer respectable, and in losing their self-respect they had become serfs. The fighting was left to a few men. But, thought Durant, hadn't that always been so throughout the history of the world?

Lincoln's wide, white house that afternoon had looked secure and prosperous and peaceful. But now, as the cars rolled up the gravel drive, the house had taken on a beaten aspect, a cowering aura. Terror had come to it. There was one light over the door, and a few dim lights upstairs. The tree-toads shrilled loudly in the country stillness; a cool spring wind sang in the new trees. Somewhere a stream rippled musically, and a new moon was a silver thread in the sky. It was beautiful and calm, but the house stood there, seeming to have shrunk and drawn in upon itself, quaking, in spite of the spring night.

The door had not been locked. Durant and his officers entered with loud laughing and the banging of boots. No one was about. The family seemed to have disappeared. The officers went upstairs, and they found that in their absence all preparations had been made for them, all the family's clothing and possessions cleared away. They heard the big grandfather's clock downstairs clanging eleven, and they looked at each other, smiled, and yawned, and went to their individual rooms. "They've got Gracie locked up somewhere," said Grandon, with disappointment. "But they can't keep her buried forever."

Where the family was sleeping, or not sleeping, was of no importance to Durant. He called in Keiser to help him remove his clothing. The sergeant assisted him in silence, while Durant tried to catch some revealing expression on that blunt, dark face. It was useless, though once or twice Keiser glanced at him furtively with a faint smile.

When Durant was in Lincoln's wide soft bed he thought that he would fall instantly to sleep to the sound of the tree-toads shrilling outside. But in spite of the darkness and the comfort, Durant could not sleep. The faces of his wife and children haunted him; he wondered where they were, and if his wife was not sleeping, either. Restlessly, he began to plot how, when the day arrived, he could rid himself of his uniform and begin his search for his family. Perhaps, furtively, he could begin to assemble some civilian clothing, stealing a shirt, a pair of trousers, a coat, a battered hat, over a period of time. He thought of his uniform with loathing. Besides, in it, he was a marked man, and would become a target for murder if and when the people revolted. He was quite determined that he would not be murdered, friend or enemy notwithstanding.

An hour passed, and another, while he turned and moved as much as his broken arm would permit. Then the arm began to ache dully. In the darkness, he found his bottle of pills, which the doctor had given him, and he took two with a sip of water. He stood in the center of his big and pleasant room, faintly shadowed with the frail light of the stars, and he listened. There was no sound anywhere but the crying of the tree-toads and the light wind. This might have been a home in a land of free and happy men, yet to Durant everything was fog-filled with fear and terror. In the past, he had had his companions; now he had no one for consolation or hope. The forms of slavery moved about him in the darkness like the motions of bats which he could not see. All at once the room, the house, became intolerable to him, in spite of his pain and exhaustion. Awkwardly, over his shoulders, he pulled his long Army coat and pushed his bare feet into his Army boots. He opened his door and stepped into the long dark hall. Somewhere, one of his men was snoring. He crept down the stairway, holding to the banister. He unlocked the hall door below, and walked out into the night.

It had turned colder, and Durant shivered. A city man, he found the darkness disconcerting. Aimlessly, but breathing easier, he moved away from the house toward the barns and the barracks. It was primordial instinct which drew him; in those barracks lived the conscripted farm labor, the slaves. He vaguely wanted to be near those who were as trapped as himself. They were sleeping, of course, but their proximity, he believed, would soothe him.

The black shapes of the long, wooden barracks came into view as he passed the barns when the horses stamped briefly and the cattle stirred. Not a single light burned anywhere. Durant suddenly collided with a tree, and held back his curses. Far off, there was a faint mutter of spring thunder, though the stars remained clear. Durant stopped to rub the pounding shoulder of his broken arm. It was then that he heard very low voices. He stepped quickly behind the tree again, and tried to listen. He could see no one, but after a few moments he could identify the voices of Grandon and Bob Lincoln. Where they were he could not know; the night quiet was deceiving, and the speakers might be within three feet or ten feet. Durant pressed himself against the tree and was able to catch disconnected sentences. Grandon gave a smothered laugh once, and Bob Lincoln answered that laugh with subdued ferocity.

"—yes, a spy," said Grandon. "There're always spies, you know that. Yet they still make you mad. Anyway, I guessed all about him after half an hour."

"—kill—" muttered Bob Lincoln.

"Not so fast."

Bob's voice rose: "I'm not under Army orders, or anybody's orders. I'll find some way of killing him soon!"

Grandon laughed again. "Don't be a stupid bastard, Bob. We know who he is, and I've a good guess why he's here and what he's looking for."

"—here in this house! That's what I can't stand, Grandon. I'll find him alone and then—"

"You'll do nothing," said Grandon easily, in his gay boy's voice. "You'll leave it to me. Or the rest of us."

"—saw him looking, the goddamned swine, at Gracie! Look, Grandon, why don't you report it to headquarters?"

The voices went down to a whisper. Durant stood behind his tree in a state of shock. He had liked Grandon. He had speculated on the courage and will of Bob Lincoln. Now it was only too evident that they knew too much about him, Durant, and that he was in danger, not from any Minute Men, but from the Army and its spies. Bob Lincoln had played his part as an independent farmer and a hater of the Army very well, and Grandon had deceived him, Durant, with very clever acting.

"—should have told me before," said Bob angrily.

"Why should I? I know your temper. I wouldn't have told you tonight if I hadn't seen you were about to do something violent, you idiot. I had to warn you—"

Durant, in real fear, began to back away from the tree, praying that he wouldn't stumble over the two men in the darkness. The voices were silent. Had they detected him by a rustle of grass or a shadow? Were they watching him now? If they discovered that he had overheard them they would probably kill him. He was to be let alone, under their cunning eyes, and to be caught in his innocence! However, if they saw him now they would murder him without any compunction at all. He would be of no further use to them.

Step by step, holding his breath, Durant moved away, backwards, putting one foot behind another, tortuously. So it was that he made somewhat of a circular motion. He paused for a moment, to breathe slowly and silently. Then he saw the shape of another man behind another tree, only six feet away. He knew that square bulk, the attitude of alert watchfulness, even in the dim starlight. It was Sergeant Keiser, and he, too, had been listening to Bob and Grandon.

Keiser! Durant became rigid and very still. Keiser was spying on those two young men, as he had spied. There was only one explanation: as he, Durant, had suspected, Keiser was a Minute Man, himself, and he was in the Army for the reason that Durant was in the Army.

Without stopping to think, Durant backed away a few more feet, then whispered: "Keiser!"

The sergeant turned with silent swiftness, then came toward him. Durant motioned with his head, and the two went as fast and as quietly over the grass toward the house as it was possible to go. The sergeant put his hand under Durant's arm and propelled him rapidly. They said nothing until they had reentered the house and had gone into Durant's room. There they faced each other in the darkness.

"You heard them?" whispered Durant.

"Yes, sir, I heard," came the answering whisper, and with savagery.

I'm not alone, after all, thought Durant. It was a liberating thought, and he laughed weakly. However, for a moment he felt sincere regret and despondency. He had believed in Grandon, had reflected on him, and had had his hopes. He opened his mouth to whisper again, then abruptly remembered the Chief Magistrate's warning, that he was to trust in no one and confide in no one and was not to use his imagination at all about his comrades. It was hard, but it had to be done.

So Durant made himself whisper: "Traitors, eh? And spies?"

"Yes, sir. I've known about 'em for some time. What shall we do?"

"Nothing. Just watch them."

The sergeant moved in the darkness. "I'm sorry, Major, but I thought at first you were with them." He laughed roughly. "It makes it better that you know, too, and that you're with us."

"But we mustn't let them know we know, Keiser."

"Major, I've been in this business too long to let my tongue wag. And, Major, we mustn't let them catch on that we're watching them, must we?"

He helped Durant to remove his coat and boots. "Sent to keep an eye on 'em, Major?"

Durant answered carefully: "You know that no man lets another man know anything, Keiser, so why do you ask me?"

Keiser nodded. He straightened after he had assisted Durant into bed, and saluted. He then went silently from the room and carefully shut the door behind him.

I have a friend, thought Durant, when alone. But for his sake and mine we must pretend to be what we appear to be. No whispering together again, no glances. We know each other, but we must never recognize each other.

He began to drowse. His last thought was an angry regret that Grandon was no friend and that Bob Lincoln was a very able actor. They had guessed who he was. He was in worse danger than ever.

When Durant awoke after his brief and uneasy sleep it was to a sensation of profound despondency and dullness. He was accustomed to these storms in himself, knowing that they had their starting points in a forgotten or half-forgotten incident of no real importance but which had impinged upon some secret and acute nerve in his emotions. Now, however, he knew the cause of his intense wretchedness and hopelessness, and he reflected that the psychiatrists were fatuous when they declared that in the knowing of the source of mental anguish is the cure of the anguish. On the contrary, Durant thought. If a source remains obscure, reason can assist in the dispelling of a melancholy mood. Once known, the cancer bared, despair adds to the original dejection. "Ignorance is bliss" was a much sounder aphorism, and a much older one, than "knowledge is power." For if knowledge is impotent, and can point out no avenue of escape, its very awareness of its importance and imprisonment increases its hopelessness.

Durant told himself that too much had happened to him in too short a time. There was a quality of disorientation in his despondency. For a few seconds, after awakening, he did not know where he was or even who he was. He was not the unimaginative kind of man who, when confronted by an appalling set of facts, can throw aside his bedclothes and "rise resolutely." That attitude might have its heroic aspects, but it has in greater measure its stupid ones. Durant began to see that the Army had quite a valid argument in its contention that witless men make the best soldiers. In more intelligent days, the American people had understood that witlessness ought not to be part of a President's character. In its degeneracy, the nation had forgotten this and had elected one sinister dolt after another.

Durant lay among his tossed sheets and blankets and thought about the old maxim: "A people deserve their government." If so, then they deserved what they had now, and who was he, the Chief Magistrate, and all the thousands of nameless Minute Men, to deny them the torment they had willingly brought upon themselves from 1933 on? They had not protested against a military dictatorship; in fact, less than two decades ago, they had vociferously approved of it, had lent themselves heartily, and with slogans, to its establishment. All the records of history had been there for them to see, all the warnings of the Founding Fathers that national militarism, and any oligarchy of soldiers, leads to slavery and decline. Soldiers were sometimes necessary, in the event of an actual, but not artificial, attack. But always, until the rise of The Democracy, civilians had used the checks and balances system of keeping the witless and the doltish subservient to sound and civilian administration, using arms and uniforms only in dire emergencies and then abolishing them.

The pale gilt sun of the morning poured through the windows of Durant's bedroom. He saw the pliant and ruddy gold of a willow tree near the glass and heard, as he had never heard in the city, the clamor of busy birds, the chattering of chickens, the lowing of cattle. Again, he was struck by the incongruity of the peaceful sounds of a placid countryside and the dark terror which ruled the cities. Nature, apparently, ignored the man-pariah who attempted, over and over, to destroy the earth which nourished him, and always he was defeated by something more enormous, more intelligent, and more eternal than himself. If there was any comfort at all to be found in the dreadful world of today it was not to be found in the ugly man-exile, the intruder who had just enough consciousness to become a murderer and a horror in the universe. That comfort lay in the gigantic rhythms of nature, in the unawareness of other creatures that man existed.

"Where wast thou when the foundations of the world were laid?" God had inquired sternly of Job. Had there been contempt, and regret, in that question?

There was a knock on Durant's door, and then the door opened and Sergeant Keiser entered. Durant's first impulse was to smile confidentially at his sergeant and to say something which would strengthen the understanding of the night before. He suppressed the impulse. He might indeed have a friend now, but neither that "friend" nor any enemy must change him. He became impatient, remembering the warnings which had been given him, but he did force himself to give Keiser a mere, indifferent nod and a cool look. Apparently, Keiser understood, for he did not smile or make any overtures. He simply helped Durant to get out of bed and to dress. He remarked only: "Everybody's disappeared, except the servants around here. Guess the family don't like us around, Major."

Keiser shaved him in the bathroom, in silence. Once their eyes met in the mirror, but it was with careful blankness. Durant noticed how pale and exhausted his face was, and he was conscious of intense weariness. Though he tried to control his thoughts he could not curb his anxiety for his family, and the sense of entrapment all about him.

His officers were waiting for him in the dining room. As he had done before, he dismissed Bishop and Edwards after one glance. But Grandon was another matter, all gay boyishness and youthful vitality. "Morning, Major!" he cried happily, pulling out a chair for Durant. "Had a good night? Feeling better?"

Durant, with a strong effort of his will, kept himself from staring at Grandon with infuriated dislike. He knew this dislike stemmed in part from his own mortification at his own self-deception. Looking at that buoyant young face, at the quick and laughing eyes of the lieutenant, and remembering the conversation he had overheard in the night, Durant wanted to curse. He had once congratulated himself on his ability to detect falsity and treachery; now he told himself that he had always been a fool. Then he controlled himself, and ridiculed his own animosity. According to his lights, Grandon was loyal and faithful, a true supporter of the government and its military dictatorship. It was Grandon's acuteness which had detected something wrong with him, Durant, and in line with Grandon's loyalty it was Grandon's duty to watch his new superior officer and to betray him when necessary. Treachery, Durant reflected, was all a matter of viewpoint. He let Grandon unfold the white napkin and lay it on his knees, and he reminded himself that he must be more careful than ever with his officers. So Durant smiled, and fervently hoped that the smile appeared sincere.

"Family disappeared?" asked Durant, as his officers sat down at the well-set table. He laughed. "I like it better this way. I can't stand that confounded Lincoln and his wife. In fact, I think I'll given an order that they are not to eat with us at any time." He studied this idea, and approved of it more and more. "Grandon, you'll relay my order?"

"Glad to," said the young lieutenant, with enthusiasm. He winked. "But how about Gracie?"

"You might give an order that Gracie must dine with us at night," replied Durant, smiling with real sincerity now.

Then he became conscious that Captain Edwards was looking at him, his rocky face harsh and thoughtful. He had dismissed both the captains as mere military robots the day before. Bishop was gulping milk mechanically. It was startling to Durant that Captain Edwards should suddenly display any expression whatsoever, and that his small hazel eyes should have the gleam of a polished stone.

"Something wrong, Captain?" he asked idly.

Grandon chuckled. "Oh, Edwards is sweet on Gracie, too," he remarked airily. "We both like soft white meat, don't we, Captain?"

Edwards turned his whole rigid torso toward Grandon without twisting his bull-like neck. "I'm your superior officer, Grandon," he said. "And when I say I'll be the one to lay that girl I mean I'll be the one to lay her. Not you."

Durant sat up alertly. Bishop poured another glass of milk and regarded it approvingly. Keiser grinned.

"Pulling rank, eh, Captain?" asked Grandon. He still was smiling with his youthful gaiety, but his eyes had narrowed.

Edwards nodded. "That's right."

Durant said: "Where's our breakfast? Oh, yes, Edwards. 'Pulling rank.' Forgetting I'm your superior officer, too? Maybe I'll decide to have first run with Gracie. Now, I'm the fickle kind. You can have her next, Edwards, then you, Bishop, and maybe Grandon. Then we can end up with Keiser, here."

Edwards and Grandon directed their whole attention to Durant, and he saw their hatred. It pleased him. He rolled up his eyes and mused: "Yes, a nice piece, Gracie. I'm in luck. Think I'll send for her tonight. Give that order, will you, Grandon? Nothing too good for the Military! That's our slogan, and a very good one, too."

Keiser laughed outright. Edwards had turned crimson, and Grandon had become very white. Bishop looked at them all, his mouth vacantly open. Then Edwards said in a suppressed voice: "Regular Army man, Major?"

Negligently, Durant answered: "You could say that, in a way. It doesn't matter. Why?"

But Edwards only turned his granite stare to Keiser. Durant understood. "Oh, you mean the sergeant eating with us. There's my arm, you know, Captain. Besides, I happen to like Keiser, and need his assistance. However, if you'd all prefer to eat in the kitchen, without me and Keiser, that's your privilege."

"Discipline," said Edwards thickly. His hands, on the tablecloth, clenched. "One of us could help you, if necessary."

"Frankly, I prefer Keiser," said Durant, with ease. "Grandon, you won't forget my order about Gracie. I'm in a mood for a little fun tonight."

Edwards shrugged, though all the rugged contours of his face still expressed disciplined rage and affront. "Just so long as I'm next in line it doesn't matter to me," he said. "I'm willing to take the leavings of a superior officer."

Durant nodded. Then he saw Grandon again. Grandon was still very white, and his mouth had tightened and his eyes were tormented. He was gazing at Edwards with disgust and detestation. His hands were shaking. Why, the idiot is in love with that girl! thought Durant with pleasure. He was even more delighted when Grandon's murderous gaze turned on himself. He assumed an expression of lascivious anticipation. He said, to Keiser: "How about undressing Gracie for me tonight, Sergeant?"

Keiser replied with mock solemnity and respect: "Anything to please you, Major."

"God bless the Army," said Durant. "It gives us everything."

The kitchen door opened and Dr. William Dodge staggered in, carrying an immense silver tray which steamed. Like a dazed automaton, he put down a plate of ham and eggs before each officer. His hands, so long and slender, were rough and red, the nails broken. He went out, to return with coffee. Then he took his station, blindly, behind Durant, and stood there, bent and voiceless.

Durant remarked pleasantly on the weather, the food, the house, and the refreshing sleep he had had the night before. He made his voice prattling and amiable. He knew that Grandon and Edwards were wincing. Bishop simply devoured the food, as did Keiser. No one answered Durant. The silence had a vicious quality. It began to unnerve Durant eventually, though he continued to prattle with enthusiasm. Finally even Keiser detected something ominous. He glanced at each face alertly, and with cunning, and smiled. He looked at Durant with amusement, and his smile assured the Major that he would be well protected.

"I expect, by tonight that many of my command will be comfortably housed on most of the farms hereabout," said Durant, to the silence. "Of course, three hundred men are too much for even these farms to absorb all at one time. So, they'll rotate. A month at a time. But this farm is my headquarters, and all five of us will be here for breakfast and dinner and sleeping quarters permanently." He chuckled. "Something tells me there'll be considerable excitement on the farms of Section 7 by tonight! And considerable flutter among the farm wives and daughters. Eh, Grandon?"

Grandon said, only: "Yes, sir." Durant saw that the young man had not touched his food. This made him exceedingly happy.

"I'm wondering," said Edwards surlily, "how Washington's going to take this."

Durant waited a moment, then he said quietly: "I've been given absolute power, Edwards. Absolute power. That is the new directive. Each administrative military officer in every Section, beginning yesterday, was given absolute power."

Edwards' face relaxed a little. "Well, that's good. It's about time. The farmers have been having it too easy. It's good news that they're to feel the bite, too. Always hated the bastards, myself."

Grandon said nothing. He drank a little coffee, then waited, his eyes fixed emptily on the table. Durant, having eaten a remarkably good breakfast, felt renewed. "Let's go," he said briskly. "I've got to get acquainted with the work in Philadelphia."

Dr. Dodge drew back the chair for him. Durant involuntarily looked at the old man, and was again startled. For Dr. Dodge's eyes were no longer blind. They were alive and glowing, and the dead face was vivid with understanding. Durant was frightened. He shouted: "Get out of my way, you old fool! What are you standing there for?"

Dr. Dodge bowed his head meekly, but Durant saw him smile as if with immense relief and joy. Durant hurried from the room. Dr. Dodge, moving with incredible speed, opened the door for him. Durant ignored him, more frightened than ever, but he was not able to evade the man. Dr. Dodge, again incredibly, was holding his coat for him. The other officers found their coats, adjusted their caps, briefly inspected their guns.

Durant stood very still in the hall. He looked steadily into Dr. Dodge's eyes. Then, as the other officers turned to him, Dr. Dodge's expression again became blind and empty, and he tottered away.

"Why don't they shoot the old crow?" asked Keiser. "Funny look he gave you, Major."

The Chief Magistrate couldn't have picked a worse man than I, thought Durant morosely, as the two cars drove to Philadelphia. He ought to have chosen a regular Army man. I'm certainly making this uniform the most hated damn thing in the world!

Then he smiled to himself, and understood that this was exactly Arthur Carlson's intention, and this intention was to include the Army personnel, itself. Durant had exerted his authority upon young Grandon. He hoped, not without some cause, that Grandon, the gay and loyal young military man, would now not only hate him as the archetype of the Army but would come to question, through his infatuation of that young cow, Gracie Lincoln, the very system of which he was a devoted and unquestioning member.

All in all, Durant was exultant, forgetting the knowledge which had come so strangely to Dr. Dodge. He had avenged himself on Grandon for his emotional disappointment in the young lieutenant, he had established himself as a ruthless Army despot in the minds of his executive staff, and he had absolute power for the first time in a powerless life. He meditated on this for a few moments, and then he was alarmed. How intoxicating power could be, and how self-destroying! Now, for the first time, he became very humble and understanding. If he, reared in a religious atmosphere, taught all the principles of a dead and betrayed Republic, dedicated to the restoration of a free and just socity, could feel a personal thrill at the idea of power, how much more vulnerable were the multitudes of men who had never had his secret advantages? If it was indeed true, as Tom Paine had said, that "tyranny, like hell, is not easily conquered," then both tyranny and hell have their roots in the primordial human instincts. Man's deepest insticts, thought Durant, with gloom, are atavistic, evil in that they are atavistic, and are due for some wide overhauling and re-direction. The Church had been battling those homicidal and destructive instincts for countless centuries. In the end, as in this violent, nihilistic world of today, the instincts had won.

He was driven, today, by Captain Bishop, and sat with Captain Edwards who was disposed to be very friendly and cooperative since the breakfast conversation. He had quite forgiven Durant for having served only three years in the Army, for he was a regular Army man, himself. He listened with tolerant interest to Durant's accounts of his campaigns in England and France, in which he had been a very reluctant lieutenant. (Durant suppressed the fact that he had been with the Quartermaster Corps.) Durant was very enthusiastic about the sack of Paris (which he had never seen) and his Latin imagination overcame the difficulties of factual experience. Captain Edwards did not question any discrepancies, so colorful were Durant's accounts based on reading and invention.

Then Durant, having run out of imagination and realizing that his gaps were becoming wider and wider, questioned Edwards as to the exact powers and duties which were his. He discovered that he had complete authority over the local bureaucrats, who were subservient to the Army and took all their orders from the Army. This knowledge gave him tremendous contentment. Of course, his duties had been defined broadly by the Chief Magistrate, and his administration was loosely confined to the oppression of the farmers, but a little extra-curricular oppression of other groups would not be censored. In fact, as Durant thought about it, the bureaucrats took on pleasing possibilities. It needed only imagination.

As they drove through Philadelphia, Edwards pointed out the fine shops here and there which only Army personnel and their families, the MASTS, and the bureaucrats, could patronize. Durant saw the smug wives parading in and out of their shops, waddling under the weight of their bags and baskets. He searched for a hating and brooding face among the shabby women who were hurrying to work in their factories. They were hard to find, for most of them wore the expression of meekness and submission which marked the faces of millions of their starveling sisters. However, like bright flames in a swamp, he saw the eyes of a few of the very older or the very younger women. These flames might light the torch of revolution which had fallen into slave-degradation and docility. After all, it was the goaded women of Paris who had torn the Bastille literally apart with their bare hands.

Edwards confided that he detested young Grandon, who was always "leaping around." He suggested that Grandon be transferred. "I've had my doubts about him for some time," said the captain. "He takes too much pleasure in his duties, and adds his own little touches."

"I never heard that devotion to duty, and going beyond the confines of duty, was reprehensible," said Durant.

Edwards shrugged. Then he became interested in some of the fine homes they were passing. "Wonderful parties we have there," he said. "Washington was bright when it decided to form the MASTS. In that way, small business was got rid of; you can't trust small businessmen. They're too independent, and in the end we found them subversive."

Yes, thought Durant, keeping his face blank, great industry and wealth can always manage to strike common ground with Communism, Statism, Fascism and Socialism. In fact, they flourish best when the people are enslaved. He meditated again on certain criminal labor leaders of three decades ago, who had enlisted gangsters and professional murderers and extortionists into their ranks in order to subdue and control the masses of the workers. No wonder the "labor leaders" of today sat in such rich power in Washington and in the industrial cities, the pets of the Administration.

The flag of The Democracy hung from many windows, and the newspapers bore enthusiastic headlines about the new war and the new "war effort" and the dedication of "the people" to the preservation of their "liberties" and independence. Army bands played here and there; Government-endorsed speakers stood on corners exalting the new "struggle for freedom." "I'd like to get into action again," remarked Edwards enthusiastically. "I always hated the South American sons of bitches, with their religion and all those millions of acres still uncultivated. And the way they've always refused to help us makes me itch to teach them a thing or two."

Durant thought of the strenuous efforts of Washington, fifteen years ago, to establish dictators over the various South American countries. He thought of the direct and indirect force which Washington had exerted to make the positions of the Latin dictators secure. At the last, Washington had been betrayed by its own stupidity. The dictators might be murderers and tyrants, but they had had a profound love for their country, a passion for it, and a very realistic distrust of America. They had refused to engage in any wars to "exterminate Communism," understanding too well that America had embraced an exceedingly terrible totalitarianism of her own.

"—the American way of life," Edwards was saying. "We've got to teach them that! It's either us or them."

But never "us" together, thought Durant. Never man united against a dangerous, natural universe of disease, unpredictability, want and suffering! Always "them" who oddly seemed to stand beyond the pale of humanity, and who must be killed to "teach them a thing or two." May God have mercy on our souls! said Durant to himself. Now he understood that when men had failed each man had assisted in that failure, either by silence or by despair, by fatalism or a false sense of importance. It was men, individually, who had betrayed man.

The hotel in which he had his executive offices seethed with happy excitement. All the officers, young and old, were eagerly exchanging hopes for immediate military action. Looking at their faces, Durant understood another of the atavistic and frightful instincts of man: the urge and desire to kill. What to do about that instinct? Could its extinction be accomplished by annihilating all potential soldiers? He knew that there was a definite soldier personality, and that despite its centuries-old atavism, it continued to be born, like some living and deformed fossil which refused to die. He shook his head despondently.

He was saluted with respectful curiosity, but he held himself erect and kept his eyes coldly ahead. He found his other executive officers waiting for him, lieutenants and sergeants, and, among them, Grandon. Grandon was still white and grim, and he appeared preoccupied. However, he once glanced at Durant and Durant saw that knifelike gleam on the young man's face, quickly suppressed as Grandon turned away.

Durant sat at his fine walnut desk in his fine luxurious office, and regarded the mass of work with dismay. Grandon, in a dull voice, informed him that Captain Alice Steffens of the Department of Women's Welfare, Section 7 Division, was waiting impatiently to see him, as were numerous other men and women under his jurisdiction.

"Impatiently?" repeated Durant, frowning.

"Yes, sir. She's a very impatient lady, all the time," said Grandon, and for the first time he smiled. "She always gets in first. Very important job."

"I think I'll let her cool her ass for a few hours," said Durant. "Or you can tell her that I'll see her three weeks from next Friday."

"Yes, sir!" said Grandon, with some of his old delight. "But she's quite a piece, Major. Not like some of these old queer hags who like to dress up in uniform, and who probably shave in the morning, and keep young girls on the side. You might like to look at her as a change. You'll see the old Lesbians regularly.

Durant thought of the Army women who were as depraved as their male counterparts. He thought of their everlasting and repulsive uniforms, their big boots, their swaggers, their hoarse voices, their mannish ways, their cruel hard eyes, their short hair, and their deadliness. They were a special breed, but an ominously increasing one. Durant loathed women in uniforms, for a uniform on a woman had terrible significance. It was all right for nurses, he had conceded, up to a certain point, for nurses did not engage in murder. However, these strange creatures, this frightful third sex which had appeared during the twentieth century, everywhere, was not interested in saving lives but in taking them. Long ago they had demanded to be included in combat forces, and they had done excellently with rifle and with hand grenade and with bomb. They had, in fact, been as good as men. Finally, they had shown their true and horrible aspects, and had their female companions comfortably ensconced in little apartments. Homosexuality had, oddly enough, decreased among men during the past two decades. It had increased enormously among women, in proportion to the national decay and the national insanity.

"Send the bitch in," said Durant abruptly, and he sat back and waited, full of nausea and detestation.

Grandon admitted Captain Alice Steffens. She entered with a quick and impatient tap of heels. High heels. Durant was surprised at that pleasant and feminine sound. He looked at the small and rapid feet before letting his eyes rise to the very trim dark blue uniform on a very delectable and slender figure. There was no concealment of breast but an artful or unconsciously feminine desire to give that attribute its full measure of display. The white silk blouse was well opened on a very white and charming throat. There was, too, a bunch of purple violets on the lapel of the coat, quite against regulations. Durant, taken aback, stared once more at very seductive legs under the hem of the skirt. They were silk-clad, and the ankles were delicate. Something very pleasing stirred in him. He wanted to retain the illusion of warm, sweet womanhood before having to look at a face which undoubtedly would be coarse and masculine and vicious. However, he was finally forced to glance upward.

He was extremely surprised. He saw the face of a woman in her early thirties, and he told himself that it was probably the most beautiful face he had ever seen in his life. Oval-shaped and rosy-and-ivory tinted, it was absolutely without a flaw of any kind. The mouth might be determined, but it was full and naturally red, the color of Italian poppies in the spring. The chin was soft and dimpled, the nose arched and clear. The eyes, large and blue, looked resolutely at Durant through incredibly long black lashes, and over them were thick slashes of black brows. There was the usual military cap, of course, but it was tilted, and under it waved masses of abundant dark hair touched on the crests with a hint of bronze. That hair had never been cut, again against regulations which demanded that female soldiers' hair must never be longer than four inches. Here was a real anachronism: a smooth big knob of this wonderful hair on the woman's nape, as shining as ebony.

The officers in the room came to admiring attention. But the captain ignored them. She looked only at Durant and she said, with annoyance, and in a most entrancing voice: "I have only half an hour, Major. I've come to receive your orders, as I understand that you have replaced Major Burnes. I also thought that I might tell you something of my work."

"Sit down, please," said Durant, quite dazed.

She sat down with an almost extinct female grace, and Durant saw the straightness of her shoulders and the slenderness of her waist. He also saw that this woman had a most intelligent expression, mobile and aristocratic. She might be all business, but there was a betraying femaleness about her very disarming to a man. She might speak briskly, but there were musical intonations in her voice, and cultured ones. Now, thought Durant, helplessly, how in the hell did a woman, a real, honest-to-God woman, get into such a job?

"I'm very busy—" she began.

"Well, so am I," said Durant, smiling. He pushed a silver box of cigarets toward her, and he stood up gallantly to light one when she put it in her lovely mouth. She gave him an appraising glance as he did so, a purely female glance. She smiled a little.

"You might tell me what you do, and what you want this morning?" suggested Durant.

She tilted one black brow indulgently. "Oh, Major Curtiss, surely you know the work of the Department of Women's Welfare! The Department, though under the jurisdiction of the Army, is distinct from it. In a way, it is almost a civilian department, though we do encourage the enlistment of young girls in the Armed Forces, and we do select the best candidates for officer training."

"Very interesting," interrupted Durant. "Quite aside from anything else, what qualities do you look for in those candidates?"

The captain studied her cigaret for a moment or two, then in a curiously flat voice she replied: "Leadership, strong physique, the ability to take orders without questioning, ruthlessness, courage, uninterest in—the other sex, determination to succeed, dedication—" She put the cigaret in her mouth and blew out a cloud of smoke which momentarily hid her face but did not conceal the sudden brilliance of her blue eyes. "Emotional stability."

"And after you get all the eligible girls into the Armed Forces, what else do you do?" asked Durant.

"We are concerned with maternal welfare, the encouraging of women who want to have children. Also the health of the women who are conscripted into the war industries. We," said Captain Steffens, again studying her cigaret, "also work closely with the State psychiatrists to weed out undesirable traits among young girls, such as rebelliousness, emotional difficulties, dangerous independence and subversive thoughts. We have, as you know, special schools for such girls, under the supervision of the State psychiatrists."

"Work closely with." The phrase of the enemies. Durant forced himself to remain silent, to keep his face bland and interested, though he sickened.

"We also take care of illegitimate children, and abandoned children, and are in charge of the State nurseries which are operated in behalf of the children of mothers engaged in essential industries."

"Essential industries!" How the totalitarian phrases rolled off American lips! But then, one must remember how easily and with what felicity Americans had adopted such terminology, with the help of American Presidents and their administrators.

Suddenly, Durant became aware that Captain Steffens was scrutinizing him, weighing him.

"We have as our slogan, the slogan of The Democracy," she was saying. " 'Unity! Duty! Sacrifice!' "

Here was a woman, a woman with all the attributes of a woman, yet she was parroting the phrases of tyranny. I must be careful, thought Durant. He leaned back, negligently.

"How old are the girls whom you pick to be soldiers?" he asked.

"Seventeen."

"Nonsense! Fifteen is not too young. Or even fourteen." He stared at her. "You know, perhaps, that I have absolute power in Section 7. This is a new directive for you: Hereafter, in Section 7, all girls from twelve on are to be taken from their mothers and sent to State institutions to be indoctrinated in their duties to The Democracy. We must have soldiers! Moreover, the parents of the girls in Section 7 are never to know the whereabouts of their children. The girls, themselves, are never to come in contact with boys or men until they are twenty-five. By that time they'll be so indoctrinated that no frivolous impulses will occur to them. Unity! Duty! Sacrifice! But, of course, you understand that, Captain Steffens."

She regarded him fixedly, and turned very white. "Major Curtiss," she said deliberately, "you know the mothers would never stand for that."

"You're wrong!" he declared. "The people will stand for anything. And now that we're engaged in another war, and another war effort, to preserve The Democracy, anyone who dares to object to the conscription of their children for labor and for the armed forces should be fully prosecuted. I understand you are an executive officer. If you hear any complaints you must report them at once to me for prosecution or discipline. We dare have no subversives."

She carefully ground out her cigaret, and then regarded the debris with deep thoughtfulness.

"Of course," she said, as if speaking to herself, "the children of today are quite fit for industry. I agree with you that the working age should be reduced from fifteen to twelve. We could have barracks for them, carefully segregated from males, of course."

"If the mothers object to their girl children being conscripted, they can easily be sent to hard-labor camps. That will increase the manpower pool," said Durant, with enthusiasm. "A woman, these days, has to work as hard as any man. Too, in the labor camps they will receive no wages, and that is a saving for the national economy." He continued: "I know you agree with me, Miss Steffens."

She said: "Captain Steffens." But her pretty voice was abstracted. She moved the stub of her cigaret around in the silver tray. "You are very devoted to The Democracy, Major Curtiss."

"Unity! Duty! Sacrifice!" repeated Durant.

She nodded. Her smile was cryptic. "I shall obey your orders at once, Major. As you have said, the masses never rebel against anything, especially not when orders are accompanied by slogans, which take the place of thinking."

"You sound very ambiguous," Durant accused.

She laughed lightly. "I am not in the least ambiguous. I am merely commenting, and with approval. One can always rely upon the people to follow anywhere."

For some reason, Durant felt uneasy.

"I find you much more understanding than Major Burnes," said the captain. "He disagreed with almost everything I suggested." Again, she scrutinized Durant. "I think, now, that we can obtain our objective. For instance. Dr. Healy, who is head of the Public Psychiatric Department of Section 7, is strongly in favor of removing male children permanently from their mothers when they are five years old. He believes these children have no 'security' or normal home life while their mothers ar working, and he has suggested State nurseries for them where they will be brought up in strict conformity with democratic principles. We've heard that working parents sometimes corrupt these little ones with subversive doctrines and religious superstitions so that they need stern reindoctrination and discipline when they reach military or employment age. All this is a waste."

"I agree with Dr. Healy, and he'll have my cooperation." Durant leaned confidently toward the young woman. "Of course, the children of wealthy parents will not come under this directive, if I make such a directive."

"Naturally not. No directive is ever issued against our loyal and cooperative Americans." Captain Steffens stood up, and Durant rose also. The young woman smiled. It was a pale smile and her eyes shone as if touched by lightning. She glanced at the other officers, who regarded her eagerly, and she threw back her shoulders. She saluted Durant gravely, wheeled, and tapped smartly out of the room.

"Now there, Major, is something special," said Captain Edwards. "Not available, like Gracie Lincoln, though worth ten of that little slut."

Grandon turned to him furiously; Edwards grinned, and Grandon halted. But his face was black with rage, Durant observed, highly pleased.

"Well, she's a captain, and I'm her superior officer," said Durant. "I might have some luck with her, myself. And now, who is next?"

"Dr. Joseph Healy, of the Public Psychiatric Department," muttered Grandon.

"Now this," said Durant, "ought to be a pleasure. Send the—the gentleman in, Grandon."

Durant was well acquainted with psychiatrists. He knew their twentieth century history, their jargon, and the powerful position they occupied in The Democracy. They, more than any other single group, had been instrumental in promoting the awful degradation of the human spirit not only in America but in all other nations. Clever political assassins had used the psychiatrists to bring about the present universal dementia, the facelessness of the populations and their subjection to The Democracy. It was known to the Minute Men that every psychiatrist qualified by the Government was a member of the terrible FBHS, and that it was the particular duty of these psychiatrists to search out and betray any original or potentially rebellious young mind in the Federal schools. It was no accident that these young minds, which might have created a revolution, were soon eliminated, either on the constant battlefields, in distant labor camps from which they never emerged again, or in prisons called "schools of training." If any of them survived after their frightful ordeals they had become completely mad or completely broken.

There was a psychiatrist for every five schools in The Democracy, and the teachers had been instructed to report to their local psychiatrists any boy or girl who revealed "undesirable" traits, "emotional immaturity," "anxiety states," "psychotic symptoms," "neuroses," or "paranoid tendencies." The psychiatrists were particularly insistent upon being informed about strong "nonconformists," and those who were markedly "asocial" and who did not "fit in with their age-group," or displayed signs of "maladjustment." If the child were very young, the terrified parents were brought in for "serious discussion" about the "welfare of the child." The real object of these "discussions" was to discover if the parents had been teaching the child "religious superstitions" or inculcating him with "subversive ideas." Quite often fathers and mothers of such "rogue" children received long prison sentences to the work camps and in the mines, and the child was entered in a "school of training." Therefore, a parent would rather have been informed that his offspring had some fatal disease than to be informed that the little one was not "adjusting himself properly to his group" or was showing symptoms of "schizophrenia."

Durant knew that all this was part of the plan of Government to destroy incipient individualism, courage, intelligence, originality, pride, independent thought and genius among the children of the subjugated proletariat. To The Democracy, these children were a powerful threat.

The children of the privileged groups were not subjected to this horrible policing and destruction of the human mind, for they were trained for "leadership" over the masses of the people. Durant's own children had not yet been entered in any Federal school, and it had been the thought of what would happen to his boys in the Government breeding-grounds of anonymity which had made him join the Minute Men. He knew only too well that anonymity is the most dangerous symptom of madness, and that the obliteration of personality—the goal of the psychiatrists—results in passivity and uncomplaining and thoughtless docility. There was, for the proletariat of the cities, a program of deliberate mental and physical indignity, a future of impotent "littleness" without stature, and quiet servitude. The psychiatrists had not only formulated this plan but had put it into action.

This had no parallel in history at all. There had, in centuries past, occasionally appeared evil men who resorted to murder and torture in order to suppress "heresy," but they had been concerned only with "spoken" heresy. What a man thought in the recesses of his spirit had been of no importance to old oppressors. But in this century of complete madness and slavery, it had become of overwhelming importance to the evil men of power that potential "heresy" should be blotted out in the minds of children so that the populace should be deprived of personality and rendered harmless to their masters.

Durant had discovered that there were two kinds of Government psychiatrists: the wild-eyed and intense fanatics who actually believed that they were rendering a service to humanity in the destruction of the human identity, and the cold-eyed cynics who knew very well what they were doing, and why, and who enjoyed with sadistic pleasure, the disintegration they accomplished. There was a quality of hatred in them for their fellowman, and a loathing. The first were zealots, the second, murderers. To Durant, the zealots were the more dangerous, for they were utterly mad.

New recruits to the Minute Men were given extensive lectures on this subject. They were taught the jargon of psychiatry, and they were shown how, over several decades, the psychiatrists became so appalling a menace to the people and why tyrants had taken them into their service. These men were the new devils of humanity, the new vampires, the new sorcerers and witch-doctors, the new wickedness and degeneration. No mores of the past applied to them, no tradition, for, from the beginning, they had been men without morality. Good and evil did not exist for them as actual things in themselves. All the virtues and disciplines of the human soul had appeared to them only as aberrations and capable of disgusting interpretations. Man, to these men, had no intrinsic grandeur or heroism, no importance as a soul, no actual dignity, and all his gods were based on loathsome imaginings or perversions, and all his instincts of charity, kindness, sympathy, compassion and generosity had, as their roots, some ugly "suppression" or were manifestations of self-seeking "exhibitionism." To a godless, conscienceless and materialistic despotism, the psychiatrists, then, were invaluable.

Durant wondered whether Dr. Joseph Healy, head of the Public Psychiatric Department, was a zealot or a cynic. When Dr. Healy entered his office, it was at once evident that he was a cynic, and was therefore expedient, vulnerable to cash, and could be cowed. He was a slender man of medium height, about forty-two, well tailored in a light gray suit and white linen, quick and rather graceful of motion, and very businesslike and assured. No fanatic, he; he was well washed and groomed and every silvery-blond hair was meticulously in place on his excellent shaped head. If he was an extreme radical, as so many of his colleagues were, he certainly was a paradox, for nothing could have been finer than his dark blue silk tie, his personal jewelry, his hand-made boots. No, Durant decided with absolute conviction, this man was no zealot, but a ruthless murderer and sadist, calculating all that he did, and pocketing his profit.

Durant motioned him silently to a chair, leaned forward and scrutinized him. He had discovered that this speechless scrutiny had a disconcerting effect on frauds, though it did not move fanatics. Dr. Healy's smiling face, so narrow, so delicate of skin, flushed faintly, though he lit a cigaret with complete confidence, and made a careful ritual of the act, saying as he did so: "It is pleasant to meet you, Major. I'm glad you are a young man. Major Burnes was old, and unprogressive."

Durant grunted. The other officers moved a little closer, so as not to miss a word or a gesture. Dr. Healy ignored them, and seemed sincerely unaware of their presence. He lifted his eyes now, and Durant saw them clearly: pale, cold blue eyes, slightly protuding, coated over with the glaucous film of mercilessness.

"Director of the Public Psychiatric Department," said Durant slowly.

Dr. Healy could produce a very charming smile, not ingratiating, but deliberately friendly. He, in turn, studied Durant. A dull, doltish Army man, he decided. Trained from childhood to be an animal in uniform. He, Dr. Healy, could trace his thought processes, exactly. The man was afraid of him, as dolts were usually afraid of psychiatrists. The old fear of the brainless warrior and the cretin masses for the "medicine man," the "man of magic," thought the doctor, with tolerant inner laughter. Durant, like any other animal, was mentally but fearfully circling around him, sniffing the air, wondering if rabbits would be produced from the atmosphere or strange manifestations be evoked. Dr. Healy thought he could hear those padding footsteps, the hard breathing of apprehension and monkey-curiosity.

Dr. Healy leaned back in his chair, with well-bred negligence, and crossed his elegant legs. (His father, and grandfather before him, had been honest bricklayers.) Dr. Healy was prepared to be gently but affectionately amused, guiding and confidence-inspiring. He glanced furtively at his watch. Fifteen minutes would do it. He had had some uneasiness at the news of the new major, a young man. It took so much of a man's time to "break in" new arrivals. This, however, would be easy. The scrutiny which at first had disconcerted him was nothing but the blank stare of a robot, he decided.

"Are you in a hurry, Doctor?" asked the Major.

"I beg your pardon?" asked Dr. Healy, startled, glancing up from his watch. And then he drew the cigaret from his mouth, as he saw Durant's eyes.

"I saw you looking at your watch. Are you in a hurry?" Durant smiled. "If you are, and you have some previous appointment, I'm afraid you'll have to make other arrangements. You see, I intend to have a thorough talk with you."

Dr. Healy put down his cigaret, and the fine skin of his forehead bunched together. He watched the smoke rising from the ashtray. His friendly and paternal smile became somewhat fixed. Intangibles, to Dr. Healy, were more real than any "reality," and much more powerful. He was not the psychiatrist who "lived by the book," but by his enormous intuitive powers. He continued to watch the smoke. He was coolly enraged with himself for his superficial judgment. I must watch it, he thought; I'm getting careless. He sent the exquisitely tuned antennas of his mind into the charged air between him and Durant, and they turned all ways, like the living petals of sea anemones. And the antennas twisted, moved about, shrank and dilated, sensing danger.

"I did have some appointments," said Dr. Healy pleasantly. "But nothing of importance. Even if they were, Major, this interview is much more important."

"I'm glad you think so, Doctor. And I agree with you. It happens, too, that I have some knowledge of psychiatry."

Dr. Healy began to relax. "Knowledge of psychiatry." Good! There was no man so easy to mislead, to use, to bend to one's purposes, as a fool who confessed that he had "some knowledge of psychiatry." Use the jargon on him, pretend to be amazed at his knowledge, talk to him as if he were an equal, assume that he understands the most intricate of terms, and you had him. To disagree with you then on any point, thereafter, he would have to confess his ignorance and stupidity, and this the human ego avoids at almost any cost. I'll soon have him eating out of my hand, thought Dr. Healy, and put on a very interested expression.

"I'm glad to hear you understand psychiatry," he said. "It makes things simpler. I won't have to explain my terminology then, Major. We can proceed on a certain basis of mutual understanding."

Durant had some difficulty in keeping from smiling. He made himself nod gravely, and he inclined his head with the gesture of one who is modestly flattered. Dr. Healy lit another cigaret, and fastidiously ground out the first. "You know the work of the Public Psychiatric Department, Major?"

Durant nodded at the papers on his desk. "I've gone over these. But I'd like some things explained." He picked up one paper.

"This is the section dealing with adults, not children, Doctor. This is your last brief report, or a portion of it, dated four days ago. I'll read you one phrase: 'We must not have ambivalence toward Government. Such reveals neurotic associations with regard to a parent, and indicates emotional immaturity.' Now, Doctor, will you kindly tell me what the hell you mean by that?"

Dr. Healy lost considerable of his confidence, and again the skin of his forehead bunched together. This robot had actually confessed ignorance. A bad sign. The doctor coughed briefly. "I'm sorry, Major. I thought you understood the term 'ambivalence.'" He waited, tentatively, for the eager affirmation. It did not come. Instead, Durant grinned. "I don't," he said. And looked at the doctor with amused inquiry.

Dr. Healy became just the slightest bit alarmed. But his voice remained smooth and cordial. "I should say, in the terms of the layman—" He paused. Durant nodded, and repeated: "In the terms of the layman—'"

"Well, then, Major, it means a state where a man has conflicting attitudes toward any object, such as love and hate, acquiescence and rebellion. Existing simultaneously for a particular government, a person, or situation."

"Common enough," agreed Durant. "My grandfather was a stern old party with some hideous ideas. But very bright and imaginative and lively. I loved him even more than I did my father, and I could have cut his throat with pleasure at almost the same instant. I suppose practically everybody has this—this ambivalence, eh?"

"It's not a healthy state," said Dr. Healy, becoming the teacher. "It can build up a very active neurosis, and, in some cases, can make the patient psychotic."

"That makes practically all of us crazy, then," said Durant. He put a cigaret in his mouth, and Keiser sprang to light it for him. Grandon was listening with intense interest. The other officers, impatiently waiting for Dr. Healy's discomfiture, looked bored.

"I wouldn't say we're all 'crazy,'" replied Dr. Healy, with amused tolerance. "We all make individual adjustments. However, there is such a thing as mass ambivalence, and vigilant and informed governments are now on the alert for it and adjust it in time, before it can become dangerous."

Durant nodded seriously. "In the old days, before psychiatry, it just meant that the people became inflamed under tyranny and shot up the works—meaning the government, and set up a few gallows and guillotines on their own, and established a new government by revolution. Very common. In the old days." He smiled at Dr. Healy artlessly.

But Dr. Healy was no longer very amused. The antennas of his mind began to quiver.

"What do you psychiatric fellows do when you encounter mass ambivalence, or in the words of a layman, when you find sections of the population brooding on ropes and axes?"

Dr. Healy said, picking his words very carefully, and watching Durant with the intensity of a stalking animal: "We find the ringleaders—or rather, I should say, the ones who exhibit the emotional disturbance in a marked form—"

"And shoot them," said Durant genially.

Dr. Healy decided his cigaret was adulterated. He ground it out.

"No, Major. No. We reeducate them. We show them that they don't really hate our form of Government. They are really only subconsciously reacting to hidden hostilities toward a parent, either a father or a mother. Once they understand that, and that they have substituted our Government for the parent in their minds—"

"You send them forth with your blessings, completely adjusted, eh, Doctor?"

Dr. Healy's filmed eyes considered Durant, and his mouth opened a little. Then, he said deliberately: "Yes."

"You return them to their friends so they can do a little psychiatry on them? Amateur psychiatrists, themselves, teaching love for our Government?"

"Yes," said the doctor again.

"No more—emotional—scars, Dr. Healy?"

"None, Major."

Durant continued to smile. He thought of the torture rooms of the frightful FBHS, where brave men were crippled, blinded, murdered, and from which only a few, and they incoherent madmen, ever emerged as warnings to others who might show symptoms of "ambivalence." The physical tortures and scarrings were awful enough. But men like Dr. Healy specialized in the mutilation of minds. Durant's fingers twisted his cigaret to fragments. He glanced involuntarily at Grandon, who was almost at his elbow. The young lieutenant was grinning abstractedly, as he stared at the doctor.

Dr. Healy was thinking very rapidly. This new major was not a fool. He had made some interesting remarks, all with that bland smile of his. Dangerous remarks. Was he subtle? Dr. Healy remembered reading the full report on this major: Regular Army man, educated; parents, sound American stock; not married, completely trustworthy; devoted to the Government; formerly active in espionage. He had been passed on by the FBHS, with laudatory comments. Highly recommended by the Chief Magistrate, Arthur Carlson. Yet—those remarks. Dr. Healy considered them again. Innocent? Or baiting? Or crafty?

Durant followed his thoughts. I'm not as careful as I should be, he thought. But his own mind was a red cloud of hatred. He said: "Well, that is your department, Dr. Healy. I just wanted a little information for myself. Curious. Whatever it is you do, in your—hospitals—is probably the only thing you can do. But let's go on. I quote from your report: 'We must become even more active in reorientation courses, in view of the new war.' What does that mean?"

Dr. Healy regained some confidence. "Instead of the regular indoctrination which we have been giving to the people once a week, we must now, in view of the new war, increase the indoctrination, having three sessions a week in each locality, under the supervision of a psychiatrist. During the last war, there were too many marked neuroses arising in the population, so many, in fact, that our psychiatric resources were badly strained. Too many people—"

"Went right out of their minds or started to shoot their own officers in the back or burned down barracks or slaughtered our own soldiers on the streets," said Durant. "Yes. I remember that. It became serious, didn't it? A mob tried to assassinate the President, himself. Yes, I remember. And thousands just walked out of the defense factories or committed suicide, or broke up their machines. Very bad."

"Very bad," agreed Dr. Healy, watching Durant closely. But Durant's expression was all disgust at such behavior.

"We had to shoot down the mobs by the streetful," went on Durant. "That was in New York, Doctor, and I understand that the same thing happened elsewhere."

"Mass neurosis. We must avoid that in this war, Major. We must increase the resistance of the mass-mind and educate it to a full understanding of what this war means."

"They did it better in the old days, a century or two ago," commented Durant. "They just invented gorgeous uniforms, trained some excellent brass bands, promised loot to the soldiers, and the citizenry thought up exciting slogans and sent everybody out to murder. Ah, the happy flags in those days, and the music and the exuberance and extra rations of rum for the gallant soldiers, and the best girls of the homeland and the enemy territory for the soldiers, and the medals! Simpler than indoctrination, eh, Doctor, wasn't it?"

Dr. Healy began to feel safe. He said, in a superior tone: "It was crude, Major, though I grant you it was effective. However, wars in those days were confined almost purely to the Military, and today wars are mass efforts and the masses are directly affected. Battlefields are in every city in every street and in every house."

"All the exultation was deliberately taken out of wars," said Durant wistfully. "Hitler had color, that's why he attracted millions. But Russian Communism and British Communism brought drabness to war. Took all the joy and the gaiety and glory out of it. That's because they pulled the masses, themselves, into conflict." He smiled at Dr. Healy boyishly. "Why not reintroduce glamour into war, Doctor? Why not some wonderful marching bands, and millions of flags with tassels, and bright-colored uniforms, and drums and fifes and bugles and dancing in the street?"

Dr. Healy looked offended at this barbarism. "We live in a modern world, Major. The people know that war isn't a fiesta. They have a sense of responsibility. We must cultivate this sense to the extreme, if we are to succeed in this new war effort, without domestic upheavals such as we had in the last war. The people must feel they participate."

"I know!" said Durant, in a happy voice. "'Age groups!' 'Integration!' 'Working closely together with!' 'Sense of belonging!' 'Identification with the mass!' I told you, Doctor, I know all the terms!"

"So you do, Major," said Dr. Healy, with a patronizing smirk. He had this military robot now.

" 'Creativeness!' 'Maturity!' 'Complete adjustment to environment!' "

"Quite so," murmured Dr. Healy.

Durant sat back in his chair and beamed. Dr. Healy beamed also. Then again, he saw Durant's eyes. He half rose from his chair. "What's the matter, Doctor?" asked Durant softly.

"Nothing," said Dr. Healy. He almost stammered. He lowered himself in his chair and stared at Durant, as if fascinated.

Durant leaned his chin dreamily on his palm and looked into space. "I'm just remembering what Rauschning said: 'Wherever the typical mass character becomes universal, all higher values are as good as lost.' What do you think of that, Doctor?"

Dr. Healy was silent, but his eyes narrowed on Durant. Then as Durant glanced at him ingenuously for a reply, he said: "The modern world cannot exist without a 'typical mass character,' Major. The world is now too complex for individuality."

"Except for a few, eh?" Durant waited; the doctor did not answer. "No matter what the system, there are always exceptions, aren't there? We cultivate the exceptions, don't we? We call them the 'leaders.' "

"Yes."

"By pure coincidence, of course, these new young 'leaders' are always drawn from our military hierarchy, the MASTS, the farmers, the bureaucrats. These children don't go to Federal schools. They have private schools of their own, where their 'individuality' is cultivated in behalf of the Government. Excellent, isn't it?"

"Are you quarreling with our system, Major?" Dr. Healy leaned forward.

" 'Our system?' " Durant raised his eyebrows in intense surprise. "Did we, the Military, who rule this country, establish such a system, Doctor? Or did you, and your kind? For your own purposes?"

The officers drew closer to Durant's desk, and Dr. Healy, the intuitive, felt their gigantic hostility, their detestation, their contempt for him as a civilian. He shrank in his excellent clothing.

Durant struck his desk with his fist. "Who established those schools for the privileged children, Doctor?"

"We—we pay for them. The Government is not put to any expense, Major! The Government approves."

"The Government? Dr. Healy, we, the Military, are the Government. You are not. We are the power of The Democracy. You are nothing." Durant's eyes blazed on the doctor. "Dr. Healy, when I was sent here, I was given absolute power. We, the Military, are resuming, with full force, the power which we have allowed to drain away in the last two or three years. I am master here, Dr. Healy. And so, I now issue this directive: All private schools in Section 7 are to be closed within two days, the teachers disbanded for more important work in the defense effort. All the children in those schools are to be sent to the Federal schools, to be indoctrinated in the precepts of The Democracy."

Dr. Healy jumped to his feet. "Impossible!" he exclaimed incredulously.

"Impossible?" Durant's voice was low and deadly. "Are you, a mere civilian, under my jurisdiction, under the jurisdiction of the Military, telling me that anything is impossible which I decree?"

Dr. Healy lost his head. He cried: "You must consider, Major! Where shall we get our leaders, if we don't train them in our private schools? Major Curtiss, do you think for a moment that the parents of these children will stand for this? They'll—they'll—"

"They'll what?" Durant stood up also, and he seemed to tower in rage above the psychiatrist.

"They'll appeal to Washington!"

Durant regarded him disbelievingly. "To whom? To what? To my military superiors, who have given me full power? To the Chief Magistrate of Section 7, who has told me to do what seems wise, and who has delegated all authority to me? Dr. Healy, you sound distinctly subversive. Are you defying the Military? Are you telling me that you, a mere employee of mine, are challenging me?" He turned to Bishop and Edwards. "You've heard this man. He is questioning the authority of the Military."

Dr. Healy was terribly frightened. He flung out his hands. "Major," he pleaded, after a glance at the circle of grim faces behind Durant. "You are inferring things which I did not imply. It—it has been the custom not to send privileged children of privileged groups to the Federal schools, where there is only mass indoctrination and little education—"

Durant roared: "Are you saying that our schools, our wonderful Federal schools, are institutes to create mindless animals? Are you insulting our noble schools, which teach children the truth about The Democracy?"

Frantic, now, all his assurance gone, all his body shaking as he had made others shake, all his faculties stricken with terror, as he had terrorized others, Dr. Healy fell back from the desk. The salt dryness of fear was in his mouth.

"You have been depriving these so-called 'privileged' children of the privilege of honest education in our Federal schools, Doctor. Unity! Duty! Sacrifice! Discipline! These things the 'privileged' children must learn at once. You have heard me. If one of your private schools exists two days from now, you and your subordinates will be arrested at once."

Durant sat down. He did not have to act now. All his rage showed on his face, all his hatred and repulsion. Dr. Healy stood before him, shattered and trembling.

"Notify all the schools in this Section of my directive. And close the doors of your special schools for your special children day after tomorrow. And see to it that the children are immediately enrolled in the Federal schools, with proper ration cards for meals, and the prevailing uniforms. If any of the parents rebel, I hereby order you to report them at once to me."

Durant turned to Keiser. "Show the doctor to the door, Sergeant."

Dr. Healy hesitated, visibly stricken. "Major—"

Durant looked at him long and hard. "Dr. Healy, get the hell out of here before I arrest you."

"I—I meant nothing, Major, please! I was merely trying to explain—"

Durant considered him. This suave, this superior individual, this urbane and sadistic wretch! There he stood, quaking in his boots, as he had made saner and more honest and more decent men quake. He stood in the fear of death, as a fox or a rat or a dog might stand, and his face was like milk. Durant made an abrupt gesture. Keiser took Dr. Healy's arm in a rough grip.

"Don't, please!" cried Dr. Healy. And he turned, half staggering, and ran from the room.

An atmosphere of happy congeniality pervaded the office upon the discomfited exit of Dr. Healy. Even young Grandon relaxed his features in a pleased expression, and joined in the general laughter. In spite of his efforts he could make his voice only moderately cold and surly when he announced that a very important bureaucrat was next on the list for an interview and to present his respects. He briefed Durant on the man and his background.

"Andreas Zimmer is not only Assistant Director in the BML of Section 7—"

"Wait," interrupted Durant. "Remember—I'm just a one-syllable man and I know nothing of the present exotic alphabets. What the hell is BML?"

Grandon thought this remark somewhat puerile, as indeed Durant immediately admitted it was. "Just warming up for my act," he explained. "Of course—Bureau of Mobilized Labor."

"Zimmer, unknown to the Director himself, is also informant to the Army," went on Grandon. "He reports, secretly and unofficially, to the major in charge of Section 7—you, sir—on any deviation which might take place in his office, and also advises."

"Advises the Army?"

"Suggests, then."

Durant leaned back in his chair. "I love bureaucrats," he said reflectively. "There's something about them. They're a special breed. They even have a special smell. As an Army man, myself, I've always wanted to get my teeth in a juicy bureaucrat. This man is juicy?"

"He certainly is!" exclaimed Grandon, with fervor and anticipatory glee. "Oh, by the way, Major, as his reports to the officer in charge are always confidential, he will see you alone." There was regret on the young lieutenant's face, and regret on the faces of the others, also.

The officers went out of the room, reluctantly, and a civilian entered. Durant studied him with that sharpness developed in him during his years as a Minute Man and as a lawyer. He saw an untidy man in black, of medium height and square figure, the collar of his shirt wrinkled, his black tie askew, his clothing crumpled and unpressed. He had a short, broad neck, and a big square face of a pasty color, and a thick mass of badly cut black hair. His features were pudgy and had an amiable cast, and his smile was friendly. However, his eyes were effectively covered by cloudy, convex glasses. If one did not look at those glasses, one had the impression of an ordinary man of about thirty-five, for there was nothing sinister about his appearance. The typical bureaucrat, Durant had observed, was either anonymous in aspect, beetlelike and brisk, or pompous and imposing and utterly stupid and vicious, depending on whether or not he moved in secret or whether or not it was to his advantage, and his masters', to seem impressive.

He deposited a thick briefcase on Durant's desk, without permission, grinned boyishly and shrugged off a rather shabby, too-short and too-skimpy black coat, and tossed it on a chair. Then he extended a somewhat grubby hand. "Major Curtiss!" he said. "Welcome to Philadelphia, and Section7! Glad to see you, sir! I'm sure we'll work very well together." He had a pleasant and ingratiating voice, but Durant stared coldly and deliberately at the hand extended, and did not take it for perceptible moments. It was a warm fat hand, with a good-fellowship grasp.

A bastard, thought Durant. A deliberately disarming dog, a treacherous snake, and greedy as hell.

"Sit down, Mr. Zimmer," said Durant indifferently. But Mr. Zimmer had already seated himself. He now beamed expansively at the major. "I work closely with the Army," he informed Durant. "But the Chief Magistrate probably has told you about me."

Durant said nothing.

If the man was intimidated by his reception he did not show it. He sat in his chair confidently. He must have browbeaten poor old Major Burnes with his boyish friendliness and hinted treachery and power, thought Durant. He has the air of someone who has been indulged and who has inflicted pain and death. Nothing else would give him that look of assurance. Durant, thinking this, smelled danger.

"In the main," said Andreas Zimmer, "I've come merely to present my respects. I hope you'll be very happy in Philadelphia, Major, and if there is anything I can do, personally—"

"You're Assistant Director of the Bureau of Mobilized Labor

in Section 7, aren't you?" asked Durant slowly. "Who is the Director?"

The friendly smile congealed momentarily. "Oh, the Director? Mr. Franklin Woolcott. A very busy man, Major. And, confidentially, he knows nothing of my affiliation with the Military. But you probably know that. He knows, of course, that I, in my regular duties, work—"

"—closely with," said Durant, repeating the loathsome phrase without inflection. However, he soon understood the measure of this man, for there was a fugitive gleam behind those concealing lenses.

"Yes," said Mr. Zimmer. The affable smile tightened along the edges. "Work closely with the Military."

"In other words, you are practically a spy without portfolio," remarked Durant.

"A spy, sir?" The other's face became grave. "I'd hardly call it that. It is in my line of duty to keep the military officer of Section 7 advised, as our Bureau is very important to the welfare of the whole Section."

Durant picked up a pencil and turned it about in his fingers. "How long has Mr. Woolcott been with the Bureau?"

The disarming smile broadened again. "Only a year, Major. Frankly, I'm more conversant with the work, as I have had this position for six years or more. Mr. Woolcott relies upon me considerably."

"What have you to report to me today—confidentially, of course," said Durant.

The man picked up his briefcase at once and opened it cautiously, keeping the papers close to his chest. The typical bureaucratic gesture, thought Durant. "Well, Major, it just happens —and I'm sorry, considering this is your first day on duty—that there is an item of real importance I must report to you." He carefully fished out a thick manual, and held it up for Durant to see. *Manual of the Bureau of Mobilized Labor*. "You have this in your office, Major, but perhaps you are not familiar with it. With your permission I'll read you a section pertinent to my report of today."

He flicked a few pages, after moistening his thumb. He began to read in the bureaucrat's careful and unctuous voice:

" 'Section 12, Paragraphs one to six, Page 98:

" 'RS That it shall be the duty of the Commissioner who is the Chief of the Bureau of Mobilized Labor to appoint Directors of Sections.

" 'The duties of the Directors of Sections shall be to enforce the laws, rules and regulations now in force or which may hereafter be passed. That it shall be the duty of Directors of Sections to supervise and have in their possession at all times a complete and full roster of the available labor in their Sections. The

Directors shall from time to time make reports to the Commissioner in Washington with reference to any surplus labor, unemployed or unemployable or otherwise unavailable, existing in their Sections which might eventually be eligible for absorption in the Labor Pool.

" 'That from time to time the Directors of Sections shall visit various factories and industries or other places of employment and confer with supervisors, superintendents or employers, of labor, to ascertain their needs and also the spirit of efficiency and morale, and whether or not labor is being used to fullest capacity in the interest of production for defense or for the war effort. The Directors of Sections shall make a full and detailed report in proper and sufficient copies to the Commissioner in Washington on each and every occasion of inspection.

" 'The Directors of Sections can, if, in their opinion an emergency exists, call upon the civilian population, not heretofore mobilized, with the following exceptions:

" '(a) All those persons essential for the well-being of the MASTS actively engaged in the defense or war efforts in cooperation with The Democracy.

" '(b) All those persons essential to the well-being of the heads of various Bureaus and Sections and Departments of The Democracy.' "

As a lawyer, Durant was well versed in the circumlocution and double-talk and tortuous language of bureaucracy. It had always enraged him. He composed his face in an expression of an Army man's total and simple-minded bewilderment.

"Me," he said. "I'm just an officer. Boiled down, what does that all mean?"

Mr. Zimmer gave him the superior smile of the bureaucrat. "It's really very simple, Major. Our Bureau supplies conscripted labor. The Directors of Sections report available labor to Washington. However, they have authority, if they see fit, to conscript it, themselves. The reporting is just for Channels and proper procedure, but the Directors have full power in their own Sections."

"I see," interrupted Durant. " 'The proper and sufficient copies' are just to make work and keep up offices."

The bland smile disappeared, and Durant saw he had made a serious mistake. There was nothing else to do but look receptively idiotic and attentive.

"I'd say it was to keep all records complete and orderly," said Zimmer, closing his *Manual* as if it were his Bible.

"Go on," said Durant, trying to make his voice as fatuous as possible.

Zimmer rubbed his chin thoughtfully. Durant noticed that the man had not shaved for at least twenty-four hours.

"Now we come to a slight difficulty," said Zimmer. "You will remember, Major, that certain classes of labor are exempt from conscription into industries engaged in essential work, etc. 'Essential for the well-being of the MASTS . . . and the well-being of the heads of various Bureaus and Sections and Departments of The Democracy.' "

Durant had some struggle with himself to preserve a listening neutrality. He failed a little, for his dark eyes began to sparkle vengefully. "In other words, domestic labor such as valets, chauffeurs, butlers, maids, washwomen, gardeners and scrubwomen employed by the MASTS and bureaucrats. Yes, I see. What's so important and 'difficult' about all this?"

Zimmer stiffened portentously. And now when he spoke there was a faintly threatening note in his tone. "It is, indeed, very important and difficult. Because Mr. Woolcott has arbitrarily decided that essential industry should not be deprived of this 'unavailable' labor pool, though the *Manual* distinctly states that this kind of labor is exempt from the labor conscription clauses. He intends to begin active conscription of this labor two weeks from today, and he is in process of preparing the necessary directives."

Durant's face became inscrutable. He remained silent though Zimmer waited for his comment. Then Zimmer said impatiently: "To boil it down, as you say, Major, it is essential to the well-being of the MASTS and important Government officials everywhere, and also in this Section, that domestic labor be let alone. But Mr. Woolcott emphatically insists on conscripting it for assignment to the Coal Mine Brigades, since recent mine explosions in this Section have depleted the labor camps in this vicinity."

Durant's heart began to beat with rage. He remembered that only a month ago a coal mine explosion had killed two hundred mine workers, men, women and children, and had crippled several hundreds more. It had been a frightful explosion, and had been attributed to "saboteurs." Of course, no one had questioned inferior equipment and the brutal disregard of the mine owners for their wretched slaves.

"If this heretofore unavailable labor is conscripted, the well-being of the persons mentioned in the *Manual* will be seriously imperiled," went on Zimmer.

Durant could not control himself at all. "In other words, the wives of the MASTS and bureaucrats will have to do their own scrubbing, cooking, washing and baby-tending. This will destroy the 'well-being' of the husbands who will be compelled to witness this heart-breaking sight."

A look of livid menace fixed itself on the big face opposite Durant, and there was a cunning flash behind the thick glasses.

Durant sat up suddenly in his chair and pointed a finger at Zimmer. "And you disagree with Mr. Woolcott, do you?" he shouted. "You believe that the welfare of The Democracy should be subordinated to the welfare of a few individuals? The safety of The Democracy is less than the comfort of a handful of minor and privileged groups? Is that your idea of patriotism, Zimmer?"

The man, attacked in this terrible fashion, began to tremble, and the menacing expression on his face changed to one of awful fear. He stammered: "Major! I—I didn't say that at—all! I merely quoted from the *Manual*, and the customary procedure. I—I haven't anything to do with it! It comes from Washington—"

Durant moved in more rapidly. "Yet, you've said, yourself, that the Section Directors of the Bureau of Mobilized Labor have full authority to conscript any and all labor! Mr. Woolcott appears to me to be a very patriotic man, completely aware of his duty. Yet you come to me and report what you consider deviations on his part. I think you are the deviationist, Zimmer!"

Utter terror seized the bureaucrat. He jumped to his feet. "Major! I—I'm afraid you don't understand! If—if domestic labor is taken away from what you call the privileged groups there'll be serious dissatisfaction, and we can't afford it during this new war effort. It—it could be dangerous—"

"You mean that this minor group would dare to rebel against the authority of The Democracy, that they might embarrass The Democracy, that they might even plot the overthrow of The Democracy?"

Panic overcame all Zimmer's caution and training. "I didn't imply that, sir!"

"You did! In fact, I shall so report to your superior."

Zimmer screamed, clasping his fat hands together in an attitude of desperate appeal. "You can't do that, Major! I work closely with the Military. Mr. Woolcott isn't to know about that at all. If you'll read your papers about me—"

Durant sat back to enjoy the full spectacle of the man's rout, fright and disorder. He watched Zimmer's shaking body with intense satisfaction, and with even more satisfaction he studied the other as he mopped his forehead with a dirty handkerchief.

Zimmer leaned over the desk. "Major," he pleaded. "You do understand, don't you? I had to make my report to you, in accordance with instructions from Washington. I've quoted nothing but what is in the *Manual*."

"It seems to me," said Durant threateningly, "that some measures will have to be taken in this Section to maintain discipline. I'm referring to those who employ domestic labor. They've got to be put in their places. Who is running this country, the Military or the MASTS and the bureaucrats? I think we must have a definite show-down. The Military is becoming lax in some respects."

"But Washington has already laid down the rules and regulations," begged Zimmer.

"Those rules and regulations were laid down by bureaucrats, and bureaucracy is subservient to the Military. Or have you forgotten, Zimmer?"

Overcome, shaken from his lofty position, Zimmer could only stare and tremble, the glasses glimmering with frustrated hatred.

"How many domestic servants do you employ, Zimmer?"

"Three, sir." The voice was craven, now. "I've got two children, Major, and my wife isn't—isn't very strong. We have to have a nursemaid, a housekeeper and a laundress."

"I'm afraid," said Durant, smiling, "that your wife will have to recover her health in two weeks. All for The Democracy, Zimmer. All for the War Effort and Essential Industry, Zimmer. Or are you going to inform me that your wife is more important than defeating the Enemy?"

He picked up the telephone receiver, and asked that Mr. Woolcott, of the Bureau of Labor Mobilization be called. Zimmer leaned weakly against the desk, his pouting lips quivering. Durant continued to smile with pleasure.

Then a voice answered him, impatiently: "Woolcott speaking. I understand Major Curtiss is calling. Is this Major Curtiss?"

Durant's hand closed convulsively on the telephone, and his breath stopped. For the voice purporting to be that of Mr. Woolcott was the voice of Durant's best friend, Benjamin Colburn, leader, a year ago, of Durant's division of the Minute Men in New York. Colburn had been captured, a year ago, and reportedly killed by Arthur Carlson, Chief Magistrate of Section 7. His body, in a sealed box, had been sent to his family for private burial. Durant had loved him devotedly, not only as a dear friend, but as the most able man he had ever known, a dedicated and fearless young man. It was incredible that it was his voice which had come to him at this time. It was the voice of the dead.

"Who is this?" the voice was demanding. "Major Curtiss? Is anybody there?"

It was indeed the voice of Ben Colburn, short, sharp and impatient. A long shaking ran over Durant's body and his eyes misted. Ben! Ben Colburn. Durant began to breathe slowly and with deliberate evenness.

"Yes, this is Major Curtiss. Major—Andrew—Curtiss. Mr. Woolcott," he answered, spacing his words. "Major Curtiss of the Army of The Democracy, just appointed as Military Officer to Section 7, in Philadelphia, and just arrived from—New York, under the direction of Chief Magistrate Arthur Carlson."

He glanced up at Zimmer, who was listening only with apprehension, concerned only with his own affairs, and his own coming loss of domestics.

There was a silence on the line.

The voice came again, slower, full of meaning. "Good morning, Major Curtiss. We haven't met. But I hope to see you very soon. I'd like you to meet my assistant, Major. Mr. Andreas Zimmer. I believe he is in his offices, now, Major. Or he was, only a few moments ago. A very able man, Major. Very efficient and painstaking. He never misses anything, Major. Very able. Is there something I can do for you, Major?"

Durant's hand involutarily loosened from the telephone, and he caught the receiver just as it was about to fall. He stared at it incredulously. Tapped. By whom? Of course, it was tapped by the Federal Bureau of Home Security. Even the Military was not exempt from the surveillance of the FBHS spies, who spied upon each other, also. However, Durant had thought that the Military had the complete trust of the Government. He began to sweat.

"I'd like to talk over a little matter with you, Mr. Woolcott." His voice shook in spite of himself. "A little matter of no particular importance. But I'd like to meet you. Shall we say for lunch?"

"That will be splendid, Major. Let me see: it is almost one o'clock. Suppose I pick you up at one-fifteen at your office. We can meet downstairs." Colburn paused. "And in the meantime, Major, I want to assure you that this office wishes, as in the past, to—"

"Work closely," said Durant, with solemnity, "with the Military." Again, he glanced at Zimmer, who was replacing his papers in his briefcase and who had apparently lost interest in the conversation. "And one of these days, soon, I'd like to meet your assistant, who, I understand, often is of assistance to the Armed Forces."

"We do what we can," replied Colburn, and Durant, from the tone of his voice, knew that he was smiling. "After all, we are under Military supervision. By the way, Major, I've just glanced at my watch, and I see it is slow. Time's running out, I'm afraid. I have only a few minutes—"

Durant hung up, and his joy at hearing the voice of his friend disappeared. For Colburn had communicated to him the fact that he was in deadly danger and that he might be exposed at any time and that in that event, for the sake of all Minute Men, he must commit suicide. Durant turned to Zimmer. "Your superior officer sounds like a very cordial man. I suppose you have no difficulty with him?"

Zimmer hesitated and peered at Durant, who waited, artlessly, for his answer. Then Zimmer coughed. "As secret advisor to the Military, Major, I'm forced to confess that I am, indeed, having difficulty with him. For reasons of security, and because I don't have full information as yet, I can't even suggest my suspicions to you. When the time arrives, I will tell you everything."

He became important again, though he was still shaken. "And, Major, I don't suppose you would change your mind about agreeing with Mr. Woolcott on the issue we have discussed?"

So, even spies were sometimes indiscreet, thought Durant, understanding at once that this wretch was not only a bureaucrat, a spy for the Military, but also a member of the deadly, invisible and omnipresent FBHS. Here was Colburn's danger. Zimmer had come upon something. Durant's spirits rose a little. He would discover what Zimmer knew, when the time came, and some way would be found not only to save Colburn but to eliminate this man. So he hesitated, as if considering. Then, with a bluff and hearty manner, he slapped his desk.

"I'll tell you what I'll do, Zimmer. I'll talk it over with Mr. Woolcott. At any rate, I don't think anyone should be too hasty in this matter."

"Good! Thank you, Major!" crowed Zimmer, thrusting out his hand in delight. "I've been worrying about my poor little wife. And I'm sure, sir, that after you give the matter your full consideration, you'll prefer to abide by the law."

Durant controlled his sudden anger at this insolence. He made himself smile. He stood up and shook the other's hand, and winked. "I'm new to all this, and perhaps zeal carried me away a little. Something tells me you and I are going to work very closely with each other, very, very closely."

Highly elated, and freed from all panic now, and believing that his logical and superior arguments had swayed this stupid military man, Zimmer was completely disarmed. He parted from Durant in a state of affable exultation, and the officers waiting outside, eagerly expectant, were extremely disappointed. They trooped in sluggishly.

"Well, boys," said Durant, grinning. "Feeling dejected? Let me tell you an old proverb: it's sometimes better to send a fox after his own scent."

They were puzzled, and waited for an explanation. But Durant announced he was going out for lunch with Mr. Woolcott, and the officers became more cheerful. Keiser solicitously assisted Durant with his coat, and Durant left them.

The stench of the streets of Philadelphia was not quite so bad as in the streets in New York. Even though laboring under despair and degradation, the people of Philadelphia still retained some faint pride in cleanliness. The pavements and the roads might be as broken and as full of craters as they were in New York, but there was little rubbish though the gutters were thick with mud. Here, too, there was a faint smell of spring and the light shone clearer. Durant, having emerged from his hotel, began to wonder at the wisdom of Arthur Carlson who had sent him from the black terror of New York to a city which might, even in the smallest way, contain some hope for the future. Was it possible that the smaller cities suffered less from the claustrophobia of New York and so might dream of freedom and the wideness of liberty? His father and grandfather had told him that it was the very hysteria of the packed masses of Manhattan, their very insularism and lack of a sense of national obligation, which had permitted them to become the victims of criminals, gangsters, murderers, evil politicians and madmen for the past fifty years. Long before the final calamity of the present military dictatorship New Yorkers had easily assimilated the doctrines of slavery and had swayed like grass in the winds of every demented "ism" blown from the noxious swamps of Washington. Thrust cheek-by-jowl with their fellowmen in New York, they had not learned to "understand" their neighbors. They had only learned to hate and fear them, and to absorb their mania.

The street outside the hotel was crowded with soldiers and officers and a few members of the Picked Guard. Here were his men, thought Durant. Young men. But militarism had inevitably degraded them, had brutalized their faces so that one man resembled another so closely as to be barely distinguishable from each other. Some of them must once have had the light of intelligence in their eyes. The light had gone. The uniforms had debased not only their bodies but their minds, and the authority they had acquired over the subject proletarian masses had given them an air of bestial arrogance and cruelty. They stood solidly on the walks, and the people, men and women and children, crept meekly by them in the gutters, heads bent, lips moistening humbly, eyes averted. It was necessary only to look into the eyes of any soldier, thought Durant bitterly, to see the corrupting and maddening effects of power.

The officers and men came to attention upon seeing Durant, but he hardly noticed them. A long, sleek black car was drawing to the curb, marked with the insignia of the Bureau of Mobilized Labor. The soldiers stared at it stolidly, and with the contempt of the all-powerful for a lesser tribe. Durant said to himself: Careful. Careful. A door swung open and a uniformed chauffeur emerged, saluting. He was followed by a man with fine gray hair and a quiet face. Durant, about to approach this man, halted, his heart beating with dismay. This man, tall, slight, apparently middle-aged, with a white tense face and a very slight smile and with tired and sunken eyes, could not possibly be Dr. Benjamin Colburn who was only thirty-five and who, when Durant had seen him last a year ago, had been full of humor and gaiety and confidence. This man limped perceptibly and moved like an old man.

"Major Curtiss?" asked the stranger, holding out his hand. Durant stood like stone and his heart sickened. He recognized the voice. And now, looking into those faded eyes, he knew that this was, indeed, Dr. Benjamin Colburn. He could not speak.

Colburn took the cold and flaccid hand of Durant. "I'm Woolcott," he said. And then he smiled reassuringly, and warningly, and it was the smile of a friend. He looked at Durant's broken arm and a faint crinkle appeared between his eyebrows.

"I'm Curtiss," Durant mumbled. My God, my God, he thought. He let Colburn's hand drop and followed his host to the car. The door closed after them and the car moved on smoothly, skirting the craters. Durant leaned back in his seat and shut his eyes. I'm too emotional, he thought. This is no job for me.

Colburn was saying casually: "This is a great pleasure. I thought it might be a good idea to get acquainted like this. I might be able to tell you something about the city and the work we do here. Have you ever been in Philadelphia before, Major?"

"No," said Durant. He kept his eyes closed. Colburn went on, but now Durant felt a hard pressure against his ankle. "I think you'll like this city. I've lived in this region all my life, and know all the territory hereabouts. I thought you might like to have lunch out in the country; the weather's fine, and there is an inn especially reserved for us about ten miles out. Have you the time?"

The hard pressure became insistent. Durant opened his eyes. "Yes. I've cleared up most of my work for the day. Besides, I've had an accident recently, and must be careful." He stared emptily before him.

"Good," said Colburn. "Then we needn't hurry." He said to his chauffeur: "Joe, under the circumstances I think we'd better drop you off at the office. I believe Mr. Zimmer wants you to drive him somewhere this afternoon in the other car. I'll take this one."

The chauffeur saluted indifferently. He glanced in the rear mirror and Durant caught the shaft of pure hatred sent in his direction. He knew that look by now, and he was dimly pleased. Apparently the Military was much more hated in this city than in New York.

Colburn said pleasantly: "Are you a New Yorker, Major? I thought so. Been in the Army long? Ten years! Well, I was in for four years, and then I was appointed to various positions in Section 7. I was glad to return to Philadelphia, and I hope you'll find the city as comfortable as I've found it. We have some nice parties, and know a number of agreeable people in town, and after a week or two you'll make friends. Have you a family, Major? No? Neither have I."

There was no change in his pleasant voice. Durant thought of Colburn's wife and his two young daughters, and his uninjured hand clenched. He regarded Colburn's profile briefly. It was noncommittal and friendly and very calm.

The car stopped before a large and well-kept building which

had once been the Philadelphia Chamber of Commerce. The chauffeur stepped out, and asked Colburn solicitiously: "Are you sure you're well enough to drive by yourself, Mr. Woolcott?"

"Quite sure. Thank you, Joe." Colburn turned to Durant and laughed. "My old leg wound still bothers me some, and I had to have a slight operation on it about a month ago. Suppose we go up front, Major?"

Colburn took the wheel, nodded at his doubtful chauffeur, and he and Durant drove on by themselves, in silence.

Then Colburn said: "I've heard a rumor that in spite of the new war there'll be some money to mend the streets. I hope so. We broke two springs last week, and that's expensive for the Government. We can't afford extra expense with the new war effort. It's a terrible thing. Why does The Democracy have to be attacked every few years? Why can't the rest of this damned world leave us in peace? Who would have thought that those goddamned South American countries would have blown up the Panama Canal on us without a warning?"

Durant turned to his host impulsively, but Colburn gave him a stern look. Durant felt chilled and stifled. Was the menace here with them, within the confines of this car? Colburn was pointing through the windshield at the motor. Durant involuntarily grasped the window handle and let the window slide down. He must have air. Claustrophobia had taken him by the throat and he had a smothering sensation.

He made himself say with simulated anger: "Sometimes I think it's about time we cleaned up the whole—world! We've been too easy. Well, I don't suppose South America will take long. They've had it very good down there all these years. No wars, no need to defend themselves. We were always here to take care of their interests, while they became rich and prosperous. Maybe when we control them they'll learn their lesson. They're bursting with nitrates and copper and food and chemicals and other natural resources. We can use them."

The two men laughed but their eyes were savage. Colburn said: "I've made four trips to the South American countries. While we were defending this hemisphere and blowing our natural resources away in defensive wars, South America grew fatter and more arrogant. We'll teach them a lesson. Some of my friends don't agree with me, but I'm convinced that all of the South American republics are out for imperialistic control of this hemisphere. They think we're weakened and now is the time to strike. I don't believe their hydrogen bombs are as good as ours. They've hardly perfected the atom bomb. We'll have their cities in ruins in two months!"

He went on, then, to explain the work of his Bureau to Durant, who made appropriate and interested comments. Colburn was very enthusiastic. "We've done an excellent job in this area. The people cooperate very well, and understand the gravity of these constant emergencies. Their conscript wages aren't too large, but they'll be willing to sacrifice in the way of new taxes. Besides, they've been promised a thousand extra calories a day in the factory cafeterias. They're pleased, too, with the increased rations for their children in the school meals. I think you won't find a more cooperative mass of people than you'll find in Philadelphia, Major."

The car rolled out into the brighter sun of the countryside. Colburn did something to a dial on the dashboard, and the motor suddenly spluttered, caught, spluttered again, then stopped. Colburn swore. "I thought the carburetor had been attended to," he said. "Know anything about motors, Major?"

"No," said Durant. Colburn sighed. "I know very little myself. I wish, now, that we'd kept Joe. Well, there's nothing to do but to get out and see what's wrong."

They stepped out into the warm spring sunshine. The roads were empty, staring white at the sky. Colburn, muttering profanely, lifted the hood of the car. Durant stood beside him. Colburn pointed to a mass of wires and parts, and Durant bent down to peer. There, almost completely hidden under the motor block, was a small black box. Couburn said cheerfully, making a pretense of adjustment: "There, I think it's all right now. Probably some dirt in the gas. Would you mind turning on the ignition for me, Major? I'll stand here to see how it goes."

Durant got into the car, turned the ignition key, stepped on the gas pedal. The motor roared. He saw that Colburn had something small and white in his hand on which he was writing. Durant recognized the object. It was the gelatine pad used by Minute Men for communicating with their fellows. The thin sheet could then be chewed and swallowed and completely digested. Colburn shouted: "Fine! Everything's all right!" He painfully climbed back into the car and handed Durant the almost transparent little sheet of paper. He had written:

"Carlson sent you? God, I'm glad to see you, Andy! Thought I'd collapse when I heard your voice. Things must be moving fast. Time's running out."

Colburn said, watching the road: "We ought to be there in ten minutes. Nice little place, and good food. Reserved for the various bureau officers." He pushed the pad and pencil in his pocket, and Durant folded the slip of paper, chewed it carefully, and when it was liquid, swallowed it. He had noticed that the paper had a small watermark: "Best for cigarets!"

Durant reached into Colburn's pocket, and using his uninjured hand, wrote: "Carlson, yes. How many of us around here that you've recognized?"

Colburn glanced at the slip, shook his head, and quickly pointed one finger at his friend. Durant then ate the paper again. Only two, then, who knew each other.

"Look at that view," said Colburn. "Let's stop here a minute. It's my favorite spot. You can see the mountains in the distance, and some water. It's been a hard winter, and I want to enjoy every minute of this weather. Let's walk around a little."

They got out again, and strolled away, chatting inconsequentially. Durant saw that Colburn was carefully measuring the distance from the parked car. The walked off the road and reached a small high knoll of green grass and pale green poplar trees, the new leaves glittering in the sun. Not a soul was in sight, though in a distant field cattle moved about contentedly, and beyond them stood a red silo and farmhouse. The two men halted in the little grove of trees.

"Ben!" said Durant, in a low voice.

Colburn turned to him and put his hand on Durant's shoulder. "Andy," he said. They smiled at each other uncertainly. Colburn went on: "We can't stay way from that damned car more than a couple of minutes, or there'll be suspicion. So, I'll talk fast. I don't know where my family is, and I don't suppose you know where yours is, either. Andy, the worst part of it for me is not being able to practice my profession. Never will, I suppose. Let me look at your arm. They broke it, eh?"

"And your leg," said Durant hurriedly. "Damn it, do they have to cripple us?"

Colburn lifted his brows with a quizzical expression. "You forget that it all has to look genuine. Then men who 'crippled' us are authentic Picked Guards." He glanced at his watch. "Never mind. Christian? Our friends?"

"Eight killed. They talked. Christian and I were the only ones of our Ten Group who survived. I don't know where Christian is, except that he is to help force the wealthy into revolt. I have the farmers."

Colburn nodded with satisfaction. "Good. And I do in this Section what Christian is to do where he has been sent. Andy, be careful. Don't trust anyone. This will probably be the last time we can talk alone. We mustn't be seen together too often nor must we appear to be too friendly. Remember: everything you say anywhere, in your offices, your rooms, is overheard. And you must never let anyone suspect that you know you are under surveillance. If they learn you know, then you'll disappear, as old Major Burnes disappeared."

He pressed Durant's shoulder hard. "The major was a harmless old soldier, all honor and pride. He was seventy, and he had never known what had happened to this country. Until one day when he found out that his rooms were wired, and his car. He tore the whole apparatus apart, raving mad. He knew, then; the whole thing burst in on his mind. He couldn't stand it. No, he wasn't arrested, or murdered. He committed suicide, before they could get to him. You see, he and I had become friends; he trusted me. He sent me a letter just before he shot himself. What they did with his body is something I'll never know."

Colburn's voice was insistent yet flat. He dropped his hand from Durant's shoulder and stared over the peaceful countryside. He began to talk as if to himself. "There's nothing left, for any of us, but to do the work we must do. You've been told that. You must never forget it. We have no life of our own. We can have no friends. Andy, I think of the days when we worked together, in secrecy. We had hope and excitement and youth. We haven't any of them now. We can't even have a memory, not of our families or of our past lives. We will make the future, but the future isn't for us."

Durant's mouth set in stubborn silence. He looked at the worn and exhausted profile of his friend, who had removed himself from any friendship. Durant shook his head slightly. He said: "You implied to me that Zimmer knows something about you, Ben. Do you know what it is?"

"No. But he does know something. He's an FBHS man. He isn't sure, and he won't report me until he is certain. Then, I'll have to die, as the major died."

"Why you, Ben? Why not Zimmer? It's important that you live, and that he die. We're at war, Ben, and we're fighting. Zimmer must die, and soon."

Colburn turned to him, and said musingly: "I've thought of that. I've thought of killing him, myself. But I suppose I'd be immediately suspected." His hands became fists, and he spoke faster. "He's a murderer, a thief, a spy, an extortioner. I happen to know of a few wretches he's been blackmailing and torturing, under threat of some trumped-up exposure. But who will kill him?"

Durant glanced down at his broken arm, grimly. "I could do it myself, but for this. I was well trained in commando action. A gun's out of the question." He smiled. "But I'm an expert knife-thrower. I think I put him off the track. Imply to him, tomorrow, that you're thinking of not issuing those directives conscripting the domestics of the MASTS and the bureaucrats. Be sincere; consult him. Listen to him. Pretend to be persuaded by his arguments, unwillingly. Don't do anything at all—until he is dead."

Colburn regarded him gravely and sadly. "I am a physician, and I've never killed yet, nor authorized anyone to kill. But this is what they have driven me to do. Andy, you can't throw a knife with that arm. You'd—"

"Leave it to me," said Durant. "There are ways. Accidents, for instance. Don't think of it again. I'll find a way."

Colburn leaned against the trunk of a tree. "I'm tired," he whispered. "I'm awfully damned tired. You'll be tired, too, before it's over." Then he straightened up, and pushed Durant affectionately. "Don't let me discourage you. It's wonderful to see you; I couldn't help letting down when I saw you again. From this time on we're merely new acquaintances. So it's really good-bye, Andy, for the sake of our work and our lives. And now, let's go back to the car."

Durant looked at him with consternation. "You're sending me back to my isolation? Just when we've found each other?"

"Yes. That's how it has to be. But we'll be in constant communication, officially, of course, and always on guard. Don't forget: never trust anyone."

He walked on a few steps, but Durant hung behind, studying the ground somberly. With some anxiety, Colburn beckoned to him, then returned, and Durant said, with a bitterness that seemed to pour uncontrollably from him: "I don't know! It's getting worse. I start to think— What if we can't trust ourselves, either? What, when we overthrow this military dictatorship Will we step right into their shoes? I tell you, Ben, I'm afraid. Oh, I know we'll take over for a 'little' period of adjustment, and then we'll delegate all authority back to the civilian authority! That's what we say. Now."

Colburn nodded thoughtfully. "I've been thinking of that, too. In more senses than one, man can't trust himself or his neighbor Modern civilization, as long as sixty or seventy years ago, having rid itself of theology, thereby lost all sense of obligation to anything or anyone. There is the root of our confusion. We have enlisted the best of the clergy, we Minute Men, because we know that materialistic confusion must give way to a supernatural order by which men can establish their own physical and temporal codes. We are striving for a point of reference, and the only one which can ever be pertinent to man is the Divine point of reference. Only then will affirmations have any verity."

Durant frowned. Colburn continued: "There'll be some among us who will be fascinated by sudden power, and will want to perpetuate it for themselves. We've got to believe that there are more of us who will always remember why we fought."

Durant burst out: "I've about come to the point of believing this foul world isn't worth saving, anyway!"

Colburn smiled. "Yes, it is, Andy."

"For my children?" Durant spat.

"No, for myself. The only reality you'll ever know is your own, and what you make of it. What duty you owe to any man you owe to yourself, and your own salvation."

Colburn sighed. "I get discouraged, too. Andy, isn't it strange how even such an absolute thing as totalitariansim takes on the worst characteristics of its particular people? Russian totalitarianism was a medieval one, suggestive of black dungeons, moats, drawbridges, dark towers and secret passages; German totalitarianism was the utmost in a modern, glittering nightmare, all efficiency and heart of chromium. British totalitarianism, though military like all of the other enormities, had a drab Cockney flavor, a fish-and-chips-and-tea dreariness, a colorless monotony. And ours—ours took on the raw confusion, the noisy superficiality, the blind expediency and kindergarten ruthlessness, which have distinguished our national character in the twentieth century. They all had only one central uniformity: hatred, and the will-to-power which hatred breeds."

Durant said: "It's an old aphorism, but without hatred there would be no armies, and without armies there would be no generals, and without generals there would be no military dictatorships. It all comes back to the people, themselves. We've had only about two Presidents in this century who preferred peace to war, and how the rainbow generals flayed them! And how the people enjoyed the spectacle! Bread and circuses. The old formula."

They got into the car, and Colburn said cheerfully: "Well, that's where I'd like to build a house! Restful, away from the city."

"I don't know why you don't just move in on the country folk, as the Army is doing now, according to my directive," said Durant. Colburn uttered an exclamation of genuine astonishment, and then he laughed aloud. Durant laughed, also. "Nothing too good for the Army, Mr. Woolcott! Nothing too good for the Government people, either. Why not move in on them, too?"

"There won't be room enough when you get all your men quartered," said Colburn, with delight. "But if there is, let me know. It'll be a great pleasure to follow your example. Why shouldn't we bureaucrats enjoy good food and fresh air as well as the farmers? Besides, the countrymen have become too arrogant. They forget who rules this country."

Durant, enjoying himself, thought that he could hear many ears prick up with interest somewhere back in Philadelphia. For the benefit of these ears, he said: "Let's think about it, for you Government men, as well as for the Army."

Upon his return to the city, Durant visited his doctor and dentist. They were fawning and servile individuals, and, looking at them with contempt, Durant remembered what his father and older friends had once told him of the ancient and honorable profession of medicine. There had been a time when physicians had been men of independence, pride and stature. They had reached this present level of degradation not so much by pressure of governmental totalitarian agencies as by their own lack of self-respect and courage, their own unwillingness to fight for the liberty of their profession. True, there had been hundreds of incompetents among them, twenty or thirty years ago, who could not make a living in free competition, and who had been eager to surrender their freedom for a nationalized salary. But these had been a minority. It was the cynicism, the absence of character and resolution among the majority of the profession which had reduced it to a slave service.

"Long before the enemy beats on the door of your house, you have opened the farther gates to him," one of Durant's teachers had told him.

The dentist misinterpreted Durant's visible contempt for him as a man for the military officer's contempt for him as a mere civilian. He prattled nervously of his son's elevation to the rank of second lieutenant in the Army, trying to ingratiate himself with this scowling terror in uniform. Durant merely grunted. The bridge which replaced his lost teeth was excellent. He wanted to express some gratitude, but held it back. He pounded noisily out of the dentist's office, in glowering arrogance. The doctor was a younger man, and there was an expression of sensitivity and weariness on his face. Durant had noticed this before, with interest. So, he rallied, harassed and annoyed the doctor as much as possible, sneering at his profession, baiting him as a civilan and therefore of no particular importance. He was gratified to see, that, in spite of the doctor's silence and attitude of quiescence, there was a sudden gleam of hatred in the other man's eye.

Durant found himself too weary to go to work. He suggested that though it was only half-past three he and his officers return to Lincoln's farm. Then he detected disappointment on the faces of all of them, and upon questioning, the older officers confessed that they had all been invited to a party to be given that evening by a very wealthy industrialist. Durant, against his better judgment, then suggested that they remain in the city and recruit some ordinary soldier to drive him back to the farm, they to retain one of the military automobiles for their own use later in the evening.

He then turned to Lieutenant Grandon, and said: "Will you call Lincoln and tell him I'd like Gracie's company tonight?"

Grandon said, in a dull monotone, looking away from Durant: "I've already telephoned him." He did not let Durant see his face or his eyes.

"Good," said Durant cheerfully. The other officers beamed their thanks at him. Not a "heavy" military bastard after all, they thought; not a "rank-puller." Maybe, though, he just wanted to be alone with Grace Lincoln. At any rate, they were happy, and wished him well with the girl.

The faceless young soldier recruited for Durant's service fastened his motorcycle to the back of the military car, and began to drive out of the city. His mind was as characterless as his features, and Durant, lying back in the automobile, mused again on the devastating effects uniforms and regimentation had on the human spirit. His own Army service had been enough; as a powerful commanding officer today, as a force in the military dictatorship of The Democracy, the horror of militarism was even more evident to him.

As the car rolled carefully through the broken streets, Durant became aware of a strange excitement among the people and the soldiers on the sidewalks. They were holding newspapers with large black headlines, and for the first time in many years Durant saw delight and laughter on the congregated faces. Something had broken up mobs of civilians and soldiers into mirthful groups, freely exchanging comments with an unfamiliar abandon and pleasure and much hoarse mirth. Soldiers, who always stood apart from civilians, now mingled with them, shouting and swearing and grinning, and slapping their legs. Durant ordered the car stopped, and a paper brought to him. He already had some suspicion. When the car moved on again, his suspicions were confirmed. The headlines shouted: "Major Andrew Curtiss quarters Military on Farms in Section 7 Area! Issues Directive to Replace Gold with Ordinary Currency in Grange Banks!"

The paper then went on to say, with laudatory side comments, that Major Curtiss was an "expert" on agricultural matters and had been angered by the "misery of the people who were being exploited by the farmers in violation of the spirit of the law as laid down by the Military." There were exultant accounts of the "fury" of the farmers and their leaders, and there were implications that "some spokesmen for the farmers" were expressing defiance and uttering threats. "If this is so," said an editorial, "it is about time that the people of The Democracy, not only in Section 7 but in all other Sections, study the whole agricultural picture thoroughly, and come to a decision whether any group—and we mean 'any group' with all overtones—should be privileged to enjoy benefits at the expense of a patriotic public. The Military has lived austerely, as the people have lived, in spite of the fact that the Military is our Government and has unlimited power, especially in periods of national emergency. Only the farmers have ruthlessly assigned to themselves privileges above and beyond what either the Military or the people have assigned to themselves. Major Curtiss' bold and justifiable action in quartering the Military upon the farmers reveals the deep concern of the Government for all the people. That the farmers and their leaders are alleged to be expressing sentiments of defiance and anger should convince even the most conservative and tolerant that the agricultural sections are hotbeds of treason and subversion, as well as arrogance and greed. Major Curtiss, our new and youthful ruler, is to be congratulated on his action."

Durant, with immense satisfaction, looked through the car windows and smiled. Tonight three hundred officers and men would sleep well and soft in the farmhouses of this area, and scores of farmers would be desperately muttering together in their haylofts and in their fields under the darkness of night. But what of the other Sections? What would Washington have to say about all this? Durant tried to remember the Chief Magistrate's reassuring promises, but he began to wonder, somewhat uneasily. However, there was one consolation: the joy and delight of the Military in Section 7 would impress the men in Washington. Any attempt to reverse Durant's decision would enrage the Military in other Sections, would convince the Military that the civilian authority was treacherously and slyly attempting to supplant them, and there would be fresh outrages and oppressions instigated against the people in general. Durant lost his uneasiness, and was much cheered.

Within a week, he said confidently to himself, the Military everywhere would be quartered on the farmers, wherever it was possible. Millions of fat and wealthy and privileged farmers muttering together in haylofts and at night, all over the country! Rich, well fed and heretofore privileged as third in importance in The Democracy, they would not accept their debasement and spoliation with the meekness and humility they so heartily approved of for the cities. Would they dare to strike? If so, dozens of them would be openly shot. But this would not subjugate men heavy with beef and money and power. It would only incite them further.

On a back page of the newspaper he found news of the directive he had given to Captain Steffens. It was reported with enthusiasm, if inconspicuously. That was bad, commented Durant to himself. However, within a few weeks the tortured parents of the children in Section 7 ought to feel that the end must come, and by their own efforts. There was no news about the closing of the special schools for privileged children. That would be a matter to keep discreetly quiet, and Dr. Healy was a man of discretion. There would be no occasion offered to the people in general for rejoicing over the humiliation and oppression of wealthy bureaucrats and the MASTS. The fires of rage would burn, but it would be behind expensive draperies and heavy doors. However, the intensity of the fire would not be the less because it mounted in secret, nor the explosion less violent when it burst through plate-glass windows.

Then Durant had an alarming thought: his new directive pertaining to the farmers would make the Military popular in the cities. There was but one thing to do, and that was to reduce the rations of all city workers, with the exception of the bureaucrats and other privileged groups, increase the hours of work, and pass a new Section 7 tax on the meager conscript wages of the people in general. He must give harsher orders to the Military under his command with regard to the populace. He began to formulate these orders. All in the name of the new "war effort," The Democracy, and "Unity! Duty! Sacrifice!" Perhaps, in spite of all the evidence of the decades, the tormented masses might finally be goaded into action of some sort.

Lincoln's slave workers were still in the warm fields when Durant arrived at the farm. He passed one group, which was being bullied and cursed by Lincoln's older son. Young Lincoln looked at him in surly silence, but Durant glared at him with cold fury and the other man touched his forehead hastily and went about his work. The car rolled into a garage, and Durant pocketed the keys and dismissed his driver, who returned to Philadelphia on his motorcycle. Then Durant clattered noisily into the cool and pleasant shadows of the house. No one was about, so Durant shouted angrily. In a few moments Dr. Dodge appeared, his glazed eyes as motionless as the eyes of the dead. He stood in the doorway of the living room, and waited.

"I want to see Lincoln, at once, and I want some ice and some whisky," said Durant. "In my room."

He went up the stairway, threw off his hat and sat down in a comfortable chair. His arm was throbbing, and his head was aching, and his weariness was like a tremendous pain all over his body. "You'll be tired, too, before this is over," Colburn had told him. He was already tired. The ugliness and cruelty and viciousness he had encountered were too much for his soul. The sweet wind blowing the curtains of the windows could not assuage his desperate exhaustion; he looked with apathy at the golden willow and the blue sky beyond it.

The door opened and Lincoln, himself, brought in a silver pitcher of ice and a bottle of whisky. The farmer's face was livid and his eyes sunken. He put down the pitcher and bottle on a table near Durant, then burst out in a trembling voice: "Major! You don't mean that about Gracie, do you? Gordon called—Why, Major, I don't believe it! You ain't that sort of man, are you, Major? My little girl. Why, she's had everything, been taken care of, by her Ma and me—"

Durant studied him with hard coldness. "Is your daughter better than the daughters of other men in this country? What makes her so special, Lincoln? Is all the sacrifice to be done by the people in the cities, and not by the farmers? What kind of deviation is this, Linocln?"

The farmer stood before him, broken and pleading, his hands extended. "But, Major, we been patriotic people; we done everything for the country." He relapsed into his old, semi-literate speech. "We sacrificed—"

Durant did not have to pretend fury. He jumped to his feet. "What did you farmers sacrifice for The Democracy, at any time?" he yelled. "You were always tax-exempt; you always had your barns and storehouses loaded with food. You've had your cars, your comfort, your sons, your daughters, your fat and well-dressed wives! Many of you lied about your neighbors and were permitted to confiscate their farms. Your banks are piled high with gold. When the cities starved, you ate well; when the cities went ragged, you wore the best and warmest of clothes. While city dwellers fell into ruins, your houses became more luxurious, and you filled your rooms with the belongings of others. You kept your cattle from the stockyards, until you had your exorbitant prices; you threw away millions of gallons of milk, while babies died in the cities. You burned grain when the Government suggested you reduce your price: you killed off your chickens because you could not get their weight in gold. You fed your vegetables and your corn to your stock, while the people of the cities picked in the gutters. You kept your sons safely at home, while the sons of better men died in the wars. What did you sacrifice, Lincoln, to anybody, to anything?"

Lincoln opened his dry mouth, made an impotent effort to speak, then merely stood, his jaw slack, his body quaking.

"The Government should have collectivized you long ago," continued Durant, in wrath, "just as it collectivized labor. But you held a gun to the heads of politicians, and they did what you asked them to do. That day is past, Lincoln. We, the Military have issued new directives."

Lincoln stammered hoarsely: "I don't care what else you do, Major, but my little girl—"

"I want her up here at ten o'clock tonight," said Durant, with a brutal gesture of dismissal. "Now, get out, Lincoln, or I'll kick you out. Or perhaps you'd prefer a bullet from this gun?"

The man literally fell from the room, grasping the side of the open door to keep himself from falling headlong. Durant slammed the door hard behind him, then dropped into his chair again. He was panting with his loathing and hatred. He tried to put some ice into a glass and to pour some whisky. But his hand shook with weakness. He cursed, twisted himself into a better position. But his fingers felt paralyzed. It was then that he saw that Dr. Dodge had mysteriously appeared.

The old man took the bottle and the ice from Durant and expertly mixed him a drink. Durant was frightened and newly enraged. "Were you listening, you old fool?" he demanded. Dr. Dodge gave him the glass, silently, and Durant took it, watching the other man speculatively. What did it matter? The blind eyes were fixed on a point behind Durant, and Dr. Dodge gave the appearance of a dead man inexplicably moving and standing upright, never speaking.

Durant began to talk in a low voice: "Look at you, Dodge! You had time, years ago. But you, and others like you, prattled of 'liberalism' and 'orderly social revolution.' You watched the ruin come; you saw the fall of the Republic. You helped the Republic to fall, didn't you? Then you were alarmed. But it was too late. Are you happy that you betrayed America, Dodge? Do you like what you see these days, all the things you helped to bring about?"

The blind eyes still stared emptily at the window, the delicate worn hands dangled at the sides of the emaciated shanks. He was beyond all comprehension.

"All the fine colleges!" said Durant, dropping his voice still more. "All the shining schoolrooms, where you and your kind taught at your desks! There you sat, and cynically spouted your deadly materialism, and smirked over the 'new progress' and the 'new era which is emerging from the old capitalism, the era of social significance and consciousness.' You uttered the name of God with ridicule, and as if it were an obscenity. Nothing was sacred to you, was it? Neither honor, nor honorable work, nor justice, nor self-discipline, nor self-control, nor religion, nor virtue, nor manliness, nor self-respect, nor courage, nor dignity. You sent out your intellectualized young men and young women, poisoned and depraved, instruments of destruction. Now they are slaves, and you are a slave, also. At the last, you tried to expiate your sins against humanity by a single act of protest. But it was too late. Too late, Dodge."

Dr. Dodge did not move. He was apparently deaf as well as blind.

"How you laughed at the Constitution, Dodge!" Durant whispered fiercely, leaning toward him. "How some of you admired Soviet Russia and Socialism! Well, do you like this now? Do you like totalitarianism, this system which you praised so highly?"

Then Dr. Dodge moved like an automaton, and Durant watched him. The doctor lifted a picture on the wall, and, to his horror, Durant saw a small black object attached behind it. Wires dangled, loosely, from the object. With swift movements of his hands, Dr. Dodge attached the wires, showing Durant mutely how it was done.

Durant gasped. Dr. Dodge turned to him and put his finger to his lips. So, the old man had deliberately detached the dictaphone before his, Durant's, entrance! What subtlety remained in that broken man that the mind could guess that there would be times when Durant would not be able to control himself? Durant began to sweat.

I'm no man for this, he thought, with self-hatred. But Dr. Dodge was putting the glass of whiskey in his hand. Durant shouted: "Didn't I tell you half an hour ago to bring that whisky? Here I've been sitting and waiting, while you took your time about it, Dodge. If this happens again—"

Dr. Dodge looked at him, and the scarred face smiled and the eyes came to life.

"No respect for the Military!" Durant continued to shout. "We've been too lenient. Well, I can tell you now that things are going to be different, with the new war effort and the necessity for sacrifice and obedience. Get the hell out of here, you damned old fool!"

His hand reached for some paper on the table, and a pencil. Awkwardly, he wrote: "How long has it been there? Who put it there?"

Dr. Dodge held the paper far from him and read with an amazing swiftness. He bent his grayed head and wrote in answer: "At least two years. The FBHS. This was Lincoln's bedroom." His handwriting was sharp if unsteady.

Durant let out his tense breath slowly, and nodded. He wrote: "Why did you do it? What do you know about me?"

The old man smiled, shook his head at the pencil which Durant offered him. Then he crept from the room. He closed the door loudly behind him. Durant drank noisily, but his alarm returned. "Trust no one," Colburn had told him. How had he betrayed himself to Dr. Dodge? The latter had known from the very beginning. As an actor, I do very well, thought Durant with bitter irony.

This was worse than he had expected. As a Minute Man, among known friends and known foes, there had been some exultation and excitement, as well as danger. Now there was danger alone, and of the ugliest and darkest kind. He got to his feet and walked furiously up and down, pausing now and then to look grimly at the innocent landscape on the wall behind which lurked the obscenest of enemies. He remembered what his father had told him when he had been a child! It is not work that kills a man, but the travail of his soul.

There was no travail like that of working in the night, and alone.

In his exhaustion, he must have fallen asleep, for he next remembered the sudden blaze of lights in his eyes. He started up in his chair, cramped and aching, to see Mrs. Lincoln, her face streaming with tears, carrying a large silver tray of food. Her outlines appeared to have melted in the heat of terror and grief; her fat features and big, gross body had blurred.

She set the tray on the table at Durant's elbow, and stood before him, wringing her hands and regarding him imploringly. She burst out hysterically in a high, shrill voice: "Oh, Major Curtiss! I can't believe you want to hurt our Gracie! Major, she is such a nice, innocent girl. Her Daddy and I are willing for her to marry you, Major. We—we've got lots of money. We'd give you anything! We'd like a major in the family—"

She began to pant, hoarsely, and came closer to him. He made a gesture of repulsion, which was completely involuntary, and she stepped back.

"Marry Gracie!" he exclaimed. "Are you out of your mind!" He regarded her with detestation. Then he said abruptly: "Get out of here."

She retreated in panic to the door, then turned with a new freshet of tears, and said hopefully: "You won't want Gracie—I mean, Major, you won't bother about Gracie? We'll do anything, Major, anything, or give you anything!"

He sat, his uninjured hand clenched over his knee, and she saw his hatred and malignance. He spoke slowly and clearly: "I want the girl up here at ten o'clock." He added, with fresh detestation: "You'll give me 'anything'? What have you? Except what you have stolen and expropriated from others? Will you give me the lives of children who have died because you withheld food from them?"

She cried out, utterly reckless in her maternal terror: "We didn't do nothing, Major, except what the Government let us do, or said we could do!"

Durant paused; he flashed a glance at the landscape on the wall. He said, loudly: "Are you accusing us of giving you permission to starve the people, Mrs. Lincoln? Are you saying that the Military plotted with you to deprive the people of food?"

"No! No, Major!" She wrung her hands again, with renewed fear. "We always worked with the Government! Our record's clear—"

"Yes you farmers dare to say that the Government connived with you to deprive the people of food," Durant interrupted. He made a disgusted sound. "I shall make a report on this, Mrs. Lincoln, a full report of your accusations. My superiors must understand what the farmers believe, once and for all. This is dangerous. If the people should begin to imagine that the Government is plotting with the farmers against the rest of the population, then we might even be faced with a revolution!"

He stood up. "Get out!"

Completely routed, Mrs. Lincoln gave a smothered scream, and ran from the room. Durant fell back in his chair, and began to curse furiously and loudly, expressing his opinion of the farmers of The Democracy and their outrages against the Military. He shouted his opinion that the Military had endured enough insults from civilians, especially from the countrymen. He then, with obscene oaths, expressed his sentiments toward civilians in general, including the bureaucrats. He threatened and raved. The Military had been too soft; he must communicate with Washington immediately, and he must call the Chief Magistrate as soon as possible. He dredged up from his memory all the vile words he had learned in the Army, and delivered them with oratorical flourishes. He stamped up and down the room, pausing to give his best volleys almost directly in front of the landscape.

He sat down again, quite exhilarated by his dramaturgy, laughing silently to himself. He could imagine the anxious flurry among those of the FBHS who were doubtlessly listening intently. He hoped he had singed their ears and had inspired fright among them. He was confident that he had. Then he had a qualm. What if the FBHS attempted to murder this rambunctious and obstreperous military brute? Then the qualm subsided. He had threatened like one given all authority, and he doubted if a single hand would dare to raise itself against him, in spite of panic. He had routed Zimmer and the others too well, today.

The meal Mrs. Lincoln had brought him was very appetizing, and he ate with sudden and overwhelming hunger. He smoked one or two cigarets, then realized, with dismay, that he had nothing to read. This was a catastrophe to him. He forgot everything else as he prowled through all the rooms on the second floor looking for books or magazines. He found some publications in Captain Edwards' room, all lewd and lascivious, but not a single book of any merit. But I ought to have known, he thought, remembering how all literature of value or seriousness had been suppressed for the past decade by the Government. The people were encouraged to read only propaganda or novels extolling militarism, "patriotism, devotion to the public welfare, the history of democratic wars, sacrifice of personal interests, and the moral disease of private enterprise and capitalism." Literature of a free and valuable and thoughtful kind had been one of the first victims of military totalitarianism, for the latter could not exist in an inquiring society.

Becoming almost frantic at the thought of having no reading matter, Durant descended to the first floor. There was not a single soul about, though every room was lighted. He went from room to room, and his footsteps echoed. The infection of militarism had driven every living thing from this house; he saw his uniform in long gilt mirrors and stopped to look at it with aversion. His flesh crawled and itched. He moved up and down, opening cabinets and drawers, searching for a single book. He found garish magazines, published the supervision of the Government, and he tossed them aside. He threw himself into a chair and stared before him, disgustedly, and smoked several cigarets in quick succession.

The great clock in the hall struck nine, and Durant started, rousing himself from his brooding irritation. He went upstairs, walking as softly as possible in order not to hear the hollow sound of his own footsteps. Someone had removed his tray, he found, and this disconcerted him, for he had heard no one, and had seen no one. On the table he found a pile of old and tattered books, and, somewhat disturbed, he examined them. There had been part of ancient sets: Thoreau, Balzac, Tolstoi, Dickens. There was also an *Iliad,* and a copy of Dante's *Inferno,* and Milton's *Paradise Lost.* They had appeared out of nowhere, these ghosts of a noble past. Who had brought them? Who had known of his unspoken need? It could only be Dr. Dodge. A prickle of sweat broke out on Durant's forehead. The old man was a desperate danger. He surmised too much.

However, the books were an irresistible lure, and Durant picked up one. He examined it carefully. It had been published in 1945, twenty-five years ago, and the pages were already so brittle that little slivers of stiff yellow paper sifted through Durant's fingers. Inside the cover he found a book-plate, with faded writing: William S. Dodge. He stared at it, and all at once he was overcome with the pathos of the books, and the muteness with which they had been tendered to him. Durant stroked the book gently.

There was a faint knock on the door, and Durant, managing a frown, put down the book. He expected Dr. Dodge, but when the door opened he saw that Grace Lincoln stood there, her face as white as the breast of a chicken, her eyes flooding with tears. She shrank as he looked at her, and clasped her hands tightly together. She was terrified of him, and Durant let himself enjoy this for a moment. Then he was ashamed, and obscurely angered.

"Come in, come in," he said irritably.

She crept to a chair, and sat on the edge, looking at him in paralyzed silence. Her pretty hair was disheveled, her mouth open and drooling with her fright. Durant studied her dispassionately, she had not closed the door behind her, and he finally got up and shut it. She began to tremble then, and raised her clasped hands convulsively to her breast. She tried to speak, and could only utter a whine.

"Well, Gracie," said Durant, in a jocular tone. "Glad to see you at last. You're ahead of time, too. I like promptness."

The girl, after a struggle to speak, broke out into wild sobs, covering her face with her hands. Durant stood near her, frowning. Now, what the hell was he going to do with this wench? He felt no desire for her, and nothing at all but an impatient pity. He had forgotten her entirely during the last hour or so. He yawned elaborately, to mask his rapid thinking, while the girl continued to sob distractedly.

"I'm tired, Gracie," he said loudly. "Get undressed, and let's go to bed."

The girl crouched in her chair and her sobs became wilder. Durant stood, irresolute. He could dismiss her. But that would not save her from the other officers. Hell, he thought, why should I care? Let them have her. She was no better than millions of other defenseless girls who had been ruthlessly sacrificed to the Military. She was certainly less to be pitied than hundreds of thousands of starving young women who had prostituted themselves in The Democracy for a little extra bread, or a bit of meat. Her life had been spent in pleasant luxury and protection and warmth, while her betters had died of malnutrition, from overwork in the terrible war-factories, in the fields of their masters, the farmers, and on actual battlefields in Europe and Asia. She was a parasite; she had lived delightfully on the bodies of her sisters, and had been happy in the fact.

Besides, her despoliation would increase the frenzy and active despair and hatred of her parents, and probably of her brothers. She was a weapon to be used against oppression. Let the other boys have her! She deserved nothing better.

Durant listened to the girl's helpless weeping, and tried to harden himself against her. "Shut up!" he exclaimed. "And get your clothes off. Are you a patriotic American girl, or are you a traitor? Answer me that, you fool!"

He began to curse her. He raised his hand and slapped her cheek violently; the sound was loud in the room. Grace stopped sobbing; she screamed faintly, and cowered before him. She crossed her arms over her breasts and bowed her head to her knees. Durant glanced at the landscape; the girl had her back to it. He went to the wall swiftly, lifted aside the picture, and, with delicate care, detached the wires.

He went to Grace, and tore her hands from her shoulders. "Listen to me!" he whispered fiercely. "You've got to get out of here. Have you any money? Have you your identification papers handy? Your cards?"

She lifted her drenched white face, bewildered and astounded. "Hurry!" he went on. "Have you money, your papers? The keys to your car?"

Glazed with fear and bafflement, she could only nod. "Leave a note for your parents. Tell them you ran away from me, while I was asleep. Get into your car, and drive as far as you can, tonight, and all day tomorrow. And hide yourself, somewhere. Don't communicate with your parents at all." He paused, and said with harsh sincerity: "If you do, I'll have them shot. Do you understand?"

She pushed herself to her feet and stared at him with intense concentration. She was a danger to him, Durant thought. He said: "Remember, your parents will die if you write them, and I'll hunt you out, too. I'm giving you a chance, Gracie. You have five minutes to leave."

She whimpered: "Why, Major—"

"If you stay, you idiot, the others will get you. I don't know why I'm doing this— Get out!"

She gasped. Then, before he could stop her, she had caught his hand and was kissing it. He wrenched it away from her. Then he seized her and pushed her rapidly and roughly from the room. "Five minutes," he whispered. "If you're here after that, God help you." Her hair fell over her face; she tossed it back, and gave him a quivering smile of joy.

She ran now, and was so far recovered that she could slip off her shoes and rush down the stairway in her stocking feet. Durant went back to the hateful little black box behind the landscape and reattached the wires. "That's a good girl, Gracie," he said, making his voice hoarse. "Into bed with you, now."

He imitated Gracie's whimper, sat on the bed and bounced up

and down rapidly, so that it creaked. He began to laugh at himself, and he wondered again why he had rescued this silly, petty and worthless girl. Nevertheless, he felt no real regret. He got up cautiously, and went to his window, after first turning off the lights. The stars were bright and clear, and he could see the garages. A slender figure moved silently below; the door of one garage opened with the slightest of noises. A moment later a car rolled out silently down the incline to the road. It was not until it was some distance from the house that Grace Lincoln turned on the ignition and the headlights. Then she was gone into the darkness, and there was nothing but the soft swish of trees, the cries of tree-toads and the chirp of crickets in the night.

Durant sat and read, being careful to make as little sound as possible. The curtains flapped against the windows in the warm spring wind. The clock downstairs struck eleven, then half-past. A horse neighed at a distance, and there was a drowsy flutter of disturbed fowl. Gradually, the deep silence of the country night began to oppress Durant, as it had done the night before. He stood up, restlessly, and moved up and down on quiet feet, smoking quickly and with impatience. He stood at the window and looked at the outlines of the barracks where the slave labor slept. Was Dr. Dodge there, or asleep in his attic? Were the other wretches sleeping, or staring sightlessly at their anguished memories? As he had been drawn to them before, Durant was drawn to them now. They suffered, as he had suffered, and was still suffering.

He took off his boots, crept to the door, and opened it inch by inch, so that any vigilant listeners in Philadelphia would hear nothing. He closed the door after him, and went like a shadow down the stairway. Everything was dark. He had heard no movement, but someone had turned off the lights. This gave him an eerie and anxious sensation. He waited in the hall below, scarcely breathing, and listened. He turned on his pocket flashlight and stabbed the beam into every corner. Only the gleam of paneled walls and the folds of draperies and the glisten of polished floors started in the darkness. He snapped off the light and opened the outside door, and the sweet scents of earth and grass and trees rushed at him. It was a great effort, closing the door behind him, soundlessly.

With some difficulty, he put on his boots, fumbling with his one free hand. Then he moved across the wet grass in the direction of the barracks. They loomed blackly against the stars, the dull glass of small windows glimmering a little in the starlight. If living creatures lay behind those windows and rough wooden walls it was not the least evident. Some windows were slightly open; Durant stood before them, listening. He could hear no groans, no sighs, no murmur, no mutter of any sleeper. He glanced back at the farmhouse; only his own light fell in a sharp stream to the ground. He toured the other side of the barracks, hopelessly. Then he heard the breath of a rustle.

He stopped, "freezing" as he had been taught in the Army. The rustle of new leaves? But the wind had dropped, and everything was still. Now he heard it again, and it came from behind a partially opened window, and he recognized it as the whispering of men. Someone grunted, someone sighed, someone moved; a bedspring creaked.

Durant ran to the door, opened it quietly. Stale dank air, loaded with the smell of sweat, hit him in the face. There was only silence, and he closed the door after him and stood in utter darkness. He put out his hand and foot cautiously, feeling for any object. He raised his hand and fumbled at each side. He encountered splintering wooden walls and knew that he stood in a corridor. He moved, holding his breath, bending down in a crouch. There were doors along the corridor. Step by step he slipped along, listening at each door for that rustle of whispering. He began to despair, stopping now and then to orient himself. He reached another door, which was probably the last, and pressed his ear against it. Now he heard the whispering again, hoarse and indistinct. He dropped his hand to the doorknob, and opened the door. No one saw him in the blackness, but now the whispers were very close and the stench of sweat very strong. He stood, stiff and unmoving, knowing that he was alone with several men. He let his hand grip his gun tightly, and now his heart quickened. He listened intently.

"I tell you, it won't be long, Henry," someone muttered. "You must believe that. No, I can't tell you what I know, but it has to be soon."

"You expect us to believe that there can be any deliverance?" whispered another man, in despair. "You tell us these vague things, and believe they'll be of some comfort to us. But we can't wait much longer. We'll break away, somehow, or—"

"Or, we'll kill, and take the consequences," said still another voice.

There was silence, now, very profound, broken only by one miserable sigh.

Then another voice spoke, gently: "Kill. Yes, it will come to that, I suppose. But not yet. There are things I know. You must be very patient, very patient. The hour is coming; I have reason to believe it is almost here."

"You're old, Dr. Dodge," said a voice, bitterly. "And you're resigned. You try to cheer us up, but it's no use. What do you know?"

Durant breathed as shallowly as possible. Dr. Dodge. His hand fell from the gun.

Dr. Dodge spoke again. "I can't tell you, Henry. I can only assure you I'm not speaking only in an effort to give you hope."

"Hope!" Someone laughed miserably. "What hope is there for us? The Army's here now, remember? Curtiss and his other murderers. I'm forty, Doctor. My family is scattered, perhaps dead. I can think of nothing for myself, not even freedom; I can only think of killing. And the word's around now that Zimmer's going to impose new restrictions on all farm labor. What more can we do, except hang chains on us?"

"Zimmer!" someone said, with a smothered exclamation.

"Zimmer!" said other voices, with hate and loathing.

Zimmer! thought Durant. Now there was a throbbing of excitement in his throat.

"If there was some way to get to the city!" whispered a voice.

"That's impossible," said Dr. Dodge. "Yes, I've heard the rumors about the new directives Zimmer is formulating. They'll be more oppressive than ever. He hates three of us in particular. You, Henry; you, George. And me. We were teachers, and Zimmer has always had a particular hatred for teachers. Do you remember how he came out here last month and laughed at us, and taunted us? He would like to kill us."

"He was my classmate," a man recalled, and Durant heard the sound of spitting. "A rat, but a cunning one. He always had it in for me. There was still a little freedom left, in colleges, and I took all the honors. He never forgave me." The man inhaled viciously. "When the time comes to kill Zimmer—if it ever comes, God help us!—I want to do it!"

Someone laughed faintly. "How? How will you get to the city, George?"

There was a noise as if a fist struck a knee. "I don't know! But I'll find a way."

Andreas Zimmer, thought Durant. The enemy of Ben Colburn, the dirty-nailed, scheming spy for the FBHS, the crawling slime of mercilessness which called itself a man!

Durant fumbled in his pocket and brought out his flashlight. He suddenly turned on the narrow beam. He saw before him a group of five men sitting on the edge of rumpled cots. He had blinded them with his light, and they sat there, petrified, every gaunt brown face fixed in the sudden brilliance, every eye blazing, every mouth open in stupefaction.

He let them sit transfixed in the light for a moment or two. He saw Dr. Dodge standing beside a cot, white as death. And then he saw Dr. Dodge smile curiously.

"Don't move, you dogs," said Durant grimly. "So, you want to kill do you? You want to murder a member of our Government. You sit here and plot, in your slavery, plot, when it's too late. Too late, do you hear me? You might have been men, instead of sweating animals, if you had plotted years ago. But no, you buried your sniveling noses in your books, poured dust on your heads in your mildewed libraries. You were afraid to see, you refused to to see. And now, in your own death, you talk of killing!"

One of the younger men, his face stark and murderous, began to rise slowly from his cot, his hands clenched. But Dr. Dodge put his hand on his shoulder and gently pressed him down. He looked at Durant steadfastly, and his curious smile deepened.

Durant pushed the flashlight in his swollen right hand, and took out his gun with the other. "Don't move," he repeated. He grinned at them. "Brave men! Noble men! Scholars and teachers! Men of mind! Well, you've come to this, and you did it to yourselves. You turned the musty pages in your musty books, and whimpered that it wasn't true. You watched a whole nation die, and you withdrew deeper into your learned stalls and pretended that it was only a nightmare. You might have saved your students, years ago; you might have scoffed a little less, and prayed a little more. But no, you never knew anything about prayer, did you? Look at you! If there are chains on you, you put them on your own hands, on your own legs. What are you now, you teachers? Beasts of burden in the fields, without family or friends or hope or life!"

No man moved. But no face showed rage or despair. Every eye was turned on Durant, and every man listened intently, gravely. Dr. Dodge watched the officer with profound reflectiveness, and his eyes sparkled in the beam of the flashlight.

"Look at this uniform," said Durant. "You helped put this on me, didn't you? You put this gun in my hand. By your silence, by your weak acquiescence, by your docile belief that I was only a violent and passing phenomenon! After all, you said to yourselves, mind is greater and more powerful than force. The mind always conquers, you said. Even when death, and repeated death, and death ten thousand times over, walked in the streets and marched in the streets and drummed in the streets, you refused to believe it. After all, there had been a Dark Age before, you told yourselves. Did you ever remember that Dark Ages last for centuries, and nations perish in them?"

The circle of faces became even graver. One man swiftly raised his hand and touched his eyes; then he turned aside his head. But this was the only gesture from any of them.

"Yes," said Durant, bitterly, "mind is very strong. Especially evil minds. You gave them their power, for you betrayed your young men and your young women and made them powerless before wickedness. They had no arms, no armor, for you had stripped these from the young with your skeptical laughter, your learned jokes, your intellectual sneers. There was nothing worth fighting for, living for, dying for, you taught. There was no virtue in the world, no banners to respect, no God to worship and obey, no trumpets of honor and nobility. The deepest instinct of a man's soul was only superstition, an inheritance from the childhood of man. That is what you taught. And that is why you were condemned to death."

His face was on fire; he looked at them with abhorrence. He moved backward toward the door, and they followed him with their eyes. Then Dr. Dodge held out his hand.

"Your car keys," he said softly.

Durant stopped abruptly, held by those calm and smiling eyes. Then Dr. Dodge fumbled inside his ragged shirt and brought out a broad-bladed knife which flashed its own light. He threw the knife beside the man he had called George, and the man seized it. "Your keys, please," said Dr. Dodge again, still holding out his hand.

Durant began to smile. He said: "Zimmer?"

The other men rose slowly, and looked at him. Then he reached in his pocket and brought out his keys. He tossed them on a cot. George closed his hand over them. Durant regarded them keenly. Then, with irony, he lifted his hand and saluted. He turned off his flashlight and walked out into the dark of the corridor. There was no sound at all in the barracks, not a movement, not a whisper.

He crept back to the house, and up the stairway to his room. He extinguished the lights, then moved to the window, watching the garage. He waited a long time, trembling. He began to have desperate doubts. He saw the shadow of trees against the stars. Coldness ran over his body. What if the car were detected in the city? What if one of the men, tortured beyond endurance, betrayed him? A thousand things could go wrong. The streets were always patrolled by soldiers. Would these wretches be cautious enough, strong enough? They had shown no manliness before, no courage, no strength or power. They had talked of killing, but scholars invariably talked and rarely acted.

Two shadows appeared at the door of the garage, and Durant saw the door lift. He waited, and his shirt was wet on his flesh. He saw his car backing out, as Grace Lincoln's car backed; the vehicle rolled silently on its velvet wheels. Someone was assisting it on the downgrade. Now it was in the driveway, rolling faster. Durant heard the engine catch, but no lights went on. The car was swallowed up in the darkness.

He began to pray incoherently. If the men were caught, what would happen to him? To his friends? How would they seek out Zimmer? How would they gain access to him? What if they were only running away, in his Army vehicle, to be apprehended within a few hours when daylight came? He cursed himself silently for his rashness. His legs became weak, and he sat down on the floor near the window and closed his eyes. His head roared with confused noises. Then, involuntarily, it dropped on his chest and he plunged into exhausted sleep.

When he awoke, it was to find the sun striking on his face, and all the birds were singing. And on the floor beside him were the keys to his car.

It was difficult for Durant to get to his feet. His broken arm had stiffened during the night, and his body ached with weariness. He held the keys of his car in his hand, bouncing them a little so that they jingled. Was Zimmer dead? Was another enemy of the American people silent and impotent now? With the logical part of his mind he hoped so, fervently; with another side, he felt a bitter sadness. A foe extinguished was one foe the less. But a man, soldier though he may be, could never forget that he had caused the death of another man.

There were Zimmers born in every generation, he reflected, with angry depression. Wise, true and honorable men refrained from creating an environment wherein the Zimmers could become oppressive and powerful. But for decades America had not been wise, true and honorable. Her governments had been composed of creatures who had striven for the extinction of individual personality, in order to perpetuate their own mighty positions. They had replaced the Republic with the law of mass-rule, which had led, inevitably, to mass-barbarism, and this, in turn, had led to mass-deterioration, crowd-slavery, and herd-death. And, the rise of the ever-born Zimmers.

Durant rang the bell for Dr. Dodge, and his somber thoughts beset him more and more. He tried to remember that the Minute Men never recruited their membership from among faceless men, but from the fast-diminishing ranks of intelligent individuals who had the potentialities for rescuing mankind from mass-barbarism. The Minute Men knew that the deliverance of a people from objective tyranny depended upon fearless and thoughtful individuals, only. They also knew that deliverance could be merely temporary if the people could not be awakened to a spiritual rebirth, for liberty had died in the Republic because her people had first decayed morally and ethically. Were there enough mature and reverent men even among the Minute Men to insure that the Republic would have a spiritual renaissance?

Dr. Dodge came in, silent and shuffling, his head bent, his eyes glazed and blind as usual. It was almost impossible to believe that this beaten wretch was the same man who had stood among his fellow-slaves last night with fervor and understanding blazing on his haggard face. Durant looked at him speechlessly, and displayed the keys in his hand. Dr. Dodge merely stared at them as a baby might stare. Unaccountably irritable, Durant pulled a piece of paper toward him on the table and wrote awkwardly: "All fingerprints wiped from car? Zimmer?"

Dr. Dodge peered at the writing without any change of expression. Then he smiled faintly. Very carefully, he tore up the stiff paper into small pieces and put them in his mouth. He chewed them with difficulty, and Durant smiled. Durant then said: "Where is that damn girl? I woke up this morning and found her gone?"

Dr. Dodge said in his lifeless voice: "I don't know, Major. She isn't about the house. Shall I shave you, and then bring your breakfast?"

Durant was shaved and washed by the old doctor, who assisted him into a fresh uniform, and then brought him his breakfast. This was done in silence, under the crushing chaperonage of the sinister thing behind the landscape on the wall. There were moments when Durant wanted to run and tear it from its wires and throw it upon the floor and trample it. He understood the fury of old Major Burnes. He made himself listen to the sounds of the farm, and it was with relief that he heard the snorting of the motorcycle of the young soldier who was to drive him into the city.

He went downstairs, which gave off an empty echo. Neither Lincoln nor his wife nor any other member of the family was to be seen. Durant guessed that they were having their own mean and secret triumph at his "discomfiture," no matter how fearful they felt after reading Grace's note about her impending "flight" from her frustrated "seducer." The thought that they were probably chuckling about it in corners together made Durant boil.

He was driven into the city by the healthy young robot of a soldier and deposited at his headquarters. He saw the excitement of his soldiers on the street near the hotel, and in the lobby, itself. He had also seen that the streets had been unusually full for that early in the day, and that many bright cars flashed about filled with grim-faced and well-fed men. The farmers, gathering for a conference with Morrow. Satisfaction returned to Durant, and it was with joviality that he greeted his staff in his offices. Grandon did not reply to the greetings; his young face was white and he appeared ill.

Edwards asked, with a wink: "How was Grace, Major?"

Durant frowned angrily. "I went to sleep before she arrived, and I found out this morning that she had run away." He threw his cap on his desk with violence.

"No!" exlcaimed Keiser, Bishop and Edwards. But Grandon began to smile, then looked frightened. Durant saw this, and said carelessly: "Who cares? Let her run. I'm not going to send out an alarm for the wench. She probably hasn't much money with her and will have to end up in some war factory, somewhere. That's all to the good. She won't dare to return home as long as we're there."

Grandon, as if relieved from some misery, bustled about with alacrity, placing papers on Durant's desk, explaining them. He 'it a cigaret for Durant, with a flourish. He smiled and joked incessantly, but once or twice Durant caught that knife-edge flash on his youthful face. Grandon, too, was enjoying a triumph at Durant's expense, and this Durant had to endure with patience.

"Morrow's meeting with all the farmers today at the Grange headquarters," Grandon informed him. "At eleven o'clock. They've probably communicated with Washington by now. Hope the whole damn thing doesn't blow up in your face, Major."

"It won't," said Durant, with much more confidence than he felt. "By the way, we'll attend that meeting, too, at eleven. With a squad as escort. Any visitors this morning?"

"No," said Grandon. He rubbed his chin thoughtfully. "And that, Major, is queer. Always a mob of them waiting for the commanding officer. But the waiting room's empty today. Something's going on; the whole city is seething. Better increase your bodyguard, Major." And he laughed, and the others with him, all in a mood of happy fellowship.

Durant studied a paper. "I thought Zimmer would be around," he remarked. "There was some unfinished business."

"No," said Edwards, "he isn't here."

Durant wrinkled his forehead. Was Zimmer dead, or not? Surely, if he were dead the news would be about the city by now. He directed Grandon to call Zimmer at his office. Grandon did so, then remarked: "Zimmer isn't there. Would you want to talk with Mr. Woolcott, Major?"

Durant nodded, and Grandon handed him the receiver.

"Woolcott speaking," said Ben Colburn's grave voice.

"Curtiss," replied Durant, keeping his voice as indifferent as possible. "Sorry to disturb you, Mr. Woolcott, but I thought Zimmer might be around to see me this morning. Perhaps I'm wrong, but I was under the impression that we were to discuss some unfinished business. Apparently I was wrong, for he isn't here."

There was the slightest of pauses, then Colburn said, with even more gravity: "I thought perhaps you knew, Major. Mr. Zimmer was murdered sometime during the night, by some unknown assassins. The alarm has just been sent out for them. Mrs. Zimmer," continued the concerned voice, "is in a state of collapse. It seems that about four this morning her husband was called to the telephone. Mrs. Zimmer went back to sleep, and it is believed that Mr. Zimmer admitted the murderer, or murderers, himself. At any rate, when Mrs. Zimmer woke up about two hours ago she heard her maid screaming, and she ran into the living room. She found her husband lying on the floor with his throat cut, and his face smashed to a pulp."

Durant cried out, with horror: "Impossible! Isn't there any clue at all, Mr. Woolcott?"

"Investigators are on the premises, I understand," said Colburn. "I am keeping in touch with them. It's very important to me, as you know. I've just received the last report. A woman in the same building thought she heard some scuffling in Mr. Zimmer's apartment, about half-past four. She lives in the apartment below. But she heard no body drop, and only that brief scuffling. She was curious. Women are always curious," added Colburn slowly. "She watched for anyone in the main hall, but it's evident that the murderer, or murderers, escaped by way of the fire escape in the rear."

"No other witnesses? No fingerprints? No other clues?" Durant kept the fearful anxiety out of his voice by a great effort. "Is it known if the murderers—or murderer—walked, or came in a car? Surely the military police must have seen someone at that hour. The streets are well patrolled against such contingencies. A car would have been noticed, or civilians out at that time—"

"No other witnesses," said Colburn, sorrowfully. "No fingerprints. No other clues. Every official car on the street has been accounted for, at that hour. No civilian cars. If the murderers came by car, they must have hidden it somewhere, outside the city. No one has reported any car whatsoever from the suburbs or fringes of the city, itself. The patrols have reported, just half an hour ago, that they saw nobody on the streets, except the Military."

Durant let out his breath slowly. "A neighbor?" he suggested. "Someone from the same building?"

Colburn coughed very delicately. "We have had the same idea, Major. Every neighbor in the apartment house has been interviewed. We have no reason to believe that their stories are untrue. Mrs. Zimmer is under some slight suspicion, for a neighbor or two has reported that there was a somewhat violent argument between husband and wife at about ten o'clock. Contents of argument unknown. Mrs. Zimmer is being closely questioned, but now she has collapsed." He cleared his throat again. "We have one other lead, Major. It is understood that Mr. Zimmer was on rather bad terms with the head of the FBHS. This may be only a rumor, for I doubt if Mr. Zimmer ever came into intimate contact with that bureau, or knew anyone there very well. Bureaus keep well separated, as you know, Major."

"Who is the official?" demanded Durant eagerly.

"It's very distressing," replied Colburn, with anxiety. "But Mr. Sheridan is somewhat vague about his whereabouts early this morning. He claims that he attended a small party given by three of his subordinates in a distant tavern about twenty miles from the city. We've questioned those officials. Two of them deny that Mr. Sheridan was with them at all; the other official says he was. The owner of the tavern said he was not, and that only the three other men were there."

Colburn stopped talking, and the wire between the two men hummed significantly. Durant was stunned. Alex Sheridan was infamous for his crimes as head of the local FBHS. But—and this was portentous—why did two of his own men deny that he was with them, and why did the owner of the tavern affirm their statement?

Durant almost stammered: "Did Mrs. Zimmer say if her husband mentioned who his visitor, or visitors, were to be? After all, he certainly wouldn't have admitted anyone about whom he had any doubts, at that hour."

There was a prolonged silence, then Colburn said with elaborate reluctance: "Mrs. Zimmer, before her collapse, and while she was in a state of hysteria, said that her husband had told her that Mr. Sheridan was coming to see him on a very urgent matter which could not wait until morning. She said she was very surprised at this, at the time, for she was not aware that Mr. Sheridan and her husband were on any terms at all, except somewhat bad ones, They have never had any real contact with each other. As why should they? They had no business with each other at any time."

Two birds with one stone! thought Durant exultantly. He made his voice sound very shocked. "Mr. Zimmer may have been deceived. As you say, he probably didn't know Mr. Sheridan very well, or his voice, if at all. Or, if he did—and this seems remote—someone imitated Mr. Sheridan's voice, someone who knew Mr. Sheridan very well."

"An enemy of both of them," agreed Colburn.

"What were the bad feelings you mentioned as existing between them, Mr. Woolcott?"

"It's rumored that they met casually, once or twice, in public places, such as restaurants, and had been overheard to remark to friends that they had no good opinion of each other. It seemed a matter of mutual antipathy, on slight acquaintance."

So, that was how these two evil men had contrived to keep down any suspicion on the part of anyone that they plotted together, and that Zimmer was a secret member of the FBHS.

"Is Mr. Sheridan in custody?" asked Durant.

Colburn sounded pained as he answered. "Unofficially, Major, unofficially. I'd rather say that he is being politely questioned in his own home. Ah, here is another report." A paper crackled over the wire. "Two of the subordinates are now sober, and they swear, vehemently, that Mr. Sheridan was not with them this morning. They have made official statements to that effect. And we now have the full statement of the tavern owner. Mr. Sheridan, he has sworn, was not with his men this morning; he also states that Mr. Sheridan was last in his tavern two weeks ago."

"It's very mysterious," suggested Durant.

"His throat cut. Apparently with a very sharp weapon," said Colburn. "It's been suggested by my investigators that it was an Army knife." Was that anxiety in the other man's voice? Durant smiled a little.

"I'm never where there's any excitement," he said, with irritation. "But my broken arm keeps me tied down. As a soldier, I could probably tell, approximately, how the thing was done, and with what weapon."

Colburn sighed. You idiot, thought Durant, with affection. Colburn said: "We've had an Army expert on the job. The weapon wasn't found, of course. But soldiers often lose their knives, in spite of the severe penalties. It's very possible that the enemy, or enemies, of both these men, had found a lost knife. Unless, of course, Mr. Sheridan is guilty."

"You'll keep me informed?" Durant said briskly. "The Military wants to render you any assistance whatsoever."

"I'll keep you informed of all developments, Major."

Durant turned to his assistants, who had been listening avidly. "Zimmer's been murdered, and there's some suspicion about Mr. Sheridan of the FBHS," Durant informed them unnecessarily. He gave them some details. "I hope you boys all have an alibi," he said, with a laugh. "Everybody see all of you at your party?"

They laughed with him. Grandon said: "Zimmer is—was—a swine. But it's too bad about Mr. Sheridan. Of course, he isn't guilty. What could he have had against Zimmer?" Grandon looked pleased, and the others, interested .

Bishop said: "Probably his wife after all. She's a mean bitch, from what I've heard, and Zimmer chases other women. But why should she name Sheridan? And how about his own men, two of them, saying he wasn't at their party? And the owner of the tavern, too?"

The danger wasn't over, thought Durant. He marveled at the skill and intelligence the enslaved scholars had displayed. Who, among them, had known Sheridan well enough to imitate his voice and to convince the FBHS spy that he was Sheridan, himself? Zimmer had been a wary and suspicious scoundrel, and he must have known that his life was in constant danger. He would have taken all precautions, and would never have admitted anyone to his home if he had had any doubts. Something stirred vaguely in Durant's memory. Dr. Dodge had been personally prosecuted by Sheridan in a widely publicized trial! It was Dodge, then, who had imitated the voice of the man he had known so well and so tragically. Dodge, too, must have known of the secret connection between Sheridan and Zimmer. But it had been one of Dodge's companions who had murdered Zimmer. All this had not been done on impulsive plotting, at a moment's notice. The plot had been well laid. There had been only the obstacle of getting into the city at the right hour. If any civilian had been abroad, in the suburbs or in the fringes of the suburb, he would have seen only an official car and the matter would have passed out of his mind. Durant breathed easier.

He said: "Almost eleven, boys. Call the squad. We're calling on Walter Morrow, and his farmers."

The offices of the Grange of Section 7 were housed in a magnificent modern building, all gray stone and immense glass windows and glass doors. It stood in the center of a row of high business buildings which were all decrepit and sifting, and the contrast was significant. Almost all the buildings were only a third occupied, and quite a number of their windows, having lost their panes, were boarded up. The streets around the Grange building glittered with scores of brilliant cars, lashed with precious chrome, sparkling with scarce polished steel, blazing with expanses of glass. The members of the Grange met every month, and this display of luxury was no new thing on the streets. Nevertheless, it always gathered a shabby and starveling crowd who admired in humble silence. Occasionally, a bolder man than the rest would even stretch out a timid finger and touch the gleaming fenders or run a slave's meek hand over the chromium. Most of the cars boasted chauffeurs, who would snarl behind the glass or would stare with haughty contempt at the bedazzled mob.

The Grange had met only a week ago, and there was a faint simmering of excitement in the furtive crowds on the broken sidewalks. They whispered together that something must be going on, for the cars were more numerous than usual, and unexpected.

The excitement grew greater as Durant's car, followed by a squad car, roared up to the Grange. It grew intense as Durant, getting out, became visibly infuriated at discovering that every available spot was occupied by farmer's cars. He ordered Bishop and Edwards and Keiser and Grandon to "clear a place for the Military." Fascinated and eager, in spite of their terror of the Army, the mobs huddled together, one collective ear and eye. The officers, delighting in their work, told several chauffeurs to "get their damned dragonflies away from the entrance." The chauffeurs, bewildered and astounded, drove their cars off in silence, with long backward stares at the officers. Then the Army cars swung into position.

Durant studied the crowd carefully out of the corner of his eye. A few men and women were smiling secretly, and with intelligent pleasure. Durant, apparently unaware of the people, shouted: "Who do the bastard farmers think they are, anyway? Do they think they run this country, besides starving it to death? We'll show the fat-bellies with their cars who had the upper hand around here!"

Even the dullest in the mob was pleased and intent. The intelligent faces became thoughtful.

Durant, followed by his officers and his tramping squad, pounded into the building. The first floor was one huge square of blocks of shining marble, black and white. Along the walls stood comfortable red and green leather chairs and sofas, and broad oak tables holding severe lamps of copper and leather and big crystal ashtrays. At the other end of the square was a row of bronze elevator doors, highly polished. Durant looked about him. "They do themselves well, don't they?" he remarked. "This is going to give me more good solid satisfaction than I'd anticipated."

The elevator men, in dark-green uniforms, regarded the invasion of the Army with vacant curiosity. One of them informed Durant, with apologetic hesitation, that the Grange was now in session, on the third floor, with Mr. Morrow, and it was doubtful of "Mr. Morrow could see anyone right way, sir."

"Mr. Morrow," said Durant, entering the elevator, "will see me at once. With the Grange."

Two of the elevators carried officers and men to the third floor, where they trooped out into a wide corridor paved with marble. They found themselves faced with a wide door on which gold letters announced that this was the meeting hall of the Grange. Grandon, smiling happily, threw open the door at a gesture from Durant, and Durant stood on the threshold, looking about him.

He saw a vast and well-decorated hall alight with broad sheets of glass. The hall, with its green leather chairs studded with brass nails, could seat over two hundred. All seats were occupied by ruddy-faced farmers in fine tweeds and polished boots, smoking excellent cigars and pipes. The smoke floated in blue streamers over their heads and flowed through half-opened windows. On a platform sat Morrow before a desk of oak and leather. The entrance of Durant had interrupted him. He looked up, frowning, then his face changed. Now every other face in the hall turned abruptly and stared at Durant and his companions, and a mutter broke out involuntarily. Each eye sparkled with sullen rage at this intrusion, and a few men half rose in indignation from their chairs.

Then every man sat in petrified silence as Durant and his officers marched to the platform, and mounted it, and the squad, rifles in hands, disposed themselves strategically, under the direction of Sergeant Keiser, around the walls. The silence was so deep that the boots of the men rang loud on the marble floor.

"Chairs!" barked Grandon to Morrow.

Morrow's hard brown eyes became flat and cold, but his broad face smoothed itself into an expression of complete and polite calm. He got up, without speaking, and courteously pulled forward four comfortable chairs from their position against the wall for Durant, Grandon, Bishop and Edwards. He waited until the officers had seated themselves noisily, then inclined his head with a slight smile at Durant. "Glad to have you with us, Major," he said. "It's probably a good thing that you decided to be present at our discussion."

The four officers faced the many farmers seated below them, and they studied the jowled countenances, the contemptuous and outraged eyes. Durant searched for Lincoln among them. He found him at the rear, but Lincoln did not look at him.

"How far have you proceeded?" asked Durant, turning to Morrow.

"Not far at all, Major," replied Morrow. He regarded Durant without hostility, and with an odd reflectiveness. Now his eyes glinted a little as if with suppressed amusement. "In fact, I had just called the meeting to order."

He let his eyes wander slowly over the stiff soldiers along the wall, whom the farmers were ostensibly ignoring. Morrow's mouth twisted swiftly, then relaxed. He ran his hand over the stiff gray bristles of his hair, and coughed. Durant was puzzled, and became alert. Morrow showed no signs of anxiety or of intimidation. There was assurance about him, and his broad and portly body sat at ease in his chair. Has something happened? Durant asked himself. Has Carlson countermanded my orders as too radical? Has he gone back on his word that he would never interfere with me? In short, have I been a damn fool to move this fast? He jerked his head at Grandon, who rose and, with elaborate slow ceremony, put a cigaret in his superior officer's mouth and lit it.

"I suppose your—men—know my orders?" said Durant casually.

"Yes, Major, they do." Morrow's voice was thoughtful. "In fact, the Army has already 'moved in on them,' as you directed. Every man here, and others who are not here, have soldiers quartered in their homes." He stared at Durant with a peculiar frankness. "And they know your directive: the gold to be exchanged at Government banks for paper legal tender."

"Do they also know," said Durant, on inspiration, "that they must report their full crops to me, and that I am empowered to pay them what I decide is a fair price?"

"I thought that would come next," replied Morrow politely. But the farmers evidently had not thought so, for again that menacing growl of rage rose from them like a swarm of buzzing wasps. Again, several started from their seats, and this time they did not fall back into them. Morrow tranquilly struck his desk a blow with his wooden hammer. "Quiet, gentlemen, please. And please remain seated. We must be orderly."

The scoundrel is too assured, too complacent, thought Durant, with increasing uneasiness. He stole a glance at Morrow's desk. It had two sheets of paper on it, and it was evident they were official telegrams. Durant felt dampness steal about his collar. Morrow turned to him.

"Then," said Durant, with what he hoped was supreme confidence and briskness, "there's no need to say anything else."

Morrow tapped his desk with his blunt fingers. "I sent a telegram to the Chief Magistrate after my last talk with you, Major."

Here it comes, thought Durant, and his dark face flushed. In a moment or two he would be publicly humiliated before these farmers and his own men. But Morrow was not looking at him; he was regarding the farmers. In turn, they regarded their leader tensely, and every face bulged and reddened with angry impatience. It was as if they were commanding him: Throw out the military fool and show him our power!

"I'll read you a copy of my telegram," said Morrow. He picked up a paper, carefully adjusted the pair of glasses he withdrew from a case on his desk, and scrutinized the paper in his hand. "Yes. Here it is, addressed to the Chief Magistrate, Arthur Carlson, in New York City: 'I, as president of the Grange of Section 7, have been directed by Major Andrew Curtiss—' " he paused, and said to Durant courteously: "It is 'Andrew,' isn't it, Major?" He peered at Durant and waited for his answer.

"Yes," said Durant grimly. The dampness around his neck became water.

" '—by Major Andrew Curtiss, Military officer in charge of this Section, to accept paper legal tender for the gold in the Grange Bank of Philadelphia. Major Curtiss has also issued orders for the Army to be quartered upon the farmers of this Section, orders to take effect immediately. I respectfully call the attention of your honor to previous decisions specifically exempting farmers from these directives, signed by the President of The Democracy. Are the directives of Major Curtiss to take precedence over laws now in operation? The farmers of this Section, through me, their representative, anxiously wish to know if these unprecedented directives have your authority and approval. We assure Your honor of our fervent patriotism and our desire to serve our country in this new emergency with all our strength and devotion. Signed,' " added Morrow, " 'Walter Morrow, president of the Grange, Philadelphia, Section 7.' "

It was more with a desire to hold off the ultimate and inexorable mortification than with real rage that Durant shouted: "You dared send that telegram without my approval or the approval of my office?"

The farmers began to grin broadly until the hall was full of florid smiles. Eyes flashed to eyes knowingly and with fatty satisfaction.

"Major Curtiss," said Morrow coldly, "you are apparently not aware that the farmers, as well as the heads of the various bureaus, have direct and private access to the Chief Magistrate, without censorship." He continued abstractedly: "And can communicate with the Chief Magistrate without first clearing through the local Military Administration Officer."

Some of the farmers chuckled; some laughed out loud. Durant, without turning, could feel the fury of his officers. He could only gaze at Morrow's placid face savagely, and wait.

Morrow directed his attention to his farmers: "Through all the wars and the national emergencies, the farmers of The Democracy have served their country well and patriotically. There's never been a time when they were found wanting. Isn't that so?" he asked the men.

They exclaimed in one voice, which was a roar: "Yes! Yes!"

"They have given full measure of their work and have obeyed all laws exactly. No one has ever supported the President more heartily. Isn't that so?"

"Yes! Yes!" The voices rose in hoarse and excited thunder. Now the farmers stood up, eagerly, and with triumph. They stared at Durant in exultation.

"Like Cincinnatus, and Paul Revere, they have been ready to serve their country at a moment's notice. Isn't that so?"

Now the farmers surged toward the platform, yelling: "Yes! Yes! By God, yes!"

Paul Revere! thought Durant, with awful bitterness. He studied the swollen bodies, the massive faces of the vehement farmers, and he thought of the Minute Men whom Revere had represented, and now his blood rushed to his face with hopeless violence.

"That is what I told the Chief Magistrate a month ago, and he agreed," said Morrow.

The farmers in their joy and their hate and victory, were about to storm the platform like an irresistible force directed at Durant. He heard the abrupt scraping of the chair behind him, and knew that his officers were rising and drawing their guns. The soldiers around the walls held their rifles ready and Durant could see the lustful desire to kill shimmering on their young faces. It was this, more than the farmers themselves, that sickened him; it was this, more than his humiliation, his drop from power, that turned his heart over. I'll never get used to it, he thought dazedly, and looked at Sergeant Keiser.

Morrow held up an unperturbed hand. "Gentlemen, please," he urged. "Go back to your seats. Let's have no—confusion."

Durant could feel the quivering lust behind him, which reflected the lust of the soldiers. His men were ready for murder. Involuntarily, he said: "Sit down, Grandon, Bishop, Edwards. And you, Keiser, at ease."

The farmers directed one annihilating and contemptuous look at Durant, and, grinning, returned noisily to their seats and fell into them. They had shown him! They, the farmers, all powerful, had brought the hated Military down to where it belonged! No one would dare interfere with them now; they had demonstrated their might and their invulnerability. The soldiers against their walls were their servants and would be thrown out of their houses.

Morrow took off his glasses, and rubbed his eyes. Then he rubbed his mouth with the back of his right hand. He ignored Durant and studied his farmers.

He said, quietly: "Therefore, I was astounded at the Chief Magistrate's answer, in his telegram."

The sudden silence in the hall had the weight of iron. Durant sat up in his chair. The farmers' mouths opened and their jaws sagged.

"I'll read you the reply of the Chief Magistrate," Morrow continued, in a voice almost of indifference, so abstracted was it. " 'It is directed that all the commands of Major Andrew Curtiss be obeyed at once, without further discussion. Major Curtiss has full and complete authority in all matters in Section 7. Signed, Arthur Carlson, Chief Magistrate."

The silence prolonged itself to an unbearable point. The farmers had turned sickly white. They sat, stunned, in their chairs. They could only gaze at Morrow, stupefied, incredulous; and their bulk diminished as though they were melting.

Durant's mouth opened slackly, also, to draw in a long breath of air. His relief made his whole body shake. He was no less stupefied and incredulous than the farmers.

The farmers were suddenly released from their terrible spell. A voice cried out, high and frantic: "Why, I don't believe it! It ain't true—!"

"It is," said Morrow, very sadly. "That's how it is, gentlemen."

"We won't stand for it!" another voice squealed. "Why, they can't do this to us! We're good citizens of The Democracy. Ain't we done all we could, every time, when the President asked us—?"

"We won't stand for it," faltered other voices.

"No! No!" exclaimed still others, in panic and disbelief.

"Can't be. Can't be," stammered some farmers at the end of the hall. "Putting the soldiers on us. Taking our gold. Taking our crops. Can't be. Something's wrong."

"The President," suggested one farmer, hopefully.

"The President!" His fellows took up the cry.

Morrow stood up. "The President, gentlemen, does not interfere with the directives issued locally in the various Sections. Any message you'd send him would be sent to the Chief Magistrate."

He said, to Durant, with a complete lack of interest: "You might want to speak to us, Major?"

Durant rose, and his wrath turned his eyes to bits of fire. "Yes," he answered harshly. "I do. And I want as many of you as possible to come to the windows, and I want you to look down on the street."

The farmers did not move, in their crushed paralysis, until Morrow accompanied Durant to the window and beckoned to his men. Then, about fifty lumbered uncertainly to their feet and followed. Their fellows stood up in the hall, and waited and listened, some fumbling at their chins, some blinking their eyes stupidly as if they had just received a staggering blow, some of them biting furiously on their cigars and pipes.

"Look down there!" said Durant, in a loud, slow and bitter voice. "See those people scurrying to their jobs. Look at their clothing, their faces. Are they well fed, like you? Look at their bodies: have they bellies, or fat on their legs or on their arms, like most of you? Look at their flesh, the color of onion skins, and think of your own faces, red and greasy from good food and clean, honest sun. Their clothes are patched and ragged, and their shoes are broken. Look at your wonderful clothes and your polished boots and the rings on your fingers and the jewels in your cuff-links, and your silk ties! Show me a car down there that doesn't belong to you! Show me a single man, down there, who walks like you, a free man. Tell me of a house in this city without a leaking roof or with heat in it, except the houses of the MASTS and the bureaucrats. And think, then, of your own big homes, your barns heaped with food, the fires in your rooms, your good, soft beds, the carpets on your floors."

Morrow leaned sideways against a window and looked down at the street with an air of polite indifference. The farmers craned their necks and stared down, sullenly, without answering.

"Then you talk of your 'patriotism' and your 'service'!" cried Durant, his face now congested with loathing and rage. "What have you farmers 'sacrificed,' as you call it? When have you sacrificed anything at all, for forty years? Do you call your gold-stuffed banks 'sacrifice'? Do you call your privileged status 'sacrifice'? Why, you bastards, you've sucked the life-blood of this country for forty years and made Presidents and politicians and a whole people pay for the right to live and eat what you produce!"

Even the most courageous and defiant were silent now. The jaws might set grimly, and the eyes narrow with scorn and avarice, but no one spoke.

"The cities have been your slaves, and all the people in them," continued Durant. "They've been like cattle, waiting for you to slaughter them. You've take the gold from the teeth of men and women, and the last rings from their fingers, and the hard-won treasures of their houses, and the lives of their starving children. For your own profit. You've thundered in Washington, for forty years, and threatened, and challenged, and withheld your produce, and intimidated your Senators, until you got what you wanted: the bodies and souls of a nation. Because men have to eat. Because men want to live." His voice dropped, became hoarse. "Because men want to live."

Morrow stirred and regarded him closely. The farmers shifted on their big feet. They stared at Durant with the heavy hatred of countrymen.

He turned his back to them, and now his voice was almost inaudible.

"You agreed to every war, and to more wars, and then more wars, so you could become richer and more powerful. When a President tried for peace, you wouldn't support him. You created inflation with your parities and your prices, until thousands in the nation died of starvation because they couldn't buy what you had to sell. That is your 'sacrifice.' You sacrificed a whole country."

Morrow lifted his body away from the window, and now he looked at Durant piercingly, at the passionate gestures, at the pale dark face, all in such violent contrast to the low voice.

Durant lifted his left hand. "But now you've come to the end of the road, you farmers. We have a new war. Your parities are gone, as of today. You'll sell at a price I'll fix, myself. Your bank accounts will be paper, not gold. You'll be permitted to eat only what the people in the cities eat. You'll have your ration cards, and not a single piece of your meat will be yours, except what is allowed on these cards. You'll begin to pay taxes on your income back to January first of this year. You'll pay taxes on every single, solitary thing in your houses. No exemptions for you. No more privileges. If the cities die, then you'll die with them. You'll starve with them, right in the very center of your fields and your barns. You've never had any fear of any God or any man. Today, you'll begin to fear."

He studied each appalled and aghast face. He saw the deep pallor on every man's cheek, and the terror in every man's eye. and he saw the hatred and silent rage and the stiffening of bodies.

"Yes! Look at me!" he went on, with a malignant smile. "I'm your master. I'm the Military. You gave me my power. You put this uniform on me. You put those guns in the hands of my men. So we could protect you and help you. Look at me! We're your masters, after all. And the laws and the power you gave us will be used against you, for the welfare of The Democracy."

He turned to his officers. "All right, that's all. Let's go."

Then Morrow said very quietly: "Major, could I see you alone for a minute?"

Durant was about to refuse, then he said: "Yes. For one minute."

He followed Morrow out of the hall, in the thickest silence he had ever heard. Every eye followed the two men, and it was as if statues were staring. Morrow led him into a small room at the rear of the platform, which was luxuriously furnished as an office. "Please sit down, Major," said Morrow, indicating a deep leather chair. Durant sat down. His breath was still hard and rapid, his face still very pale. "Cigar, Major?"

"No," said Durant. He twisted his left wrist and glanced at his watch.

Morrow sat down behind the leather and mahogany desk in the

center of the room. He clasped his hands on it and gazed at Durant with the utmost gravity.

"I suppose, Major, that because the Chief Magistrate has approved your directives for Section 7 that all the other Sections will follow your example."

"Of course," said Durant.

Morrow studied his hands. He said softly: "The farmers have had their privileges and their wealth and their security so long that they won't give it all up—very easily. They'll—make a fight of it, Major."

Durant was silent.

Morrow began to smile inscrutably. "You're very eloquent, sir. Very eloquent."

"What are you leading up to, Morrow?" asked Durant irritably. "Are you trying to intimidate me with your threat that the farmers will 'make a fight of it'?"

Morrow's smile broadened. "No, Major. Not at all."

"Then what are you trying to say?"

Morrow turned his big gray head so that he could look at the paneled wall. "I'm merely saying that the farmers will fight. And hard. They're very strong, Major." He turned back to Durant. "Isn't that what you want to hear?"

Durant sat very still. He could not speak for several moments, then he blustered: "I want to hear—I want to hear—that the farmers understand their new position, without any doubts."

Morrow nodded. "They understand. As I said, you're very eloquent, Major."

Durant stood up. He looked down at Morrow, whose smile was more cryptic than ever. He could not prevent himself from saying abruptly: "Who are you, Morrow?"

"Me?" Morrow lifted his gray eyebrows, as if puzzled. "I'm president of the local Grange." He paused. "I've been president for two years."

"Were you ever a farmer?" asked Durant, feeling something strange in the atmosphere.

Morrow shifted in his chair. "No, Major," he said thoughtfully. "I was never a farmer. I used to be what you soldiers call a bureaucrat. I was once Assistant Secretary of Agriculture. That was five years ago. The farmers owe a great deal to me." He glanced at Durant, and those hard brown eyes shone with secret amusement.

He stood up, and offered his hand to Durant. "I'll tell the farmers they can do nothing. Of course, that won't prevent them from doing what they can. And, Major, we'll probably meet again. Somewhere."

Durant, his head buzzing, all his instincts stirring so strongly that they confused him, found himself shaking hands with Morrow. Morrow's smile began to broaden into a laugh. "Tell the

Chief Magistrate, when you see him again, that Walter Morrow will cooperate with him fully, at any time, and with you, Major."

He opened the door for Durant and bowed him out. The farmers were standing as they had left them, and now they searched Morrow's face eagerly. It was very quiet and very solemn. They still stood, watching their leader, as the officers and men marched out.

"Well, that finishes the farmers!" said Grandon happily, in the elevator.

But Durant made no comment. Something's very damned wrong, or something's very damned good, he thought, dazed. Whatever it is, the tempo's got to be stepped up.

Durant could feel the city simmering with excitement all around him. It was a new and heartening sensation, a unique one, for a man who had known only the excessive and humble docility and the suppressed violence of New York, which had been merely the violence of despair without hope. But this simple excitement had a warmth of humanity about it, which indicated that Philadelphia was not yet completely dead. Even his directives against the workers of the city—reduced rations, increased hours of work and a new tax—had not thrown the people into fresh misery. For they now had companions, their ancient enemies: the farmers, the bureaucrats, the MASTS. Therefore, the workers had accepted the insupportable directives against them almost with amusement. They had so short a way to fall; the others were falling mightily, into chaos, into ruin, into the very bottomless pit that held the whole of Section 7 now.

Durant tried to sense if behind the people's exaltation in the fall of their traditional foes there was a hint of revolt. He knew that hope had a way of being born when a man's spirit was even momentarily released from its awful preoccupation with its own agony. The clergymen might deplore that one man's suffering could appear to lighten his neighbor's. But there it was; it was part of the character of humanity, and it was a factor which only a fool would ignore and not use in his reckoning. Yes, there was some possibility; once all the people were united against the Military, and there were exemptions for none in a common slavery, revolt could be expected, or at least hoped for.

The new war was hardly mentioned these days in the papers. There was always a war and the people had become conditioned to war as an ox becomes conditioned to the whip. The papers still rang their mechanical bells of "Unity! Duty! Sacrifice!" but they were mostly preoccupied with the alarm, rage and indignation expressed by the Public Psychiatry Department because of the new directive that the children of the privileged groups were to attend the Government schools. Dr. Healy had recklessly stated that he was "certain" that this directive of the new major would be rescinded by the "proper authorities." He had gone to New York to see the Chief Magistrate, himself. Dr. Healy did not return for a week or two, but the news of that meeting had rushed to Philadelphia before him. The Chief Magistrate had declined to interfere.

It was reported that the bureaucrats, the MASTS and the farmers were gathering repeatedly for "discussion," and that the meetings were notable for their expressions of anger and outrage. However, it was carefully noted, the meetings invariably closed with new avowals of loyalty and devotion to The Democracy. It was all really a "mistake." "Something" would be done. Washington, said a spokesman for the privileged groups, would not allow its dedicated classes to be ruined, would not permit the nurseries of "leadership" to remain closed very long. The President would intervene. It was rumored that the Chief Magistrate had been called to Washington. No word of disrespect against Arthur Carlson was uttered; every man affected by the new directives was very eloquent in his words of admiration for and fidelity to the Chief Magistrate. One or two gentlemen went so far as to speak of the "youth" of the new major, and his apparent "unfamiliarity" with "certain problems," and they piously hoped that he would soon "understand."

The privileged groups, then, received the dismayed Dr. Healy with equanimity, and talked with him in private.

Their equanimity was severely shaken at the directive, which came later, that the formerly "unavailable labor" assigned as servants to the privileged groups would now be assigned to "essential industry." No sound reached Durant of the loud and furious outcries of the wives of the privileged when their house-and-garden slaves were called to labor in the war plants and in the fields. However, Durant was quite sure that husbandly ears were torn to shreds by the screams of sleek and impudent women in the privacy of secluded bedrooms. A man, he reflected, could endure a great many more important calamities with considerable calm, but he could never endure the shrieks, complaints, threats and tears of his wife. Even the new directive that the privileged groups were no longer to be exempt from the ten percent tax on all personal and real properties would not reduce the powerful to such despair as the rampagings of their outraged women-folk.

From such mean, trivial and ignoble sources, Durant thought, often came the fires of revolt. He prayed that the women, deprived of slaves who ministered to their gleaming bodies and who filled their kitchens and houses, would incite their husbands, by their nagging, tantrums and acidulous shrieks to a blazing revolution.

Seize a man's body, annihilate his soul, reduce him to serfdom, Durant told himself, and centuries would pass without a murmur from him. But touch his purse, touch his privileged comfort, and he would shake the very foundations of the world with the blows of his rage, and he would set the very cities on fire, in a few hours, a few weeks, or a few months. Take away his liberty, destroy his dignity as a man, and he would only murmur weakly, then forget. But take away his gold, his pomp and circumstance, his little personal power, and even hell would quail at the measure of his vengeance. What a thing was man! What a mean and contemptible thing!

Yet, out of the very contemptibleness of man could heroic things be born, not voluntarily, not by contemplation and prayer and earnest seeking, but merely as a side product. Oh, was it as Arthur Carlson had said, that the revolt of the self-serving gave opportunity to good men heretofore kept silent?

It was from the office of Dr. Benjamin Colburn that the directive had come that all personal, and real, properties held by the MASTS were to be taxed the prevailing ten percent. A delegation called upon Durant with anxious recriminations against Mr. Woolcott, director of the Bureau of Mobilized Labor. It was all very well, said the well-tailored gentlemen, for the farmers to be so taxed, as directed by Major Curtiss, for, who were the farmers?

"Who, indeed?" agreed Durant.

Encouraged, the gentlemen congratulated Durant upon his directives against the farmers, who were, really, only rustics and illiterates. But it appeared that Mr. Woolcott had a personal prejudice against those whom The Democracy had recognized as very important personages, and who had been granted exemptions accordingly. As Major Curtiss was the Military commandant, he would surely inform Mr. Woolcott that this directive should not, and could not, be enforced. There was also the matter of servants. A gentleman and officer, such as Major Curtiss, quite understood that it was not to be expected that the wives of very important personages scrub their own kitchens, take care of their own children and cook their own food.

Major Curtiss, the officer and gentleman, listened pleasantly to the well-bred complaints. Then he said: "Before any Bureau can issue any directive it has to clear with me. Gentlemen, I regret to say that every directive to which you are objecting has received my approval. And, gentlemen, you are well aware of the fact that I have been given absolute power in this Section. The Military, gentlemen, must, and shall, be obeyed."

The delegation looked at him with consternation. It was understood, naturally, that the Military was supreme—

"It is," interrupted Durant, still smiling pleasantly. "I'm glad you know that. It seems that for some time there has been a misapprehension about the matter. I'm here to correct the misapprehension. We have a new war, gentlemen. A new war. We must Labor; we must Live Austerely; we must Pull in our Belts." This new emergency had created an unprecedented situation in The

Democracy. All, now, were to be called upon to Sacrifice Everything. "But everything," Durant emphasized. He was certain that the gentlemen understood, and that, as loyal citizens of The Democracy, they would stand United Against the Common Enemy, working shoulder to shoulder with every other citizen, sleepless in their devotion, Giving their All.

They listened to this unctuous and sonorous speech with expressions of delicate distaste, though some were discreet enough to nod soberly and agree, but—

"But, what?" asked Durant seriously.

"The morale of Those Who Lead," suggested the spokesman, a very urbane gentleman with an air of sweet reasonableness. "Our morale might be injured. I might even say it would definitely be injured. So, for the sake of The Democracy, and in order to conquer the new Enemy, it is most necessary that the morale of the leaders be sustained."

Durant regarded them in silence, his eyes narrowing. The silence became prolonged, until some of the gentlemen shifted uneasily in their seats about Durant's desk. Then he said very softly: "And the morale of the people, Mr. Remington?"

Mr. Remington shrugged. "Oh, the people," he answered indulgently. "They do as they're told."

"And you're implying that you won't do as you're told?"

Mr. Remington was alarmed. "I did not say that, sir! I am merely implying that we are men of intelligence, and the people are only morons."

Durant leaned his elbow on his desk and studied Mr. Remington with intense curiosity. Mr. Remington was a man in his late sixties, short, thin, aristocratic of feature, and with a thick mane of very silvery hair. He was a manufacturer of diversified war materials, and some twenty years ago, when he had been forty-five, he had been called upon as advisor to the President then in office. It had been his duty to "coordinate manpower." Durant had never met him before, but he knew his history. Mr. Remington, twenty years ago, had been fervent in his praise of the Common Man, and the Common Man's propensity for unity, duty and sacrifice during wars. All civilization, Mr. Remington had said, rested on the broad shoulders of Labor. Without the brawn and the devotion and the intellect of Labor the whole world would be engulfed in barbarism and slavery.

"Some twenty years ago," Durant said, "you, Mr. Remington, declared that only the people, only Labor, was significant, and you didn't spare the adjectives. Now, you call them 'only morons.' Have you changed your mind about them, Mr. Remington, or were you a hypocrite? For your own purposes?"

Mr. Remington did not flinch or look embarrassed. He laughed richly. "Come, now, Major, you know very well that one must always lie to the mob, always flatter it, so that it will do what you want it to do. An apple for a horse, a carrot for a donkey, a bone for a dog, flattery for the people. It is all one and the same thing." He laughed again, and waited for Durant to laugh, also. But he did not laugh. Mr. Remington, then, was for a moment a trifle disconcerted. "If the people had any intelligence, Major, they would never have listened to flatteries and cajolements all through the centuries. They would have used their minds. Not having minds, they must be led, as the ass is led, broken to work and service. If there is any design in the universe, the Common Man was created to serve his betters. That's always been understood by the rulers of all nations."

Durant kept his face bland. "I quite agree with you, Mr. Remington."

Mr. Remington glanced triumphantly at his colleagues. "Good, Major! Very good!"

Durant lifted his hand. "In fact, Mr. Remington, we, the Military, regard all civilians, without a single exception, as horses, donkeys and dogs. We, the Military, see you, and all your friends, as no better than any of the wretches who work in your factories and your houses and your mills. You, too, are servants of The Democracy and the Military. You made the Military your rulers, believing we would be your robots. You put guns into our hands in order that we might make a whole nation your slaves. You forgot that a robot can never be trusted not to swing blindly on his metallic heels and shoot down blindly the man who made him. A robot sees no difference in any human creature. He makes no distinction. I, gentlemen, the robot created by you, see you as only flesh and blood—like the slaves at your machines and the slaves at your blast furnaces. You put me into motion, by the turn of your screws and destiny—a destiny you designed—and I can't stop in my tracks. You made me incapable of stopping. So, gentlemen," and now he shrugged, "I can't stop. The monster of steel you made commands you. And you can't crush me. I haven't a heart to beat or flesh to feel or a mind to think. Gentlemen, I am the Military."

He smiled at them engagingly, and Grandon, Bishop and Edwards and Keiser smiled also, and swaggered a little behind him.

Mr. Remington had become quite pasty, and his colleagues were aghast. "But, Major," said Mr. Remington, "if, as you say, we made you, and we did, then—"

"I'm your robot, your slave?"

Mr. Remington did not answer. He rose, with dignity, and his friends rose with him. "I know you are to be informed of any message sent to the Chief Magistrate. We intend to ask his opinion." With that, the elegant delegation turned as one and left the office.

The Chief Magistrate, when petitioned by the MASTS to set aside the directives regarding taxes, privileges and servants, replied politely that he had given Major Curtiss full and absolute power in "this present emergency," and that Major Curtiss was to be obeyed to the letter.

Nothing of the dismay, horror and hate and rebellion of those now oppressed, who had oppressed, came to Durant's ears. But he could well imagine what went on in secret, what hasty meetings were held, what defiance was uttered, what plans were being made. He could even feel it in the air, in the movement of the wind, in the very light that fell over the streets of the city. But how soon would the former privileged, the farmers, the securely wealthy, MASTS, the bureaucrats, revolt? Would they meekly obey, after all? No, they would not. They had been too well fed; they had lived too luxuriously; they were swollen with privilege. Out of their rage and resolution the revolt would come, and they would utterly destroy the robot they had created, and, as they had done so often in the past when they themselves, were threatened, they would restore liberty and overthrow what they had built in their avarice.

They were so stupid. They never understood, after all these centuries, that the tyrant is invariably chained by the evil he has conjured up to chain others, that the despair he has inflicted shall blacken the doorway of his own house, that the murderers he has paid shall eventually dig his own grave.

They always burst the prisons they had erected, and, in freeing themselves, they inadvertently, and without intention, freed those they had set within the bars and under the whips of the torturers.

An old, old story. But they always forgot the Magna Carta and the barons. This time, they always told themselves, they would succeed. They never succeeded.

The excitement in the city rose to a subdued frenzy when it was learned that Mr. Alex Sheridan, director of the infamous and terrifying Federal Bureau of Home Security, had been arrested, by order of Major Curtiss, for the murder of Andreas Zimmer.

Durant, the lawyer, intended to put into motion the swift machine of jurisprudence. He looked forward, with deep pleasure, to conducting the trial, himself. Juries had long been dispensed with, as had the writ of habeas corpus and all the other entangling and delaying impedimenta of justice and law. Now, the military officer in charge was both judge and jury, and from his sentences there was no appeal. Sheridan would die, not for a murder he had not committed, but for all the anonymous murders he had committed in the soundproofed rooms of the fearful FBHS. His victims would stand, an invisible jury, at his judgment.

And then Durant received a message from Arthur Carlson, the Chief Magistrate. Mr. Carlson, Durant was informed, was coming to Philadelphia within four days, to conduct the trial in person. "The case of Mr. Sheridan was so important, and would have so many far-reaching consequences, that it was necessary that the Chief Magistrate, in these days of desperate emergency, preside, himself, at this momentous prosecution."

Alex Sheridan had been a great favorite and friend of the powerful, from whom he had received much secret wealth and support. The fact that he had not only been under suspicion, but had actually been arrested and would be tried, affrighted them. If Alex Sheridan, the friend and confidant of the President, was no longer secure, no longer safe in his person, and could be prosecuted like any common criminal, then no one could boast of immunity!

The people were elated. Their monstrous enemy, the shadow that brooded over them day and night, who fell upon them from around corners and in their beds and at their meager tables, was confined in the noisome prison which so many of them knew only too well. They speculated upon him; they even dared to gather in groups under the windows of the prison and jeer faintly until the soldiers dispersed them with obscene threats. They began to adore Major Curtiss, who was now oppressing those who had oppressed them. They hailed his car on the streets. This alarmed him. He had reduced their rations to a point where a little less would cause them to collapse of starvation. He had issued the most intimidating directives against them. But they still adored him. Bad, very bad, when it was designed that their very enemies should lead them to freedom.

He was even more alarmed at the coming of the Chief Magistrate. Didn't Carlson trust him? Did Carlson fear that he would not punish Sheridan severely enough? Had he failed, somewhere? Had Carlson heard that he had not succeeded in arousing even the slight possible resistance of the people to him? In desperation, Durant ordered wholesale arrests and disappearances, and, before Carlson arrived, the people hated and feared him as had been originally intended. When one night eight of his soldiers were murdered on the streets—something which had not occurred for over two years—he was heartened again. Some of the people, at least, had weapons of a sort, and this, too, had a cheering effect on Durant. They had brought out these hidden and secret weapons, and they had used them. Possible resistance, possible revolution, had become probable.

There was only one consoling thought in the coming of Arthur Carlson. Somehow he, Durant, would discover how it was with his Maria and his children. He had done good work; Carlson was not a stone. He could, perhaps, be moved by some human compassion and sympathy.

Waiting, with some apprehension, for the arrival of the Chief Magistrate, Durant felt his loneliness descend upon him more heavily than ever. He often talked with Ben Colburn on the telephone, on matters of new directives, but he never saw him socially, or even had a glimpse of him. The ambiguous Morrow never crossed his path, though Durant knew that his oppressive directives against the farmers were being carried out with what seemed extraordinary zeal on the part of Morrcw. Dr. Dodge was blind and deaf to an incredible degree, though Durant, in his presence, disconnected the wires of the thing behind the landscape. Durant had talked with the two FBHS men who had sworn that Sheridan had not been with them on the crucial evening in question. They were typically bureaucratic, anonymous in appearance and apparently devoted to their work of endlessly turning out new regulations against the people and arresting scores of suspected "saboteurs" and "subversives." Were they deserting Sheridan because they wanted his position? Durant began to consider that possibility with disappointment. Or were they Minute Men, placed in that strategic spot by Carlson? When talking with the men, Durant studied them searchingly, but they merely returned his regard with the complacent stare of bureaucrats and answered his questions with the usual circumlocution of their profession. There was not a single gleam of eye, a sudden faint smile, a slight gesture, which would lead Durant to believe that they were other than what they professed to be. Of course, he tried to reassure himself, if they were Minute Men they would be well trained and would not trust him, just as he had been told not to trust anyone.

Still, his loneliness and depression mounted. What do you want? he asked himself irritably, a secret Club of Anonymous Minute Men? Do you want to ferret out possible Minute Men for cozy chats, and so expose all of us to suspicion and ruin and death? The safety of the Minute Men, the hope for the country, was imbedded in silence and lack of recognition.

Durant, in his hunger for human companionship, even tried to cultivate the superficial friendship of his officers. But though he had served his time in the Army, he had never mastered the obscenity of military men, had never been interested in their lives and knew next to nothing of their jargon. He was not one, even casually, with Grandon, Edwards and Bishop, and he knew they knew it. As for Keiser, he must be avoided for the safety of both of them, though they often exchanged knowing glances. As the powerful Military Officer in Charge, Durant had been invited to numerous parties at the homes of the privileged. He had courteously refused. Since his frightful directives against them he had, naturally, not received any more invitations.

He rarely, if ever, saw the Lincolns or their sons, except at a distance. They were like furtive rats scurrying from his path, though occasionally he saw Lincoln's gray face, Mrs. Lincoln's anxious body flitting through a doorway and the three sons working sullenly in the field with their slaves. So he spent his nights reading, praying soundlessly, cursing as soundlessly to himself and desperately worrying about his family. I have the plague, he thought, the plague called Militarism.

He had worked, and had done good work. But what about the other Sections in the country? Were they copying his directives against the farmers, the MASTS, the bureaucrats, the wealthy? He could not know, for each Section was almost hermetically sealed against other Sections. Of course, there were rumors, but Durant preferred facts. He studied the newspapers closely. If they mentioned the other Sections it was only to report with enthusiasm that the farmers were producing more than ever, that beef would be plentiful "shortly," that weather was good in the agricultural Sections, or bad, that "production had gone up," or had not gone up, in the purely industrial Sections. There was news of "the war" and the grim determination of "the people to resist the new aggressions of the Enemy," and the naval bombardments and bombings of the great cities of South America. But how much of this was true, and how much downright lies, Durant had no way of knowing.

The Press was as dead as all the other freedoms. Most of the pages were devoted either to eulogy of The Democracy, "and our great ideals which no enemy has ever vanquished, and our national vow that our liberties shall never be destroyed," or to speeches by the captive President, or to news of enthralling murders, or to foolish and trivial fiction extolling military heroes, women spot-welders in the factories, women farm-workers, devoted male workers in every industry, lascivious cartoons and pages and pages of "comics." If the Press had died, it had not been struck dead by Washington. It had been delivered up to death by the people decades ago, the faceless, stupid, benighted and greedy mobs who had struck down freedom with their ape-fists, and had permitted their unions to be dominated by criminal elements and had regarded that domination with a sort of chuckling and idiot pride.

There was no surcease, anywhere, for the beset Durant. Sundays had long been abandoned as holy days, since religion had been severely restricted. Sunday was only a day of labor, except for higher officers in the Military, and then only if their services were not needed. Durant was careful not to make a point of taking each Sunday off. But on the Sunday before Carlson's arrival in Philadelphia, he decided that he would not go into the city.

He had not been able to sleep the night before, in spite of the sedatives he had taken. So, wearily and heavily, he walked out of the silent house in the morning, dragged himself across yards and a field, and found a small swell of ground on which grew five poplars in close formation. It was a very hot day in midsummer, but here the shade was thick and blue and fragrant, and gentle with the dark and holy silence of trees. Durant sat down and gloomily smoked cigaret after cigaret, brooding on his wretchedness and his fear for his family and the awful muteness of his life.

The great white house shone in the early morning sun through its banks of glittering trees. The barracks stretched behind it, and the red barns and the silos. Cows were toy figures in the distance, as were the men who worked in the wheat fields and the vegetable gardens. The sweetest warm wind blew through the poplars, and they sang mysteriously. All the earth shimmered with the circumambient light which fell down upon it from the sky like a cataract. A few fair-weather clouds gathered and drifted in the intense blue sky. There was a holiness in this quiet, on this land, which no directive, which no insane Military, which no mad government or enslaved people, or war, could befoul. The fewer people, the less dementia, thought Durant, and the thought was not a happy one, considering that men were immortal souls as well as bodies.

Immortal souls! All at once, the idea was grotesque to the young man brooding under the poplars. If "immortal souls" had created all this evil in the world, then something was wrong in the universe, something distorted and horrible and witless, or, perhaps, something wicked and malignant. Had Satan disenthroned God, after all? Durant looked at the sky; the ghost of the full moon stood there, a small rounded cloud, in the very midst of the blaze of the sun. Were the smirking scientists right, and was there no significance to life, no Good, no personal Deity, and nothing whatsoever except some pointless Law and Order among wheeling and meaningless suns? Was man's dream of God a lie, as his old dream of liberty and dignity was a lie?

It was useless for Durant to tell himself that in the past centuries there had been wars and oppressions and tyrannies and massacres. He knew that these had been local matters, and not universal ones. Now the whole world was mad. Europe, broken, disorganized and completely ruined, was one chaos of anarchy, with starving multitudes surging back and forth over a whole continent, mingling with disordered and disorganized armies constantly and senselessly killing for the mere pleasure of killing. There were not even a few hidden churches and monasteries left, where devoted men and women would record the history of the ages, and its sciences and its arts, in deathless books. There were no governments except tribal or local ones. The blasted cities were not being rebuilt; the torn fields were not being plowed. Only plunder and fury and death and starvation prevailed, while ancient walls toppled and mountains of rubble were overgrown with weeds. War had done this, war born of man's intrinsic hatred for his species. The Century of Man's contempt for Man! Immortal souls!

He had not seen or heard anyone approach him, but all at once he was aware of a presence. Dr. Dodge was beside him, carrying a small silver tray on which stood a glass of whisky. Durant started violently, and his cigaret burned his fingers. He began to swear, then saw Dr. Dodge's face. The blindness and deafness was gone;

the old man was smiling. He murmured: "I thought you needed this, Major. I saw you from a window."

Durant, staring at him, took the glass of whisky. He put it to his lips, and with the quick motion of despair, he swallowed the liquor. Dr. Dodge stood rigidly beside him, but now he was looking over the fields and at the distant mountains. The alcohol began to spread warmly through the bitter coldness in the heart of the younger man, and something relaxed in him. He, too, for long minutes, watched the glowing countryside with the old man.

"The churchbells," murmered Dr. Dodge, as if he were speaking to himself. "One misses them. They should be heard over all this land, from the villages. It is the time for prayers. It is a time for God."

Durant remembered his church, from the days of his childhood, before religion was proscribed. He saw the white altars, the shining candles, the exquisite statues, the tall golden crucifix, the stained glass, the marble floor glimmering in the holy dusk. He heard the tinkle of the bell, the chant of the priest. The altar boys were genuflecting; the choir soared out in a triumphant voice. The pillars of the church shook and there was a light on the faces of the kneeling people. Suddenly, Durant bent his head on his knees.

"Man has abandoned God, in all the world," said Dr. Dodge, dreamily. "But, has God abandoned man?"

"I don't know, I don't know," answered Durant, in a muffled voice.

"I often think of the story of Jonah and the depraved city of Nineveh," went on Dr. Dodge, in his murmurous voice. "Jonah went out from the city and sat on the east side of it and contemplated it. Then God made a plant to grow overnight to shelter Jonah from the heat of the sun, and Jonah sat under it and waited for the destruction of Nineveh. But the next morning a worm gnawed the plant, and the plant died. Jonah, attacked by the merciless blaze and the wind, fainted, and said to himself: 'It is better for me to die than to live.' "

Durant waited, his eyes fixed on the other man.

Dr. Dodge smiled sadly. "God asked Jonah if he had pity on the plant, and God remarked on his pity, with understanding, though the plant had come up in a night and had perished the next night. And God said: 'And should I not spare Nineveh, that great city, wherein are more than sixscore thousand persons that cannot discern between their right hand and their left hand—?' "

Durant did not move, but only listened, and it seemed to him that everything about him—the landscape, the clouds, the distant figures of men and beasts, the very ghostly moon and the fiery sun—listened, too.

"There is a legend," said Dr. Dodge, and his voice was full of sorrow. "When Moses and his people had escaped over the dry bed of the Red Sea, the following Egyptians were drowned in the waves of the ocean. It's said that the angels wished to sing a song of triumph, and God said to them: 'My children lie under the sea, and you would sing?' "

He looked down at Durant. "There is no record in history that any nation was ever just and good and lived by the laws of God. Yet, God has had mercy on them all, and will continue to have mercy, and will deliver us from our own evil."

Dr. Dodge gently took the glass from his hand, shook his head, and walked away like an automaton, a tall figure tottering over the grass. Durant was alone again. Then, all at once, he felt he was no longer alone, and the distortion he had seen left the landscape and the sun poured down its rivers of light on a world not yet dead.

He lay back in the cool grass under the poplars and fell into a deep sleep.

When Durant arrived at his offices the next morning, there was a message awaiting him. One of his staff stenographers, a little beetle of a man, told him of the message with an air of great if subdued excitement. Chief Magistrate Arthur Carlson was now in the city. At ten o'clock, "precisely," an escort of the Picked Guards would call for Major Andrew Curtiss and conduct him to the "Philadelphia residence" of the Chief Magistrate.

Durant's junior officers appeared apprehensive, though when Durant asked them why they could give nothing but confused answers. Bishop and Edwards and Keiser murmured that a similar summons had arrived just before "old Major Burnes" had disappeared. Durant glanced for confirmation at Grandon and caught the young lieutenant indulging himself in a secret and unpleasant smile. Durant shrugged. "Nonsense," he said. "We all know that the Chief Magistrate is coming to conduct the trial of Alex Sheridan, himself, because of the importance of it."

Grandon smiled again. "The old Major always conducted all trials, and there was one, two years ago, which was equally important."

"The Picked Guards," said Bishop. "I hate the bastards. Why shouldn't they be part of the Military? Why are they a separate organization? They look like ape-men."

"Old Major Burnes never allowed himself to be escorted by them," added Edwards. "It was tried once, and he kicked them out of his office, and went with us. That's the last time we ever saw him."

Durant smiled. "Much as I'd like to gratify your curiosity, boys, and take you along, I'm going with the Picked Guards."

At ten o'clock, "precisely," an escort of four Picked Guards arrived at the hotel. Durant knew they had come by the very vague and disturbed sounds about him seconds before Edwards announced that the Guards were in the corridor. Durant saluted his junior officers with an unconcerned smile, and joined the Guards, all huge men with meaty and brutal faces. They saluted him indifferently, arranged themselves about him, and walked off with him. It reminded him disagreeably of the night of his arrest; their boots clanged, they kept their hands on their guns and did not even glance at the awed and hating soldiers and officers who were standing in the lobby of the hotel. It was their mission to intimidate, and even the Military could be intimidated by the very presence of the Guard.

The Guard car, painted the dark-green official color of their organization, was waiting below. In utter silence, Durant entered the car, and the Guards settled around him. He maintained an air of amiable indifference, attempted no conversation, made himself yawn once or twice, and tested his newly healed arm. He put a cigaret to his mouth, and one of the Guards lighted it for him with scrupulous politeness. If he felt himself oppressed by them, he did not show it. His mind was busy.

They drove down cratered Broad Street, then out beyond the suburbs. Finally, they were rolling in the country where the late August sun gilded fields and mountains and houses with hot gold. Durant could smell the sweet fragrances of drying hay and clover; all the countryside murmured with bees. Clouds of yellow dust followed them on the empty highway. The Guards sat heavily and stiffly beside Durant, and stared ahead and looked nowhere. Once or twice, large groups of men working the fields looked up at the sound of the car, but recognizing it, they hurriedly went back to work. Durant smoked contentedly, but his throat felt sick and his heart was beating with unreasonable speed. He had nothing to fear, he told himself. The sending of the Guards was a courtesy. However, he could not keep down his senseless apprehension.

The car swung and turned off onto a country road, rutted and narrow. It swung between the green arches of trees, and the air, cool and fresh, struck on Durant's face. Then there was a gravel road, broader, now, and suddenly an expanse of green parklike land, dotted here and there with a great oak or isolated elm. In the distance stood a large brick house with a red roof and ancient chimneys and windows, diamond-paned, glittering in the sun. Durant noticed that no trees were very near the house. He had never seen this place before; he had never known that Carlson possessed a "Philadelphia residence." No one stirred about the grounds; no one appeared at the windows. But he knew, instinctively, that almost every window was a watchtower, and that every watcher was armed with a machine-gun. He knew that he and his escort were being scrutinized by unseen and coldblooded eyes, and that the men in the car were being counted and that the way they had come was being studied for any possible follower.

Durant had become accustomed to the silence of the countryside by now, yet it seemed to him, as he alighted from the car, that the silence of this place was too profound and had a quality of terror about it. Durant and his Guards walked up the brick walk to the front door. The door opened without a sound, and revealed at least two squads of Guards in the cool dusk of the hall.

Evidently this was a confiscated mansion, for the floor was of dark marble, old and gleaming, and the walls were of paneled mahogany. A monster chandelier, splintering the sun which shot through the door into a thousand prisms of light, hung from an immense beamed ceiling. A great wooden staircase, polished and curving, rose from the hall. Durant stood uncertainly, then felt a slight pressure against his thigh and discovered that his gun had been deftly removed. He started, uttered a profane exclamation. One of the Guards informed him, politely, that this was "customary" whenever the Chief Magistrate interviewed "anybody." Durant was about to protest when he saw a very disconcerting sight. He caught the wolflike and ominously silent shadows of tremendous dogs ranged along the walls in the dimness of the hall.

Durant knew all about watch-dogs, and knew that they always set up a wild barking at the approach of anybody, stranger or friend. The fact that these dogs were so quiet informed him that they needed only a gesture, or the slightest known word, to spring at his throat and tear him apart. In truth, his exclamation had brought them to the alert, ears cocked, teeth soundlessly bared. They were even more formidable than the Guards, and even more deadly. They were trained and intelligent murderers.

Durant was careful not to utter another word, to make the smallest untoward movement, as he mounted the stairway with his Guards. It was ludicrous, even to him, that he kept well and cautiously in the very center of his escort, for protection. He could feel the savage eyes of the animals following him, and it was all he could do to prevent himself from running. Now he was really frightened, and he confusedly thought of Carlson, not as a secret Minute Man but as a sinister enemy.

They walked down an empty wooden corridor, lined with doors. Then at one door a Guard knocked, three short blows, followed by two spaced ones. The door opened and a blaze of sunlight momentarily blinded Durant. It was some seconds before he could see a large and splendidly furnished room with wide windows standing slightly ajar. And then it was a few seconds longer before he could see the two men waiting for him—one, Arthur Carlson, the other, a stranger.

Carlson and the stranger sat and looked indifferently at Durant. He heard the door close behind him, and by the thick dullness of its movement he knew it was sound-proofed. He stood there and waited. Carlson did not smile at him. He was, as before, the cool aristocrat with his pale hair and slender, ascetic face, delicately at ease and detached. "Sit down, Major," he said, at last, and there was no inflection of friendliness or interest in his quiet voice, no secret undertone.

Durant sat down. Then Carlson rose, and carefully closed the windows and locked them. Instantly, the room was a tomb from which no voice could emerge. Durant felt the oppressive closeness, and his old, mysterious claustrophobia clutched at his throat and weighted down his chest. To hide his discomfort, he looked at the stranger, and recognized him at once from newspaper photographs he had seen. He was the Director General for the frightful Federal Bureau of Home Security, Hugo F. Reynolds, whose office was in Washington, and who controlled all the directors of the FBHS in the various Sections.

Hugo Reynolds was a very tall, very thin man in his middle fifties. Everything about him was gray, from his sleek thin hair to his clothing. He was the very personification of anonymous evil, intelligent, lethal and omnipresent. His eyes were gray, his skin had a grayish cast, his motionless hands were ashen, his lips had no color. Nothing about him shone or caught the light except his brilliantly polished and narrow boots. Beside him, the patrician Arthur Carlson was vivid in his green uniform of the Picked Guards.

Carlson sat down, and still unsmiling, said: "Mr. Reynolds, the Military Officer in Charge of Section 7, Major Andrew Curtiss."

"Good morning, Major," said Reynolds, and Durant thought that his voice was gray also, with an intonation like fine grit.

Now Durant really felt panic. His naïve imaginings that he and Carlson were to have a friendly hushed talk with each other disappeared. Something was wrong here. He swallowed deliberately, to calm his fear and desperation, then involuntarily he braced himself. He had faced death before. Death sat opposite him, scrutinizing him with those pallid and unblinking eyes, and he thought: If it's come, then it's come. He did not glance at Carlson for reassurance. Carlson had become a stranger, also.

"Mr. Reynolds, Major," said Carlson, very coldly, "has come here to defend Alex Sheridan. The circumstances are very grave. His office had conducted a private investigation of the conditions surrounding the murder of Andreas Zimmer, and Mr. Reynolds thought the results of the investigation merited his own presence."

Then Durant knew something terrible had gone wrong, and that Carlson could not, would not, help him. "You will stand alone," Carlson had told him months ago. "For the safety of all of us, you can't expect any assistance if you betray yourself in any way. If you fail, or are stupid, you will find yourself abandoned, surrounded by the silence of friends or associates."

Arthur Carlson was powerful beyond the power of the loathsome Director General of the FBHS. Yet, for the sake of the work he was doing he would desert Durant immediately, if the necessity arose, and would deliver him up to the FBHS. He dared do nothing else. He sat there in his chair, looking at Durant with cold expectancy. Out of the corner of his cye, however, Durant saw that the aristocratic hands were just slightly tensed. Durant gave his attention to Reynolds.

"I should like to ask you a few questions, Major," said Reynolds.

If I've failed, and something has gone wrong to imperil all of us, then I'll just have to die, thought Durant. His panic left him; all his muscles became taut and ready. He regarded Reynolds with the proper expression of interest. "I'm ready to answer all questions, Mr. Reyonlds," he said.

Reynolds picked up a sheaf of papers on the table beside him, and he studied them closely. He withdrew a silver pencil from his pocket, and impaled one item on the papers. Without looking up, he said: "I have here, Major, the report of your own investigation of the death of Andreas Zimmer. A very good and detailed report." He waited. Durant did not answer. "I see that you've carefully interrogated two assistants of Mr. Sheridan, who claim Mr. Sheridan was not with them on the night of the murder. You have also interrogated the third assistant, who swears that Mr. Sheridan was with the three of them. I see that you held the tavern owner in custody for three days, and that your questioning was very adroit and exhaustive but could not break down the statement of the man to the effect that Mr. Sheridan had not been in the tavern for two weeks. Yes," continued Reynolds musingly, "a very complete and rounded report. I congratulate you, Major. You are not only a military man, but have a skilled lawyer's ability for interrogation. Did you ever study law, Major?"

Durant said: "I never studied law, Mr. Reynolds. But thank you for the compliment." He felt the sweat running down his back.

Reynolds lifted those dreadful pale eyes of his. "You never studied law, Major?"

"I never studied law, Mr. Reynolds."

Reynolds glanced at Carlson. "You've known Major Curtiss for a number of years, Arthur. It's strange that you never guessed that he had the makings of an exceptional criminal lawyer." He smiled slightly.

Carlson smiled in return. "Major Curtiss and I discussed the possibility of his studying law, Hugo, a few years ago. He is, as you say, an expert in interrogation. However, I thought it best for him to act only as a military officer. His work has been excellent. That is why I am promoting him to the rank of colonel."

Durant let his pent breath leave his mouth.

Reynolds scrutinized him again, and said, almost idly: "Any French blood in your family, Major—Curtiss?"

"Not that I know of, sir." He made himself smile.

Reynolds said: "I've gone over your whole history, Major. Very, very good." He waited for Durant to answer, but Durant only inclined his head as if pleased by the compliment.

Something was not pleasing Reynolds. He frowned delicately. Carlson's face was smooth.

Then, without the smallest gesture, without the smallest rise of inflection in his voice, Reynolds pounced.

"Major Curtiss, I see that you've carefully gone over the possibility that the murderer, or murderers, of Andreas Zimmer may have arrived from some point beyond Philadelphia. You've advertised for witnesses who might be able to give any information as to any car or other conveyance. None appeared. You went into the matter exhaustively. You inquired as to whether the murderers might have come on foot. You questioned everyone in the neighborhood of Zimmer's apartment. Nothing more was learned. Yet, Major," and his slow voice became slower, "my own secret investigators have discovered something very serious."

He stopped, and waited. Durant controlled his features. The sweat was a river down his back. But his mind had become cold and still.

"I'd be interested to hear about it, Mr. Reynolds."

Reynolds regarded him in silence for a few moments. "Major, we've found two witnesses who swear that they saw an official car running rapidly, without lights, from the direction of your farm residence on the night in question. We've found two more witnesses who saw that car returning, still without lights, along the same road, about an hour after the time of the murder. The witnesses say that there were at least three men in the car."

My God, thought Durant. He made himself frown as if incredulous. "Was the car traced?"

"No," said Reynolds, still watching him. "It was seen only on the road."

Durant smiled very convincingly. "There was only one official car at the house of John Lincoln. It was mine. My junior officers did not accompany me home that night. They stayed in town, for a party."

"And you, personally, locked the car, and retained the keys?"

"I did."

"And you found the car exactly where it had been left, with no signs that it had been used—without your knowledge, Major?"

"It was not used. I had the keys."

"There was a slight shower that night, Major, I've learned. The car was not spotted, or dusty, or soiled in any way?"

Durant raised his eyebrows. "I never knew of the shower. The car was not spotted in the slightest. I'd have noticed. I'm particular about those things, Mr. Reynolds."

Reynolds tapped the papers reflectively with his silver pencil.

"It surprises me, Major, that under the circumstances you did not question anyone closely at the farm about the car, or wonder if anyone could have used it that night."

Now Durant really smiled inwardly. The trap was so childish, to his lawyer's mind, and almost all his fear of this lethal man drained away.

"You forget," he said, "that I knew nothing of what you call these 'circumstances,' Mr. Reynolds." He made his voice subtly and deliberately authoritative, the voice of a military man who has permitted a civilian considerable liberties and who has decided not to permit them much longer. He felt, rather than saw, that Carlson had begun to smile a little. "My car," continued Durant, "never left the farm that night."

Reynolds studied Durant with hard new attention.

"Moreover," said Durant, staring at him directly, "I don't believe your witnesses saw an official car on the road to and from the farm at all. I believe they are manufacturing evidence—possibly, it could just be possibly—for a fee."

"A fee?"

"Or for some excitement, or in a spirit of self-importance. Call it what you wish. It isn't unusual, in law, for witnesses to spring out of the earth with made-to-order evidence, tailored to fit any—buyer."

"And who do you think would be the buyer, Major?" asked Reynolds softly.

Durant shrugged. "I don't know. Frankly." He added, "and I repeat, I don't believe your witnesses saw an official car. They know that Zimmer was murdered; they know there's a reward out for the murderers, or murderer. They are probably looking for the reward."

Reynolds was coldly amused. "Let's leave that for the moment, Major. You didn't question anyone at the farm because your car was not used, as you say. Tell me, do you know Mr. Sheridan?"

"No." Now Durant was all the rigid military man. "I keep my contacts with bureaucrats at a minimum. I"—and he looked at Reynolds straightly—"call them on the telephone—to tell them of my new directives—or I write them, or send a messenger."

Reynolds ignored this not too gentlemanly insult. "Did you know Andreas Zimmer, Major?"

"I met him once. When I told him of a new directive, the one, sir, about the new assignment to essential industry of the so-called 'unavailable' labor exploited by the formerly privileged groups."

Reynolds lifted an eyebrow musingly. "You do not care for the civilian bureaus, do you, Major?"

"They have a function. But their functions, as I have had reason to remind them recently, are all subservient to the Military." He said this calmly.

Reynolds sighed. "A very correct officer, Arthur," he said to

Carlson. "You train them well." But Carlson only smiled in the friendliest manner. Reynolds turned back to Durant.

"You had no reason to dislike either Sheridan or Zimmer, Major?"

Durant frowned. "They were civilians, sir. I neither liked nor disliked them. I knew Sheridan as the local director of the FBHS, and Zimmer"—he gave Reynolds a long look—"as assistant to Woolcott of the Bureau of Mobilized Labor." He leaned forward in his chair, as if he had had a fresh idea. "I assume your interest in the matter is to defend Sheridan, and that Zimmer matters no way at all to you. Would you mind telling me, if you will, what other evidence you've been able to obtain? I'm only curious. After all, I conducted the preliminary investigations."

"Only the witnesses to the official car, Major." The cold voice bored at him.

"There was no 'official car,' sir. Your witnesses are either mistaken, honestly, or they are lying. Or, if there was actually a car, it did not come from my direction. Or were you suspecting that I, who had a broken arm at the time, drove into town and killed Zimmer, myself?" He grinned at the other man derisively. "And, if I accomplished that remarkable feat, what would be the reason? If I had wanted Zimmer killed, or Sheridan, for that matter. I'd have employed no mysterious coming or goings. I would simply have ordered their arrest, and their execution, with as little delay as possible. After all, sir, I am the Military."

"Major," said Arthur Carlson, rebukingly, "you are being insulting. Mr. Reynolds is merely conducting a full investigation."

Durant was entirely the junior officer who was losing his temper in the presence of the despised civilian, even if that civilian was a powerful and dreaded man. "I meant no insult," he said to Carlson, allowing indignation to touch his voice. "But apparently the Military, through my person, is being insulted. If you'll excuse me, sir—" And he actually got to his feet and managed to convey his pretended wrath by cleverly upsetting his chair.

"Sit down!" Carlson's voice was sharp, and cracked with authority. "You'll not leave, Major, until Mr. Reynolds is finished questioning you on an entirely routine matter. You should give him that courtesy, whether it is necessary or not."

Durant blunderingly righted his chair. He protested: "I'll not be insulted by a—" And his voice rose.

"Sit down!" said Carlson again.

Reynolds watched all this, narrowly. He saw Durant's inflamed face. He heard the icy anger in Carlson's voice. He saw this military man's trembling hands and mutinous hot eyes as he obeyed his superior.

Durant thought to himself: I've saved Dodge. I've saved the others. I've saved myself, and all of us. He was almost enjoying his own histrionic performance. It had been a desperate maneuver, and he hoped it had succeeded.

"There is no other evidence, Major," said Reynolds indifferently, ignoring the whole immediate episode. "However, I'm not prepared to accept, as you have accepted, that the witnesses are lying, or mistaken. We'll go into that at the trial. But can you explain to me, Major—and this is just by way of casual conversation—how it would be possible for three men to deny the presence of Sheridan at the tavern, and one other man to affirm it?"

"I understand that it often happens that way, during trials. Conflicting witnesses, Mr. Reynolds. Judges invariably accept, unless there are other circumstances, the word of several witnesses as opposed to the word of one. As you know, I interrogated the three denying withnesses. They displayed no animosity toward Sheridan."

"You didn't—let us say—intimidate them, did you, Major?"

Durant was outraged. "'Intimidate' them, sir?" He conveyed incredulity. "Why should I?"

Reyolds ignored this. "Tell me, Major, do you think it possible that the farmer, Lincoln, or any of his sons, could have driven into the city that night?"

The temptation was strong, but childish, Durant thought regretfully. He shook his head. "If they did, it was in my official car. I doubt very much if they went in one of their own."

"I've been informed, Major, that Lincoln's daughter disappeared that night, from her father's home."

Durant put on a sheepish and sullen expression. "I'd rather not go into that matter, if you please."

Reynolds permitted himself a frigid smile. "By the way, Major, do you know a man at the farm, who is conscripted labor, by the name of Dodge?"

Now fear tore at Durant again. "Dodge? Do you mean the old house servant Lincoln has around?"

"You don't know who he was?"

"Good God!" cried Durant. "He's an old imbecile fool! 'Who he was?' Was he ever anything?" He showed his impatient bewilderment.

"He was once a very famous scholar. But scholars wouldn't interest you, would they, Major? After all, you are a military man." The voice was shaded with derision.

"I doubt if he was ever a scholar, Mr. Reynolds. I'm sure you're mistaken."

But Reynolds did not answer that. "Have you ever known him to drive a car?"

"Of course not. He's half blind, and almost totally deaf. The walking dead, we call him." Durant laughed. "Like thousands of other civilians one sees every day."

Reynolds swiftly took another direction. "You don't care if Sheridan dies for a crime he didn't commit, Major?"

"I'm convinced he did commit it, sir. There are witnesses, recorded in my report, who swore there was bad blood between the two men. Why, I don't know. I never found out. It seems, apparently, that they either quarreled at some time, or had a mutual antipathy. It often happens that way." Then he showed signs of a bright inspiration. "I can see that the evidence against Sheridan is very slim, in spite of the witnesses, and in spite of what Zimmer's wife has testified, herself. No one saw him near Zimmer's house. There were no signs of blood under his fingernails, or on his clothing. There is no absolute evidence that the two men ever really quarreled. Sheridan is a married man; he perhaps had a female friend, unknown to his wife, and he is protecting her. It is possible he was with her that night. For some time I've had the vague suspicion that Zimmer's wife might have done it, herself."

"But you had her examined, Major. She, too, had no blood on her clothing, or under her fingernails, and the murder weapon has never been found"

Durant appeared to be all crestfallen. "You're quite right, sir. I've no evidence against the woman, except the gossip of the neighbors. No, sir," he added resolutely, "I'm afraid Sheridan is guilty. After all, Zimmer was a wary and careful man. At least, he gave that impression. It isn't likely he would have admitted anyone he didn't know. And he told his wife that Sheridan was coming."

Reynolds put his papers meticulously together. He rose. "I'm finished with the major, Arthur. Or is he now a colonel?"

"He is." Carlson was suave and genial. "You won't have lunch with me, Hugo?"

But Durant was rudely importunate. "Mr. Reynolds, what would Zimmer have to do with Sheridan, anyway? Zimmer, assistant to Mr. Woolcott?"

Reynolds regarded him with distant aversion. "I'm sure I don't know, Major. It's very mysterious, isn't it? I suppose you'll be at the trial?"

Durant was properly rebuked for his insolence. "If Mr. Carlson wants it, yes. Otherwise, no. What have I to do with civilians, except to give them directives?"

Reynolds overlooked him entirely, now. "No, thank you, Arthur. I must get on with this investigation. But tomorrow?"

The two men left the room, talking together as equals, leaving Durant behind. He sat down and lit a cigaret with wet fingers.

Carlson and Reynolds were gone a long time. Restlessly, and smoking too quickly, Durant went to the window. He saw Reynolds leaving in his limousine. Carlson was standing in the driveway. He waved affably to Reynolds, and the chauffeur started the car and drove away. Carlson continued to stand in the driveway, as if waiting. Then Durant saw an old black car, nondescript and common, glide with an astonishing swiftness from behind the house. A man sat in it, a little dark-clad man with a sharp and intelligent face. Carlson nodded, and the old car took off at a safe distance behind Reynolds' car, careful to let clouds of dust envelop it.

Well, thought Durant, and his anxiety went away. He sat down and lighted another cigaret with equanimity, and congratulated himself. When Carlson entered the room, he stood up and saluted. Carlson's face was quiet and wryly amused. "Colonel Curtiss," he said, and held out his hand. "And now, here's a letter from your wife. The last one, I might as well warn you."

Arthur Carlson ordered that lunch be served him and Durant in the closed room where Hugo Reynolds had interrogated the young man. Durant's reverence and almost fearful respect for Carlson took on a warmer tint, and his release from the tension of the past hour made him exuberant. He was full of questions, but Carlson, showing more and more of a suppressed and sternly controlled humanity, suggested that Durant first read Maria's letter. So, while they drank whisky and Durant's nerves quieted, he concentrated on the letter from his wife, the envelope of which was not postmarked and did not reveal by any address her present whereabouts.

Maria's letter was filled with love and concern for her husband, and with quiet confidence. She was very happy, she said, and was living obscurely "in the sort of place where I have always wanted to live." (That means a farm, somewhere, thought Durant eagerly.) Maria, who had once been a teacher of English in a New York school, had a gift for description, and it was soon apparent to her husband that she was artfully giving him hints as to her location. "The scenery is so lovely," she wrote. "I missed the hills which we used to visit on our trips to the Catskills, but now the brilliant flatness of the land, and the color of the earth, and the strange and fiery flowers, seem to me to be more beautiful than the strong cold green of New York mountains." (California? No, California had hills and deep valleys. Florida? Louisiana? Georgia?) The letter went on: "Flowers long finished blossoming just about the time they start to bloom at home! And flowers just coming up which will bloom by Christmas in a warm, calm sun! Dear Andy, how little we ever knew of America." (Florida? Florida!) "Do you remember, Andy, how we admired the Guernsey and Holstein cattle on the farms in New York and how you planned that we'd breed them ourselves some day? You don't see that kind of cattle here, for they're mixed with the Brahmin cattle." (Yes, Florida!) "The children love to play in the water, though it's strange to them." (Durant had a moment's bafflement.

New York City was surrounded by the salt ocean, except for part of the Hudson River—Then he remembered, with excitement, that he and Maria had never taken the children to the seashore, because all the hotels and beaches had been appropriated by the Military for many years. They had had to accustom themselves to fresh water pools and little streams and lakes in other places in New York. So, the children were swimming in the sea. Taken all together, it must be Florida, he thought.)

"They tell me we are quite safe here, and though I work hard, it is worth it. The children are so healthy and brown, such as they never were at home. In fact, I never want to return to New York. —They say I must never plan on seeing you again, and that I mustn't have false hopes. But I pray constantly. Father Martin always told us that God never ignores a prayer—When I am most lonely, I remember that you are working for our country, and that is the greatest consolation. It was not only wise that you should have a new identity, but that your family should not be near you to distract you. Without us, you have less fear, and can give all your devotion to our dear America."

Durant, deeply moved, turned to Carlson, who said gravely, "Yes, I have read the letter. It was brought to you, passed from hand to hand, by brave men who were instructed to destroy it at any sign of danger. It has taken months to arrive. We always permit our men to have one last letter from their wives and families. It relieves them, and frees their minds. But this will be the last letter you will ever receive from your wife. There is too much peril involved for men who have too much to do to act as postmen."

He held out his hand commandingly for the letter. "You know you can't keep it, Durant. It would endanger you, and us." So Durant, with a last look at his wife's handwriting, gave up the letter reluctantly. Carlson set it afire, methodically, and when it was reduced to ashes he opened the window and gave the ashes to the quiet wind, fragment by fragment. He can say what he wants, thought Durant. But some day I shall see Maria and the children again. I shall—Arthur Carlson spoke quietly from the window. "No. No, you won't." And he closed the sealed window again and returned to his chair. He did not speak of the letter again. The subject was done.

Two Picked Guards brought in their meal on trays, and left the room. While the two men ate, Durant talked exhaustively, and Carlson listened. Carlson made no comment until Durant smoked after the meal was finished. He was sunk in thought. At last he said: "Good." Durant waited, but no further praise came, and he was momentarily disappointed. Carlson went on: "Dr. Dodge. Of course he will allow himself to be tortured to death if necessary and if Reynolds, who apparently knows that Dodge was prosecuted by Sheridan, has any real suspicions. Durant, we must never forget that there are men, not Minute Men, who are also conducting solitary fights for America, on their own initiative."

He smiled his cool and wintry smile, and all the ascetic planes of his face sharpened. "I rarely make a mistake in choosing my men. I knew you had wit and artistry and flair for drama and acting. Section 7 is the most important Section in the country. It needed an intelligent, keen and dynamic man to set it ablaze, a blaze that would light up the other Sections. Time is growing too short. Improvising was necessary on a bold and reckless and courageous scale. I want to tell you now that you've succeeded even better than I expected, and in a shorter time."

Carlson went on: "I doubt if you had an actual method worked out in your mind when you arranged for the murder of Zimmer, who was a desperate threat to Colburn and all of us. I've learned, incidentally, that he knew too much. He even had his suspicion of you. A week later, he would have set an earthquake under us, and would have shaken Section 7 from border to border. Your impulsive improvising to bring about his murder was marvelous; I think, though, it was more intuitive than anything else. Mind you, I don't underestimate intuition. I've always believed it is the very essence of enormous intelligence, a subconscious summing-up of intangible factors."

"Yes, it was improvising, and impulsive," said Durant. "I just saw, in the flash of a moment, how it could be arranged. I had no definite plan in the beginning." He was gratified, and his dark face beamed. Then he said: "But what of the other Sections? Are they following us? I'm so damned alone—"

Carlson replied: "I often think of what Ibsen said: 'The strongest man upon earth is he who stands most alone.' Your strength has been in your aloneness, Durant. There was no one you could consult, at any time. Consultations weaken, raise disastrous doubts. Stultify. Had you men with whom to consult, you would have been in danger. You might have been paralyzed, for some of the men might have been too cautious, too slow of action, too reasonable. In desperate situations we need desperate men, not rational intellects."

He sat and watched Durant for a little. "You ask me about the other Sections. I can tell you this: as soon as I learned what you were doing—and don't ask me how the news traveled to me so fast—I went to Washington and had a talk with my father. Then we went to the Joint Chiefs of Staffs, those greedy and avaricious rascals, who live only by wars, their pockets and their bellies. Within minutes after we received news of your directives, and long before we received furious protests from the privileged groups, we saw the full possibilities. Of course, you know," and Carlson smiled again, "you interfered somewhat with matters not concerned with your actions against the farmers. For instance, the man who is working against the bureaucrats was at first annoyed with you, and then he began to appreciate your action and enlarged on its potentialities. He is a little too cautious. You excited his imagination—

"But I'm wandering a little. My father and I, in our secret sessions with the Joint Chiefs of Staffs, who are great friends of ours, soon convinced these mechanical brutes that the new directives and new taxes would bring them enormous personal fortunes, even greater than their present revenues. One or two were somewhat doubtful at first, but even they joined the general delirium when they fully understood. They've already arranged to triple their salaries, out of the pockets of their former friends, the members of the privileged groups. They've received protests from this Section, at their offices in Washington, but what are protests from groups already being oppressed and shorn of their golden fleece compared with more money and more power for professional soldiers? Also, they highly approve of you, Durant. One of the generals said you have 'restored the authority and majesty of the Military.' General Anderson suggested that your rank be raised. Another general even demanded you be made a brigadier-general! I bring you their love." And Carlson smiled dryly.

"But what of the President?" asked Durant, exhilarated, and proud of himself.

"The President is the captive of the Military, as was the President before him. We flattered him that he had been hiding these very plans in his mind, long before we approached him. He has always had an affection for the Military, and he is toying with the idea of announcing himself as General Supreme of the Army of The Democracy. The Chiefs of Staff were not too pleased by this, but President Slocum is very excited and will probably succeed. After all, we have a new war, and news wars need resolute commanders. Quote, from President Slocum."

"So—!" cried Durant, moving to the edge of his chair in his impatience.

"So, as of a week ago, the directives you have applied to the farmers, and the other directives against the MASTS and the bureaucrats, went into operation in all the other Sections. The country is seething. The pot is beginning to boil. The day and the hour are almost here. We must work even faster. We dare not let anything occur which will destroy all the work which has already been done, and we mustn't minimize the danger.

"I understand," Carlson continued, "that the farmers already have formed a League for Freedom, and the MASTS are holding impassioned secret meetings in every large city, and the bureaucrats, preoccupied with their disaster, are issuing fewer and fewer petty directives and regulations. There is not only a League for Freedom now, but a League for Free Enterprise as well as a League for Constitutional Liberty! Just think of it: bureaucrats forming a League of Constitutional Liberty!"

Durant burst into wild laughter. I started it, he thought. I started it!

The Carlson, as if reading his thoughts, said seriously: "You may have begun it, Durant, but the time was ripe. Ideas are never confined to one man. If it hadn't been you, it would have been another Minute Man, somewhere, somehow.

"But let's get on. The harsher directives you issued against the masses of the people have been adopted in other Sections, also. The docile mothers of children affected by those intolerable directives are maddened, in spite of decades of oppression. The people are awaiting a leader, or leaders. They'll get them. It is only a matter of applying a little extra pressure here and there to precipitate a revolt. A bloody revolt," added Carlson, looking at Durant with his cold eyes. "A revolt in which hundreds of nameless Minute Men will die. Including us."

Durant became abruptly sober. He saw, now, completely, how frail was his possibility for survival. As the Military, hated by the whole country, he was the enemy which must be struck down first of all in any revolt. Somewhere, a Minute Man who hated him as the embodiment of all the anguish and tyranny of the country was waiting to kill him upon the giving of a signal; somewhere, a brute in the employ of the farmers, or the MASTS, or the bureaucrats, was sharpening a knife for him or oiling a gun. His life was in imminent peril. Today; tomorrow; next week. A month. A few months. Men like him, working desperately in the dark in the name of freedom, in every Section, would be murdered in the name of freedom.

Carlson said: "You're not so expendable as yet, Durant. You must take every precaution against premature action. You must never be alone, even in your own room. Even then"—and Carlson smiled as if the thought amused him ruefully—"you can never be sure that one of your bodyguard won't put a bullet in your back or a knife in your ribs. He may be a Minute Man, himself, having joined the Army to do exactly what he will do."

Durant's hard mind tightened stubbornly. I'll survive! I'll find a way!

"In this new uproar, secret as yet, but gaining momentum every day, the war is almost forgotten by everybody," said Carlson. "Did you know, Durant, that we have friends in Europe and Asia, and in South America? They have been notified that when they hear that this nation is in revolt against its oppressors they can safely bring off revolts of their own. Durant, I think we can begin to hope. It may be fifty years before the world is completely free again, and civilized, and at peace. But it will come. We can be sure of that. And we have the consolation, even when we die, that we are the hidden saviors."

Very good, thought Durant. But I shall see Maria again, and

the children. If a new world was about to be born, he would be present at the birth.

"I am appointing two Picked Guards as your personal attendants. They have my orders, Durant, to guard you and never leave you alone for a single instant. And, Durant, they are not Minute Men."

Durant was dismayed. The thought of having two Picked Guards constantly about him, even sleeping in his room and following his every footstep, horrified him. He was about to protest, feebly, when Carlson rose, indicating that the interview was over.

"Tonight," said the Chief Magistrate, "I should like you to join me at dinner at the home of a friend. I will send a squad of the Picked Guard for you."

Durant was driven back to the city by four silent Picked Guards. Two of them remained with him. His own men greeted the news with surly surprise. Grandon, especially, scowled, and turned away to hide the scowl. Even the news that Durant was now a colonel could not decrease the irritation of the junior officers.

Durant waited in his office, alone with the two Picked Guards. The autumn night pressed somberly against the windows, and the dark wind muttered ominously. Durant tried to work at his desk, but the presence of his Guards oppressed him. He glanced at his watch. It was half-past seven, but he was not hungry. It was not possible that Arthur Carlson had forgotten him. He looked at the Guards' heavy and expressionless faces, and he wondered how many decent men they had killed with their truncheons and their guns. They looked back at him impassively. Rain began to beat on the windows, and it was loud and melancholy in the silence. Durant rustled some papers. But it was useless to attempt any work. A listlessness came over Durant, a conviction that all was hopeless. A thought swam through his mind like a silent fish through water: What did it matter, eventually, whether good or evil prevailed? Men lived and died, and they managed to survive, some way, under any system of government. Why did a few men invariably struggle to give the people ideals, to gentle them, to incline them to peace and justice and love? They never succeeded.

It was then that a curious emotion took possession of Durant, without violence or anger or disgust. He felt it, and examined it, with surprise, and recognized it for what it was: pure hatred unadulterated by any personal passion or coloration. It was a hatred directed against everything and everyone, including himself. He was not appalled by it; he regarded it with curiosity, and felt its intense and concentrated power. It was a phenomenon, objective and subjective, a thing that was, disassociated from any human touch, unsoftened by shame. He recognized it as evil, and not actually part of his own personality; it was as substantial and real as a stone, existing alone and undiffused, having its own intellect and directions.

He glanced up, with growing surprise and excitement. The two Guards were looking at him. They appeared uneasy; they shifted on their feet, as they stood by the door. They could not look away from him. Had they felt the emanation of that pure, undistilled hatred of which Durant had suddenly became aware, that evil which had its own enormous mind? Durant was sure they had.

"What's the matter?" he asked them abruptly. "Something frightened you?"

One of them stammered, and became red: "Why—why nothing, Colonel. I don't know about Tim, here. But—but it was like a ghost, or something—come into this room."

Yes, thought Durant, a presence. He tapped the papers on his desk with his pen. He remembered what he had been taught as a child, that evil was an actual and sentient thing in itself, an eternal spirit. The priests had called it Satan, Lucifer. They had said it was an entity, as God was an entity. He, Durant, had not accepted that when he had become a full man, and had smiled a little indulgently to himself. Evil, he had believed, was intrinsic in the human spirit, as good was also intrinsic. It was an abstract. Let simpler minds accept evil as outside themselves, against which they could battle more or less ineffectually. Now, he was not so sure. Could it be possible that Lucifer did indeed "roam the world, going up and down ceaselessly through the night, seeking whom he might destroy?" Durant remembered that when this thing had touched him he had felt unemotional hatred and great power and invincibility.

Did the wicked men of the world, the tyrants and murderers and oppressors, know this presence very often? Was that their motivation, their guidance? Very mystical, thought Durant, trying to smile. The emotion had gone from him. Had he resisted it? Had something in him, inviolate and virtuous, turned it away? He could not flatter himself. He remembered that when it had been strongest, there had been no virtue in him at all, nothing but that hatred and strength. And there had been no guilt, no horror. Now he was oppressed; he felt emptied and undone and very tired.

A squad of Picked Guards arrived for him, thundering sharply on his door. He went with them into the chill and watery night. He sat in a car between his personal Picked Guards, and he saw that the other Guards drove in one car ahead of him and some in the car following him. The wet and broken streets shone in the light of a few feeble lamps. Few were about and these scuttled through wide puddles and stumbled over crumbling pavements. Durant's oppression became almost unendurable.

The long red-brick procession of attached houses rushed by the windows of the car, streaming with water. Here and there a yellow light broke through the solid walls. Solitary soldiers patrolled, huddled in their coats miserably. They exchanged challenges at each corner, mechanically. Suddenly the cars halted. A detachment of soldiers appeared briskly; within their ranks straggled four beaten creatures, three men and a woman, and by the light of a street lamp Durant could see the blood on their faces. "Enemies of the people!" Durant leaned forward and studied them sharply, and he saw their ragged clothing, their pain and despair. This was not an unusual sight; it was very common in The Democracy. But all at once it had a strange significance for Durant, though he had seen similar things before.

He remembered that he had often been part of the spectators who watched the arrest and brutalization of men and women who had dared raise a cry against oppression and tyranny. He had kept his silence, as a Minute Man, while the rage roared in him and the hatred for the soldiers had become more grim and determined. If the prisoners died, their death only hurried the day when their fellows would be free to kill those who had killed. But now Durant looked at the soldiers, and suddenly he was filled with compassion for them, compassion because they had become murderers, compassion because they had lost their humanity, compassion because other men had made them beasts, and because they had accepted their beasthood without a struggle.

He glanced at the brutal Guards about him, and his compassion rushed out to them, also. He wanted to talk to them, for some overwhelming if obscure reason. He said: "I wonder what those—those criminals—have done?"

The Guard nearest him was surprised that the colonel had condescended to speak to him. He answered eagerly: "Hasn't the colonel heard? It happened about two hours ago. Mr. Hugo Reynolds, of the FBHS, was murdered, and I guess they're arresting people."

Durant was very still. He saw, again, the little insignificant man in his little insignificant car who had been given a signal by Arthur Carlson that very afternoon, after Reynolds's limousine had rolled away from Carlson's house. He said, in a smothered voice: "Who did it? How did it happen?"

The pleased Guard, proud of being addressed by the colonel, was only too anxious to be informative. "Why, Mr. Reynolds was in his car, see, Colonel? It was getting dark, and it had just started to rain. Mr. Reynolds was going to his hotel. His car was turning a corner, and all at once, this car—a little old car—appeared kind of from nowhere, like it was in a big hurry. It hit Mr. Reynolds' car, right in the middle, and when it did it exploded. It was full of dynamite, or something. Mr. Reynolds' car was bullet-proof, like the cars of all the big fellers, and was reinforced against hand grenades, too. But the explosive was too much for it. Mr. Reynolds' car and the little old car and the man in it went up together. Nothing left but a lot of blood and wreckage. Mr. Reynolds was killed, and so was his secretary and driver. They say it was something to see," added the Guard, with relish. "Hole in the street like a bomb crater. Funny thing, though, there was nobody right in the vicinity, and so nobody else was hurt. Looked like it was all planned to happen so nobody else would get hurt."

Durant thought of that little insignificant man who had gone resolutely and calmly to his death, knowing that it must be done. There had been no honors for him, and never would be. There had been no one to help him or give him courage. His help and courage had been in himself. Would I have been as courageous as that? Durant asked himself with humility. Even though I was often in danger, there was always the possibility of rescue or escape. At the very least, I knew I was not alone. But that anonymous little man had been alone, and his name had died with him, and it had meant nothing to him in the face of his duty.

So many would die for the death of the lethal Hugo Reynolds, innocent men and women who had long been under suspicion of secret and "subversive" activities. Durant thought: Hurry! Hurry! We must move faster if we're to save the brave and decent among the people!—The soldiers and their prisoners had disappeared in the dark and windy distance. There was no end to the Hugo Reynolds. Hurry! Hurry! sang the wet tires of the cars. Now Durant was no longer oppressed, and there was no memory in him of the evil he had felt, himself, but only compassion. Something strange was rising in his mind, a new emotion, a startling idea.

The wind and the rain increased to a sudden violence of sound. Another voice added itself, autumnal thunder, and a glitter of lightning fled through the sky. The cars were passing through wider yet darker streets, impressive streets lined with fine old houses. Durant saw the huge bulk of what had once been a famous library. It had been transformed into a barracks for women conscripted by The Democracy to work in war plants, women imported from smaller cities from all the Sections. These women were under the special guidance of the Department of Women's Welfare, of which Captain Alice Steffens was the local head. There was a nursery for the women's children in the basement, but there were few children and the mothers rarely visited them, preferring to leave the care to nurses and teachers.

Years ago, Durant had watched his wife's tenderness with her children, and her constant watchfulness, and her uneasiness when the boys were out of her sight. He had wondered about that large percentage of women in the war plants who bore their children indifferently, and abandoned them with actual eagerness to the hands of others. He had studied these women in the factories, and he then had had the answer. Almost uniformly, they were of a certain type, with large hard bodies, coarse-grained skins, rough loud voices and pulpy features, striding about in their big thick shoes and workmen's blue overalls and shirts. They were brutes, with the anatomical outlines of the female figure, but with nothing else to distinguish them from men.

He had discussed it with his father, for he had been a much younger and more naïve man then, and his father had said thoughtfully: "It happened in Germany, Russia and America, this emergence of strong physical masculinity in a percentage of the women. It was like another sex. The women preferred working in masculine trades, and rushed to the factories, first voluntarily for a long time, and then by conscription, which they didn't mind at all. It was the beginning of the era of the degradation of womanhood. Perhaps the emergence of this masculinized sex created that degradation or vice versa. It's something one can't tell, but it's a fact that when this kind of woman emerged, Communism made great advances. The Church tried to do something about it, urging the women to remain with their children. But it was no use, with that breed of creature. They had no maternal instincts. First the factories, and then the armies—and they liked it. It was all necessary to them. They are the monsters bred out of Communism, and recreating it."

From these women had come the vicious wardens of the women's prisons, for brutality came naturally to them. They officiated as members of firing squads, and enjoyed it. They also enjoyed the beatings they administered to their charges. They were forewomen in the factories, and were extremely efficient at forcing the fainting and exhausted female workers to final efforts. They were much extolled for their "patriotism" in the "war efforts." They were the only women workers who were given extra rations of food and clothing. However, they rarely dressed becomingly; they preferred their big flannel trousers, which they stuffed into their rubber boots in the winter or into their leather boots at other seasons, their bulky shirts, their short square coats and the scarves which they pulled harshly over their heads and tied under their chins. They strode on the streets arrogantly, pushing and thrusting their way through crowds, their dull eyes fixed.

What shall we do with these animals, when the Republic is restored? thought Durant. They were even more dangerous than men, for they were instinctively of a totalitarian nature and could adjust only to a totalitarian system. Would it be necessary to pass laws to forbid the employment of women in factories in the future or their enlistment in the armed forces? World-madness had made them manifest. In an era of sanity they might disappear, as all anachronisms disappear when the environment becomes untenable to them.

Durant saw that, while he had been thinking, the cars had stopped. He saw a large detached house surrounded by a rain-soaked lawn which in turn was surrounded by a high iron fence. A Picked Guard was opening the gate. The night was so dark that Durant could get only a confused impression of the house, looming against the pouring sky. A window or two was lighted. He got out of his car, and, surrounded by his ubiquitous guards, he walked to the house and entered it as the door opened. He found himself in a small severe vestibule, where the Chief Magistrate was waiting for him.

Arthur Carlson dismissed the guards with a quick gesture, and he and Durant were alone. He gave Durant a slight smile, and then his eyes sharpened. "Has anything happened?" he asked.

Durant said: "I've just heard about Mr. Reynolds'—accident."

"Yes. Unfortunate, wasn't it?" The cold smile shone for a moment in Carlson's eyes. "Some fanatic, no doubt. Who else would give up his own life like that?" He took Durant's arm with a friendly gesture, opened the door and led him into a large and pleasant room, softly lit with lamps. A log fire burned on a brick hearth, and a semi-circular sofa faced it. A woman sat on the sofa, and she turned her head with a smile when the two men approached her. Durant was taken aback, for this pretty woman with the dark-blue eyes and black hair, and clad in a charming gray dress, was Captain Alice Steffens.

She gave her white hand to Durant, and the jeweled rings on it sparkled. "How are you, Colonel?" she asked, and smiled again. "It is colonel now, isn't it?" Durant sat down beside her, and stared. This amused her, and she began to laugh. She glanced up at Arthur Carlson, who was standing near her, and the blue eyes glowed.

"Yes, Alice, it's 'colonel' now," replied the Chief Magistrate. He looked down at the girl and there was a change in his expression, tender yet withdrawn. He turned quickly to Durant and said: "Alice is one of us, as you've probably guessed."

"Department of Women's Welfare," said Durant unkindly, thinking of the barracks he had recently passed, and annoyed for some obscure reason.

Alice touched his arm briefly, and laughed again. "Colonel of the Army of The Democracy," she added. Her face sparkled a little mockingly, as if she found him amusing. Her round white neck was like satin in the firelight. She was all feminine assurance and gaiety, and a sweet perfume hovered over her, a tangible excitement.

"Is your name really Steffens, Captain?" asked Durant, who had begun to watch Carlson with curiosity and understanding.

She smiled. Carlson said quietly: "Is that question necessary, Colonel?"

"No." Durant, embarrassed, began to glance about the room.

The lamps were concentrated in the center, so that shifting shadows filled the corners. In one of these distant corners sat a man, silently smoking. It was hard to see him clearly, but Durant caught an impression that this man was very thin and tall and not young, and that he had a distinguished narrow face and long legs. He puffed at his pipe, the bowl of which he kept in his hand. In spite of the dimness, Durant felt a strength and gentleness in this stranger, and immense intelligence.

Carlson said: "We have another guest, Colonel. Alice's father, Mr. Steffens. Mr. Steffens, Colonel Curtiss."

Mr. Steffens nodded, and said: "Good evening, Colonel." Durant stammered something in return. He liked the sound of Mr. Steffens' voice, for it was strong and gentle and full of thoughtful control. He tried to see the other man's face more directly, but the hand holding the pipe partially concealed it. However, Durant's face was illuminated by lamps and firelight, and it was evident that Mr. Steffens was studying him.

Carlson asked: "Wine or whiskey, Colonel?" He walked to a table on which stood four glasses and two bottles. "Whiskey," replied Durant. He added, inanely, for he was becoming uncomfortable under the scrutiny of Mr. Steffens: "You live here, Captain—I mean, Miss Steffens?"

She nodded graciously. "Yes, Colonel. But my father does not live here." She was no longer smiling. She sighed. When Carlson gave her a glass of wine her fingers touched his, and lingered. He removed them, quickly, and brought Durant his glass. He sat down, but not too near Alice. He said: "It's usually unwise to let our members know each other, but I thought you ought to know who Alice is, Colonel. For the tempo of our work will have to increase rapidly. It will soon be now or never. You can assist Alice, and she can assist you. She has been telling me that the mothers under her immediate jurisidiction are becoming more and more desperate as their younger girls are removed from them and sent into farm labor camps and factories. Some of their letters to their children have been confiscated. And found 'subversive.' Alice has the idea of spiriting the girl-children away so that their mothers won't know their whereabouts, and this will make them frantic."

Alice said, with sadness: "I think it's very necessary to do so, if the women of this country are to revolt soon. Of course, unknown to them, we are keeping a file system of the children's addresses, and the children will be restored to their mothers at the proper time."

"It was the women of Paris, and not the men, who tore down the Bastille," said Mr. Steffens comfortingly.

"All this pain, all this misery," murmured Alice restively.

"We didn't make it. We are trying to destroy it," said Carlson, in a cold and reproving voice. "The people willed it, and we're trying to rescue them from their own wretchedness, and their own stupidity. We're goading them into action. If we fail—and we might very well fail, considering the mentality of the majority of men—we've done our best. We have our own leaders ready when the time comes, and we have thousands of anonymous men and women all over the country quietly inciting the people." His words were reasonable enough, but they were icy with contempt. "I sometimes wonder if the people are worth our efforts." He stared grimly at the fire. "We've lost two hundred good men in the past two months, men we can't spare, for they're the seed corn of freedom. They died—for what?"

Mr. Steffens said, from his corner: "For the Republic, as you've often declared, Arthur. Do you think a nation is an abstract idea, that liberty is a thing apart from man?"

Durant listened to this with surprise. He had never heard that note in Carlson's voice before, so gloomy and so bitter.

Carlson went on, as if Mr. Steffens had not spoken: "We always fail, throughout history. We're always defeated, at the last."

"But we also always triumph, and we always overcome our defeat," said Mr. Steffens. "Colonel, what do you think of all this?"

Durant hesitated. Once more, he thought of his eerie experience in his office. He felt Carlson watching him with sudden and intent interest. "I've often thought as the Chief Magistrate thinks," he admitted. "And then, tonight—"

"I thought there was a change in you," said Carlson, with some amusement. "What happened tonight?"

But Durant could say nothing. He drank from his glass, hastily. Mr. Steffens said: "I remember what Christ said: 'I have compassion on the multitude.' You've never had much compassion, Arthur."

"Compassion?" Carlson laughed shortly. "Compassion for people who allowed their liberty and sovereignty to die, without a struggle, and with complacency? Who permitted totalitarianism to establish itself in America? Who looked at traitors and murderers and never lifted a hand to destroy them? Who elected, and elected, and elected, year after year, criminals and mountebanks and fools who enslaved them more and more? Who bent their heads meekly under every oppressive law, and did not protest? Who, because of spite and envy and greed, allowed brave men to die? Who knew nothing of States Rights, and raised no outcry when these Rights were abrogated by a malignant and centralized Government? Who regarded the slaughter of Negroes and Jews and other minorities with ugly satisfaction? Who eagerly engaged in war after war, and shouted idiot slogans? Are we to have compassion for the millions of these, who everlastingly overthrow liberty and set tyrants over themselves?"

" 'I have compassion on the multitude,' " repeated Mr. Steffens, in his strong and quiet voice.

"Forever?" asked Carlson.

"Forever," agreed the other man.

Durant thought of the farmers, the bureaucrats, the MASTS, the soldiers and the Picked Guards and the depraved women and the timid men. He thought of Andreas Zimmer, and all his tribe, and of Hugo Reynolds. He held his glass in both hands and looked down at the yellow puddle of whisky at the bottom. He said, as if speaking to himself: "That's what I was thinking tonight. And I'm thinking, now, that the good men always hesitate too long and have no strong convictions, but that evil men always act with immediacy and are full of surety. In a way, then, the good men are as guilty of the destruction of a nation as the evil men are. Perhaps they're even more guilty, for they know what honor is, and virtue and decency, and they do nothing about it."

"They're in the minority," said Carlson.

"No," said Durant, shaking his head. "The evil men are in the minority. They just know what they want, and they set out to get it, while the good talk or shrug their shoulders or tell themselves they're helpless. They never are; they're just weak."

He looked up at Carlson. "We could goad and goad the people, and they'd do nothing at all, no matter what happened to them, unless they were, the majority of them, waiting and hoping for deliverance. They haven't any voice of their own. When we give them a voice, they'll explode into action. Even if there were twice the Minute Men there are now in America, they'd be impotent without the people behind them. And the people will soon be behind them. I once thought that when we oppressed the oppressors, they'd rise up and lead the people, themselves." He shook his head again. "That is part of the answer, but only a part of it. The people are the answer."

"Yes," said Mr. Steffens. He blew a cloud of smoke from his pipe, so that his face was completely hidden for several moments. "Colonel, I was once a soldier, myself. I was a four-star general of what was once the Army of the United States. I—shall I say? —retired. That was twenty years ago. I had seen, over a long period of time, the gradual decay of the people's liberties, and the numbing of their conscience, and their indifference to the destruction of their nation. I saw the increasing number of intense, fierce-eyed men going about their dedicated business of establishing totalitarianism in America. And I saw them succeed. They did it with such surety and conviction that the people were persuaded. And I saw good men keep silent. I say, as you've said, that they were the more guilty, for they knew the end and did nothing to rescue the people. Were they afraid? I think not. I think they were cynical. It's strange that good men are cynics, and evil men never are."

He said, to Carlson: "Before the colonel arrived, Arthur, you were speaking of the fact that most of our great natural resources have been blown away in endless wars, and that no scientific discovery of any real good or importance has been announced for over twenty years, with the exception of a few antibiotics, and that the whole business of the world, for decades, has been the business of death and tyranny. Granted that, scientifically and constructively, we've not advanced for these twenty years. But the people remain, and when they are free again they'll make up for the lost time." Durant had the impression he was smiling. "Not even science exists apart from mankind. It isn't an abstract. We'll invent or find new resources, to replace those we've expended in wars."

"Nevertheless, it will take a quarter of a century or more for the world to recover materially and scientifically, and perhaps fifty years for it to recover the morality, stability and peace it had before 1914," said Carlson. "If we take two steps forward, we take one back."

Durant observed that Alice had stretched out her hand toward Carlson and that the latter was not even aware that her fingers were pressed comfortingly over his. The young colonel's deep sentimentality was stirred, and he was irritated that Carlson was so oblivious of all that beauty and love which was being offered him so touchingly. He studied Carlson's sharp profile, and then he was not so certain that Carlson did not know, for there was a shadow, deeper etched than usual, about his eyes and mouth. So Durant, not hearing the conversation about him, gave more of his attention to Alice Steffens, and he was fascinated by this personification of what a woman was meant to be, all gentleness, sweet strength, loveliness and color. He thought of what the proletarianizing of America had done to its women, how it had deprived them of their particular female glory, had drained them of coloration so that they resembled animated figures made of mud. Ideas, then, he thought, can either make man's physical body radiant with splendor; and other ideas, gross and vicious and malignant, can blur all its cutlines and deform it. The disease of the soul was reflected in the flesh. It was not just a theory of priests; it was an actual phenomenon.

Darkness, ugliness, and deformity could not endure the existence, in the same world with themselves, of light and grandeur and beauty. And as evil things are usually more powerful than the good, Russian and American totalitarianism had set out, each in its own way, to destroy what was intolerable to it and which threatened it. That is why, thought Durant, Russian Communism has never created great artists or exalted scientists, and why, for several decades, America has produced nothing glorious and sublime or heroic. The business of totalitarianism was not only the death of the body but the death of the soul.

Durant became aware of Mr. Steffens' voice, and now it seemed to him that that voice was no longer just thoughtful and kind, but full of authority. "Man casts a long shadow only at morning and at sunset. He stands in his own shadow at the height of his noon."

Carlson was walking up and down the room now, as if obscurely agitated, and Durant wished that he had listened these last few minutes. Mr. Steffens was speaking again, and the authority in his voice dominated the room: "If God does not exist, then man is without significance. He is only an animal, and no one need be concerned about him. For only God gives man meaning."

The Chief Magistrate did not reply. He continued to walk up and down, followed by Alice's beautiful and anxious eyes. Then he stopped abruptly before Durant. "Your Guards are ready to take you back to the farm," he said, and his voice was impersonal.

Durant stood up obediently, but annoyed. Why had he been brought to this place at all? Certainly, it had not been a social visit, for Carlson had hardly spoken to him, and Alice had given him only a few vague if charming smiles. It seemed to him that Mr. Steffens, alone, had been interested in him, and that interest had been slight. The business in which they were all engaged was too important for time-wasting, and this evening had been wasted. Durant saluted Carlson, bowed to Mr. Steffens and Alice, and went out, stiffly.

After the departure of Durant, Carlson turned to Mr. Steffens, and smiled. "Well, sir?"

"An excellent young man," replied the other. "He is all that you have said. And more. You've done well, as usual, Arthur. Guard him. I don't think he is expendable."

"We can guard him only so far," said Carlson. "I'll do my best. Of course, at the end, he must take his own chances with the rest of us."

Mr. Steffens left his corner and came into the full lamplight and firelight. His thin face was implicit with authority and strength for all the thoughtful kindness of his eyes. He sat down beside his daughter, and took her hand.

"How much does he know?" he asked.

"Only what I've told him, and what he has discovered himself."

"And I imagine that he has discovered a great deal, Arthur. He has a very active and subtle mind, and a contemplative one. The others I have seen tonight are also fine men, but two of them, at least, are too much inclined to take orders and to act on them precisely. The colonel uses his imagination, and he has rebelliousness in him. Good."

"How do my men compare with the men in the other Sections, sir?"

"There are excellent men in every Section." Mr. Steffens smiled, and the worn furrows in his face became less pronounced. "Don't try to get me to flatter you too much, Arthur." He became grave. "I think, before long, that we can give the signal. More death, I'm afraid, but it has to be done. We'll win; of that, I'm certain."

He looked at Carlson. "Arthur, I must ask you again not to consider martyrdom on your part the only solution. In the coming years, you could be invaluable."

Carlson laughed a little. "The people must have a devil. Remember, they're simple-minded. It would confuse them to have their devil suddenly become a saint. They'd begin to doubt."

Alice turned very white. She stood up, resolutely, and held out her hands to Carlson. "Arthur!"

He looked at her hands, and hesitated. Then he took them, gently, and said: "Alice, I want you to withdraw as local head of the Department of Women's Welfare. I want you to disappear. Go into hiding, before it's too late."

"Why?" she demanded, and held his hands tighter.

He hesitated again, and said: "It would make me happier. Because I'd like to remember, at the last, that you're still alive, and safe. I'd like to think that you'll marry, when it's all over, and that your children will rebuild America."

She said, oblivious of her father: "I want those children to be ours, my dear." Tears began to run from her eyes and over her cheeks.

Carlson shook his head. "That's impossible, Alice. I've told you that so often. What I must do, I must do. There's no room in my life, and never has been, for the things other men have. You know that; you knew that from the beginning."

Mr. Steffens got to his feet and put his arm about his daughter, who had covered her face with her hands. "My darling," he said, "I am beginning to understand. Arthur would not have been able to accomplish what he has accomplished had he not been the man he is. Some men are inexorably born to heroism and martyrdom, and nothing can change that plan. Let him go."

Carlson smiled at him with deep appreciation. "And you'll persuade Alice to leave tomorrow, sir?"

Alice let her hands drop, exhaustedly. "No. I'll stay. Nothing can make me go. Not even if you refuse to see me again, Arthur." She was no longer weeping; her pretty face had become stern. "Let's not talk about it again. As you've said about your men, I'll have to take my chances, too."

"It will make your father very unhappy, Alice."

She smiled sadly. "He must take his chances, Arthur."

Mr. Steffens let his arm drop from her shoulders. He sat down wearily, and puffed at his pipe. They watched him as he stared at the fire. Finally, he spoke: "I'm sixty-five years old. For most of my life I was a soldier. I was retired at my own request, because, I said, my health was failing. But the truth was, as you both know, that I couldn't stand the wars any longer, the senseless and hopeless wars, the permanent militarism, the design for endless death and destruction. When I accepted the mandate of the Conclave that I become President of the United States when tyranny is overthrown in my country, I felt it was my duty to accept. Now, I'm not so sure. I'm not sure I can face, again, the pattern of violence which will inevitably emerge before we can restore liberty and the Constitution and peace. The evil in this nation, and in the world, is so well established now that it won't give up without enormities. Can I face that? Can I remember to be a soldier again, firm and without fear or tiredness? I don't know."

Alice was alarmed, and forgot her own wretchedness. "Father, you were almost elected president at one time, and only fraud and lies defeated you. You were willing, then. Why should you consider changing your mind now, when we need you so?"

He smiled at her affectionately. "I'm not sure a military man should ever be president, let us say, not even a military man who has always hated militarism."

Carlson said, with cold and angry emphasis: "It is because you were a military man who hated militarism that you are best fitted to lead the restored Republic, sir. You would be the first to discover the incipient signs of the disease whenever they appeared."

Mr. Steffens was silent. Carlson waited, then spoke bitterly: "You aren't deserting us now, sir?"

The older man winced, then smiled. "No. I'm not deserting you. I only hope I am strong enough—"

He stood up, drooping, and appeared to have forgotten Arthur and his daughter. His face was the face of an old and disillusioned man, carved by sorrow and suffering. Then, very slowly, his shoulders straightened, and he turned away, walking firmly and stiffly from the room as a soldier might walk to his post. Carlson and Alice watched him go, in silence, and they heard the door close behind him.

The fire muttered on the hearth, and the autumn wind became a roar in the quiet. Before Carlson could move or speak, Alice had put her arms about his neck and pressed her body to his. She did not cry again; she only stood, fiercely silent, and held him to her until he, involuntarily, closed his arms around her and let his cheek fall upon her hair.

"It's no use, Alice," he said.

But she held him and would not let him go.

When Durant entered the vestibule on his way outside, he discovered that his Guards had been changed for two others, younger, quicker and slighter men, and officers. They saluted him, and informed him that they were under orders not to leave him alone at any time, and that they had replaced the first two Guards at the directive of the Chief Magistrate.

"What was wrong with Tim and Jack?" asked Durant irritably. "Sergeants, but good fellows. Why do I need two lieutenants? I'm swarming with men from the regular Army as it is—a lieutenant, two captains and a sergeant."

One of the guards smiled a little disdainfully, but replied with politeness: "We have our orders, Colonel, and the Picked Guard is now your bodyguard." He and his companion saluted, and courteously stood aside, waiting for him to leave the vestibule.

Durant decided he liked neither of his bodyguards, and he debated going back and asking Carlson to be relieved of them. He looked at the Guard at his right, a young man with a lean, smooth face and eyes like polished blue glass. "What's your name, Lieutenant?"

Again the smart salute which had in it the faint scorn of the Picked Guard for the regular army, a scorn just perceptible because it was so elaborately courteous. "Beckett, sir. John Beckett." Durant shrugged, having been fully aware of the scorn, and turned to the other young man, his eyebrows raised. "Sadler, sir. Chard Sadler."

There was something about Sadler which caught Durant's lively attention, something vaguely familiar. Sadler's face was slightly gaunt, with a prominent nose jutting sharply from it. He had a straight thin mouth and brown eyes so inflexible in their expression, and so unyielding as he stared at Durant, that the latter was taken aback. Then even as Durant studied him, the expression went from his eyes and they revealed nothing at all but disciplined blankness. Why, God damn it, thought Durant, he looks as if he hates me!

Disturbed, Durant said: "I've seen you somewhere, Sadler. And you've seen me. Where was it?"

Sadler frowned and tilted his head, puzzled. "I never saw you before, Colonel." He had a harsh, clipped voice, and the intonations were not new to Durant.

"We both arrived yesterday, from Section 2," said Beckett. "We never saw you until tonight, sir."

Durant, still disturbed, went out into the night. The rain had stopped. He got into his car with his Guards, who sat one on each side of him; the driver, a regular Army youth, started the car and they rolled away in silence. Durant almost forgot Beckett on his left, for his whole attention was centered on Sadler. The latter watched everything they passed with the alertness of a savage animal, yet he made no movement of any kind and hardly seemed to breathe. I know I've seen him somewhere, thought Durant, with increasing uneasiness, acutely aware of the intent and unblinking ferocity beside him. It gave him a rueful little satisfaction to make, openly, the sign against the evil eye. If either of the Guards saw the gesture, Durant could not tell. He hoped they did; he hoped they knew what it meant.

Unlike the other two Guards, these could not be drawn into conversation. He was determined that they should not dog him at every moment. He occupied himself with little plans. His aversion for them became almost intolerable. He remembered the compassion he had felt for Tim and Jack, but there was no compassion in him for these two.

The car had to halt at a black and windy corner, for a fleet of mighty trucks was rolling across the intersection, loaded with war materials. They rumbled and roared in the empty darkness, their malignant headlights glaring before them, washing up a tide of livid light on the brick walls and cold windows of the sleeping houses. They passed, and the car went on. Now Durant could see the distant pulsing and ebbing of the fiery chimneys of the war plants; they threw a shadow of dull flame against the cloudy night sky. Infernal fires lit to the mad gods of war, fires which sleeplessly devoured a nation's substance and a nation's life, thought Durant, with a fresh onset of despair. Hurry! Hurry! he said to himself. Almighty God—hurry!

He remembered the news he had read earlier in the day. It was reported jubilantly that Rio de Janeiro and Buenos Aires had been subjected to "another atomic and hydrogen bomb attack by our fliers." So many lies were circulated by the Government that Durant felt a little hope that this was a lie, also. He thought of those white and brilliant cities with their great boulevards and grand parks and statues, and he shivered. According to official reports all this now lay shattered and broken, and the mountains looked down on steaming and blazing ruins. "Three million dead!" the newspapers had screamed. Almighty God, repeated Durant in his heart, let it not be true. The hope died in him, and the despair was a heavy sickness in his flesh. He seemed to see the whole violated world before him, with its smashed cities and polluted fields, and its multitudes streaming in wild hunger from place to place, falling upon each other to kill and rob in their insane frenzy and in ther insane desire to live another hour, another day, another week. Dialectical materialism! Man was paying with his blood, and the reddened earth was paying with him, for the disease which he had embraced. "—pray for us sinners now, and in the hour of our death—" Pray, pray, but hurry, hurry!

"Cigaret, sir?" asked Sadler. Durant, hardly knowing what he did, fumbled with trembling fingers at the package offered him. A light flashed into his face, and he looked into Sadler's eyes. He could not turn away; those eyes hypnotized him. For they had lost their inflexible expression, and were narrowed and curious and reflective, and the hatred in them had gone.

Sadler applied the light to Durant's cigaret, then blew it out. Durant smoked, his throat dry and his heart throbbing. What had he done that had changed Sadler's eyes? What movement, in his distress, had he made? He could not know that, but he knew with stronger and frightening certainty that he had seen those eyes before, and that very look. An impression, dim and fleeting, came to him of greenness and quiet and a voice. What voice? A voice lower and slower than Sadler's and without its harshness.

The car gathered speed in the empty streets, and soon it was rolling out into the country. Absorbed both in his fear and despair, Durant came to himself with a start as the car turned up the driveway of the Lincoln house. Only one light showed in a lower window. His men had gone to bed, and he was alone with the Picked Guards, and he must get rid of them some way. They entered the house, the Guards carrying their packs, and Durant looked about for Dr. Dodge. But the old man was not in sight. Silently, the three men climbed the stairs. Neither Beckett nor Sadler glanced around them with any interest. But when Durant attempted to enter his room first, Sadler murmured something, brushed by him, hand on gun, and turned on the lights. Durant, harassed beyond control, exclaimed: "Good God, do you expect a murderer in here?"

"Orders, sir," replied Sadler. Durant watched him as he walked rapidly to the closets, opened and examined them, and scrutinized every possible hiding place.

"I give orders here, Sadler," said Durant, with exasperation. He sat down on the bed, fuming. Beckett had stationed himself at the door, and Sadler pulled down the shades at the windows.

"We have our orders from the Chief Magistrate, Colonel," said Beckett, staring at Durant with his glassy blue eyes. Durant began to feel excessively foolish and angry.

"I don't know where you fellows will sleep. All my men are on this floor. And you can't expect to get in bed with me!" Durant laughed shortly. "Look, I've lived here for months and nobody's even fired a blank cartridge at me. Why don't you go downstairs and sleep on the sofas, or sit there and look into each other's eyes?"

"One of us can sleep, but one of us must stay awake," replied Sadler. "Orders." He repeated the word mechanically.

"The hell with your orders!" said Durant, getting up. "I can trust my men." He went to the wall and pulled a rope. "I don't know about you, but I'm going to have some whisky before I go to bed. On second thought, it's an 'order' for you, too."

He went to his chest of drawers. In one of them he kept the box of drugs which he had had to use when his broken arm had been healing. Powerful sedatives. Surreptitiously, he palmed two capsules. Both the Guards were watching him with disciplined attention, and he hoped fervently that they had not seen his actions. He opened another drawer, pretended to be searching for something. He overturned a heap of his Army shirts, and then stopped, rigid. Under them was a neat pile of old civilian garments, a shirt, a pair of trousers, a thin coat, a tie.

Durant could feel his face turning white. He smoothed down the Army shirts, and his hands shook. He closed the drawer. It could only be Dr. Dodge, he thought. He turned as a knock sounded on the door. "It's all right," he began, but Sadler had wheeled, had taken out his gun. Beckett's gun was also in his hand, and he was opening the door slowly, poised for action.

Dr. Dodge stood on the threshold, blind and mute and automatic as ever. He gave no sign that he saw either of the Guards or their guns.

Durant muttered an obscenity. "I called for him, you fools. Put away those damned things. You'll scare the old man to death. Dodge, these are my Guards. Don't let them frighten you. They're just boys, playing. It's all in fun. Bring us some whisky."

Dr. Dodge advanced feebly into the room, catching Durant's slight and furtive gesture. "Whisky?" he murmured. He came closer to Durant, then stopped at Beckett's command. Beckett approached, ran his hands briefly over him.

"Leave him alone," said Durant, and caught the old man's arm. "You'll have him fainting on us." He slipped his hand down Dr. Dodge's arm very rapidly, and pressed the capsules into the other's palm. They disappeared immediately from his fingers. Beckett moved away.

It was only clever acting, of course, but Dr. Dodge started from Durant as if struck. "There, you see, you've frightened the hell out of him," Durant said. And then he saw Dr. Dodge's face. The flesh had turned ghastly, the dead eyes had come alive, and were protruding and glittering, blazing with incredulity. The sunken mouth was open and shaking. All at once, the old man began to tremble violently, and a horrible gasping sound came from his throat.

Astounded, Durant followed the direction of Dr. Dodge's eyes. They were fixed on Chard Sadler. Sadler had become as pale as death, and as motionless. Beckett had gone to his post at the door, and was occupied in replacing his gun and tightening his belt.

Then Durant knew. He looked from one face to the other, and he knew. These were father and son. The features he had thought familiar, and the voice he had believed familiar—all this was not his imagination. after all. He was profoundly shocked.

"Something wrong?" asked Beckett, from his post. "What's the matter, Chard?" He made a step toward them.

Durant said, and his voice was hoarse: "There's nothing wrong. You've just frightened this poor old man." He stepped between Sadler and Beckett; he seized Dr. Dodge's shoulders in his hands. He shook him, and turned him so that Beckett might not see his face. "Dr. Dodge," he said urgently, and shook him again. "Don't be afraid. Do you hear me? Don't be afraid."

The old man's trembling became less violent, but he gazed over Durant's shoulder with passionate intensity. He was silent now. Durant could feel Sadler behind him, not moving, only standing there and gazing back at his father.

"Don't be afraid," Durant repeated. "Only my Guards, which the Chief Magistrate assigned to me tonight. Beckett and Sadler." He said, very slowly yet emphatically: "Beckett at the door. Sadler, right here. Sadler."

"Sadler," whispered Dr. Dodge. And then his eyes filled with tears and his mouth worked, and his shoulders, so stiff in Durant's hands, sagged. His head dropped on his chest, and his feeble breath came raggedly.

"What's the matter with the old fool?" asked Beckett, from the door. "Need any help, sir?"

"You've just frightened him," said Durant, impatiently. Then Sadler was beside him. Sadler took Dr. Dodge in his arms. He held him a moment, then dropped him into a chair. He said to Durant without emotion. "It looks as if the old man needs the whisky, Colonel." He looked into Durant's eyes, and Durant saw fear or depression in them.

Durant thought rapidly. He turned to Beckett, who was all alertness. "There's a cabinet in the dining room, against the wall facing the door. You'll find glasses there, and whisky. Better bring them up here. The old man's almost out of his wits because of you fellows. Probably has reason to be, too. Go on, Beckett."

Beckett saluted briskly, and went out, closing the door after him. Durant waited a moment, then tiptoed to the door. He opened it a crack and peered out. The hall was empty, and Beckett's boots were clattering on the stairs. Durant shut the door. Sadler was standing before his father, and they were regarding each other in agonized silence.

"I thought you were dead," whispered the doctor at last. Sadler made a distracted gesture to quiet him. Durant said: "I know, Sadler. You remember I thought I'd seen you before."

Sadler wheeled toward him. Durant recoiled in alarm, with an exclamation. Dr. Dodge caught his son's arm.

"Don't!" he murmured. "We are friends."

"Friends!" muttered Sadler, his hand involuntarily feeling for his gun. "He's reduced you to this, and you call him a friend!"

Dr. Dodge put his hand over his son's. "We must talk fast, Clair." His voice was strong and quick. "I'm here as house labor for Lincoln, a farmer. This young man—" He stopped, and smiled weakly at Durant. "What does it matter? We have no time to talk, now." He laid his cheek against his son's sleeve, and closed his eyes. "My son, my son! I thought they had killed you. They told me that. They said you were dead—caught as a Minute—"

"Hush!" whispered Sadler, with fierce tenderness. He put his hand on his father's head, and Durant saw the fingers trembling. He glanced imploringly at Durant. "I'm sorry, sir. But my father—" He halted.

"Can we trust you, Colonel?" he asked, urgently. "Surely you wouldn't injure this old man more than he has been injured?"

"How could I injure him?" asked Durant. "I've only been a little kind to him. I know nothing about him, except that he is your father. If you enjoy being a member of the Picked Guard, that's your own business." He regarded Sadler without expression.

Sealed in from each other, for the sake of each other, thought Durant. Never knowing each other, never daring to know each other. He made a rapid gesture, and Sadler moved away from his father, and Dr. Dodge leaned back in his chair in a collapsed attitude. A moment later Beckett came in, carrying a tray of glasses and bottles. He placed the tray on a table and regarded the bottles with satisfaction.

Dr. Dodge pushed himself to his feet and tottered to the table. Durant watched him anxiously. He saw one capsule drop into one glass, and sighed with relief. The old man poured the whisky into the glasses, moving as slowly and carefully as possible. His son stood at a distance, inscrutable and still pale. Durant thought: I was probably marked out by Sadler to be killed, when the time comes. I can rest easy about that, I suppose, if Dodge ever has the chance to talk to him. Just the same, it's not a very happy idea.

His thought ran on, while Dr. Dodge carefully added a little water to the glasses. Had Sadler joined the Picked Guards as a self-elected "devil's advocate"? This opened up a vast area for speculation. How many hundreds of thousands, perhaps even millions, of solitary men, on their own initiative, and without assistance from the Minute Men, and without knowledge of the Minute Men, were working in lonely silence for the restoration of the Republic? Herioc men, without friends, unaware that friends were all about them, though unrecognized! Men who had no support, no consolations, no way of knowing that they were not alone!

Should he, Durant, inform Arthur Carlson that Chard Sadler was such an isolated and dedicated man? Or did Carlson already know, and was Sadler ignorant of the Chief Magistrate's information? Remembering Dr. Dodge's attempted mention of the Minute Men, Durant wondered if, after all, Sadler had been a member of that organization. It was very involved. Durant was determined that he would keep his own silence; however, he was deeply apprehensive. What if the sane and heroic men started to kill each other off in a wholesale fashion, under the delusion that they were enemies? Carlson had often spoken of the possibility, but he had implied that this would happen only to the Minute Men.

Durant had another disturbing thought. There was the slightest chance that Sadler, in despair, cynicism and hatred, and hopelessly convinced that the people of The Democracy were not worth saving but deserved all evil, was actually and wholeheartedly a member of the Picked Guard. It was very confusing. The only thing, Durant commented gloomily to himself, is to keep my mouth shut. More men have been hung by their tongues than by ropes.

Dr. Dodge, weak and unsteady, gave Durant his glass. He handed a glass to his son, without glancing at his face. He gave Beckett the drugged whisky. Durant asked his Guards to sit down, sipped at his glass, pronounced the whisky excellent. Sadler dully agreed. Beckett took a long drink, then made a wry face.

"If the colonel will excuse me, I think this whisky is rotten," he said. "Bad taste."

"What do you mean?" demanded Durant indignantly. He drank a little of his whisky with a critical air. "It's wonderful. How about you, Sadler?"

Slowly, very slowly, Sadler's eyes traveled to his father, then to Beckett, and came to settle on Durant. He considered the latter with stony intenseness. Then, as Durant had done, he sipped at his glass. "Tastes all right to me," he remarked casually.

"Give Lieutenant Beckett another dash," Durant directed Dr. Dodge, who had become rigid. The old man started, then brought the bottle to Beckett, and poured another portion into the latter's glass. Beckett drank again. "A little better. But bitter."

"Perhaps it's because we haven't had any decent whisky for a long time," Sadler suggested. He drained his glass. "I thought mine was bitter at first taste, too."

Durant lay back on his bed and held the glass to the light. "I've been better treated than you boys. Best of everything. Nothing too good for the Army."

"That's right," said Sadler impassively. But Beckett scowled, then hastily concealed the scowl in his drink. He drained the glass, and wiped his lips fastidiously with his handkerchief. For the first time, Durant noticed that the young man had faintly effeminate mannerisms. The whisky was beginning to affect him. He regarded Durant with an almost ogling friendliness. "Decent of you, Colonel, to invite us to a nightcap. Not that we can sleep; we're here to guard you."

"Against whom?" asked Durant idly, putting down his glass.

The lean smooth face began to soften and blur. Beckett winked. "Against assassins, sir. The news is out that the people are sick of the Army—begging the colonel's pardon—and that there is a real danger of a sudden and spontaneous revolution. I don't believe that; we've got them too well under our heels. But some of them might start using knives and old guns. We found an arsenal in Section 2 only two weeks ago. Outmoded stuff, but it could be useful—in killing. In fact, five Picked Guards were murdered in one bunch just before we found the arsenal. It wasn't an organized killing, just an insane and impromptu one. You've lost soldiers in your own Army, too, haven't you, sir?" The blurred slackening became more and more evident.

"Over fifty, in the last few weeks," admitted Durant, with reluctance. "Isolated cases, though. In back alleys and suburbs and less patrolled streets. Done by individuals, our investigations showed. We caught two of the murderers, who didn't even know each other."

But Beckett was giggling softly to himself. He leaned toward Durant with a confidential air, and the three men in the room watched him.

"Nobody's going to kill the colonel while we're around," he confided. "Chief Magistrate said maybe there're assassins right in your own office, or in this house. No way of knowing. Maybe your own fellows, in the other rooms." And he made a wide and exaggerated gesture in the direction of the door. "Maybe some of the labor around here. Maybe the farmer who owns the house. Been kicking the farmers around, haven't you, Colonel? Good thing, too. They're being kicked around in the other Sections. Picked up your idea, Colonel?"

"Shut up!" exclaimed Sadler, with hard violence.

Beckett turned to him in surprise. "What's the matter with you, Chard?"

"You talk too much." Sadler got to his feet and began to walk up and down the room. He passed Beckett once, and Beckett put his hand fondly on his arm and restrained him. "Good old Chard," he wheedled. "Never opening his mouth. Nice boy, though."

Sadler stood still. He said, in a slow and penetrating voice, looking at Durant: "Beckett's all right. He's a real picked Guard. Born that way, educated that way, enlisted that way. You can rely on Beckett being exactly what he seems to be."

Durant raised his eyebrows, affecting puzzled innocence.

Beckett raised his empty glass in a gallant but somewhat uncertain salute. "That's right, Chard. Honor of the Picked Guard. Everything for the Picked Guard. The hell with everybody else."

"Good," commented Durant. "Dodge, give the lieutenant another drink." He watched Sadler, alert for any motion of protest or anxiety or concern. But Sadler only nodded, patted Beckett's shoulder. Still, thought Durant, it could be pretense.

Beckett drank from his glass with relish. "The colonel's right," he exclaimed, touching his forehead with a drugged and drunken salute of apology. "Whisky's wonderful." He considered his remark, and was deeply affected by it. His glassy eyes moistened. "Sorry I insulted the colonel's whisky. Apology—"

Sadler, who had been studying his fellow guard with penetrating attention, said: "Johnny, I'll stay up here with the colonel.

There's no guard downstairs. Suppose you patrol the first floor. Anybody could get in."

"Right! Right!" cried Beckett enthusiastically. He stood up, caught the back of his chair, shook his head affectionately at Durant. "Colonel's made me a little whoozy with his damn good whisky. But, as Chard says, you can rely on old Beckett. Won't even close my eyes."

Durant said: "Dodge, go with Lieutenant Beckett downstairs, and make him as comfortable as possible. If he needs anything, give it to him. If you can't find what he wants—come back up here and let me know at once."

Beckett put his arm tenderly around Dr. Dodge's bent shoulders. The old man staggered for a moment, and Sadler made an involuntary movement to go to his assistance. But he stopped it almost at once.

"Don't leave Lieutenant Beckett tonight," said Durant to Dr. Dodge, but looking blankly at Sadler.

With some difficulty, Dr. Dodge assisted Beckett from the room. Then Sadler ran lightly to the head of the stairs, and watched the descent of the two men. Durant could see the apprehension on the young man's face for his father.

"Close the door," said Durant indifferently. Sadler obeyed. He returned to the center of the room, frowning and thoughtful. He picked up Beckett's glass, tasted the dregs. Then he smiled somberly.

"Good whisky?" asked Durant.

"Very good whisky, sir."

Durant got to his feet, yawning. Then, under the eyes of Sadler, he went to the landscape on the wall, and moved it aside. There the thing hung like a big spider, its wires detached and dangling impotently.

"My God!" muttered Sadler.

"Don't let it frighten you," said Durant easily. "It wasn't originally put there because of me, but it remains, because of me. The FBHS spies on everybody, even the Army. So your father and I have a little joke between us: he detaches it before I come back here at night, and attaches it—later. You see, sometimes he and I have talks we'd rather not have overheard." He added: "But your oath, Sadler. You'll probably have to report your father for—irregular—activities, won't you?"

Sadler said nothing. "I didn't attach it, or have it attached, right away, when we came in tonight," said Durant. "I don't know why. I suppose it was because of all the excitement between you and your father. It wouldn't have been so good for you if your conversation had been overheard, would it? Or good for your father?"

He picked up the wires, and sorted them out. "Mustn't rouse their suspicions. They've got it all figured out how long it will take to get here from the city. If we don't begin talking, with this thing attached, they'll start wondering."

"Wait!" cried Sadler. Durant turned to him, as if in surprise. The young man's face was working desperately. "I want to talk to you, Colonel."

Durant went back to the bed and stretched out. "Better not," he said. He glanced at his watch. "In two minutes I'm going to attach that thing, and we're going to talk about something having happened to the car. I don't know, though. Probably an FBHS spy right behind us on the road, or perhaps in this house. Save your breath, and start thinking. We're twenty minutes overdue, even allowing more time than usual to get here."

Sadler came to the bed, and looked down at Durant. "I want to tell you," he began hurriedly. But Durant lifted his hand. "No," he said.

"But you've got to know something, sir!"

"I want to know nothing. I never saw anything. I never heard anything. You're my Guard. The less you talk the less trouble you'll find."

"My father—"

"—is a house laborer. I've been kind to him, in my way. That's all you need to know." He pointed to Sadler's gun, and laughed. "Been planning on using it on me, Sadler?"

There was a silence. Slowly, Durant lifted his eyes to Sadler's face. Then Sadler whispered: "Yes."

For a long time they just looked at each other. Then Durant made an almost imperceptible gesture. At once, Sadler replied with an answering gesture. Durant smiled, and held out his hand. "That's all," he said, as Sadler took it and shook it.

"But don't ever try to have any talks with me, Sadler, in out-of-the-way places." His relief was tremendous. "And remember, don't trust anybody, not even me. Just as I won't trust you. We go our own way, do our own work."

He got up and attached the wires, and said: "Well, Beckett's established downstairs, Lieutenant, and if you have to, you can stay in this room with me. I don't see the sense in it, myself. My men are right on this same floor, and the doors are always locked." He made his voice sound impatient and irritable, and he gestured commandingly to Sadler. "I've wasted too much time, arguing with you boys downstairs."

The young man cleared his throat, then said, almost naturally: "I'm sorry, sir, but orders are orders." He raised his voice, turned in the direction of the landscape, and said, louder: "Nobody will dare to try anything here! But nobody! Not while I'm around, Colonel."

So, there's been some information that the FBHS might try to murder me, thought Durant, with discomfort. Then he laughed silently. Let the FBHS speculate, and wonder. Let them, without any sure knowledge, suspect him. He had a Guard, now, a dedicated Guard, who might, under other circumstances, have contrived to commit a murder.

With considerable satisfaction, Durant undressed and went to bed. Sadler seated himself on a chair with his back against the door. He had insisted on a small lamp being kept lit, and Durant had raised no objection. Sadler's gun was no longer in its place on his hip. He kept it on his knee, and his hand over it. Durant's last impression, before falling asleep, was of a sleepless Guard who would never, even for an instant, take his eye off him. It was a comforting thought.

It was Durant, after all, who conducted the trial of Alex Sheridan for the murder of Andreas Zimmer. Carlson had sent him a message that "urgent reasons connected with security" necessitated his return to New York. Durant was particularly gleeful at the prospect of prosecuting Sheridan, and in this case he was not regretful that ancient procedure, and the guarding of the rights of the accused, had been abrogated by a depraved people. Had they not, ten years ago, eagerly agreed with a malign Government that all "enemies of the people" be dealt with by the Military without the "flummery of legal impediments"? And had they not, at the urging of the President, assented to the dissolution of courts of appeal, including the Supreme Court? Sections of the press had only too delightedly danced in the wake of the debased Government, shouting that the "enemies of the people" constituted all politicians and private citizens who exposed Communists in Washington bureaus and the great labor unions. Other enemies, according to the White House and its subservient press, had been newspaper men who had denounced the growing power of the Military, and men and women who had testified in court as to Communist activities in public means of communication. (Still other "traitors" had been designated as those who belonged to the American Legion, for the Legion had been too vigorous in its condemnations of all radicals, Communists, "progressives," and other nondescript bleeding-hearts and do-gooders with a grudge against prideful and self-respecting men. The Legion had been outlawed.)

Even while "foreign" Communism had been under violent attack by Washington as a prelude to the third World War, the American Communists had received preferred treatment in both public and private employment. All attempts to prosecute them in the courts had come to nothing. Though many of them had been caught in the very act of transmitting vital secrets to Russian agents, their cases had been dismissed, or silence had enveloped them. They had continued to work strenuously and anonymously in the Cabinet, itself, and had directed foreign policy. They had raised their voices only when they had denounced "reactionaries," that is, men and women who were desperately concerned over the growing influence of Communism in every phase of American life. No honorable citizen had been immune from their attacks, which took the form of persecution by various bureaus, including the Bureau of Internal Revenue and local police departments. At the end, these infamous creatures had turned against their milky friends, the so-called "liberals," when the latter had awakened to the nightmare which had invaded their nebulous reality.

It had been piteous enough when the "liberals" had finally understood what they had been enthusiastically supporting for several decades in the name of Socialism or "progressive democracy," or "social justice." When fully confronted by the monster they had helped to bring into being, they had been aghast, and had attempted a pathetic revolt. They had cried a feeble warning to the people. But the warning had come too late, not only for the people, but for themselves. The full fury of the monster had been turned against them, and they had died by the thousands or had fled underground with their mental and physical wounds. For a few years they had hoped that the people might come to their rescue. Their disillusionment had been complete. Hundreds of them committed suicide, not out of fear, but out of despair. Those they had innocently betrayed to tyranny knew nothing of their personal tragedies, or, if they had known, it was with indifference.

Heroic death was not for them. No opportunity came when they could appeal on the scaffold to the unthinking mobs. They were murdered in secret, or they fled in secret. They hid in the universal darkness or occasionally emerged, in silence, to look at the ruins which they had helped to create. They could not join the Minute Men, for they were people without vigor or passion. It never occurred to these numbed and stricken "liberals" to become individual "devil's advocates," for they lacked power and anger. Gentle, unrealistic, without belligerence and indignation, robbed of all faith in "the spirit of the people," unfamiliar with religion, which they had once called "the opium of the masses," they had no fortitude and no sustenance in their anguish. Reality was too much for them; they had lived with dreams too long.

Durant, as a private attorney, had had his practice confined to trivial matters, such as petty theft, divorce, minor crimes, infringements of obscure little patents, vandalism and kindred insignificant affairs. As a private citizen, he had never been present at the Military Court, and knew little of its procedure except that it was abrupt, violent, arbitrary and arrogant. He was given a Military manual, and soon learned that all criminals brought before the Military Courts were accused of one crime only: "Crimes against the People of The Democracy." These "crimes" ran from utterances of discontent in war plants, disrespect toward the

Military by word or gesture or deed, private or public questioning of any Governmental mandate or directive, desperate rebellion against any order issued by any bureau, failure to obey the Military in small or large matters, black-marketing, having in one's possession the ancient flag of the Republic or failure to report friend, relative or neighbor who "unlawfully secreted or reverenced" such a flag, or "uttering, in public or private, any Article or Section, of the former Constitution of the Republic of the United States of America, or teaching it to children or to pupils," to the graver capital offense of murder, or attempted murder, of any Governmental official or member of the Armed Forces, and treason and other "high crimes" directed against the People of The Democracy and their "security."

Each one of these "crimes" had subdivisions and supplementary clauses, so that any citizen, who was considered "dangerous," might be proved guilty under them. Durant studied the manual exhaustively. As an attorney, he had had a brief course in it some years ago, but now it occupied his absorbed interest. When a young man, he had been aroused to loathing contempt upon reading it; now he was enraged. He had always known of this abomination. But it had come closer to him in these last months, and he had applied some of its provisions against the bureaucrats, the MASTS and, especially, to the farmers who were his own province.

It was not a necessity for the Military Court to "prove beyond a reasonable doubt" the guilt of the accused. The Court had only to be "convinced," even without evidence. However, any trial under the manual was given tremendous publicity in the press, in order to assure the people that their "rights" were being fully protected by "their servant, the Military," and to deter them from committing such crimes themselves.

The prosecution and judgment for crimes which did not warrant the death penalty were usually disposed of by the commanding officer of any Section, or his appointed deputy, without assistance from other military officials. But "grave capital offenses" had to be judged not only by the officer of the Section, but also by two lesser officers. Moreover, at least two members of the Picked Guard had to be present. This, said the Government, virtuously, was a provision especially provided "to protect the interests of the accused."

Durant chose Lieutenant Grandon and Captain Edwards for his officers, and John Beckett and Chard Sadler as his Picked Guards. He then had to find an attorney for Alex Sheridan, for alleged criminals were no longer permitted to employ their own counsel. The reason for this was explained with immense nobility: "It is only just that the best counsel be obtained for the accused, who is not always in a position to engage proper defense. Therefore, it is the duty of the State to provide the accused with counsel who can protect the interests of the accused, without cost to the accused." In consequence, men and women brought to trial in the Military Court were represented by counsel drawn from a list of lawyers "whose probity is beyond question, and who have the approval of the State."

Durant studied the list carefully. Those who had "lost" the most cases to the Military Courts had their names prominently marked. Durant noted that these lawyers seemed to have appeared the greater number of times. Durant picked a name which was not only capitalized but underscored, and it needed very little perspicacity to understand that this name was in high favor. He showed it to Grandon, who laughed maliciously, and to Edwards, who remarked that Pellman was a good man, though he never happened to get his man off very often. Further inquiry on Durant's part brought out the information that Mr. Pellman lived in one of the best sections of Philadelphia, had a son in a Government bureau in Washington, and a wife who was an aide to Captain Alice Steffens of the Department of Women's Welfare. For a man who consistently "lost" cases to the Military Court, and whose fee, paid by the State, was comparatively small, Mr. Pellman appeared to be doing very well, indeed.

The arrest and impending trial of Alex Sheridan aroused enormous interest in Section 7. The newspapers polished up their most vituperative adjectives against the accused man. (It was taken for granted that he was guilty.) Durant rightly conjectured that a signal had been given to the newspapers to vilify Sheridan, even though he was the head of the local FBHS, and Durant had his suspicions that the signal had come from Arthur Carlson. Ordinarily, on the rare occasion when the powerful head of a bureau was accused of any crime, the newspapers were wary. If released, such a man might soon be out for revenge against any publication which had denounced him.

The people were very excited. This hated man now stood where so many thousands of their relatives and friends had once stood, and it was very probable that he would face the firing squad, as those relatives and friends had faced them. So many innocent citizens had been tortured by the FBHS, or had "disappeared" at the instigation of Sheridan, that the people could hardly contain their joy. But they had learned to be discreet. They did not mention the name of Alex Sheridan. FBHS spies were everywhere, and if Sheridan were adjudged not guilty even the most poor, the most insignificant or wretched creature, was not safe from bloody reprisal if he had been overheard denouncing Sheridan. However, among those they could trust, the people exulted.

Durant brought the case to trial on a wild and bitter day in November. An early snow blew down like a gray curtain; the wind screamed through the city. As early as dawn, groups of shivering and ragged men and women gathered outside the building where the Court held its sessions. Soldiers, scowling, kept them in line, but did not disperse them. Colonel Curtiss had issued a specific directive that the people be permitted to gather, "in order that they might discover for themselves that the Military Courts were just." No private citizen, of course, was allowed in the building.

They stood there, the people, in a rapidly gathering crowd, silent but expectant. They did not speak to neighbors, but their faces reflected their hope that Sheridan would be condemned to death, and their eyes blazed with eager expectation. They looked for the arrival of Durant and his men, but Durant slipped through a rear entrance, which the soldiers had kept clear.

The immense edifice which housed the Military Court was also the Military prison for civilian offenders against The Democracy. Old warehouses had been torn down to erect this building, which was of gray stone. It stood thirty stories tall; broad and grim, it stared over the surrounding slums. At night, a red beacon on its top, in the form of a pouncing eagle, bloodied the sky. It was guarded at every door by soldiers, and soldiers patrolled outside, and officers came and went constantly in official cars, and black automobiles brought fresh prisoners. No one ever again saw the victims who were dragged behind those ominous bronze doors, except on the very few occasions when they were released after being found "not guilty" of the crime charged. The building had a name: Democratic Justice Department. The people called it The Morgue.

Durant was led through the administrative sections on the second floor, pleasant enough in bronze and paneled wood and diffused light. He entered the agreeable room called "the judge's chambers," where all was warmth, red leather, handsome rugs and polished floors. Here he found Mr. Stephen Pellman waiting for him. The lawyer rose quickly at Durant's entrance, and Durant's first impression was of a flare of white teeth, very big, very prominent, and curved affably. The next impression was of a carefully and expensively dressed man of about forty-five, with a rich pile of gray hair on a high skull, a tiny little nose, a gleaming forehead, and a pair of sparkling and mendacious brown eyes. Durant felt those eyes sweep over him, catalogue him, and consign him to a particular niche. He guessed, with considerable intuition, that Mr. Pellman had decided that he was not in the least formidable and not very intelligent. He was so far right that in less than four seconds Mr. Pellman had conjectured that he would be on the way home in little more than an hour.

The presence of Beckett and Sadler did not disconcert Mr. Pellman. He was not in the least afraid of them, and gave them no more than a second flare of teeth and a quick glance. He would have refrained from bestowing even these on the men had he not observed that they were officers. He waited until Durant had seated himself behind an absolutely blank desk, and then sat down, himself, with a care for the crease in his trousers.

Durant let his eyes become empty and glazed, as he contemplated the lawyer. He put a cigaret in his mouth, and Sadler lit it for him. He puffed at the cigaret, and continued his contemplation. The flare of teeth came and went, each time a little less brilliantly and a little more mechanically. A very bright scoundrel, thought Durant, looking more empty second by second. He watched his cigaret smoke curl idly in the warm air. The gray snow blobbed against the tall windows; the winter gale swept by in a long gray swirl. Hurrying footsteps sounded in the corridor, a subdued voice. But everything was silent in the chamber; the Picked Guards stood on each side of Durant, and regarded Pellman stonily.

Then Durant said: "Pellman?"

The smile flashed out electrically to its full capacity. Pellman half rose and stretched his hand across the desk. "Colonel Curtiss!" he cried, and Durant noticed that he had a full and singing voice. Durant gave the big pink hand a brief shake, then dropped it. Pellman sank back in his chair, disconcerted.

"You've seen your client on a number of occasions?" Durant asked idly.

"Indeed, yes, Colonel! Several times. I've gone into the case extensively."

"Well?"

Mr. Pellman's face took on the solemn curves of distress. He affected to hesitate. He sighed. "I shall do my best for Mr. Sheridan," he said.

Durant watched the cigaret smoke again. He knew that Pellman was waiting for a signal. He allowed him to wait. Then he remarked: "I covered this case, myself, from the beginning. It's a queer one. Sheridan has a prominent position in this Section. Tell me, what do you think of Sheridan, personally?"

Pellman was confused. Had he been told to defend this case honestly, an almost unprecedented event, or had he been told to lose it? He had listened to Durant's intonations, the shading of his words, and was baffled. He cleared his throat. "Well, Colonel, I have known Sheridan for a long time—" He paused, and waited again for another clue.

"Would that prejudice you for or against him?"

"I shall do my best for Mr. Sheridan," he repeated. "I haven't any prejudice for or against him." Then he was desperate. "Should I have?"

"What?" asked Durant.

Pellman was silent, but he watched Durant closely. During old Major Burnes' tenure, victims frequently escaped with their lives or a small sentence, and a lawyer had only to watch the old major's face, which usually expressed disgust and loathing for his work and sympathy for the accused, to know how to plead the case. Before Major Burnes, the commanding officer of the Military Court had been a malign individual, nicknamed "Old Thumbs Down" by the irreverent, and under his jurisdiction, too, matters had been simple for the lawyers. But this new man—was he a dull military fool, as he, Pellman, had at first decided, or was there something sinister and elusive about him? There he sat, just staring, and saying again: "What?" Pellman smiled, but his teeth barely glittered. "I just said that I haven't any prejudice for or against Sheridan. I shall just do my best."

"Good," said Durant, pleased with the other's discomfiture. He walked out of the room without another word, followed by his Guards. Pellman watched him go. What was he to do? How was he to conduct this case? He would just have to try to catch clues from this man as the matter proceeded. He suspected that Durant had baited him. If so, this was alarming. His very position depended upon pleasing the commanding officer. He caught up his briefcase and hurried toward the courtroom.

The day of the large public courtroom was gone. The Military Court was held in a chill room hardly more than thirty feet square. It contained the commanding officer's bench, the chairs of the accused and his counsel, a single long bench for the witnesses, and a row of stiff seats for newspaper reporters which were rarely occupied, and only when the commanding officer permitted. Below the judge's bench were two chairs for the other officers who assisted in capital cases.

Because of the "gravity" of this case, the immense excitement it had aroused, and the prominence of the defendant, the reporters' seats were already filled with newspaper men; photographers stood beside them, tense with expectation. Grandon and Edwards were seated, with properly solemn expressions. On the bench for the witness sat four men, stolidly gazing before them. At Durant's entrance with the Picked Guard, all stood up. Lights went on and revealed in full the utter starkness of the room. Behind the judge's chair hung the flag of The Democracy, flaccid in the cold air. The wintry gale hammered the barred windows. Durant seated himself, and his Guards stood beside him. He acknowledged the presence of Grandon and Edwards, and they saluted and sat down. Soldiers stood along the walls, guarding the doors, their rifles ready in their hands. Now the atmosphere quickened. Durant examined the papers on his desk with deliberation, rereading his own reports of the case. The accused was in his seat, and Mr. Pellman leaned toward him in his own chair. There was no need, in these days, for tables and many papers. Even capital cases rarely continued longer than three hours, and there was little ceremony and no rebuttals and no "objections." No matter what the commanding officer might say, no lawyer was permitted to challenge him. There was no jury to be convinced or swayed or confused. Oratory must be directed at the military judge, who could cut it short if he desired, make his decison, and leave with nothing more to be done. From his decision there was no appeal. The two officers under him might ask a few questions to clarify the situation, but they had no other function.

Slowly, Durant lifted his eyes and scrutinized everyone in the courtroom. The reporters scribbled feverishly, recording his appearance and expression. The heavy silence lay over everything like a mist of death.

Alex Sheridan sat rigidly in his chair. He was a small gray man, middle-aged and slender, with wisps of hair on a small tight skull, long thin features intelligently and delicately set, and pale sunken eyes withdrawn behind his polished glasses. As Durant studied him, he straightened even more, and there was a natural dignity in that movement. It was hard to believe that this man, so inconspicuous, so quiet of manner and face, was a murderer and a creature of dread to millions of people. Though Durant had talked with him several times, it was incredible to him, still, that countless thousands had died at his ruthless word. For Sheridan appeared to have all the well-bred reticence and gentle thoughtfulness of a kindly schoolmaster, or a clergyman, or a secluded scholar of famous reputation, and his voice was reserved and modulated, his conduct temperate.

Durant forgot everyone else in the room but this man, and Sheridan regarded him in turn with a detached remoteness such as one bestows on a stranger. Durant thought of all Sheridan was, and all that he had done. Suddenly, unable to control himself, his face blackened. His eyes glowed in the stark lights overhead. Pellman, watching him with absorption, relaxed happily. He had his clue. That intense expression of hatred, that bitter mouth, was enough for him.

Durant returned to his papers, and was amazed that his hands trembled so, and that there was such a constriction in his chest. He manipulated the papers into a neat pile, looked up and addressed space.

"How does the defendant plead?"

Pellman got to his feet, and his whole figure drooped with sadness. In a dolorous voice, he said hesitatingly: "Not guilty, Colonel Curtiss."

The faintest shadow of a smile touched Sheridan's gray lips. He knew that he had been judged and condemned to death during those moments when he and Durant had regarded each other in that pressing silence. He did not shrink or tremble. He only sat beside his lawyer, his hands folded neatly in his lap, his eyes contemplating the distance thoughtfully.

Durant snapped: "First witness. Alfred Schultz."

Schultz rose clumsily, approached the bench, and stared

truculently at Durant. He was a big fat man, untidy and none too clean, and there was defiance in his manner.

"Your occupation?"

"I'm a tavern keeper, sir."

Durant said: "It won't be necessary to ask too many questions of any of the witnesses. Schultz, look about you and identify those who were in your tavern until closing hours on the night of the murder of one Andreas Zimmer."

Schultz wheeled slowly and turned to the witnesses' bench. He pointed to one man, a short, stout fellow with graying yellow hair, a large intelligent face and narrowed blue eyes. "Mr. Schaeffer." He pointed to another. "Mr. Kirk." Mr. Kirk was an emaciated man in his thirties, with a cynical mouth and the long features of a hunting dog. Schultz then pointed to the third man on the bench, an old and wizened man with old-fashioned pince-nez and neat, old-fashioned clothing. "Mr. Goodwin."

"Look at the defendant," directed Durant, noting that Mr. Goodwin's wrinkled old face had become passionate with indignation as he returned Schultz's gaze. The other witnesses smiled a little, exchanging furtive glances.

Schultz looked directly at Sheridan. "Was the defendant with the three witnesses at any time, at any hour, of the night of Zimmer's murder?" asked Durant.

Schultz drew a deep and beery breath. He met Durant's eyes belligerently. "No, sir, he wasn't."

Schaeffer and Kirk were called, denied, without emotion, that Sheridan had been with them and Goodwin. At their testimony, Goodwin's indignation increased, and he wriggled on his chair. Pellman, drooping with sorrow, questioned them gently, and then, with an excellently acted gesture of resignation, sat down again.

Durant had questioned Schaeffer, first assistant to Sheridan, and Kirk, second assistant, several times. Their story had never changed; they had answered him easily and quietly. Who were they? What were they, that they should lie and put their director in jeopardy? Schaeffer, perhaps, might covet Sheridan's power, for he was next in line for the position. But Kirk? Kirk was an enigma. The two men seemed to have some secret understanding. Durant studied them keenly, and they looked back at him with open interest and bland eyes.

Sheridan had listened to their testimony with frozen indifference. He had not even turned in his lawyer's direction when Pellman had questioned the men. He displayed no interest whatsoever. Sometimes he examined the gold signet ring on his hand, and sometimes he glanced at the stormy windows. If he expressed anything at all, it was cultured politeness.

Then Mr. Goodwin was called; and the frail old man almost ran to the bench in his indignant eagerness to be questioned. He looked up at Durant, and quailed for an instant. Then he gathered his slight body together and threw back his head. Under questioning, he insisted, in a high shrill voice, that he and Sheridan and the two other witnesses were all together on the night of the murder, and did not separate until dawn. He became more excitable as he talked. He made the stiff fierce gestures of the elderly when they are emotionally involved, and angry. An honest man, thought Durant. He probably believes that he is serving a free and righteous and democratic State, and he serves fervently, meticulously, and with all his heart and mind. Durant's eyes lightened with dreary pity and tenderness. Then he saw that Sheridan was gazing at the man who was defending him with gray and shadowy contempt.

Durant said, sharply: "That's enough, Goodwin. You're screaming. You are either mistaken about the night, or you are lying. Which is it?"

Goodwin quivered with wrath. "I'm not lying, and I'm not mistaken, sir! I'm telling you the truth, the whole truth, and nothing but the truth, so help me God!"

The old words, so long forgotten except by the old, so strange in this Court, struck poignantly on Durant's ear. He regarded the old man with deep sadness. There had been no oaths taken by the witnesses, for this formality, too, had been set aside. But Goodwin had raised his gnarled and shaking hand in the resolute gesture of the ancient oath, and his wrinkled face blazed. The newspaper photographers took a second picture of Goodwin, and the reporters scribbled more feverishly than ever, and grinned derisively.

Durant suppressed a compassionate smile. "How old are you, Goodwin?"

"What has that to do with it, sir?" quavered the old man, who had forgotten his fear. "I'm seventy-one, but I'm not senile, and I've been in the Government service for fifty years. I do my work well, I hope and believe, and have full possession of my faculties."

The newspaper reporters wrote: "Colonel Curtiss showed great consideration for Goodwin, who was incoherent and revealed every sign of senility, and apparently had no respect for the Military. The colonel was much amused when the old man, to emphasize his point, employed an oath long abandoned."

Goodwin turned slowly and scrutinized his fellow bureaucrats. He frowned at them, made a vague gesture of pleading. They merely smiled a little. Goodwin returned to Durant, and in a decisive and heart-broken voice, replied: "They're lying, sir. I don't know why, but they are. I—I don't understand it. Mr. Schaeffer and Mr. Kirk always liked Mr. Sheridan, I guess. They—they were good friends. Always together; used to meet for cards at each other's houses. And I—"

"Yes?" said Durant gently.

The dull flush of the old stained Goodwin's cheeks. The veins swelled in his concave temples. "Well, sir, I worked for both Mr. Schaeffer and Mr. Kirk. I didn't see Mr. Sheridan very often. I—I don't think he liked me very much." He glanced at Sheridan, imploringly. "But I did my work well, and Mr. Schaeffer, especially, always seemed to like me. He used to give me as much as two hundred dollars on Christm— I mean, on Democracy Day, December twenty-fifth." He was trembling more and more. "So, when Mr. Schaeffer and Mr. Kirk and Mr. Sheridan went to that tavern, Mr. Schaeffer used to invite me. Once, when my wife was sick, he sent us some extra blankets. I surely liked Mr. Schaeffer, sir! And Mr. Kirk, though he came only three years ago, was considerate, too. I—I just don't understand, sir." Tears rushed to his eyes, and he blinked them away, his features quivering with distress. Then, embarrassed, he straightened resolutely.

Schaeffer and Kirk listened intently to the old man's words. They watched him with pitying kindness, then exchanged glances. Their eyes flickered.

Durant recalled both Schaeffer and Kirk to the bench. He said: "You've heard Goodwin. What is your opinion? He bears neither of you any malice; in fact, he is deeply grateful to you."

Schaeffer's large face softened. He replied: "Remember, he's seventy-one, sir. And old people forget. It's true we four were together, but that was two weeks before the murder."

"He often forgets things," added Kirk. "He's old enough to have been retired years ago. I've spoken of this to Mr. Sheridan several times. However, we came to the conclusion that Goodwin's small pension wouldn't support him and his wife. Then," added Kirk, with the utmost solemnity, while his eyes bored into Durant's "the President has said—again—that we must prepare for the new conflict with our—enemies. Unity! Duty! Sacrifice! Every man must be available."

Durant was silent; he kept his face expressionless. Then he scratched his chin. "Ah, yes, of course. Unity! Duty! Sacrifice!" He motioned to Pellman. "Your witness."

Schaeffer and Kirk went back to their seats. For the first time Sheridan displayed interest. He turned in his chair and examined his erstwhile aides. They met his eyes; their own changed subtly, and Durant was not too surprised to see their cold hatred and derision. Sheridan smiled almost imperceptibly, settled his elbow on the arm of his chair and contemplated nothing, again.

Mr. Pellman came to Goodwin. He was all solicitude and sorrow. "You must have a certain point of reference in your mind, Mr. Goodwin, which fixes that night in question in your memory. Will you please tell us what it is?"

Goodwin hesitated, bewildered. "Why, uh, it was one of the nights—we used to go to the tavern on certain nights—once a month. I was used to it. Of course, sometimes I wasn't invited, but that wasn't Mr. Schaeffer's fault. My wife is often sick, sir." His lips trembled, dried. He moistened them.

"Was your wife ill around that time, Mr. Goodwin?"

"Well, sir, she was just recovering. She said I could go. She liked me to have the outings."

"How soon was it, after her illness, that this party assembled in the tavern?"

The old man was silently and frantically searching his memory. Then he stammered: "Maybe a week, maybe two weeks."

"Then," interrupted Durant, "you can't set the positive date?"

"Yes, I can!" Goodwin cried, with spirit. "I remember reading about Mr. Zimmer's death, and I thought to myself: 'It was last night, while we were in the tavern.' "

Schaeffer said, from the bench: "May I ask Goodwin a question, Colonel?"

Durant paused, then made an assenting gesture. Schaeffer walked casually to the old man, smiled at him with encouragement. "Goodwin, do you remember the Pinchard case? Do you remember discussing it with me, and coming to the conclusion that Pinchard ought to be arrested?"

Goodwin nodded. "Yes, Mr. Schaeffer."

"Well, then, we had that discussion two weeks before the murder. We had it the day before we had the party at the tavern."

Goodwin gazed at him with protruding eyes. "Are you positive, sir?" He was shaking again.

"I can show you the report, Goodwin."

The old man was speechless. Schaeffer took him by the arm. "There, now, don't let it upset you." He appealed to Durant. "I'm afraid he's going to collapse, sir."

"Let him sit down, then." Schaeffer led Goodwin, who was tottering with agitation, back to the witnesses' bench. Once seated, the fragile old man turned his fearful and pleading gaze from Kirk's face to Schaeffer's, his mouth working. Both men nodded to him kindly, and Kirk put his arm protectingly over the narrow shoulder.

Durant cleared his throat, and went on with pompousness: "The FBHS is under my jurisdiction in Section 7, though it operates more directly from Washington than any other bureau and has its own directives, though it must try all its cases before the Military Court. I want it on record that the Military is concerned only with justice, no matter the bureau or the person or the accused, or any other institution or citizen."

Goodwin was wiping his shriveled face and hands, and listening. His lips twisted like a child's. He said, almost inaudibly: "I'm too old. I forget. No one needs me any more." He pressed his handkerchief to his eyes in a gesture of simple grief.

Durant addressed himself to Stephen Pellman. "You may speak in behalf of the defendant."

Pellman rose. He moved with dramatic slowness to the bench. Every gesture, every movement, expressed his dejection and his courageous dignity. He held up his big hand, and paused while the lights flashed again. He drew a deep breath. He turned eloquent eyes upon Durant. Then his voice, sonorous and ringing, filled the courtroom; and every pen began to scribble frenziedly.

"Colonel Curtiss." Pellman bowed deeply to Durant. "Whatever any speaker of falsehoods might say, it must be evident to everyone in this room that the commanding officer is a gentleman of tolerance and consideration, giving every advantage, straining every opportunity for fairness, in behalf of the defendant. Neither Mr. Sheridan, nor I, can cavil at one word, nor challenge any statement, of the commanding officer. We accede to that; we admit that with respect and gratitude."

He stopped; he was overcome by his emotions. Sheridan began to smile his gray shadow of a smile.

"We are faced by insurmountable difficulties. We have the statements of both Mrs. Zimmer and Mrs. Sheridan. The poor ladies, naturally prostrated, were in no condition to appear at this trial. Mrs. Zimmer can offer only hearsay evidence, received from her husband's lips, that her husband told her of the impending visit of Mr. Sheridan. Mrs. Sheridan's testimony, in the preliminaries, means nothing insofar as our case is concerned. She states that her husband returned shortly after dawn. I preferred not to have her appear, even if she had been able to do so."

He whirled out a fine linen handkerchief and applied it to his face in a mopping gesture of despair, and paused again while his photograph could be taken. Then he spread out his hands, surrendering, to Durant.

"There are three witnesses against my client, and only one witness for him, a witness, treated very tenderly, who has virtually admitted that he might be wrong. What can we say, Colonel Curtiss? To reiterate that my client is not guilty would put me in an absurd position. I prefer not to waste time in urgent denials. And so"—and he gestured dramatically—"we throw ourselves on the mercy of the commanding officer. We plead with the commanding officer. He has demonstrated his boundless capacity for mercy and patience and justice. We ask him to remember Mr. Sheridan's long and faithful service to The Democracy, his unrelenting and steadfast devotion to its principles, his inexorable administration, his brilliant performances in the past. Surely, these must be taken into consideration. We do not admit his guilt, as such. If, in a moment of passion, or in the belief that Andreas Zimmer was dangerous to our country, he killed him—or, should I say?—he executed him, ought he to be punished for this act?"

Durant listened in silence. He chewed his thumb nail, then suggested: "Execution is not a private affair. If Mr. Sheridan were convinced of Zimmer's guilt, he ought to have delivered him to justice. Besides, there is no evidence of Zimmer's treachery. I have Mr. Sheridan's statement that he never knew the man, had seen him only at a distance."

Mr. Pellman sighed mournfully, shaking his head. "I cannot circumvent or set aside Mr. Sheridan's admission. Again, Colonel Curtiss, we can only throw ourselves on your bountiful mercy, and beg you to remember Mr. Sheridan's faultless and dedicated administration. A prison term, perhaps—"

Durant was tired of him and his theatrics. "Andreas Zimmer was equally dedicated and devoted. He was murdered horribly, for no reason we can discern, unless it can be a despicably personal one. In order not to prejudice your client, I shall not suggest that perhaps Mr. Sheridan is not what he seems, and that he is an enemy of The Democracy, murdering those who adhere to its laws and serve them without question. No, I shall not suggest that. It would be unfair. Let your client, if he wishes, take the stand in his own defense."

Mr. Pellman was all joy. He bowed again to Durant. He bounced rapturously on his toes, and flung out his arm to Sheridan. "Mr. Sheridan, sir, take the stand! This has rarely happened before, in my experience. Defend yourself, sir!"

Sheridan did not move for a few moments, and more photographs were taken of him. Then, with a faint gesture of well-bred scorn and impatience, he got to his feet and approached the bench. He stood there, gently patrician, his eyes gleaming behind his glasses. He smiled with amusement. He studied Durant, and his pale lips curled.

"The Military Court," he said deliberately, in his modulated accents, "is determined to destroy me. The colonel has his own motives, which I am not interested in questioning. But the colonel must understand that I have some faint suspicion of those motives."

"Mr. Sheridan!" protested Pellman, in tones of wretched sorrow.

Sheridan gave an aristocratic gesture of disgust. "I don't need your oratory, Pellman. Don't you remember? I know you too well; I've used you, myself, too often."

He directed all his attention at Durant: "There is no use, of course, in attempting to defend myself. The effort would be ridiculous. Nevertheless, the colonel is as sure as I am that I am not guilty of the murder of Andreas Zimmer."

The men in the courtroom were aghast, and looked incredulously at each other. Pellman withdrew from the vicinity of his indomitable client as from an obscenity. But Durant smiled darkly. "The defendant is wrong, very wrong. I know he is guilty of murder."

"The colonel might be convinced that I am guilty of what he might call murder," said Sheridan, softly, coming a little closer to the bench. "But not of Zimmer's murder."

"You might elucidate," suggested Durant.

Sheridan shrugged. "The colonel came only recently to this Section. The colonel is an equivocal gentleman. A gentleman," he repeated, and his colorless eyes surveyed Durant mockingly. "But, of course, the colonel will never be questioned."

Durant was startled, and his throat tightened. But he said, stolidly: "Go on. I am at a loss to understand you, Mr. Sheridan. However, a man in your position can be ambiguous. I was sent here, as you know, by the Chief Magistrate, Arthur Carlson. So, I will dismiss your remarks." He said to the newspaper men: "Mr. Sheridan is not himself. You may delete what he has said these last few minutes."

Sheridan's calm smile widened briefly. "The colonel confirms my opinion." Then his quiet face became stern. "I wish the colonel to know that I do not intend to plead for mercy, or grovel. I really prefer to die. For the colonel must understand that I can live only in an environment I have chosen, which is an environment natural and suitable to me. Outside that environment, I could not exist." He paused, and now the pale eyes were steady on Durant's face. "The colonel would not be here, and would not have his power, if an era which I could not endure is not about to appear violently. It would be untenable to me, to my nature. The colonel will be doing me, not only a great honor, but a great mercy, in condemning me to death."

Durant said, and felt his words were inane: "The defendant fears further strengthening of the Military in The Democracy?"

Sheridan laughed a little. "I wish the colonel very good luck," he said, with reserve. "There is no static society, I see. I knew there would be an end some day. I prefer not to be alive when that end arrives. The colonel is a young man. He will eventually be disillusioned. It's regrettable, just as it is regrettable for me, now. However, I am somewhat tired, and I loathe the thought of the future. I loathe, in truth, all that the colonel represents."

Durant addressed the press weightily: "You have recorded that Mr. Sheridan is strongly apposed to the just dispensations of the Military, and is an enemy of the Military?"

The newspaper men nodded vehemently. Sheridan laughed again, then appeared thoughtful. However, he said no more.

Durant let a very dramatic silence fall. "Much has been revealed here. Mr. Sheridan has practically admitted to murder. Worse, perhaps, he has admitted that he is a traitor in his heart." He struck his hand on the bench. "Therefore, with regret, I must condemn Mr. Sheridan to death, and to order his execution, at dawn. In the meantime, I order that he be confined to solitary confinement and that he receive no visitors."

Sheridan said, with surprise: "Does the colonel fear that I might speak—to anybody? The colonel is naïve. The colonel does not know that I no longer care. I have done with the future, and I know, now, that the future is inexorably approaching."

He went back to his seat, composed and uninterested, and again remote.

Durant looked down at his aides. "Captain Edwards; Lieutenant Grandon. Have you questions?"

They shook their heads in the negative. "Then, I hereby order Mr. Sheridan to be delivered to the soldiers who are his guards, and conveyed to his cell."

He stood up. He could not help glancing at Schaeffer and Kirk. They were smiling, but only a little, and they considerately did not look at Durant. He waited until Sheridan was surrounded by the soldiers and taken out of the room. Only then, did he leave, himself.

Durant, for some reason he could not explain, felt a repulsion at the idea of returning to his offices immediately. So he went to the judge's chambers, sat down and began to smoke. He felt suddenly ill and beset and outraged. He asked his Guards: "Well, how did it go?"

Sadler replied imperturbably, his face noncommittal: "Wonderful, Colonel. You gave Sheridan every opportunity." Then he smiled.

Beckett was more enthusiastic. "Seeing it was the colonel's first trial, it couldn't have been better. Why, I've seen trials in Oregon; disposed of in fifteen minutes, and the defendant never even called or permitted to testify! Rough, sometimes." He gave Durant a light for his cigaret; the glaucous blue eyes had a queer expression of satisfied awareness, which Durant could not interpret. He did not like Beckett, and this was not only because of his implied effeminacy on occasion. In truth, he was unable to say why he disliked the Guard, who was handsome, efficient and intelligent.

He said restlessly: "I'd like to look over Sheridan's dossier again. Beckett, would you ask the warden for it? And tell him that I'd like to have Sheridan in these chambers in about half an hour."

A curious look passed very rapidly over Beckett's face, but he saluted and went out. Durant made an abrupt gesture to Sadler, who nodded, and began, very rapidly and systematically, to examine every portion of the room, searching under the carpets, through the desk, under chairs, and behind the fine engravings on the walls. He lifted the telephone, delicately touched its underplate. He ran his fingers along baseboards, under windowsills, climbed on a chair to examine the fastenings of the blue velvet draperies at the windows. He tapped the walls, listened intently for hollow echoes. He pressed down heavily on the leather sofa, testing it. Then he shook his head at Durant. "So far as I can see, there's nothing. Probably because the room isn't used very much. No papers in the desk, no marks on the blotters."

Then he went out and closed the door behind him. Durant listened, straining for a sound and saying a few words. Sadler returned, lifting his eyebrows questioningly. "I couldn't hear your voice, so it's soundproofed," he said. "Hear me?" Durant answered with a shake of his head. He relaxed. "Found out anything about Beckett, Chard?"

"Nothing at all. We've been together for four years, in the Guard. He's just what he seems to be. I've visited his family in Oregon—successful lumber merchants. He wanted me to marry his sister." Sadler smiled again.

Durant said restively: "Sounds all right. But there's something about him—Chard, you haven't been stealing out to speak to your father at any time, have you? Nothing Beckett could put his finger on, or suspect?"

"No. I know, sir, that a man in your position can't trust anybody, and I must remind the colonel that he, himself, told me that I wasn't to trust him, either."

Durant laughed. The door opened and Beckett, exuding good nature and efficiency, came in with a folder and laid it on Durant's desk. Durant began to read, trying to find, again, some clue which would tell him why Sheridan was what he was. So far, the clue had evaded him. Sheridan was sixty. His father had been a professor of English Literature at Harvard, and had evidently enjoyed a fine reputation. His mother had been graduated from a now defunct women's college. Sheridan was their only offspring, and, judging from the famous schools he had attended, they had cherished him. He was graduated from Harvard. An excellent student, apparently, and even of the genius type. Law at Yale. Those were the years of the Depression. Had that young man been tremendously moved at the plight of a destitute and desperate people? Durant considered this for an instant, then dismissed it as absurd.

Sheridan had married the daughter of a wealthy copper and aluminum fabricator and he had joined the legal staff which that manufacturer employed. Those were the days of strikes; President Roosevelt had not been able to restore any semblance of real prosperity to the nation. His regime had been strengthened and consolidated and made infinitely powerful by war. Sheridan's father-in-law had extracted enormous profits from that war. Was that a clue? Durant mused. No, Sheridan was not a man to be disgusted by war. He had not served in that conflict, nor in the others that had followed; he had remained with his father-in-law the time, when he joined the FBHS. An even enough record; a smooth account of a success story. His relations with his wife were excellent. In private life, and in Government, he had proved able and even brilliant. His friends were many. Evidently he had made no enemies, except in the case of those he had prosecuted as head of the FBHS.

His wife had inherited a fortune, and as her father had been a member of the MASTS she had been permitted to keep the major part of that fortune. Her brothers were still engaged in the business. So, no poverty anywhere, in Sheridan's history, no strife, no objective stress. Durant lay back in his chair, and thought. The clue to Sheridan, as Sheridan had, himself, said, was in his own nature. What was that "nature"? Something stirred uneasily in Durant's memory, but refused to surface. What does it matter to me what he is? he asked himself. It's no concern of mine. In less than twenty-four hours he'll be dead.

Nevertheless, he wanted to know. This demand in himself was not mere curiosity; he believed that if he understood Sheridan he would know what motivated so many men like him in the service of The Democracy. It was necessary for the nation to understand such men so that they could be recognized immediately on appearance and rendered harmless.

The door opened silently, and Sheridan appeared. Durant said at once, to Beckett: "Stand outside, and see that no one interrupts us." Was it his imagination, or did Beckett's face really tighten, his eyes really narrow? It was just a fleeting impression, gone in an instant. Beckett saluted and went out, shutting the door after him. Sadler remained.

"Sit down, Sheridan," Durant directed. Sheridan sat down on a leather chair, and simply waited with that remote and polite patience of his, a gentlemanly patience conferred on a rather boorish stranger. I must suffer the intrusion of this person, implied his attitude; very tiresome, but it must be endured, I suppose, for the sake of the amenities. Durant's collar became warm.

He indicated the dossier on his desk. "I've been reading this again," he said. "I wanted to reassure myself that no injustice had been done to you today."

"Indeed," murmured Sheridan. "Very kind of you, Colonel."

"Aren't you interested in my final conclusions?"

The gray eyebrows lifted quizzically. "I thought you came to your conclusion long ago, Colonel."

Durant studied him, leaning back in his chair. He could find no immediate words.

"Perhaps I might be able to assist the colonel," Sheridan said, gently. "The colonel is a young man. Faithful—shall we say?—to his faith. And a very young man. The colonel is puzzled; he won't be puzzled when he is my age. In short, the colonel, who has studied my dossier very carefully, as only a lawyer would study it, or one with a lawyer's mentality, is wondering why I am what I am. Is that correct?"

Durant felt both foolish and alarmed. "Yes," he said, and his voice was unnecessarily loud.

Sheridan laced his delicate fingers on his knee. "I'm afraid the colonel, who I have heard is not an admirer of psychiatry, nevertheless has absorbed some of that science. He believes there is an explanation for all human behavior, that men are not born as they are but are made what they are by environment. He also believes in heredity. Now, may I ask the colonel if he found anything in my heredity or environment which has given him some food for conjecture?"

"No," said Durant. He fought down sudden anger.

Sheridan studied the ceiling thoughtfully. "The colonel, who is a young man, can possibly have what used to be called a conscience. He has probably rationalized his subconscious emotions about me; he has probably said to himself that I must be destroyed. Yes," said Sheridan softly, "he believes I must be destroyed, and that he must know what I am so that future generations may recognize my kind. Nevertheless, the colonel is not at ease. He subconsciously—quite subconsciously—wishes to be reassured that he was justified in condemning me."

Durant's face turned hot. He said unevenly: "I don't know what you're talking about, Sheridan. Don't you remember me? I'm just the Military. I'm just a steel-jacketed moron. You're crediting me with emotions I don't possess, and don't understand."

Sheridan gave him the friendly glance which a schoolmaster would give an obstinate but intelligent student. "I think the colonel understands," he observed. "And I'm willing to assist the colonel in quieting his conscience." He waited, then; as Durant did not speak, he continued: "I told the colonel before that I could never live in the environment he has sworn to restore, where there are conscience and other unnecessary emotional impediments to intelligent Government."

"Why not?" blurted Durant involuntarily.

"Because," answered Sheridan patiently, "that environment is an insane and impossible one, a fantastic dream which was never based on reality. It is not based on human nature. It is a religious concept, and man has never truly embraced any religious concept at all, not once, through all the ages. That ought to be clear evidence, even to a fool, that religion is antipathetic to man, alien to his nature, unnecessary for him. I, Colonel, am a realist. I was born a realist. There are only the weak and the strong in the world, whether living things are beetles, birds, fish, animals, or men."

"Not a very original conclusion," said Durant. "Beetles, birds, fish, animals and men discovered that long ago, ages ago. But a newer concept was given us, also a long time ago: that man is neither a worm nor a dog, a weasel, nor an animal only. He has a mind, an ego. He is aware of himself. Becoming aware of himself, he became aware of abstracts and his ability to reason in abstracts, something other creatures don't possess. I won't make you smile by speaking of the soul—"

But Sheridan interrupted, and his face was serious. "The colonel misunderstands me. I do believe in the soul."

"Well—" began Durant. And then he stopped, and he remembered that strange experience he had had in his office, his knowledge that a tangible presence had moved close to him, a presence of incredible and absolute evil, utterly amoral, utterly omnipresent. He looked at Sheridan, and his volatile face paled.

Sheridan nodded. "I think the colonel comprehends now."

The evil that invaded everything was always defeated, and always triumphed. The evil that was part of every man, but only a part in lesser or greater degree, in the majority. But the evil which was, in some rare men, supreme, unqualified. It was born in them as a perfect entity which did not admit the presence of any other emotion or motivation. Was that evil madness? Durant, who had once considered evil to be a form of insanity, no longer believed that. Sheridan was completely sane.

Durant leaned toward Sheridan and studied him with something like fear. He said: "One of my teachers once taught me that Man is noble, but men are ignoble, or worse. When Man becomes men, only, there emerges a universal paranoid state of mind that dwindles off into death or explodes in a suicidal catastrophe." He did not know why he should speak like this to a man he had condemned to death, but something irresistible was urging him. "What do you say to that, Sheridan?"

Sheridan smiled at him pleasantly. "I was not mistaken in the colonel, I see. I've considered what the colonel has said. His teacher was quite correct, I must admit. Correct in a 'moral' or religious concept. But, may I remind the colonel that we, in this century, are a Society of Men, and that Man is an outlaw, an anachronism? It always happens. Men finally overcome man. Man never wins for very long, but he leaves behind him a trail of transcendental error, shining with stars, perhaps, but an error. There is no reality in it." He shook his head. "What the colonel has called a 'paranoid' state of mind is neither paranoid nor deathful. It is pure reality, and can never be overcome by any theory or set of benign laws which are based on the nonexistent nobility of man's personality."

Durant felt cold and vulnerable. He protested: "Hitler thought that, and Stalin, and our present State, here in America, and tyrants thought that for thousands of years before! And they always were defeated."

"And they always triumph, again and again," said Sheridan,

almost with compassion for this young fool. "And, some day, they will triumph permanently. Not in your generation, perhaps, nor in your children's children's generation. But eventually. Truth, you see, cannot help but establish itself."

"Or evil?"

"It has many names," said Sheridan indulgently. "Call it what you will."

Durant examined his own fingers, his face dark, his forehead wrinkled. Then he said: "You told me you believed in the soul, Sheridan. So, death doesn't matter to you, does it?"

"No, Colonel, it does not. For, you see, I know that men of my kind are born forever, preparing to kill you, you who believe in dreams and fantasies. Shall I say, to make it clearer, that what I am is forever born, and that you can do nothing about us? As an entity, I don't know whether I shall exist after tomorrow; but as a reality, I shall always exist."

A faint roar reached them even in this room, a sound like a rising and stormy sea. Durant ran to the window. The crowd outside had reached tremendous proportions; it overflowed the streets; its tentacles extended into other streets, into alleys. Someone had told the people that Sheridan was to die tomorrow. The snow blurred the multitude of faces below, but Durant could sense the crowd's jubilation, their ecstasy. "Come here!" he cried to Sheridan. Sheridan rose without hurry and joined Durant at the window.

"Look down there," said Durant, pointing. "The people. They know you have been condemned to death. Their enemy. They are overjoyed that one evil is going to be eliminated."

Sheridan studied the crowds thoughtfully. Then he laughed, his soft, patrician laugh. "No, Colonel, you are wrong. For, you see, they created me; they gave me power. In the past, they've created thousands of other men like me, and made them powerful, and they'll do the same in the future. They hate me because the thing which they made, and to which they gave authority, has injured and frightened them. Their uproar does not mean that they are hoping for freedom, and are beginning to detest slavery. It's only an immediate and transitory thing. It's even an ugly emotion, according to your concepts, for there's nothing 'virtuous' or 'sublime' or 'aware' in it. That cry is the cry of the mob which killed the Gracchi, and Jesus and Socrates, the cry at the guillotine or at the gallows or at the auto da fé. The cry of purely emotional hatred, which can be directed at anyone."

He touched Durant gently on the chest. "The same cry which was raised against your kind, Colonel."

He is right, and he is wrong, thought Durant desperately. Then, all at once, he was flooded by a strange quiet. "I have compassion on the multitude." Christ saw; Christ forgave; Christ understood. And Christ knew that under all the hatred, all the horrible stupidity and ignorance and bestiality and evil in man, there lived the true reality: the divinity, like a secret kernel, there planted in beneficent soil could become a great and immortal tree. A tree of life, filled with fruit, airy with flowers, glittering in the sun.

Durant turned to Sheridan. He wanted to speak. But Sheridan's ghostly eyes were laughing.

The young man moved away, his arms folded. He had forgotten Chard Sadler. Now, startled and bemused, he saw him. Sadler's face was very stern, and his eyes were full of a sterner sadness. He smiled a little, after a moment; never had he looked so like his father.

"Perhaps the colonel might remember," he said, "the old saying that the children of darkness are wiser in their generation than the children of light."

"Yes?" said Durant.

"But the generation passes, too, and if men like Sheridan are born, again and again, as he says, the children of light also are born. Perhaps, one day, they'll never die."

He put his hand on his gun. "Just the same, sir, if you'll permit, I'll stay with Mr. Sheridan in his cell, until tomorrow morning. So nobody will disturb him, you see."

Early December snow yellowed on the broken streets of Philadelphia, and melted in the gutters. A dull yellowish wind blew over the city; even the sky was juandiced, especially at night.

Durant was suffering from a particularly severe depression, a psychic listlessness. He adjudged some cases in the Military Court, meted out harsh sentences, for public effect, with the result that his melancholy became blacker day by day. His isolation had never seemed more terrible to him. He dared talk with no one. An intangible coolness, if not open hostility, settled down between him and his officers, with the exception of Sergeant Keiser. Keiser, he sometimes reflected, might be a fellow conspirator, but there was something about the man which he could not like. There was a sullen expression on young Grandon's boyish face these days and, as Durant had become extremely unpopular with the local wealthy families, few invitations came to Edwards and Bishop. Durant knew that those families were his malignant enemies; before his directives against them he had ignored all their overtures. Since the directives, the submerged but none the less savage hatred they had for him was a palpable thing which he felt when he accidentally came into contact with them. Finally, when he commanded Bishop and Edwards not to accept any further invitations, the hostility of the officers became manifest to him in surly side-glances and silence.

He dared talk with Dr. Dodge no longer, for fear that bringing him into his own presence, and into the presence of Sadler, the resemblance between father and son would soon be seen by others. He did not talk with Sadler, either, even when they were alone. He found it hard, indeed, to have any conversation with anyone.

There was also another reason for his misery. He remembered, from the days of his childhood, the happy anticipations of December twenty-fifth. He remembered the Midnight Mass on Christmas Eve, the gleaming tree, the presents, the seasonal dishes, the laughter and gaiety and prayer and song. All these had been sucked down in the gray mud of universal proletarianism. In December it seemed to him that that mud was everywhere, on the faces of the people on the streets, under his fingernails, in his hair, on his clothing, in his food. And, worst of all, in his very soul.

He would think to himself: Can we really ever eliminate this horror from the spirits and memory and habits of the people? What of the young folk, who had known nothing but rough and shabby clothing all their lives, nothing but military despotism, nothing but the drabness of Americanized Communist philosophy, nothing but the worship of the State, nothing but oppression and materialistic indoctrination? All these had become a way of life to them; they probably could imagine no other type of existence, no other world. There was no spot on earth which had not been ravished, no smiling land of freedom anywhere, no rumor of any splendor or human dignity, by which they could make comparisons with their own nation. There was nothing they could emulate; they could restore no standards, for they had awareness of no standards but their own. They had been born in times of war, had lived in times of war, knowing nothing but war and regimentation. Beauty and peace and reverence and joy had never been part of their knowledge. Emancipated, what would they do? Cast adrift on their own responsibility, faced with the demand that they live like free beings, forced to meet the exigencies of individual enterprise, was it not likely they would be thrown into confusion and panic and fear?

It was without much hope that Durant reminded himself that their parents remembered, and might be able to reeducate their young people. After all, their parents, years ago, had betrayed the Republic, themselves, in the name of "security," and if they now regretted it, their age, their sufferings over decades, might very possibly have diminished their initiative and their faith, if they had not entirely extinguished them.

In all eras, Durant thought drearily, older men looked to youth for encouragement and strength and enthusiasm. But now we must look to the old, no matter how tired they are, no matter how numbed. They, and only they, could save their children, even in the days of deliverance. Veined and withered hands must take up the lights to banish the darkness; youth might follow, quaking with terror. To them, the darkness had been the day. The light might be too much for them. The parents had surrendered their children and their children's freedom to the enemy; from the enemy they must rescue them.

The old would have to restore old meanings to present terminology. Unity; duty; sacrifice; discipline; freedom; democracy. These had been corrupted and perverted to mean regimentation, slavery, forced labor, thought control, war and death. A whole new lexicon had come into being by direction of evil men. Words were not changeless things, abstractions. They were symbols of emotion, which was never static. The young were the victims of evil semantics; the idiot jargon of time-serving scientists had become part of the vocabulary of the schools. The scientists had been among the very first to betray America, and though they were now controlled by the Military, their enthusiasm for The Democracy had increased through the years. Not to the scientists, then (once considered by sentimentalists to be the clear-eyed sages of the centuries), but to the homely old and middle-aged would youth have to turn for the nobility of words. Not to teachers and instructors and professors would youth be compelled to appeal for the meaning of charity, pride, courage and faith, but to old clergymen now starving in cellars and attics.

Age, which in its youth had invoked the terror, must now destroy it. The murderers detested and feared the middle-aged and the old, for they distrusted their memories. Their harshest laws had been directed against those who might remember the days of freedom and faith and private enterprise and honor, and who might still cherish within themselves the thought of God.

It was a most frightful and pressing problem, not only for America, but for all the world. The Dark Ages must always be overcome by those who have immediate memory of light, or the Dark Ages endure for centuries.

Haunted by these thoughts, Durant felt in himself the wild necessity for haste. Yet, nothing happened but dull routine, dull silence. He could not endure his present existence. Sometimes, with alarm, he found himself thinking as a military man, acting like a military man. By empathy, he could realize the predicament of thousands of secret men like himself: temporarily, at least, they would discover themselves thinking in accordance with their behavior. How frail a thing was human nature, how easily seduced, how easily self-betrayed!

There was no amusement, no recreation for Durant. He never attended the State theatres or "festivals" or parties. He rarely, if ever, saw Colburn or Alice Steffens or the ambiguous Morrow. He caught infrequent glimpses of the Lincolns; they scuttled away each time they glimpsed him, bending their heads so that he might not see their faces. He told himself that "things were going on behind the scenes." If they were, he had no inkling. His very eyes became less quick. Had they been alert he might have noticed that the soldiers on the streets were haggard, their expressions strained, and that they no longer patrolled singly or in mere pairs, but in squads. He might have noticed that they whispered among themselves furtively. He might have seen that the faces of the people had become tense and turbulent, and he might have smelled the fire of subterranean violence in the dank air of early winter. Because he was waiting for something huge and dramatic, something explosive and universal, he missed the very signs which he should have observed.

It was true that a war plant in the suburbs of Philadelphia had burned down. But he considered it only a baseless rumor that sabotage was behind it. Over a hundred women had invaded the food warehouses in the city, and had made off with considerable provender, but Durant believed this to be a mere desperate act of starvation. A very prosperous farmer not far from the Lincolns had been shot in his open field; two homes of influential MASTS had been destroyed by fire only two weeks ago. A freight train, carrying tons of war materials had been derailed near the city, and the contents had mysteriously exploded. Durant discounted the rumors that this, too, had been sabotage. There was a rumor, not even recorded in the newspapers, that in Section 17 a group of five officers, emerging from their cars, had been clubbed to death on the open streets of Chicago by assassins who disappeared in a crowd which strangely swallowed them up. Another rumor, reported to Durant by Bishop, was to the effect that four members of the FBHS had been found dead of knife-wounds in their offices, in Cleveland. There were more rumors of desertions by young recruits from the Armed Forces in various Sections, and an even wilder rumor that in Minneapolis a mob had set upon a detachment of soldiers who were leading traitorous men and women to the military prison, and had freed the victims. There was a rumor of an abortive revolt in Section 10, which had formerly been called Canada.

Rumors, rumors, said Durant, impatiently. There were always rumors. He refused to listen to any more, finally. He was waiting for the loud call to arms; he was waiting for spontaneous and gigantic events. He forgot that small and smoldering fires in a forest usually merge together to become a destroying holocaust. He was beginning to breathe the tainted air of drabness into his lungs; what should have excited him, what should have had tremendous meaning for him, escaped him entirely.

Democracy Day had been substituted for Christmas Day, and it was the only holiday which the people were permitted to enjoy. Celebrations were stimulated; the President spoke enthusiasitically from New York. There were parades for the children, indoctrination parades, in which huge and obscene images of "capitalists," "enemies," and "traitors" were carried through the streets, led by blazing bands. Extra rations of food were issued, even whisky was temporarily available for the people. Speakers exhorted in gaily decked halls and in what once were churches. And irony of ironies, banners appeared everywhere displaying the image of the great Statue of Liberty, mingling themselves with the flags of The Democracy.

In fact, the whole national attention was turned in the direction of that statue. The President was always flown over it, to drop flowers on its mighty shoulders. Wreaths were laid on its majestic feet. Its crown streamed with lights, which illuminated the massive features below. Tugs shrieked as they gushed by it, and warships saluted with thunderous salvos. At twilight, on Democracy Day, the President would deliver his speech on "our great liberties, derived from the blood and sacrifice of noble men." The people, temporarily freed from uniformity and colorlessness, would become almost insane with rapture and release. The cities, feebly lighted all the rest of the year to save coal, bathed themselves in brilliance. It was a great day, a day to be anticipated all year. It was a day which had no other significance for the young; in the dimmed minds of the old and the middle-aged it was a day of mourning for a God who had been banished.

A week before Christmas, Durant arrived at his office, even more depressed and dull-eyed than usual, even more disheartened. He found on his desk, which had been cleared for its presence, a sealed letter from the Chief Magistrate. He had received no other letters from Carlson before, except infrequent directives, and these had been unsealed. Durant's officers were all excitement, and Grandon called his attention to the letter immediately. He opened it, his hands shaking. It read innocuously enough.

"I know you are extremely busy these days, and so you need not interpret my invitation as a command. However, if you have time, you might like to come to New York for the celebration of Democracy Day. I understand there will be even more enthusiasm displayed this year than in other years, because the people are extremely determined that the present conflict be resolved as soon as possible in order that peace and prosperity may be restored.

"We are very pleased with your work, and I shall make it a point to bring you to the attention of our beloved President, even if you cannot spare yourself from Philadelphia in these arduous days.

"The celebration of Democracy Day in Philadelphia ought to be very pleasant for you, and so you must not regret it if you cannot visit New York on this occasion. Though Philadelphians are more staid than New Yorkers, I understand that they are not too restrained on this day.

"In the event work keeps you, I must reconcile myself to

your absence, and, in the meantime, I send you my personal expressions of regard and affection."

Durant put down the letter. He could hardly breathe; he knew his face was suffused. His officers were waiting eagerly for his comment. He took out his handkerchief and mopped his face. "Warm in here, isn't it?" he remarked. His voice sounded queer in his own ears. Then he made himself laugh. He tapped the letter. "Nothing important, boys. Just an invitation from the Chief Magistrate to visit New York on Democracy Day. I don't think I'll go, however."

They were disappointed. Grandon lingered for a moment, then walked away. Durant was alone at his desk, and he struggled to control his fierce agitation. The first alert! There would be three, if possible, or at least two. He reread the letter, carefully decoding. Only a short message: "Insurrections and incidents mounting daily in all Sections. Our men inciting, aided unknowingly by the privileged groups. Do not leave your post. Do not leave your post! Guard yourself constantly; increase pressure. Wait the next alert. Destroy this letter immediately."

Beckett and Sadler were watching him closely. He became aware of this scrutiny when he happened to glance up. Beckett's mouth was slightly open, his eyes slightly narrowed. Sadler looked strained and pale. Had he betrayed himself in any way? He cursed the mobility of his face, and said to his Guards: "I suppose you boys would like to go to New York? I'd like to, myself, but it's impossible." They saluted, but made no answer.

The presence of the Picked Guard was very irksome to Grandon, Keiser and Bishop and Edwards. They felt themselves insulted, their honor called into question. They ignored the Guards, and the Guards ignored them. They never spoke to each other. Durant was sometimes impatient with them all, but understood.

He left the letter carelessly folded and tossed aside on his desk. Unknown to him, three pairs of eyes concentrated on it, three minds began to plot ways and means of knowing its contents. Durant's intuition, or extra sensory perception, began to detect the intensity and desire of those minds without his conscious knowledge. He only knew that under all his enormous excitement was a faint flutter of uneasiness. Finally, in the midst of his planning for the immediate future, in view of the commands in the message, his eyes kept straying back to the letter which lay negligently on a corner of his desk. Impatiently, he abandoned his greater plans for the moment, and began to think of a way to destroy the letter without arousing the most minute of suspicions.

It came to him with a kind of thrilling shock that matters must indeed be moving desperately one way or another for Carlson to have written him in the new code of the Minute Men, which enemies even now might have broken. It had been a terrible risk, yet Carlson had taken the risk, Carlson the extremely cautious and wary. Apparently, it will soon be time, and the risk has to be taken, thought Durant. We either succeed, in one last gigantic effort, or we die. The days of waiting were ended. He stared at the letter. He pretended to be engaged in the deepest thought, and began to move objects abstractedly on his desk, picking up a pen, writing a few words on a report, dropping the pen, yawning, lighting cigarets, scribbling absentmindedly on a note, throwing the note aside, scratching his chin, rubbing the back of his head. He did not glance at his officers and Guards; he appeared to have forgotten them. Yet, all the time, the flutter of uneasiness in him sharpened, became more immediate. He picked up the letter, yawned widely again, leaned back in his chair, scanned the contents of the letter, threw it aside impatiently. He laid it face down on his desk, took up his pen again, and asked Grandon to bring him the dossier of Mr. Remington, the local spokesman for the MASTS.

Grandon brought him the folder, Durant opened it and began to scribble rapidly on the back of the letter, as if it were a mere scrap of paper to be tossed later into the wastebasket. Once the letter was actually under his fingers, the uneasiness subsided a little. He could give his attention completely to his plans.

"Increase pressure." He wrote down Mr. Remington's name first, followed it with others, made notes. How to increase pressure more? He had it! He called for the folder of Walter Morrow, who was head of the Grange, and for the thin folder of Karl Schaeffer, now the district director of the local FBHS since the execution of Alex Sheridan. He called for the folder of Ben Colburn, or "Mr. Woolcott," of the Bureau of Mobilized Labor. He mused as he glanced through the letter folder. He had seen his best friend but three times during the past months, and then only formally, on matters of business.

He lifted the telephone receiver and put in a call for Colburn. He said coldly: "About that Trenchard matter, Mr. Woolcott. What has happened to it?"

Colburn answered as remotely: "We could get very little evidence. Possibly a malicious neighbor. I'm afraid we'll have to let him go. We tried our usual methods, but elicited nothing."

"Well," said Durant warningly, "be sure to investigate everything. After all, two people said he was in the vicinity of the intersection where three of my soldiers were assassinated." Then he let his voice become friendly. "By the way, are you going to New York for Democracy Day? I've received an invitation from the Chief Magistrate, but I'm afraid I can't accept it."

He waited tensely for the reply. It came, casually enough: "Yes, I did receive an invitation, but like you, Colonel, I can't accept, either."

So, all the Minute Men had been alerted, everywhere; Durant's voice became cold and threatening: "I'm not questioning your thoroughness, Woolcott, but I really want an exhaustive investigation of Trenchard. He's no fool; he was once a newspaper publisher, and though he's now a machine shop worker in a plant, he probably harbors subversive thoughts. Send him over to me tomorrow. You know I only want justice. I'm thinking of sending for some other men, too, and I'm going to ask reporters to be present in order that the people can see that the Military are not the oppressors traitors report us to be."

Colburn replied: "I'll have Trenchard there at ten o'clock tomorrow, Colonel. We always wish to cooperate fully with the Military, as you know."

He hung up, then made other calls. He was aware, more than ever, of the alertness of at least three men in the room. He scribbled more notes on the back of Carlson's letter, scratched out some, added others. Finally as if he had completed that immediate work, he put the letter in one of his pockets, and announced he was going to the washroom reserved for him. Accompanied by his relentless Guards, he left his office. Sadler went ahead of him, as usual, entered the small washroom, examined every possible hiding place for bombs or any other automatic lethal objects which might have been placed in strategic positions. This took some time. Durant said impatiently: "What if I have diarrhea one of these days, while you boys fool around? The washroom's always guarded on the outside by a soldier, anyway, and there's no window."

Sadler answered, in his neutral voice: "Perhaps there might be a traitorous soldier, Colonel." He smiled at Durant, and continued: "In the event of diarrhea, we'd have to take a chance."

Durant went into the closet, but before shutting the door, he asked: "Would one of you fellows like to stand in here with me, too?" He slammed the door irritably while Sadler and Beckett laughed. He took the letter out of his pocket. He'd have to eat the damned thing; he dared not burn it because of the two immediately outside the door. Stiff official paper. His mouth and throat were dry enough. Moodily, he carefully tore off a piece, while he flushed the toilet noisily. He put the piece in his mouth, and was astounded when it dissolved like butter on his tongue. He could thrust big sections into his mouth, and they would melt away into a liquid which he could swallow without effort. In a few seconds the whole letter had gone. He was much intrigued; apparently his saliva had a disintegrating effect which water might not have had. The paper had not been the gelatine affair of the old means of communication between the Minute Men. Now Durant was more deeply impressed than ever by the gravity of the situation, and the need for haste. Carlson must have some sheets of this paper which so completely resembled official paper; the fact that he had taken the risk of using it was another indication of the pressure of immediate events.

Durant removed a sheet of notes, which he had made a few days ago, from an inside pocket, folded the sheet so that it would deceive any watchful eye, and put it in the pocket which had held Carlson's letter. He hummed a little, opened the door and rejoined his Guards. He went back to his office. Was it his imagination, or did a number of eyes glance furtively at his pocket?

He tried to work. But his thoughts were too strong and excited, and even fearful. He began to remember the "rumors" which had been brought to him, and which he had dismissed impatiently. Apparently, they were not mere rumors. Now he recalled things he had seen only with his unconscious eye, the faces of the people on the street, the sound of louder voices on the street corners, the apprehensive expressions of soldiers on patrol work. He recalled the "smell of violence" in the air lately. Why had he overlooked these significant signs? He was disgusted with himself for his obtuseness.

He said, idly, without turning to his men: "Any more 'rumors' lately, boys?" And laughed forcedly.

Grandon came to him, and Durant glanced up. His glance had been quick; that knife-flash had appeared and disappeared on Grandon's face in a single instant. The young lieutenant grinned. "Why, sir, you said not to repeat 'rumors' to you, so maybe you won't be interested in hearing a 'rumor' that a warship, the *Sea Runner*, was blown up yesterday at a loading dock in New York. There's nothing about it in the papers this morning; there wouldn't be, of course."

Durant frowned. "If it isn't in the papers, of course it isn't true. What does 'rumor' say about any deaths, or anything, on the warship?"

"All the crew dead, including the captain. Whole harbor full of wreckage. Saboteurs. They found remnants of explosives. Must have been riddled with them; the whole ship. Funny, if it's true, that saboteurs got on board to do the job without being seen."

Durant was silent. Brave men, many of the sailors! Heroic men, dying anonymously in a blaze of hell. Dying, these young men, for the Republic of the United States of America. Durant felt humble and prayerful; he had maligned all of the young. Thousands of parents, everywhere, were not too tired, too frightened, too beaten and oppressed, to whisper the stories of old freedom and God and human dignity, to deliver their sons up to voiceless death in order that the world might be free of the madness. The oppression which had stifled Durant since the execution of Alex Sheridan, and particularly since his conversation with Sheridan, began to lift. "The children of light" might not be so wise in their generation as "the children of darkness," but they had courage and faith and nobility.

Durant's thoughts continued. If these acts of "sabotage" were being perpetrated in Section 7, then they must be occurring in all the other Sections, too. They were not mere spontaneous violences; they were acts of decision and planning. The hour was almost here.

His head began to ache with the fury and excitement of his thoughts. He looked at his watch. It was almost four o'clock. He said: "I've got a headache. I think I'll go home."

When he reached the lobby, with his Guards, he found it unusually full of soldiers, not gossiping and laughing as usual, but grim and attentive. Now he remembered that this phenomenon was not a recent thing. Who had ordered this extra guard? Bishop? Edwards? The order had not come to him. Perhaps it had just come about because of the turn of events, but Durant doubted it.

His car was waiting, and he crossed the sidewalk to it, shivering in the wet and heavy wind. He paused a moment, feeling for a cigaret. It was then he noticed that the innocuous sheet of paper which he had put into his pocket to replace the letter from Carlson was gone. He had a momentary sensation of shock. Who, during his passage from his office down the corridor, or in the elevator, or in the hotel lobby, had removed that sheet? Who, perhaps, in his very office? Friend or enemy? Spy or traitor? Minute Man or agent of the FBHS? Sadler and Beckett were looking at him inquiringly. He shrugged, and entered the car, his mind in a renewed fury of thought. Someone had wanted that letter very badly, perhaps had had orders to steal it, had been in possession of the code. Or wished to destroy it, if Durant semed careless, and had not obeyed instructions.

As the car rolled away, Durant examined Sadler's face. It was impassive. If Sadler had taken the sheet he would have indicated so, for he had seen Durant's searching of his pocket. But Sadler gave no indication. Therefore, it was not Sadler. Beckett? Durant examined that smooth lean face minutely, and was convinced it was not Beckett. He had passed through a crowded lobby; it was very possible that, in the press, the sheet had been taken. Someone, then, in the office, had notified the thief.

Not Grandon, who had plotted with Bob Lincoln in the darkness of a spring night against him, Durant; not Keiser, who was "one of ours." Bishop? Edwards? Durant recalled their typical military faces, their typical military thinking. He knew their history well. They were professional soldiers of many years. Then, who? He came back to Grandon, who had shown more curiosity about the letter than any of the others. It was quite possible that Grandon, in addition to being a soldier, was also a spy for the FBHS.

Durant was not afraid any longer. There was too much danger all about him, now, for fear. He saw that Beckett and Sadler had their guns in their hands. "Why the guns?" he asked. "Expecting an ambush?"

Beckett explained with patience: "If the colonel had been noticing, lately, he'd have seen that we've been carrying our guns openly, in our hands, for over a month."

"Orders from the Chief Magistrate," added Sadler.

"On account of the 'rumors'?" said Durant, with sarcasm.

"On account of the rumors," agreed Sadler.

The yellow sky was darkening as the car raced through the suburbs and then out into the country. Durant smoked thoughtfully. His Guards did not smoke; they watched constantly through the windows, guns in their hands, fingers on triggers. The wind, gathering force out in the open places, roared against the car, made it shiver and shake. The bare trees along the road, and on the farms in the distance, twisted and whirled in the increasing gale. At times the car had to slow down, to negotiate around a fallen limb. Durant, the city-bred, had never heard such primal thunder before, and he was awed by it and vaguely disturbed. Rain began to lash fiercely at the windows, yellowish rain, and the driver again slowed. He turned on the headlights, which revealed the tide of water falling from the sky. It glittered dully in the lights, swept up and around, blindingly.

Then the driver halted the car, trying to peer through the muddy windshield. "Big tree fallen on the road," he announced. Sadler and Beckett leaned forward to peer, also, and so did Durant. A huge trunk stretched across the road, barring their passage, its empty branches lying on flooded ground. There was no way to leave the road and crawl over the fields on either side. "We'll just have to haul it out of the way," said Sadler. He and Beckett opened the doors of the car and went outside, pulling up their collars. The driver got out, and the three men studied the tree gloomily. Durant could see them in the headlights, just faces or a shoulder or a hand, in the howling rain.

Apparently they were somewhat discouraged, for they made no effort to struggle with the monstrous tree. They talked together; Durant could not hear them. The interior of the car became too warm for him, and he wanted information. He rolled down the bullet-proof window. "What are we going to do?" he shouted.

But Sadler had begun to wade almost knee-deep in the water to the right, holding his small flashlight. He was examining something: the stump of the tree. Then Durant glimpsed his face; it had become grim and understanding. He shouted something to Beckett and the driver, and they rushed back to the car. At that instant Durant saw a vivid flash of light, brilliant against the watery and yellowish dusk, and simultaneously he felt a burning and smashing blow on his right shoulder. Beckett turned, ran toward Sadler, and standing side by side, the two men fired into the near distance where a dim tree thrashed in the wind. The crash of the guns echoed back and forth in the windy twilight, and Durant, stunned by the bullet which had struck him, and deafened by the noise, painfully, almost without consciousness, rolled up the window at his side.

His eyes blurred, and he saw the shadowy figures of his Guards splashing further into the field, and he heard another shout. The driver, now in the car, was screaming at him. A great weariness fell over him, and he leaned back in his seat and fainted.

"He's hit!" exclaimed Sadler.

"Bleeding like all hell. We've got to get a doctor fast," replied Beckett excitedly, from the front seat.

Durant opened his eyes with a great effort, and could not focus them for a moment. The driver had turned off the headlights, and a foggy darkness lay outside. Somewhere, somebody groaned and retched, and then there was the sound of a blow and a curse.

Swimming in a dream of indifference and tiredness, Durant tried to remember what had happened to him. He moved on his seat, and Sadler said quickly: "All right, Colonel? The bastard got you on the shoulder. We don't dare turn on our flashlights. Easy there; don't move too much. Johnny, don't punch that rat any more; we've got to question him before he kicks off, and the way you're punching him he'll die on our hands."

"A good thing for him," replied Beckett savagely. "Hell, he's bleeding all over me!"

Consciousness was returning swiftly to Durant. He felt the car backing, then turning. He said weakly: "Vossen's farm. Adjoins Lincoln's. Who's in the front seat with Beckett?"

"The fellow who shot you," said Sadler. "One of us got him in the belly. Faster," he said to the driver, who, much shaken, was proceeding slowly back the eighth of a mile to the Vossen farm. He said to Durant. "One of Vossen's sons, I think." And again to Beckett, more angrily than before: "Are you trying to kill him, Johnny? He's got to be questioned first." Beckett muttered something and the wounded prisoner groaned again and again so that Durant winced.

"If he dies before I talk with him, I'll put the blame on you, Beckett," he said, and his voice was strong and hard.

Sadler supported Durant gently. "Just a flesh wound, we hope. Just before you were conscious, sir, you moved the arm, so nothing's broken."

Durant said: "It's my own fault; I let down the window. He was aiming at me, not you."

Sadler grunted. "He sure was. He could have got Johnny or me if he'd wanted to. Good shot, and only about two hundred feet away. I knew something was wrong when I saw the tree had been sawed, and that it hadn't fallen in the wind. It was a road-block, so we'd have to stop, and he'd have his chance at you, sir. And you gave it to him, free and clear!"

I'm certainly a stupid damn fool, thought Durant. The wound in his shoulder had become pure white anguish. The prisoner was silent now, except for an occasional gasp. His head lolled within reach of Durant's hand, and all at once Durant was sick with a sickness that was only slightly connected with his wound. The violence had come face to face with him, and it was only beginning. He said: "I hope he doesn't die—Vossen."

"I hope so, too, sir," replied Sadler. He added slowly: "Until we can question him, anyway." Beckett, in the front seat with the prisoner, muttered again. The car was moving faster now, splashing up noisy tides of water, and the darkness was increasing.

"They're getting bold," Durant commented.

There was a little silence, then Sadler replied quietly: "Yes." Suddenly, he put his hand over Durant's mouth in an urgent gesture, then removed it.

There was something dangerous in the car with them, Durant thought. Who? The driver? Beckett? The prisoner? He smelled the danger. Now the pain in his arm reached a crescendo, and he groaned, himself. Beckett turned his head alertly. "The colonel, Chard?"

"Just beginning to feel the pain; just a flesh wound," answered Sadler. "Can't we go a little faster?"

The Vossen farmhouse appeared through the darkness, well lighted, solidly built of local fieldstone, its square bulk big and gracious. The car turned up the driveway toward it and water and mud sucked at the wheels. It was very rough going, and Sadler braced Durant strongly. The prisoner was silent now, evidently unconscious. The car stopped at the white doorway, and Durant said in a tone of authority: "Sadler, you'd better go in and call a couple of our Army doctors, and a squad of soldiers, before you help me into the house. That'll prepare the family. And, Beckett, search around the house before I get out; I'm staying right here, with my gun, until you're sure everything is safe. And you, George," he said to the soldier-driver, "cover Lieutenant Sadler's rear."

"What if this bastard wakes up?" demanded Beckett, "and you all alone, sir?"

"I've got my gun; I suppose he doesn't have his? Well, then, I'm safe, and I'll keep the windows up and the door locked."

The men were unwilling, but they obeyed. Durant watched until he was sure they had gone, then he leaned forward and spoke quickly and quietly to the man in the front seat. "Can you hear me? It's important. I've got to talk to you while we're alone—"

The head stirred painfully in the back of the seat, and a faint but surprisingly young voice answered: "I can hear you. I never passed out." The voice added, without rage or much interest: "God damn it, I thought I'd killed you."

"You almost did," said Durant, laughing drearily. "How old are you? Who are you? Why did you do it? Hurry, or they'll be back."

The head tried to lift itself. Durant took his pencil flashlight from his left hip pocket and threw the beam briefly on the other's face. Why, a kid, not more than twenty, if that! A dying child, too, if that wet lividity was any indication; Durant had a glimpse of large black eyes and a desperate young face, a boy's face.

The boy could only whisper hoarsely: "What do you care? I'm plugged; I'm going to die in a few minutes. Leave my family alone; they don't know anything about this. Good people. Stupid people. Except Dad." Now the whisper became harsh. "I'm eighteen; I'm Ken Vossen. Help with the farm work. I thought you should die—"

"Why?" pleaded Durant.

The boy was silent a moment; Durant could feel rather than see that he was pressing his hands convulsively against his abdominal wound in an effort to stop the blood and the pain. Then the boy was whispering: "Because you're the Military. Because you've killed this country. Because The Democracy is bad and we've got to get rid of the men in Washington—"

Durant said urgently: "Listen: did you have these ideas before I started putting the pressure on the farmers?"

"Yes," and now the voice had become stronger. "I had them when I was a kid. I tried to talk to Dad about them, and he was mad. Said the State was the friend of the farmers, and we had everything, and I was to shut up or I'd land in jail or in front of a firing squad." The head moved in an access of agony, and the boy groaned. "God damn you, why should I talk to you, anyway? You can't do anything more to me."

Durant said: "Ken, please talk to me. How many of you young people think as you do?"

The boy gave a ghost of a bitter laugh. "Want me to give you names, eh, so you can kill all of us? Well, I won't. But I can tell you this," and the voice was strong with passion, "you're finished. There's millions of us, millions! I know it. I hear the other kids talking when I go to the city."

Durant was silent. He touched the top of the young head very gently. "Have you been baptized?" he asked. The head moved abruptly under his hand, and the boy tried to twist a little to look up into Durant's face. But it was too dark. "Baptized?" he muttered. "I don't know; never heard I was. It's illegal, you know." All at once he began to sob, the long, deep-drawn sobs of a hurt child. "Who are you?" he cried.

Durant glanced through the windows swiftly; there was no sign of his men. He fumbled with the left door of the car, leaned down to the road and scooped up a handful of the flood water. He pulled the door closed after him, shutting his eyes against his own pain for a moment. Then he flowed the little handful of water over the boy's forehead and murmured: "—in the Name of the Father, and of the Son, and of the Holy Ghost, Amen."

The boy lay very still, his head unmoving. Then, all at once he began to gasp raggedly. Durant put his hand against the cold cheek. "Listen to me, Ken. The time's almost here, when America shall be free. Take that with you, kid. Have that to remember."

Something was fumbling at the back of the seat, and Durant caught the boy's hand. There was no life in it, but Durant, almost weeping, pressed the icy fingers. "God bless you," he whispered. "God bless and help all the kids like you. We need you, for the future."

The hand became limp in his; a convulsion shook the young body in the seat ahead. There was a long and sobbing groan, and the boy collapsed. Utter silence filled the car; now Durant could hear the fresh onslaught of the rain on the roof, the rattle against the windows. He was alone; he knew that the boy was dead. But what he was had not died. "Millions of us!" No, but enough, perhaps, to help rebuild the future, to be leaders, to be the core of the Republic. Durant bent his head, prayed for the young soul so violently separated from its body, prayed that the courage of the children like Ken Vossen would not be diminished but would grow indomitably in the years ahead. Not all the children had been corrupted; here and there, throughout the whole world, perhaps, the young were thinking, the young were plotting, the young were willing to give up their lives for the dignity and liberty of men. Durant marveled, with deep humility. Was it indeed true that the human spirit could not be entirely killed, even in chaos and death and oppression, even without the assistance of those who had once known freedom and peace? There was something mysterious in outbursts of spontaneous vitality and fortitude, however scattered they might be, something miraculous, something that could not die or be smothered.

There was a hard tapping on the window, and Durant saw that Sadler had returned. A gush of light from the open door outlined his figure. Durant opened the car door, and Sadler thrust his head inside. "All right, Colonel. Let me help you out. I called the office, but the officers had gone; they'll be flagged on the road, somewhere, and they'll turn in here. Better than just soldiers. They can't get beyond the road-block, anyway. Here's Beckett, too. Looks like this man was alone."

Durant said hurriedly: "He wasn't a man; he was just a boy. And he's dead."

Beckett came up to the car, his shoulders wet with rain. "Left the driver at the back. Here, I'll give you a hand with the colonel, Chard. And then we'll haul out that bastard."

"He's dead," Durant repeated.

Beckett began to curse savagely. "Now we can't question him! I ought to have stayed here, Colonel. I'd have gotten some information—"

"I got what was necessary." Durant felt overpoweringly weak as Sadler gently helped him from the car. The two Picked Guards supported him, almost carried him up the two shallow white steps toward the door. He closed his eyes momentarily against the light, and felt himself lifted. There was a chair under him, and all about him was silence. He opened his eyes.

He was in a large and firelit living room, very pleasant, not lavish as Lincoln's home was lavish, but comfortable and gay. A ring of people was before him, a short fat man, bald and calm, in a chair, and beside him a middle-aged woman with a white and appalled face, her stark eyes desperate with fear and grief. Behind these two a couple of young and buxom farm women and a man about thirty stood in rigid quiet. They were all staring at Durant, and their mouths were pressed hard together in stubborn wariness.

Durant watched them as Sadler expertly cut away his right sleeve. He did not glance at his wound; he was only vaguely aware that Sadler had rolled up a handkerchief and was pressing it hard against his shoulder. The pain was nothing to him; his eyes moved slowly from one face to another. Then he said, flatly, looking at the older man: "Your son, Ken, is dead."

The woman uttered a shrill and anguished cry, then put her hand to her mouth. Vossen puffed at his pipe and said nothing. One of the girls whimpered, but was almost immediately silent. The dark thin man near her tightened his mouth and glanced away from Durant. The other girl merely blinked.

Durant went on: "In a few minutes, he'll be brought in. But I want to question all of you. Your son tried to kill me, Vossen. He set up a road block. Did any of you help him?"

Vossen took his pipe slowly from his mouth, cleared his throat. He showed no sign of sorrow, and his rough voice was even: "None of us helped him. We're law-abiding people, Colonel. We don't like what you've done to us farmers in this Section, and we hope that Washington'll soon overrule you. Morrow's down there, now. But we don't go around trying to kill the Military; you've always been our friends. Up to now," he added unemotionally. If he was frightened there was no sign of it.

His wife burst into tears and rocked in her chair, moaning. The daughter nearest her put her hand on her mother's shoulder.

Now the older son spoke, as unemotionally as his father: "You've taken our crops, and fixed the price, and we get just about what the city workers in the plants get. But we hope the

Military will soon change its mind. We're not killers, we farmers. We work legal, and if we got to sacrifice, we'll sacrifice."

Durant contemplated them thoughtfully. "Very good," he said at last, with contempt. "I believe you." He hated them, hated their docility. They were regarding him with fixed attention, even the weeping mother. He could read nothing from their faces. They were pale, but they were not too much afraid of him. He began to wonder, to take hope.

The older son said: "There was always something wrong with Ken. Two years ago we took him to a psychiatrist, who said he was a psycho. That is, not adjusted. They sent him away for a year, and then he came home and we thought he was all right. Had his moods, but did his work, and kept his mouth shut. We don't know where he got the gun, sir, that he fired at you. We don't know anything at all about it." He drew a deep breath, and stared hard at Durant. "It's better this way, his being dead. No telling what he might have done if he'd got away."

There was hatred and enmity in this room, and a cold determination. Durant began to feel better by the moment. Vossen was nodding. "Better this way," he agreed. But the mother was sobbing again, her hands over her face. The older son looked at her, and his hands clenched. The daughter near her helplessly patted her head.

"Well," said Durant, "I suppose I'll have to take your word that you knew nothing about your son, or any of his activities. I could put you all under arrest, and hold you for questioning. But we need the farmers, and I've had no report against you."

He turned to Beckett. "Get the soldier and bring in young Vossen's body."

He waited, and the others waited with him, silently. Only the mother's weeping made any sound in the room. The fire crackled loudly, and somewhere a dog barked. Vossen was smoking again, and gazing at the floor; he showed no interest in his wife. Tears were running down the girls' faces; the older son stood stiffly and looked at nothing. Then heavy footsteps were heard, and Beckett and the soldier entered the room, hauling the dead body roughly between them. They laid him on the floor near his parents' feet, and his body fell, sprawled and grotesque, the filmed eyes open, the clothing sodden with blood. The mother screamed, pulled herself from her chair and knelt by her son. She took his head in her arms and held it passionately against her meager breast, as she had held it not so many years before. She smoothed the wet hair with her hands; she kissed the white face over and over. She called to her son wildly, in a heartbreaking voice, and her gray hair straggled over her cheeks.

They all watched. No one moved. The boy's blood was on his mother's hands, on her print dress. She rocked him in her arms, holding him protectingly. Durant examined the faces of the father and the son and the daughters. They were expressionless; their eyes were fixed on the mother and her dead child. But Durant felt the cold violence that lay behind those impassive faces. Then, all at once, as if some one had commanded it, every eye turned upon Durant and he found himself looking at hatred.

No, none of them had helped young Vossen; none of them had known of what he had set himself to do. They regretted only that Durant was not dead, that the brave boy had not succeeded. So, thought Durant, the farmers are just about ready to move. He had no illusions that they were inspired by any ideals, for they had lost them decades ago, or had destroyed them deliberately for profit. The old-fashioned farmer was gòne. These hated the Military because of what the Military had done to them, curtailing their power and their position and their incomes. It would be in an effort to regain these that they would strike. Good enough, commented Durant to himself, somberly. He had no pity for them, no pity for the sorrow they were repressing because he was present, and because they were shrewd and cautious. He had pity only for the mother.

A car roared up to the door outside, and he knew his officers and the doctors had arrived. He said to Beckett and the soldier: "Take the body away, and the family with it. I can't stand the sight of them."

He closed his eyes. His strength was gone; he had lost too much blood. A dizzy darkness whirled about him. He heard voices, but was too listless to care. He felt a stabbing in his arm, and movements around him. He fainted again.

Despite the objections of his doctors, Durant insisted upon returning to work within a few days. The Philadelphia newspapers were enthusiastic about "our Colonel's devotion to duty." They explained that "our Colonel is engrossed in making the coming celebrations on Democracy Day the most spectacular and eventful of any previous celebration, and is determined that the people of this city shall have happy reason to remember our Day of Days." The papers, at Durant's command, gave full coverage to the account of the attempt on his life, and, at his private order, attacked "some irresponsible farmers, long accorded special privileges by a benevolent State, who, because they are asked to sacrifice in this present emergency, are displaying violent symptoms of rebellion. A long-suffering and patient people have, too long, endured the arrogance of wealthy farmers, and this crime against our Colonel is an ominous sign that they believe they can control The Democracy and need obey no laws but their own."

The tormented people were aroused by editorials such as this, and especially by accounts of the "unlawful concealing of food by our local farmers, and the unlawful withhholding of food from the people." It was no coincidence, then, that several barns were mysteriously set aflame during the week or two following the attempt on Durant's life, and that huge supplies of foodstuffs disappeared from farm warehouses. Durant, remembering the grief of the Vossens, felt a twinge of regret that their house was, a week before Democracy Day, burnt to the ground. Fearful that his popularity with the people might become too dangerous, he ordered that all "criminals" connected with the fires and the stealing of farm goods be apprehended immediately. As a consequence, over one hundred men and women were thrown in prison on mere suspicion. His popularity was extinguished at once, and he was relieved. But there were more "outrages" against the farmers, in spite of harsh punitive measures, and two State warehouses, filled with food left there for decay, were raided one dark night by "bands of subversives who carried off tons of meat, butter, eggs, and other commodities being carefully reserved by the Government for equal distribution to the people in accordance with law."

Well, thought Durant, quite a number of families are eating ravenously these days, and gathering strength for the great revolt.

Other incidents, even more grave, occurred throughout the Section, and were followed by military raids on homes and factories. Durant, however, was careful that these raids did not result in the imprisonment of potential leaders. He imprisoned only the obviously stupid and innocent, and gave wide publicity to their punishment. He preferred that young girls and boys be the recipients of vengeance by the State, and so it was that at least ten children were sent away to labor camps from which it was known they would never return.

Now even the most obtuse could feel and see the submerged hate and rage of the crowds on the street. Heads of bureaus called for extra guards for their persons and their homes. The streets were full of soldiers, on twenty-four hour duty. It was odd, however, that the soldiers now never seemed to be able to apprehend criminals before "crimes" were committed, and that their raids netted fewer and fewer victims. But the newspapers did not write of these things. They spoke of the "enthusiasm" being shown for "our most popular commanding officer, and the increased efforts being put forth in the war plants by labor in response to Colonel Curtiss' pleas."

Three days before Democracy Day, Durant received another letter from Carlson. It was very affectionate, and expressed the Chief Magistrate's concern for the health of Colonel Curtiss and his hope that the wound had been only superficial. The Chief Magistrate regretted that his "best commanding officer" would not be able to participate in the celebrations of Democracy Day in New York. "We expect at least three million people to pay special homage on the Day to the Statue of Liberty. I have never seen such vigor and spirit among New Yorkers, and such determination that this Day must surpass all other Days." The Military and the bureaucrats were especially enthusiastic, and the MASTS, farmers in the immediate vicinity of New York and important members of the Social Economic Planning group were particularly fired by patriotism and have promised unusual demonstrations and assistance. "After all," wrote the Chief Magistrate, "these groups have a peculiar devotion to The Democracy."

Durant carefully decoded before destroying the letter. Three million Minute Men were preparing to lead the people when the third alert was sounded by Carlson. The people were ready. The new and secret organizations formed by the bureaucrats and the farmers and the MASTS, were, independently and without knowledge of the work of the Minute Men, almost ripe for revolt, and were awaiting their own guarded signals, which, unknown to them, were being readied by the Minute Men in their own ranks.

There was a postscript to the letter: "We hear, from authentic sources, that Europe will soon stabilize herself, and that the hordes of Asia are subsiding and that new and sound governments will soon be established. This is excellent, in view of our war with the South American republics."

Durant decoded: "European leaders have finally succeeded in alerting their people to move for free government and order on signal from America, and this is true of Asia, also. Our agents on both continents have signified that they are confident that the European and Asiatic peoples, on our signal, will coalesce instantly."

Durant's depression and sadness were considerably lightened by his news, and he became extremely excited. He was still weak from the loss of blood, and the blood transfusions which had been given him had not agreed with his constitution. He had suffered a slight jaundice, which had not increased his strength. But now that events were moving so rapidly his spirits rose deliriously. He listened intently to all rumors brought to him by his men, and evaluated them, especially rumors which leaked out from other Sections. Bishop told him that "the grapevine" stated that in various Southern Sections the people were particularly obstreperous, even more so than usual. Confederate flags were appearing everywhere, cheap flags contrived of old rags and paper, handmade and crude, and that the Military could not tear them down fast enough. "They say," said Captain Bishop, "that if they arrested everybody who was suspected of showing those flags, or making them, they'd have to kill off millions of people because the jails and the prisons wouldn't hold them." The grapevine also declared that young Southern soldiers were disappearing faster and faster from their regiments, and that officers were only half-hearted in attempts to apprehend them and punish them.

Good, thought Durant, grimly. The old Southern states had not been particularly alert or concerned when they had lost their sovereignty decades ago. They had shouted about "States' Rights," but their venal and treacherous representatives had steadily abrogated those rights at the command of the Government. When their Rights had gone completely, and they were reduced to faceless Sections, they had vented their tardy and futile rage on the Negro populations. Nearly one hundred thousand innocent Negro men and women and children had been slaughtered in a vengeance which ought to have been directed against the evil plotters in Washington. The State had not interfered, though it had "deplored" volubly. Let the people's fury expend itself on innocence, so that the State could become stronger! While the mob murdered, the plotters could work undisturbed on the program for the destruction of the liberty of the whole country. It was an ancient maneuver, but the Southern states, like their brother states in the North, had been stupidly and humanly blind. They never learn, they never learn, thought Durant, as he listened to the rumor about the Confederate flags. The time for action is when the disease first appears; an epidemic is almost impossible to control.

So now, in this desperate day, when the whole world lay in ruins, and America was in the full grip of a Communist Military dictatorship and its economy wrecked by wars, the Confederate flags appeared in thousands of villages, towns and cities! Good, brave gesture! A gesture almost too late for effectiveness, but still a gesture that men were living among docile slaves. What if the Southern states had forgotten their silly factionalism twenty years ago, and had joined with their Northern brethren in the preservation of freedom, and the unseating and the uncovering of vicious traitors and potential tyrants in Government? There would be a peaceful, prosperous and orderly world now, and not a world of despair and slavery. But the Southerners, even in the face of monumental and sinister evidence of the plot against all men, had vehemently defended their Senators and Representatives who were betraying them in Washington, and had denounced Northern Republican Congressmen who were warning them of the betrayal. How dared "Yankee politicians" defame the "good Southern gentlemen who represented Dixie in Washington?" The good Southern gentlemen, chuckling among themselves, had eagerly voted for monstrous taxation bills, bills shackling the press, bills restricting Constitutional liberties, bills giving the Military unlimited powers, bills abrogating the rights of the states, and had been among the very first to give assent to wars. In these, at any rate, the gentlemen of Dixie had concurred with their fellow plotters from the North, and had denounced, with them, any Senator or Representative who had lifted his voice in a cry of protest.

Tyrants never seize power, thought Durant. The people give it to them with hosannahs.

There were rumors that swarms of people were actually daring to gather together in the villages and towns and cities of the Southern Sections to sing old Christmas hymns in defiance of law. Their soldiers "tried to disperse the unruly and unpatriotic groups," and had their orders to fire on the law-breakers. But somehow, probably because of the night darkness, when the singers assembled, the soldiers were able to arrest only a few, and their shots never appeared to wound anyone.

There were rumors that in the great lumber regions unseasonal forest fires were breaking out and destroying large stands "essential for the war effort."

There were rumors that in various sections of the country crudely printed copies of the Constitution and the Declaration of Independence were being "seized" by the Military. There was even a rumor that a copy of the Declaration had been nailed right on the house door of the local commanding officer in Section 14, though the officer's residence was closely guarded. In Section 12, it was rumored, a "huge mob" had been fired upon for gathering together and singing the proscribed "Star Spangled Banner," and "had been dispersed with many casualties."

There were hundreds of these rumors from other Sections. The newspapers in Section 7 did not publish them. They spoke only of the enthusiasm of the people for the approaching Democracy Day and their dedicated work "in behalf of the war effort."

Two days before The Day, Durant sent for Walter Morrow of The Grange, Mr. Woolcott of the Bureau of Mobilized Labor, Captain Alice Steffens of the Department of Women's Welfare, and Karl Schaeffer of the FBHS, to consult with them about their speeches to be given in the City Stadium on December twenty-fifth.

Karl Schaeffer of the FBHS was the unknown quantity to Durant. He had had only routine contact with him, by telephone, on FBHS matters. He was still uncertain about the reason which had prompted Schaeffer to lie in his testimony against Alex Sheridan. Was Schaeffer "one of ours" or had he only desired Sheridan's position? Durant, in these momentous days, decided to find out.

The head of the FBHS was bland and pleasant when admitted to Durant's office, his large fair face expressing nothing but interest. He shook hands warmly with Durant, said he hoped that the colonel was completely recovered from his wounds, and that he was glad of this opportunity to discuss his speech with the colonel. He sat down, smiling amiably, and lighted a good cigar, waiting respectfully, however, until Durant's cigaret had been lit.

Durant scrutinized him, and his men and the Picked Guard regarded Schaeffer coldly and with distaste. Durant smoked reflectively; Schaeffer smoked with enjoyment. The two men gazed at each other in a silence that went on for a considerable time.

Then Durant said: "I understand you're doing good work in your office, Schaeffer. Congratulations."

Schaeffer smiled, and answered: "Thank you, Colonel. Of course, it was too bad that Potter eluded my men when they went to arrest him. Somebody must have given him a warning."

Durant closed one eye against the smoke of his cigarette. "Yes, too bad," he murmured. "By the way, his last pamphlets about the FBHS were particularly disturbing. Worst of all, thousands of them were not recovered, so we must deduce that the people in Philadelphia picked them up and made off with them. He must have set up his printing press in the neighborhood somewhere, for the pamphlets are still being printed and are being found daily in every shop and factory and on doorsteps. Can't you put on extra men, or something? Potter must be found."

He waited, smoking idly, but so alert that he began to sweat. Schaeffer's cigar, in spite of its volume of smoke, was apparently giving him trouble. He brought out a packet of paper matches. He lit one; it went out. He lit another; it went out. He lit a third, and he applied it to his cigar. But the cigar was still not giving satisfaction. He thrust his hand, muttering, into his pocket, and produced a metal lighter. He beamed sheepishly at Durant, and said: "I always forget I have this thing! Stupid of me, isn't it?"

Durant laughed, idly rubbed his right ear. Schaeffer smoked a moment, looked at his cigar, rubbed his left ear abstractedly. Schaeffer became grave. "Perhaps Mr. Sheridan would have done better about Potter, though I've done my best. He's a wily customer."

"But Sheridan was a traitor, himself," said Durant, trying to control his nervous agitation. "He was probably behind Potter all the time."

Schaeffer inclined his head. "If the colonel thinks so, perhaps the colonel is right. The colonel's opinion won't be questioned by me."

He sighed. He found he was having trouble with his eye. He took out his handkerchief, carefully folded it into a smooth wedge, and dabbed his eye four times.

Good, all good. But still, there was a possibility that the FBHS had all the signals of the Minute Men. Durant continued with the next test, wording it carefully and slowly.

"Our office, in spite of Potter, commends the work of your men. I know your difficulties. The work grows harder, instead of easier, for all of us. We never know from minute to minute what problems will arise, and the problems seem to be multiplying. Something must be done, after Democracy Day."

Schaeffer was silent; his thick light brows drew together thoughtfully. He seemed to be considering. Durant waited, and now his agitation was so intense that his fingers involuntarily clenched.

Then Schaeffer said, as slowly as had Durant: "I agree with you, sir, that the problems seem to be multiplying. The crucial point, I believe, will be after Democracy Day, if the people do not respond as expected. The work grows harder, yes, but we are adequate to the task, I believe. Difficulties, yes. We can overcome them, however, for our whole future is at stake."

The word signals had been changed only a day or two ago, as indicated in the Chief Magistrate's letter. The FBHS could not have had them so soon, or have decoded them so rapidly. They were too involved.

Durant said: "The celebrations for Democracy Day are to be more elaborate than usual. We have every reason to believe that the people will respond satisfactorily."

"I know they will," replied Schaeffer, and he pitched his voice to a certain note of enthusiasm, and to a certain intonation. "The best celebration we've ever had, Colonel! My speech, which I've been preparing very carefully with my assistants, is, I hope, more than satisfactory." He laughed boyishly, and struck the side of his right hand on the desk, three times.

Durant sighed, and smiled. Too many signals, too many signs and imperceptible shadings of voice, to be false. Durant became aware of the boredom of his men at these amiable exchanges. Even Sadler did not have these signals in their entirety. He had been alerted in the beginning, but Durant, after a quick glance, saw that he was slightly puzzled. However, Sadler would not have the more elaborate signals. They were reserved for a few leaders in the most vital fields.

A sensation of well-being and renewed hope came to Durant, though he was careful not to betray it. Morrow had refused to respond to any signals at all; it was very possible that he was working alone, if indeed he were working for the restoration of the Republic. If he were a Minute Man, or had any connections with Minute Men, there was also the possibility that he did not trust Durant.

Schaeffer was saying: "Has Dr. Healy been asked to make a speech?" A hangnail was bothering him; he rubbed it carefully.

Durant frowned, and waited. "Healy?"

"Why, yes. He usually makes a speech about the work of psychiatry in this Section, and he's always reminded the people, on Democracy Day, of the wonderful results he and his bureau are getting by 'raising up new young leaders to guide us into greater liberties and greater fulfilments.' Of course, that was before the privileged children were forced into the Federal schools. I understand he is nursing a case of violent ulcers over this and other curtailments. You might want to placate him, Colonel, and let him make his usual speech and give his side of the question. That would assure the people that you wish to preserve the freedom of the press and fredom of speech, no matter how much you disagree with him."

"An excellent idea," said Durant, with heartiness, after he had followed the tortuous hint to its conclusion. "Grandon, put in a call for Dr. Healy and asked him to come to see me at once."

Schaeffer stood up, smiling placidly. He shook hands with Durant, remarked on the bad weather, and left.

It was nearer half an hour later, instead of an hour, when Dr. Joseph Healy of the Public Psychiatric Department arrived. So Durant had very little time to assume a proper facial expression of despondency and doubt and defeat. He kept his expression while studying Dr. Healy, and made some mental notes.

Dr. Healy was not quite so dapper as before, and he had a distracted and harried air. His assurance and smirking benevolence were gone. His silvery-blond hair had definite gray streaks in it, his cold blue eyes had permanent lines of anxiety about them, and his smile was feeble if ingratiating. He had lost considerable weight, and was now very thin rather than slender. His grace had become abstracted fumbling; he sat down without the former dainty arrangement of his clothing; his delicate skin had lost its healthy flush and had become pasty. Durant felt intense satisfaction. If ever a man was chronically uncertain, that man was Dr. Healy.

In the meantime, the clever doctor was also studying Durant, and he was surprised and suddenly elated at Durant's expression of melancholy and worry. Part of his old confidence came back. He lit a cigaret with something of his former assurance.

Durant sighed. "Dr. Healy, I'm a little discouraged. I called you to talk with you about your speech on Democracy Day, which I understand you make regularly. But I also wanted to consult with you about the state of Section 7, particularly this city. Dr. Healy," he continued, leaning toward the other with a look of profound apprehension and disturbance, "I want you to be very frank with me. I'm in a quandary. Something's going wrong. I confess that I didn't quite realize the importance of what you said when we had our talk a long time ago, and though I still think you are incorrect about a number of things, I'd like a little advice and your opinion." He frowned, spread out his hands helplessly. "I've done my best, but the Chief Magistrate has indicated some disapproval."

Durant was pale enough, and strained enough, and his fingers shook authentically as he put his cigaret in his mouth. The trained doctor narrowly examined him, and was so enormously relieved that color returned to his face. An expert at dissimulation, himself, he was certain that he could detect it in others. His voice was purring and soothing as he began to make his subtle attack on this brutal military man who had caused him so much agony these past months.

He said: "Colonel, you've asked me to talk with you, frankly. When I last did so, in behalf of the State, you were furious. Forgive me, but I should dislike it very much if the colonel became furious again if I were candid. I'd do almost anything to avoid antagonizing the colonel."

Durant deliberately thought of the desperate and violent days ahead, and so without acting he could induce a look of trouble and fear. He let his mind dwell on young Vossen and the evil that had been Sheridan, and his eyes became tired and sick. Dr. Healy, watching closely, saw all this, and his elation made his heart beat rapidly.

Durant said in a worn and half-smothered voice: "Be candid with me. I promise you, in the presence of my men, that I won't take offense against you, though I might disagree." He made a gesture of pleading. "You've carried out my orders, implicitly. I've never had to complain to you." Now he was humble.

Dr. Healy's tight body relaxed. He leaned back in his chair, and a measure of his old elegance, and his feeling that he was always in command of any situation, returned. He contemplated the ceiling reflectively.

"Thank you, Colonel. I have always cooperated with the Military to the best of my ability, and I'm happy that you are pleased." He coughed. "You've mentioned that 'something has gone wrong.' I haven't made any reports to you, sir, because I thought you'd take umbrage against me. But you've asked me to be frank."

He took his eyes from the ceiling, and put on a look of serious regret. "Yes, Colonel, 'something has gone wrong.' I am a trained psychiatrist, and I know that the people are very restive these days, in Section 7. I know you have acted to the best of your ability, and have worked only in the interests of the State. Nevertheless—may I indeed be frank?—I think perhaps the colonel has moved too fast and too drastically. Perhaps events needed that, because of the new war effort. Nevertheless, the new indoctrinations of my Department, accelerated though they have been of necessity, have not been able to keep up with your directives. We have had to change our tactics too much, too abruptly, to keep pace with those directives." He paused, to let an ominous note intrude into the atmosphere. "Colonel, I can only say this: in all my years with the Department, in this Section, I have never seen the people so dangerously restless and so full of hatred."

He shook his head. "But perhaps you know all this, Colonel?"

"Only rumors!" cried Durant defensively. "Surely you don't credit rumors, Doctor?"

Dr. Healy smiled, shook his head again. "They aren't rumors, Colonel. I've seen burning barns, myself. I've heard the mutterings in war plants. I've seen distress of my good friends, the MASTS, who, though they've faithfully followed every directive, are broken-hearted. The farmers are extremely indignant. All these things have been brought to my attention. I've tried to appease the people, and our office has—brought in—many disturbed individuals, and we haven't been able to do much to reorient them. The devoted men in our various bureaus throughout Section 7 feel that the colonel does not fully understand their problems. Many of them have had nervous breakdowns. I've treated them privately, and have tried to assure them that the colonel is acting only for the best. Sir," and he leaned quickly toward Durant, "if matters are not soon alleviated, I can't be responsible for what might happen."

"Ambivalence?" pleaded Durant. "You told me all about that before. You think everybody has ambivalence?" he added artlessly.

At this absurd question, Dr. Healy smiled inwardly. The charging bull was only an animal, after all. Dr. Healy saw himself laughing with his dear friends tonight about this military brute, and promising them that things would soon change.

"It's the Minute Men! I know it!" shouted Durant, striking his desk with his fist. "I thought we'd destroyed every last one of them! Have you found any, Doctor?"

"No, Colonel. Not one. I think we have indeed destroyed 'every last one of them.' I think that the people are emotionally disturbed and dangerously rebellious, not because they are being 'led' by anyone, but spontaneously. That is very grave."

Durant thought of the secret societies set up by the farmers, the bureaucrats, the MASTS, societies doubtless well known to Dr. Healy, and doubtless inflamed by him, advised by him, and directed expertly by him—for revolution. It was not Durant's intention to have Dr. Healy reassure his friends too much, or have them slacken in their efforts. He frowned in concentration, and Dr. Healy believed that concentration to be anxiety and dread.

Durant simulated despair and anger. "We've got to do something! I've discounted rumors, but there are some things I haven't been able to explain. You've got to help me, Doctor. What do you suggest?"

Dr. Healy thought. He, too, was in a quandary. His friends were determined to overthrow the Military, and their friends, in all the other Sections, also had this determination. The Military must go, if The Democracy were to survive, and his friends must take over the State entirely, and crush the mob once and forever.

Durant waited, well understanding the doctor's thought processes.

"Look," he said urgently, "why not direct your speech at the people? I'm giving newspapers full freedom to report all the speeches. The people were pleased at my directive that the children of privileged groups are to be educated in the State schools. However, Doctor, it wasn't my intention that the other children should abuse them and persecute and torment them, the way they have been doing all these months. I sympathize with the parents. I tried to do my best, for The Democracy. So I'll publicly give my permission, on Democracy Day, for you to explain your position that the children of the privileged groups should be educated privately and exclusively, by trained specialists, in order that they may lead our nation in the future. You're persuasive. You can do it."

Dr. Healy regarded him steadily. Would this soothe his friends? Would this enrage the people further? No, it would not soothe his friends; they were too aroused. But it would enrage the people against the Military, which had changed its tactics. The people's mounting wrath would be directed against this thick dolt of a soldier, and all the Military, and they would then be more amenable to ruthless discipline and control when their superiors seized the Government. His friends had done their work excellently; their spies and inciters had been trained by himself in subtle approaches and the exactly proper methods of influencing the rabble.

Now he was excited. A few weeks, perhaps! A little extra work and effort! And it would be done! He had been hopeful at times, but more often fearful. Now he knew that he could hope fully. Durant saw him changing moment by moment, becoming what he once had been, the brilliant and dominant man and leader.

He pretended to hesitate. "Well, Colonel, I can only assure you that I'll do my best." He pulled himself up in his chair, and assumed an expression of resolute courage. "I'll prepare my speech and, in view of the fact that you have given me full permission to make a frank statement before the people, with full publication in the papers. I'll be able to state my position. With respect for the Military, of course."

Durant smiled widely and joyously. "Thank you, Doctor! Thank you!" He thrust his hand across the desk, and half rose. "I knew I could rely upon you!"

Dr. Healy shook that hand vigorously. You can certainly rely upon me; he thought, with exultation, and he mentally made a few other comments about Durant which would have shocked the ladies among his acquaintance, the poor ladies, once so charming and happy, and now so work-worn and shrewish since their servants had been removed.

"Well, boys," said Durant to his men, after Dr. Healy had left. "It looks as if we're getting somewhere!"

There was a silence, then young Grandon, with a sour look on his face, said with, however, the utmost deference: "And where does the colonel think he is going? We thought you had no use for Healy, the slimy witch-doctor!"

The young man's eyes were cold and venomous, and Durant was startled. "You've got to keep the civilians happy," he suggested.

"Why?" asked Captain Edwards.

Durant shrugged. "Temporarily, anyway. Democracy Day is coming up. Everything must be fine and enthusiastic. You know, Unity! Duty! Sac-ri-fice!"

His remark did not stir a smile. Six pairs of eyes fixed themselves on him without kindliness.

It had been snowing heavily all day, and a gray blizzard whirled over the city. Sadler remarked that though it was only five o'clock it might be best for the colonel to start home before the roads were blocked. The four Army officers were to attend a pre-holiday affair, and would probably remain in the city overnight. Durant was very tired. He was eager to go back to the warm farmhouse, so he and the Picked Guards left the building.

He was getting into his car when a voice hailed him, and the bland, good-tempered face and figure of Karl Schaeffer loomed through the white gale. "I was about to leave a copy of my speech with you, Colonel. I've just finished it," he said, unstrapping his suitcase. "I couldn't send it, for it is very confidential."

Durant was pleased to see him, but had no interest in the speech. He waved his hand, and shuddered in the cold. "You know what to do, Karl," he said largely. "As for me, I'm going home to a fire and whisky, and a book. Besides, I want to see the pre-Democracy Day shows on the television set. I understand Margaret Stanley will be especially good. Give my holiday regards to Mr. Kirk." He waved, and went toward his car. Then he heard Schaeffer say to Sadler: "Haven't I seen you somewhere, Lieutenant? Before today, months ago?"

The lieutenant shook his head. Schaeffer scrutinized him; his back was to Durant, who had paused in the act of getting into his car. Then Schaeffer, whitened by snow, paused.

"Now that I look at you, Lieutenant, I see I was wrong." He smiled, and deep friendly dimples appeared in his plump cheeks. He held out his hand. "Well, Lieutenant, if I don't see you before the holiday, I wish you every happiness. Take care of our colonel. He's a valuable man to all of us."

"Indeed, Mr. Schaffer," replied Sadler. It was only the thick and howling snow which muffled his voice, thought Durant, watching the handshaking. Then Schaeffer shook the hand of Beckett, and wished him well, also. Schaeffer waved, and disappeared in the white fog toward his own car. The Picked Guards arranged themselves on each side of Durant, and they rolled off on wheels which made no sound on the street.

"A nice feller," remarked Durant. "Better than Sheridan in

every way. And he isn't a traitor, either. I hope his speech isn't boring; I hate speakers."

Beckett answered: "I do, too. But I suppose it's part of our job." Beckett glanced at his fellow Guard. "That's the second time someone thought he had seen you before."

"Johnny," said Sadler, still in that tight and muffled voice, "you know that's ridiculous. Why, you and I have been together for years. We know everything about each other; we've practically grown up together, in training, and in assignments. Did you ever see Schaeffer before we came to this city?"

"No."

"Neither did I." He was silent for a few moments. They passed a struggling street lamp, and for some reason Durant looked at Sadler. It probably was only the reflection of the snow which made his face so taut and white, so bitterly strained.

"Johnny," Sadler was saying gently, "do you remember how we skied together, and how I hurt my leg and you carried me back, two miles or more? Do you remember the Cascade Mountains at dawn, when we were camped in the valley? Do you remember our hunting trips, when we were off duty, and how we talked at night around the fires? And when we explored the Everglades, and a 'gator nearly got us, and you beat him off with an oar? And when I was sick, and we were in the woods, and you nursed me? And your sister, whom you wanted me to marry, and your mother's cooking? And all the years we've spent together, friends, better than brothers?"

"Why, yes, I sure do, Chard," replied Beckett, surprised but touched.

"Maybe I'll go back and marry your sister, if she'll have me, and I get leave," said Sadler, and his voice became hoarse. "A lovely girl; an intelligent, sweet girl. I went away because I didn't think I was good enough for her, Johnny."

"That's crazy," said Beckett, with pleasure. "Louise always writes me about you. What better could she get than an officer in the Picked Guard?"

"And your parents, Johnny. Fine people. Your father with his books, and your mother, knitting and smiling. They love you, Johnny. They miss you."

Durant listened compassionately to these maudlin reminiscences. Of course, it was the holiday season, and in spite of Democracy Day old urges surged even in young men.

"Old-fashioned people. Not up to date." Beckett attempted to be off-hand, but his look at Sadler was affectionate. "I've had to warn my father. Mother's just a darling old girl, and I've always been her pet." He laughed, embarrassed.

"Yes," said Sadler, and his voice was somber. "You were always her pet. She cried when you left. She said she thought you'd never come back, not again, in your whole life."

"That's Ma's way," scoffed Beckett, but he sighed shortly. "Why shouldn't I go back?"

"She thought everything began and ended with you," muttered Sadler. "If—you never came back, it would kill her."

"Well, she's old," said Beckett tenderly, and he stared pensively ahead. He repeated: "Why shouldn't I go back?"

"Because these are dangerous days," said Sadler. His gun was in his hand, and his fingers tightened on it. "Johnny, if anything happens—to either of us—I want you to remember I was your friend, your best friend. I want you to remember what a friend you've been to me, even in the hard days. You took many a blame for me, for I was new to it, newer than you. You saved me a lot of time in the guardhouse. You shared your packages from home with me. We were never apart for very long. Johnny, I want you to know that outside of my—my own people—I like you more than any one I've ever known. You were the brother I never had."

Beckett was more surprised. "That's good. But why the funereal note? I expect to go on for years with you, Chard. Even after you marry Louise. Name the first boy for me, will you?" And he laughed with that awkwardness which men who love each other show at any display of sentimentality.

"Yes, Johnny," said Sadler, with heaviness. "I will. You're okay. I'll never forget you."

Because of Durant, Beckett laughed. "Why should you? We were practically told by the Chief Magistrate that he wouldn't separate us. What's the matter, Chard?"

"Nothing," said Sadler, and he slumped a little in his seat. "Nothing at all, Johnny. But just remember that we are friends."

"You sound as if you were going to disappear into the mists," said Beckett. But he was very moved. He stretched his hand across to Sadler, and they shook hands, briefly. "Good old Chard. Don't leave me, Chard."

"I won't. You can be sure of that."

Durant was not impatient. His keen intuition sensed tragedy in this small rolling world of the car. He said: "Not applying for a transfer, are you, Sadler? I think I ought to know."

"No," said Sadler, and he looked through the snow-shrouded window. "I'll stay with you, Colonel."

"Well, I'm staying," remarked Beckett jocosely. "That makes two of us."

Sadler did not answer.

A strange conversation, and, in its way, a disturbing one, thought Durant. Sadler was not a man to display emotion, and especially without any provoking element. It was the snow; it was the time of the year. Of course. A time for festivity, for prayer, for longing, for home-coming. But these men were young. What did they have to remember, about Christmas? What did they know of the love of a God becoming Incarnate?

It was something else. There was a quality in the talk between the two men which had a terribleness for Durant, and he was mystified. He pondered. The Picked Guards were a savage organization, without human sympathy or attachments. Yet here were two very young men, who had shared most of their lives together, and who loved each other as brothers ought to love, but seldom do.

The blizzard stopped abruptly as the car reached the country. The watery and yellowish snow of the past weeks, an ugly and dreary snow, had become this white wilderness, and Durant was entranced by the glittering brightness all about him. He forgot his diffused alarm at the conversation which had taken place between his Guards. He looked through the car windows and saw how the whiteness had piled itself in silent and marble mounds under an incredibly dazzling moon. Farmhouse roofs lay heaped with incandescent purity; stark trees stood absolutely still like ghostly images of themselves. Across the immaculate fields raced the sharp black shadows of fences, caught and transfixed in a moment of flight under the moon, while pearly reflections lay on the sides of alabaster dunes. All color, all sound, all motion, had ceased; a mystery had fallen on the shining earth, had steeped it in crystal light, had enveloped it within a crystal shell.

How was it possible for men to live in the midst of such beauty, such illuminated and awesome splendor, and be what they are? thought Durant. He remembered the lovely country scenes of the last summer, and looked at what lay about him now. Was this earth really purgatory, as some mystics had said, and God, in His infinite mercy, occasionally drenched the world of men with mirrored reflections of Paradise in order to lift their courage and comfort their souls and give them hope? City men should not live completely city-bound; they should run from their stony caves very often into the fields and the forests, so that they might not forget the true reality which existed beyond their darkness and their evil.

Yet, men lived among all this, and did not see, Durant's thoughts went on. Perhaps too many men were blind, and even those who had their homes where the mirages of heaven occurred most frequently were often blinder than their brothers imprisoned in the cities. The seeing spirit existed as a rare phenomenon among humanity. When it attempted to communicate what it had discovered to others it was greeted with derision, denounced as "infantile" and unsophisticated or naïve, or, as in these days, it was condemned as "an enemy of the people." When the seeing spirit was silenced, then evil souls dominated governments, and tyrants emerged from their black hiding-places. Only in the absence of faith in a whole nation could despotism triumph.

Durant became aware that only one of his Guards was interested in the enchanted wonder outside the car windows, and that one was Beckett. "We could ski on some of those hills," he said to Sadler, pointing to a range of gleaming mountains in the near distance. "Perhaps some of the farmers hereabouts have skis. We could borrow a couple of pairs. It's cold, and getting colder, and the snow'll be just right tomorrow. What do you say, Chard?"

Sadler did not reply, and Beckett repeated his remarks and questions. Sadler appeared to have difficulty in concentrating. "Ski?" he said, in a lifeless voice. "You always liked it, didn't you, Johnny? Yes. Ski," he added somberly.

"Now, what the hell's the matter with you?" demanded Beckett. "Thinking of home?"

"Yes," said Sadler. "I'm thinking of my home."

Undertones, thought Durant, becoming singularly uneasy. Beckett was sitting forward in his seat so that he could see his friend on the other side of Durant. He was staring in surprise. But he made no comment.

The car arrived at the Lincoln house; golden light poured out onto the snow from the windows. Durant, getting out of the car, breathed in the clear and sterile air of a country winter night. The cold struck his face with an exhilarating effect. He did not want to go into the house just yet; he wanted to walk in the snow, to look at the blazing moon, to exult in this pure and virgin air. It was all such a wonder to him, such a glory. A little icy wind rose, blew sparkles of brilliant snow into the air; the moon struck them, and they were silver and blue and scarlet and gold. Some of them settled on Durant's sleeve, and he was so moved at their exciting forms and perfection and glitter that he stood very still, hardly breathing.

"I think we'd better go in, Colonel," said Sadler. He stood close beside Durant, and he sounded urgent. "You know what happened when we had to stop out in the country a few weeks ago."

"Who would try anything here?" asked Durant, vaguely convinced that no violence could occur in this silent and marble world.

He walked away from the house, circled toward the rear, and then pushed his way through the snow which covered the garden. Wonder, he thought. When men lost the capacity to wonder they lost communion with God, and the capacity to be moved by anything or to understand anything.

He could hear his Guards behind him, crunching determinedly in the snow. He wished they would go away. A man wanted to be alone when he felt full of wonder. He drew the sweet and immaculate air into his lungs, with gratitude.

There was a slight scuffle behind him, and then Beckett's voice, loud and stammering: "What's the matter with you, Chard? Give me my gun!"

Durant turned as fast as the deep snow would allow him. Sadler was facing Beckett, and a gun, apparently Beckett's, was in his hand. The moon flooded down on the men's faces, and Durant could see them clearly. Beckett was stupefied, his eyes and open mouth like black holes in his face; Sadler's lips were pressed together as if he were suffering unendurable pain.

Durant's own mouth fell open with astonishment. But neither of the men noticed him; they were gazing at each other in an awful silence, standing there like two dark statues against the illuminated background of snow. Moment by moment passed, and the men did not move, but only looked at each other, forgetful of everything but each other.

Then Sadler said, quietly and with a great effort: "I've got to kill you, Johnny. Now."

Durant came to life. "Are you crazy, Sadler?" he cried. He put his hand on his own gun. His gloved hand was weak with terror, and cold sweat burst out on his face. A thousand shrieking thoughts invaded his mind, thoughts of betrayal, of violence, of confusion and dread.

Sadler did not glance at him. He was too preoccupied with Beckett, who was no longer astounded, but was standing stiff and straight in the moonlight like a wooden figure of himself.

Sadler said: "Colonel, you can go back to the house, if you want to. You don't have to see anything. I wish you'd go. It would be better for me."

Durant said, his voice trembling with anger and fear: "Put down your gun, Sadler, or I'll shoot you."

"No, Colonel," said Sadler, shaking his head, and never for an instant taking his eyes from Beckett. "I won't put down my gun. I didn't want to tell you this, but Johnny's a spy for the FBHS. He's been a spy ever since we came here, and perhaps before. I don't know about that, though. I only know that he was delegated to spy on you, and then kill you. He'd have killed you tonight, perhaps. That's why he didn't object to your walking out here; if he'd objected, I'd have known this wasn't the night you were supposed to die." Something was wrong with his voice; it had become weak and faint.

Sadler was speaking again, falteringly: "I got the signal that Johnny had to die very soon, if not immediately, from Karl Schaeffer, on the street tonight. You see, Colonel, Johnny didn't know. About Mr. Schaeffer. So Johnny's making his reports to Mr. Schaeffer, about you. He didn't report to the Chief Magistrate; his orders were to deal with the FBHS. He's already reported some things to Mr. Howard Regis, in Washington, who took Mr. Reynolds' place after Mr. Reynolds was assassinated. And Mr. Regis ordered him to work with Mr. Schaeffer. So, Mr. Schaeffer knew that it was too dangerous; all of it. Johnny had to die before any of his reports leaked out to others, the way reports always do, though Mr. Schaeffer has been very careful—"

Durant looked at Beckett. He said with some difficulty: "Beckett. What have you to say about this?"

Beckett turned his head slowly and regarded Durant with such sudden and violent hatred that there was no need of his replying. However, Beckett said: "I began to suspect you, you —— spy, you dirty Minute Man, a long time ago."

The two men watched and listened in silence, a sick and weary silence. Sadler's hand rose a little, as if he were trying to find a conclusive spot. "Wait," said Durant. He moved to Sadler's side; he could not look away from Beckett. "Where did I make my mistake, so it was evident? You're going to die, Beckett, so you might as well tell me."

But Beckett, grinning, shook his head. "Think I'd tell you, you swine? Others will come after me, when I'm dead. You'll never know. You'll just keep on making your mistakes until you're killed." Then his face changed, became contorted with rage. "Lots of us know what you're doing, and what men like you are doing all over the Sections. All that pressure you're putting on everybody! All that inciting, under the disguise of being good Military officers! We know! And we're killing you off, one by one. Did you know four of you have been killed in the last three weeks, and it was all 'suicide' or 'murder by a person or persons unknown'?" He laughed again, with a maniacal sound. "In a few weeks there won't be any of you left. Not a single goddamned one!"

So, thought Durant, shaking, that's why Carlson is taking so many chances. The situation's desperate. We've got to move fast.

He said aloud, in dull horror: "I wonder how much Regis knows?"

Beckett said derisively: "He knows everything! But he has to move under cover; lets his district directors do the work. Even Regis doesn't dare mix it up with the Military openly. Yet." Again his face became ugly with hatred. "So Schaeffer's one of you, eh? I might have known; he was too slow, and kept telling me to 'wait.' "

"But how did you communicate with him?" asked Durant. He felt so tired, he vaguely wished to lie down in the snow. "You were always with me."

Beckett laughed and laughed, and his eyes seemed to leap in their sockets. "You'll never know! Maybe through one of the Army men in your office; maybe through one of the farm laborers here; maybe someone just brushing by in the street. Live with that, you fake colonel! Live with that, you ——! You won't ever know until you feel a knife in your ribs or a bullet in your back." He paused, and regarded Durant with high mockery, and seemed so delighted that Durant dimly wondered if he were mad. "And it won't do you any good to change your Army officers; there'll probably be someone like me among them."

Durant's shaking became so strong that he had to put up his hand against a big tree near him to keep from falling. But I always knew the danger, he thought.

Beckett was speaking again, with malign viciousness: "You started it, you rotten dog! What you did here was copied in the other Sections. We knew something was wrong, a long time ago, months ago. We knew there was someone who was setting things off. I didn't know it was you, at first. Now I know it's you. That's what I reported to Regis, and to Schaeffer. You were the one we wanted, more than anybody else. I was sure of it, the way you condemned Sheridan to death, on no evidence at all."

I must be very, very careful after this. Durant told himself with painful slowness. And then he knew that there could be no more carefulness, no more caution.

Beckett was watching him, and he was laughing silently so that all his teeth sparkled in the moonlight. "You won't win!" he exclaimed. "You never win. You're too stupid. 'Rights of man'! 'Dignity of man'! 'Spirit of man'! I know all your imbecile slogans. Hell, they're so funny that it makes us laugh until we puke! We thought you'd be choked with all that manure twenty years ago, but still come up with your incantations and your pious —— about 'God,' and you still believe that men should be free and that men like myself should die, or be 'reeducated,' or something! Haven't you learned yet, and gotten it through your pork heads, that there aren't any men in the world except the strong ones, who haven't any slogans except force, and authority for themselves, and power for themselves? All the rest of you were born to serve and lick our boots! But you never learn!"

He lifted his fist and shook it over his head with fierce frenzy. "You won't win! Maybe you'll overthrow our authority this once, but we always come back and you never recognize us until we've got our boots on your necks! You even help us, until it's too late! You let governments shackle newspapers in the name of 'national security,' and you get all patriotic and submit to 'controls,' and taxes, and you march out to wars with your silly faces shining, and you worship 'free speech' and let us take advantage of it until we have you where we want you!"

His excitement became frantic. His whole body was convulsed by his laughter; his eyes shot glances of such malignance and contempt at Durant that the latter involuntarily shrank.

Then Durant said, quietly but steadily: "You won't win again, Beckett. With the help of God, you won't win, not ever again."

But Beckett shook his head and replied, with savage mirth: "We always win; you always lose. Because we use your slogans while we put chains around your necks! And we wave your flags, while we're making our own."

Suddenly, the terrible light left his face, and it became abruptly dark and grave .He had forgotten Durant in one instant. He was looking, now, at Sadler, whose gun was pointing at his chest.

"I guess you can't do anything but kill me, Chard." And now his voice was almost gentle. "I'd do the same thing in your place; if I'd known about you before, I'd have killed you. It's always you or me, all the time, isn't it?"

"Wait," said Durant, and his sickness was a huge lump in his chest, cutting off his breath. He had to struggle to speak again. "I can't have you do this to your friend, Sadler. We can put him under arrest, throw him into the Military prison, keep him there until it's all over—"

Sadler replied, not looking at him, but only at Beckett: "No, Colonel. You could order him put in solitary, but he'd find a way to communicate with our enemies. There'd be no way to stop him. And that would be the end of you, no matter how well you were guarded. The Chief Magistrate warned me, particularly, to watch you."

Beckett started. "The Chief Magistrate?"

"Yes," said Sadler, with tiredness in his voice. "I don't know if he knows about you, Johnny, but he's one of us."

Beckett sagged momentarily.

"You see," continued Sadler softly, "we really have won, after all. If you are everywhere, we are, too."

He lifted his gun, and his face was stark and gaunt in the wild white light. Durant caught his arm, and he said with involuntary passion: "I'm sick of all this killing! There must be another way—"

Beckett burst into a tremendous shout of laughter. He pointed his finger at Durant. "You think you have 'won,' you damned fool? 'Sick of killing,' eh? With your kind of minds, how can you win? You dirty weaklings!"

"May God have mercy on your soul," said Durant. No one heard him, for there was a stupendous crash of sound, and Beckett threw up his arms. He swung about once, staggered, then fell into the snow face down.

The moon poured its argent light down on the white earth. Flakes of whipped snow winged their silent way through the bright air like colored insects. But there was an acrid smell in the sweet clarity, and there was a man in the soft whiteness who was dead. A frightful enemy, who was dead. A man who was dead, a young man, thought Durant. A young man corrupted and polluted by evil, but not a man born evil. He had been fashioned into what he was.

Sadler stood with the smoking gun in his hand. His head had fallen on his chest; he seemed to be in a trance. Durant wanted to speak to him, but had no words for such anguish; Sadler was beyond comforting.

Silently, then, Durant offered up a prayer for the young man who had died. It was a bitter prayer, and Durant had to struggle to withhold hatred for the men who had perverted that soul. He found it easier to pray: "Almighty God, preserve our children from corruption by the men of evil, as this soul was corrupted. May our future generations turn from the wicked ones each hour of their lives; let them recognize the vile when they appear so that they may be armed spiritually and morally against them."

He put his hand gently on Sadler's shoulder. "Let us go," he said.

But Sadler looked down at his dead friend. Then he turned to Durant, and he was weeping. "It's cold," he stammered. "We can't leave him here in the snow. It's too cold."

He bent and lifted Beckett in his arms, and carried him ahead of Durant, as a brother might carry his brother, or a father his child. There were dark and silent and shrinking figures standing in the white fields now, anonymous figures that had been brought out by the crash of the gun. They moved aside as Sadler carried his friend, and they stared mutely at the dead face upturned to the moon, and the face above it, hardly less dead.

"There's nothing I can say to you that'll help you," said Durant to Sadler, as they waited in Durant's room for an answer to his call for the Chief Magistrate.

They had conducted an uninspired conversation concerning Beckett's "suicide" for the benefit of the spidery dictaphone behind the picture on the wall. They had expressed a dull horror, which, however, had not been hypocritical; most of the remarks had been made by Durant, with Sadler merely muttering or sighing. Now the wires had been detached, and Durant could speak with misery and pity.

The effort to talk for the edification of the unseen listeners had been too much for Sadler. He sat in his chair, which was pushed against the door, and he had covered his face with his hands. Durant watched him compassionately. He went on: "Beckett wasn't like the rest of them, like Sheridan, for instance. He hadn't been born evil. So, we've got to fight harder, now, to save the millions of our young men from spiritual obliteration, and their children from slavery."

Sadler did not remove his hands from his face, but he replied in a smothered voice: "That's the only consolation I have." After a moment or two, he dropped his hands; he was totally exhausted, and his eyes had fallen far back in their sockets and their lids were swollen and red.

Dr. Dodge knocked on the door, and Sadler admitted him. The old man was carrying a tray of whisky. He regarded his son with pain and sadness. "I've covered him up, downstairs," he said, in his feeble voice. "He—he looks very—" He stopped, for Sadler had made an agonized gesture. "I know," said Dr. Dodge. He put the tray on a table, and his furrowed face became stern and hard. He looked into space, and added: "It wasn't your fault; it wasn't even the fault of Beckett. It happened because of my generation. I killed your friend, Clair. I killed thousands like you. In my classrooms, in my writings, in my speeches. In everything I did, years ago. That's my punishment, and the punishment of my contemporaries."

The telephone rang, and it took all Durant's efforts to raise himself and answer it. "Curtiss, sir," he said. His voice was thick and uncertain. "I'm sorry to report that Beckett, one of the Guards you assigned to me, committed suicide about two hours ago. I don't know just how it happened. We were standing in the snow, then all at once—he shot himself in the chest."

There was a little humming silence, then Carlson said with concern: "I'm greatly distressed by the news. In looking over Beckett's dossier, recently, I noted that he had been confined to some mental institution when he was about eighteen." Carlson paused. "There was no reason to believe he'd have a relapse at any time, and his conduct had been sane and exemplary after his release. Please accept my regrets. And convey to Sadler my condolences. The two young men have always been very much attached to each other."

"Yes," said Durant wearily, looking briefly at Sadler who stood in the center of the room like a man caught in a nightmare.

Carlson went on, in his grave, calm voice: "I shall order three Picked Guards to fly to you immediately, Curtiss. In the meantime, don't admit anyone into your room. I don't doubt the integrity and devotion of your officers, of course, but I'd prefer that you remain closely guarded by my men, who are alerted always for any possible enemy. Army men don't always realize danger. Too confident. The Picked Guards are never confident, of anyone, at any time. Especially the men I am sending you."

Durant decoded: "You can rely on these; they are Minute Men. Some way, you've been too careless of yourself. You have a spy among your associates."

Who? thought Durant: Grandon, Bishop, Edwards, Keiser? Grandon, of course!

"In these uneasy days," Carlson resumed, "my appointed officers should take every precaution. I'm sorry to say that matters have become somewhat alarming, though I hope that it is only a temporary restlessness. In fact, I'm sure it is."

"Watch for the third and last signal," Durant decoded. "Very soon. We must move rapidly, for we're in desperate danger."

Durant said: "I haven't noticed any 'restlessness' in Philadelphia and adjacent areas, sir. Everything is calm. The people are happy and contented and are anticipating our celebration of Democracy Day."

"Good," replied Carlson. "I meant to call you tonight, even if I hadn't had this call from you. You are going to have two distinguished guests, I learned today. Mr. Howard Regis of Washington, head of the Federal Bureau of Home Security. He replaced Mr. Reynolds, you know. And Mr. Dean Burgess, head of the Confederated Association of Labor Unions, also from Washington."

Durant was greatly alarmed. There had been nothing in Carlson's last remark to indicate any private information about Regis and Burgess. So Durant stuttered: "Mr. Regis? I—I've never met him. As able as Mr. Reynolds, sir?"

Carlson said coldly: "Very able. I know him well, and Mr. Burgess is a close friend of mine. They'll be staying at my home in the country, so there'll be no necessity for you to provide quarters for them. Extend every courtesy to both these gentlemen during their stay."

Durant flushed, for Carlson had told him: "I shall tell you nothing. You must conduct yourself as if you were what you appear to be. That is the only way to protect you."

Carlson was continuing: "When your three new Picked Guards arrive, they'll have their instructions about poor Beckett's body, and it'll be removed at once for return to Beckett's parents. I shall send them a message immediately. Good night, Colonel. Take extra precautions during Democracy Day."

He hung up abruptly. Durant turned to Dr. Dodge, who was detaching the dictaphone which he had attached during Durant's conversation with Carlson. Durant motioned him to attach the wires again. He said to Sadler: "Three Picked Guards are arriving by midnight to assist you, Chard. Then you can have some rest. As for me, I'm going to sleep immediately. My arm's bothering me; after all, I've had two accidents to it in the past few months, and so I'll take a sedative. Wake me when the guards arrive. I'll have my dinner with them."

"Good night, Colonel," said Sadler abstractedly. "I'll be sitting here by the door."

Dr. Dodge detached the wires. Durant said hurriedly: "Regis is coming. I don't know what he is. From all indications, I'd say he's another Reynolds. He and Dean Burgess are going to address the people on Democracy Day."

Dr. Dodge left the room in order to prepare Durant's and Sadler's dinner trays. Sadler seated himself at the door, his gun in his hand as usual. He looked at Durant and said, with an effort: "Things are getting pretty bad, sir?"

Durant frowned. "I'd say that the heads of the State in Washington are more than just aware that something is happening. They don't dare move just yet."

He added, with disgust: "I've certainly been generous about myself! I must have been very easy to spot."

"No, Colonel," said Sadler. "I've watched you very carefully. You're a good actor, and sometimes I've thought that you actually believed yourself to be a member of the Military." He smiled a little at Durant's embarrassment. "I think you've got the FBHS spies confused; they don't know if you are just too zealous as a military man, or an enemy of theirs. You see, I haven't told you everything."

"No?"

Sadler shook his head. "Johnny and I—" He stopped and glanced away. "You see, Johnny and I sometimes talked about you. Not often, because we didn't have the opportunity. It was only lately that Johnny expressed his suspicions of you to me, and hinted about his extra-curricular activities as a spy for the FBHS."

Durant brooded on this. He exclaimed: "This is getting on my nerves! Damn it, I know it sounds childish, but how long can a man go on expecting a bullet or a knife any minute?"

Sadler smiled again, sadly. "Well, Colonel, think of all the others in the same predicament."

Dr. Dodge returned with the supper tray, and said to his son: "You don't have to examine or taste the colonel's portion, Clair. I kept watch on the food." He hesitated. "However, there was the ham which I had previously prepared for tonight. I left it on the stove for about half an hour. As usual, I gave a piece to one of the dogs." His old face darkened. "The dog died almost immediately."

Durant was freshly aghast. He swore viciously. "Who was in the house at the time, Doctor?"

"No stranger that I know of. It was this morning, before you all left. The Lincolns had had no opportunity to touch the ham, or to be in its vicinity. So, it might have been Beckett." Dr. Dodge eyed his son compassionately for a moment. "However, I don't think it was Beckett, for he and Clair were with you during that half hour. Your own men, Colonel, followed you a few minutes later in their own car."

"Or, it could be a farm laborer, or a spy in the guise of a farm laborer, right here on the premises."

Dr. Dodge said: "No. I've thought of that. Not one of them was about the house. They were at work, and our friends would have reported any absence of a fellow worker. You haven't forgotten, have you, Colonel, that our people are watching you to see that no harm comes to you?"

Then, thought Durant, it was definitely one of his four officers who had tried to kill him. If he had eaten that ham, his Guards would have eaten some of it, too. There would have been three murders, at least. They're getting desperate, Durant said to himself. They are taking all kinds of chances. Well, Durant's thoughts continued, they seem a little more desperate than we are, and that's some consolation.

He had little appetite for his supper, and Sadler ate nothing. The moon had gone; a fresh blizzard howled about the warm house. Durant drank his hot coffee, hoping that the chill shivering in his bones would subside. He could not forget the dead man lying downstairs in the glare of the lights which never went out. He could not forget Sadler carrying his friend in his arms through the snow. There were bloodstains on Sadler's uniform.

Sadler sat at the door, his reddened eyes fixed on nothing. Dr. Dodge sat in a chair near Durant, and looked at his son. The wind thundered against the windows, but this was the only sound. Durant, all at once, could not stand the waiting and ominous silence.

"What do you want me to give you for Christmas, Dr. Dodge?" he asked, trying to smile.

The old man slowly turned his face to him, and answered quietly: "A gun, Colonel."

"Chard," said Durant. "Beckett's gun. You still have it?"

Sadler looked at his father somberly. Then he withdrew Beckett's gun from his own holster and threw it at the doctor's feet. The gesture was one of weary contempt. Dr. Dodge picked it up, and his hands trembled as he pretended to examine it. "It won't be missed?"

"If it is," said Durant, "it doesn't matter. Things are moving too fast. We have to take reckless chances now."

Dr. Dodge held the gun in both his hands. Then he feebly got to his feet. "Kill," he murmured. "We helped to bring this about—all this killing." He pushed the gun in his pocket, and picked up the supper tray. Sadler moved aside so his father could leave, and though Dr. Dodge hesitated, imploringly, at the door, Sadler turned aside his head. Well, thought Durant with compassion, that's how it is. The fathers have earned the loathing of their sons.

He thought of his own children. He had not betrayed them. He was fighting for their lives, and something more precious than their lives: their right to live as free men in a free world. His fortitude returned.

He saw he could not talk to Sadler, as Sadler, at his post by the door, had forgotten him. So he picked up a book, lit a cigarette, and tried to read. However, the events of the night had robbed him of concentration. He found himself reading, over and over, that famous passage in Robert Cheswick's *The Turn of Destiny*, published just before Cheswick's arrest and subsequent execution as a "subversive."

"That which, among the ethics of men and the government of men, is not man-centered, is evil. The abstract, therefore, should be concerned only with the fields of mathematics and physics and kindred sciences, if it is to remain harmless. Once any scientist or layman or politician or government departs from anthropomorphic values, or advances any concept unconcerned with those values, society is in danger. Man is not an abstract; his emotions, his spirit, his virtues and his vices are not abstracts, and are treated so only to his peril, and to the obliteration of his personality. We have seen the evil of the abstract approach to man in all authoritarian governments, where man as a spirit has been derided and discounted, and where his flesh has been regarded as a machine. The living creature, drenched with soul, is a mysterious but none the less potent entity, fired with dreams and possessed of enigmatic memories beyond his immediate experience. Any attempt to measure these, or to control or 'channel' them, or to subject them to a slide-rule, or any other 'scientific' calculation, including what is called 'psychiatry,' is to invite madness. There is a point beyond which those who 'study' man dare not go."

The great clock in the hall below struck the hour of eleven, massive strokes full of music. Durant had often listened with pleasure. But tonight the strokes blended together in his ears in a mighty jangle of sound, discordant and without meaning. He put down his book. He was about to speak to Sadler, for he could no longer endure the silence which followed the striking of the clock, when he heard the noise of a car outside, and the robust laughter of men.

Sadler got to his feet, crouched by the door, his gun in his hand, and Durant stood up. "Only my men," he murmured. But Sadler listened, and Durant listened, also. The men were stamping into the house, speaking loudly and raucously, and joking. Apparently the party they had attended had been very satisfying, to judge from their voices. Then, all at once, there was a shocked silence. They had come upon the body of Beckett. The house still reverberated with the banging of doors, but now there was no laughter, no voices, no movement.

The officers apparently were standing there in the living room, where Beckett lay. The wind screamed suddenly against the windows, wailed away into the night. Sadler still crouched by the door, and Durant could see that his finger was on the trigger of his gun and that all his muscles were tensed. Then Sadler half turned his head and motioned fiercely to Durant in the direction of the landscape on the wall. Durant ran to it, and attached the wires. He moved away, yawned with an effort, muttered, and said, sleepily: "What's the matter? I heard something—"

"Your officers, sir," replied Sadler quietly.

There was a pounding, now, up the stairs, the tramping of heavy boots, the harsh sound of gasping. Someone struck heavily on the door, and Durant exclaimed: "What is it? What's all the row about?"

Grandon answered him, excitedly: "Beckett, sir! Down there, dead. Shot!" There was a confused muttering behind him. Someone tried the handle of the locked door. Sadler lifted his gun. Now Durant's heart began to leap and strain.

He said as calmly as possible: "I know. Beckett, for some damned reason we don't know about, committed suicide tonight. Terrible. Nothing we can do about it, though."

Who, among those men beyond the door, understood? Who, among them, did not need an explanation? The handle rattled again, and Bishop said: "Are you all right, sir? May we come in and talk about it?"

But it was Sadler who answered, in his deadly voice: "No, you can't. Orders from the Chief Magistrate. Three Picked Guards will be here by midnight.

There was a smothered and startled cursing in the hall. Grandon said: "Colonel Curtiss? Are you sure you're all right? Why can't we come in?"

Sadler pressed his body against the door. "The colonel is all right. You heard his voice. If any of you tries to force this door I'll shoot to kill. And so will the colonel."

Durant could hardly breathe, in his quick fear. He made himself laugh. "Orders from the Chief Magistrate," he parroted Sadler. "Go on to bed, boys."

"Did you hear the bastard Sadler?" cried Edwards incredulously. "He said he'd 'shoot to kill'! Kill any of us!"

"That's right," said Sadler. "Those are my orders."

"But why?" demanded Keiser truculently. "What's this got to do with Beckett being shot?"

"Nothing at all," Durant replied irritably. "We don't know why the Chief Magistrate issued those orders; we only know he did. Now, get the hell away from the door and go to bed. You woke me up, and I've taken a sedative."

They went away, but Durant doubted that they separated. He thought he could hear indignant murmurs and angry mutters for a long time. Sadler did not sit down again. He faced the door like a sentry, and Durant sat on his bed with his own gun in his hand. It was queerly like a siege. A siege. Yes. His heart continued to beat painfully, and he said to himself, as he had often said: "I'm just not the man for things like this!"

It was half-past twelve before the Picked Guards arrived. Dr. Dodge admitted them. The three young men were curiously anonymous in appearance, all of a height, all young, all harsh-faced, all with bright and wary eyes. It was Sadler, rather than Durant, who carefully examined their credentials and scrutinized each one, while Durant watched.

So, these were Minute Men. From their glances, from their quick movements, from the way they set themselves without direction in various strategic points in the room, Durant knew that they were only too well aware of the desperate danger that lived all about them. They had a covenant with death. That covenant would soon be broken, and they knew it. They looked back at Durant, and, in momentous silence, he looked back at them.

Suddenly, Durant thought of what Darwin had once written: "To survive is to be valuable. To be is to be good." Under those circumstances, he said to himself, I'm damned valuable, and I must be as good as all hell! Maybe that's why I'm sweating, he added caustically.

Durant took a sedative that night to quiet his nerves and to help lessen that awful cold trembling which had settled about his bones. But he slept only briefly, and the snatches of sleep were invaded by confused nightmares, all in vivid colors. He would awaken, drenched with sweat, to see the low lights in his room and the unsleeping faces of two of his Guards. Sadler sat there, back to door, a motionless stone of a man, and a Guard sat near the window. The other two Picked Guards were stationed outside the bedroom door, and sometimes they spoke in hushed mutters. It was extremely nonconducive to repose, and Durant after awakening, would lie with closed eyes remembering the events of the night and the pressure of coming violence.

All his muscles ached from tension. He tried to fix his mind upon his wife and children, to remember their smiles and their voices. Then he would shake with overpowering terror, not for himself, but for his family. The success of a revolt no longer meant for him the emancipation of a country, but the deliverance of his family from evil. After all, he would ask himself, isn't it impossible for any but a few of the heroes and saints to think in universal terms, in a state of self-abnegation? Man cannot divorce himself from his emotions and from his heart. Rather than be denounced for that, he should be praised and lauded and encouraged, for out of individual souls sprang the great fires of reform. Uniformity, even in virtue, was to be condemned.

He slept a little better toward dawn, but woke about eight o'clock so exhausted and undone that he could hardly move. Sadler came to the bedside, and Durant blinked up at that haggard face which had become so much older during the last few hours. Durant said: "I think I'm having a nervous breakdown."

Sadler smiled involuntarily. Durant felt so much pity and concern for the younger man that he assumed irritability in order to hide his emotions. "Don't smile. I'm not getting up. I'm going to stay in this damn bed all day. Perhaps for two days."

The idea suddenly had immense appeal for him. He contemplated the safety of his room and his bed with growing pleasure. Not to cower in his car; not to drive through broken and snow-blown streets for a while; not to look at the strained and savage faces on the streets; not to smell the fury in the stagnant air; not to plot and plot and plot incessantly! Surcease. It was a marvelous idea. After all, he consoled himself, even soldiers are permitted to rest after hard engagements.

"I'm shell-shocked," he said to Sadler. "Battle fatigue."

The other Picked Guard came to the bed and joined Sadler. He had not slept for a single instant during the night, yet his boy's face was flushed with health and his eyes sparkled. For some reason Durant became resentful, and thought of himself as an old man. "What's your name?" he asked. "And how old are you?"

The name was Tom Griffis, the age, twenty-one. Durant regarded him enviously. He flipped over his hot pillow and again announced that he was ill and that he was going to remain in bed. "Perhaps for the rest of my life," he added.

The Guards laughed, and Durant was relieved that Sadler could laugh after the dreadful night. That comes of being young, he reminded himself, regarding his thirty-one years with distaste. He felt a hand on his forehead, and Sadler said to his colleague: "The colonel does have a fever. We'd better call an Army doctor." His voice was serious. Durant was alarmed. What if he were really ill? Certainly his bones ached and his head was a furnace. He tried to sit up; the whole room swam about him and he fell back.

"I can't be sick," he said grimly. "I don't dare, with Democracy Day the day after tomorrow. No, it's tomorrow, isn't it?"

"That's why we must have a doctor," said Sadler. "At once." He picked up the telephone and called Philadelphia while Durant lay in his bed stiff with anxiety.

Sadler called in the other Guards, who looked exactly like Tom Griffis. They were so young and so boyish and there was such an aliveness about them, and there was no somberness in their eyes, no bitterness about their mouths. However, in their backgrounds, there must have been devoted and determined parents of superior mentality, and teachers who had trained them in the proscribed ideals of the Republic. That would account for their air of compact fearlessness. These young men, who had been born in an enslaved country, had seen nothing but war and regimentation about them, yet had the fortitude and assurance that must have been the endowment of the old pioneers who had originally driven back the wilderness to create a once-great civilization. In spite of his weakness, Durant's spirits rose.

"May your tribe increase," he said to them.

They grinned at him, shifted their belts and saluted.

"You boys have to sleep, sometime," Durant remarked. "You'll be with me all day; you can take turns sleeping. Sadler, you and Tom can lie down in the next room, which Captain Bishop occupies at night. Sleep for about four hours, then the other kids can have their turn."

There was a sudden and angry hubbub of protest and outrage in the hall outside, and Durant heard Edwards' voice:

"Damn you, you're only sergeants, even if you are the Picked Guard! I'm a captain, and your superior, and when I say I and Bishop and Grandon and Keiser are going in to see our colonel, we're going in!"

"Yes, sir," said one of the Guards. "That's perfectly all right, sir. But you must all leave your weapons with us, down to your pocket knives. And only two of you can go in at a time. Orders, sir; sorry, sir." He added, equably: "Maybe the captain forgets that the Picked Guard isn't subject to the Army, not even to a captain, or even a general. We take our orders only from the Chief Magistrate."

"Our colonel is an Army man." This was Grandon speaking. He raised his voice: "Colonel Curtiss! May we come in?"

"An outrage!" exclaimed Bishop. "What's the matter? Is our colonel under arrest or something? Something's wrong, somewhere."

"I'm not under arrest," replied Durant, with annoyance. "I'm just under guard. Too many incidents lately. I order you to obey the Picked Guards, boys."

There was more argument outside the door. Apparently the honor of the Military was being questioned, and the officers resented it angrily. Then the door was flung open and Grandon and Edwards marched in, weaponless, their faces dark with rage. Durant had a brief glimpse, before the door was shut firmly behind these two, of Keiser and Bishop, seething furiously, while the Picked Guard stood beside them, in possession of all weapons.

Grandon and Edwards, pointedly ignoring Sadler and Griffis, came at once to the bed. They were breathing loudly, and their salutes were short. Durant looked up at them. One of these? Grandon's youthful face was tight and his eyes were narrowed. Edward's large and sturdy body expressed his sense of humiliation, and the hard hazel eyes glittered unpleasantly in his big and rugged face. Sadler and Griffis stood close by, negligently holding their guns.

"Perhaps the colonel would be willing to give us an explanation of all this," said Edwards.

Durant pondered a little. Then he looked at them keenly. "Beckett committed suicide last night. I understand that he had some mental disturbance when he was very young. We were all out together, in the snow, and he suddenly began to rave. Before we could stop him, he pulled out his gun and shot himself."

Did Grandon's face tighten and become closed and secret, and did Edwards' face become smooth and shut? Durant asked himself. Or was it all his imagination?

"What has that to do with the assignment of three more Picked Guards, and their arrogant attitude towards us, your executive officers?" demanded Grandon.

"Nothing at all," Durant assured them. "But, you remember all those rumors you boys have been feeding me? I have reason to believe, now, that they were facts, not rumors. And so the Chief Magistrate has assigned these extra Guards to me."

"And we, your four officers, aren't enough to protect our colonel?" suggested Edwards. "Our loyalty is in question?"

Durant pretended astonished shock. "Now where did you get that idea, you idiots? The Picked Guards are merely supplementing you. The people are in such a dangerous state of unrest that the Chief Magistrate wants to take extra precautions. To be sure that I survive," added Durant.

The two officers were silent. He could read nothing from their faces.

"There's only routine work today," Durant continued. "You, Edwards and Bishop can handle that yourselves. I intend to rest. In fact, I'm sick, I think. I must be all right for Democracy Day, tomorrow."

"That doesn't explain why our guns and knives were taken away from us at the door, by our inferiors in rank," said Edwards, affronted. "Do they expect us to shoot you, or something? Our colonel?"

Sadler interposed calmly: "If Captain Edwards will permit me. We have our orders that no one shall enter the colonel's room armed, except the Picked Guards. Perhaps the Chief Magistrate was too upset, when the colonel reported Beckett's—suicide—to him, to remember to make exceptions in favor of the colonel's executive staff."

Durant waved his hand. "You boys go and collect more rumors for me," he suggested. "The doctor's coming, and, frankly, I feel shot to hell."

The two officers stalked out with umbrage, not looking again at Sadler and Griffis. Keiser and Bishop were then admitted. Durant examined them furtively. Keiser's sullen face was even more sullen this morning, but Bishop's typical Army face—stolid and blank—merely expressed angry bewilderment. Durant wearily permitted Sadler to repeat his explanations. Keiser's sullenness increased, and he stared at Durant meaningly. Bishop was more bewildered than ever.

The two officers pounded indignantly out of the room, rejoined their fellows and clattered downstairs for breakfast, making remarks about the Picked Guard that were extremely uncomplimentary and obscene. Durant laughed, in spite of his headache and general misery of mind and body. Then he sobered. He said to Sadler: "One of them? Two of them?"

Sadler gestured in the direction of the landscape, and Durant caught his breath. Sadler replied: "I think one aspirin will be sufficient, Colonel."

"A nice time to be ill," said Durant fretfully. He got out of bed with difficulty and went into his bathroom where he washed and shaved. Each motion, however small, brought cold sweat to his face. He examined himself in the mirror. He was gray, his eyes smudged with exhaustion. When he returned to his room, Dr. Dodge was entering with a large breakfast tray. The old man exhibited more feebleness this morning, and his hands shook. Griffis went to his aid with youthful kindness, chatting pleasantly. "That's too heavy for you, Grandpa," he said, taking the tray. He regarded Dr. Dodge with compassion, then patted the bent shoulder. But Sadler, by the door, did not look at his father.

Dr. Dodge straightened and turned to the young Guard. The boy smiled at him pityingly. "We'll take care of the colonel," he said. "Bet you have enough work without playing waiter."

Dr. Dodge stood there, his worn hands hanging at his side. He could not take his filmed eyes from the boy's face. His mouth quivered. Then, silently and without a change of expression, he began to weep, the slow tears rolling into the furrows about his mouth. He lifted one hand as to wipe them away, then dropped it again. His head sank on his emaciated chest.

"Hey!" said the boy, concerned. "What's the matter, Grandpa?" He took out his own handkerchief and dabbed at Dr. Dodge's face inexpertly. "Feeling bad this morning? They overwork you here? That's a damned shame!"

Durant could not refrain from glancing at Sadler, so stiff and unseeing at the door. Durant became angry. He could understand Sadler's grief for his friend, and his rage that his father helped to bring about the circumstances under which Beckett had died. But enough was enough. A man, especially an old and broken man, can absorb just so much retribution.

Dr. Dodge made a piteous effort to compose himself. He tried to smile at the young Guard. Then he turned away and tottered toward the door. Sadler moved aside. But the old man stood and gazed up at him, speechlessly, and he was visibly trembling. "You might unlock the door for him," said Durant, in a loud voice.

Sadler started, reached mechanically for the bolt. Then he stopped. Slowly, and as if without volition of his own, he looked at his father. A long moment passed. Then, with an involuntary moan, hardly audible, Sadler caught his father in his arms, and the two men clung together, clutching each other in an attitude of fierce desperation and sorrow, and one of Sadler's arms pressed Dr. Dodge's head against his shoulder.

Tom Griffis stared, fascinated, at this tableau. Durant touched his arm, and soundlessly moved his lips in the words "his father." The young Guard's face filled with astonishment, and then pity, and then commiserating anger. He sat down, stared at the floor, shaking his head over and over.

When Dr. Dodge had gone, Durant and Sadler and Griffis turned to the breakfast tray. But Sadler drank only a cup of coffee; he was preoccupied with his sorrow and personal agonies.

Durant found himself unable to eat. Only young Griffis devoured his breakfast, and even he was silent. He kept peeping anxiously at Sadler, and it was evident that he was embarrassed as well as sympathetic.

Two Army doctors arrived in a flurry. They were stopped courteously by the Picked Guards outside the door, who explained that they must be searched, and their bags, also. The doctors made no protest, evidently. The door opened and they entered the room rapidly. Durant knew them both, and, as usual, he greeted them with contemptuous courtesy. He could never forget how supinely these professional men had submitted to authoritarianism, and how meekly they had served it, some with fear, some with abject approval because of Socialistic convictions. Tom Griffis stood by alertly, his hand on his gun while they examined Durant. Then they sat down and discussed Durant's symptoms learnedly. The colonel had a fever, but there were no objective or subjective indications beyond that fever. The colonel was apparently overtired. Durant listened eagerly, and with relief. The doctors recommended a stay in bed for about twenty-four hours. In the meantime, they would leave him some sedatives and restoratives. They ceremoniously opened their bags, produced small bottles and counted out pills.

Sadler came forward. "How soon will those sedatives work?" he asked.

They blinked at him, baffled. Then one said: "In about an hour or so."

"Well, then," said Sadler, picking up the bottles and extracting four pills from the two of them, "you gentlemen will take a dose of these." He solmnly extended a blue pill and a pink pill in each of his palms. "You'll both have time to reach the city before you feel too sleepy, I suppose."

One of the doctors twittered incoherently, while the other merely looked mystified. Durant began to smile.

"You see," explained Sadler patiently, "we have orders to guard the colonel closely. He can take nothing, or eat nothing, without its first being tested. We, his Guards, obviously can't take sedatives, and we don't need the 'restoratives.' So, gentlemen, you are nominated as tasters."

"This has never happened to us before!" exclaimed the younger doctor, in exasperation. "Did you expect we might try to poison the colonel?"

"We can't take chances," said Sadler, inexorably forcing two pills into the other's hand. The older doctor accepted his with incredulity. "Water, please," Sadler said to young Griffis, who was obviously enjoying himself. The boy obeyed with alacrity, bowing as he extended two glasses of water to the doctors.

They took their pills abstractedly, not looking away from Sadler. The latter glanced at his wristwatch. "You will remain here, gentlemen, for ten minutes. Poisons, these days, are fast and potent. If you aren't dead in ten minutes, you may leave."

The doctors colored, but said nothing. They eyed each other, frowning. Their honor had been insulted, their loyalty questioned, their profession exposed to outrageous doubt. Durant began to feel much better. The grave silence in the room increased. Sadler had returned to his post, and Griffis, smiling from ear to ear, leaned negligently against the wall near Durant. He stared at the doctors, and finally the impact of his amused eyes was felt by them. As one, they turned to him, and he grinned wider. Again they colored, and sat up stiffly.

The anonymous Minute Men in charge of their accelerated oppression had done excellent work, thought Durant, much satisfied. It was very evident that the doctors were indulging in very rebellious, seditious and enraged thoughts. They smoldered with them; their teeth clenched on them; their fists knotted with them. The younger man gave Durant an involuntary glance of pure venom and hate. He would have been considerably more careful a few months ago, Durant reflected. The older doctor was absorbed in his meditations; sometimes his eyebrows would jerk up and down, and sometimes his lips would tighten.

"The ten minutes are up, gentlemen," Sadler announced, at last. "And, as you're obviously not dead, and show no indications of dying, you may leave."

They jumped to their feet, glared at Sadler with obvious detestation, snatched up their bags and went out of the room without a word. Durant was gratified that they did not speak to him with their old servility and eagerness to please. He took two of the pills, laughing. "If they haven't thought of some good, slow-acting poisons before this, they'll think of them now," he remarked. "I don't believe they love the Military any more."

Durant slept, and he dreamed. He was miles up in a radiant air, flying on hushed and mighty wings of his own. It was a majestic sensation, and he felt released and exalted. Below him flashed the earth, rolling in light, a green, blue, white and silver ball. He saw a vision of forests, of great harbors, of tilted cities, of mountains blindingly reflecting the sun, of pampas and prairies and golden lakes, of scarlet deserts and the bare teeth of yellow crags. He saw quietly rolling hills and shining bays, villages with red roofs and villages with plastered walls. He saw the herds of cattle, the coiling threads of roads, the smoke of thousands of industrial chimneys, the bulbous domes of strange metropolises, the ships of strange nations. There were peaks crowned with fire and green rivers and jungles tangled with monstrous red and yellow flowers.

And nowhere were there armies or marching men or ruined

cities, or the acrid blaze of guns or the wheeling carrion birds of war planes.

How peaceful it is, he thought to himself in his dreams. It was then that he heard the bells, rolling up to him like gigantic waves of rapturous music. They beat as one triumphant song, sometimes rising to a thunderous pitch, sometimes dropping to a mere sweet whisper. There was not a scene or a city or a harbor or a river which did not send up its individual voice to join the universal chorus. Joy rolled in the bells, and release and love and peace and thanksgiving. It is Christmas, thought Durant. And then he thought: It is freedom. The world is delivered.

The bells mingled, rejoicing, in the luminous light that engulfed the earth. There was such happiness, such surcease, in Durant that he began to weep as he flew through the pure air. There was no pain in him now. The bells thundered against each other, telling each other the glorious news, speaking to each other softly as if they were remembering, then crying out exultantly. Durant became dazed and stunned with sound; he could no longer tell where the thunder began and the light ended.

He woke to the intense silence of night and the narrow walls of his room. A small lamp was burning in a corner. He lay quietly, and he could still hear the clamoring of the liberated bells, their laughing joy, their eager tongues. The music sailed off into the night and he strained his ears to catch its last echoes. He told himself it had not been a dream, for he had been awake before the bells had been muffled.

Sadler sat on his chair before the door. Young Tom Griffis was sitting near Durant, reading one of his books. Durant said: "I heard the bells."

Sadler said unemotionally: "You've been dreaming, Colonel. A heavy sedative. Go back to sleep."

He got up, and under Tom's surprised eyes, he detached the wires from behind the landscape. Tom laughed delightedly, as only a boy could laugh. He put down his book and smiled at Durant. Durant said obstinately, sitting up in bed with his dark face full of passion: "I tell you, I heard the bells. Not Christmas bells. Just bells, all over the world. Sadler, we're on the eve."

"Yes. I know." Sadler looked less tired and drawn, and Tom was as fresh as ever. Sadler went on, with more expression in his voice: "It must be very soon. None of us can stand this much longer."

Durant thought to himself that he had forgotten that he was not the only one enduring unbearable strain. He was elated that his malaise of the morning had gone. Strength returned to him in a surge of exultation. A natural mystic, he was certain that he had heard the shouting bells of the future, a future almost at hand.

He stood up and stretched, and laughed. Then he said: "Did you fellows get any rest?"

"Yes, Colonel. You've been asleep twelve hours, and Tom and I have had eight hours sleep, in four hour shifts. We just came on again about ten minutes ago. Do you feel like going downstairs for dinner? My— Dodge is ready, and we'll get the other boys. And your own officers." Sadler eyed him inscrutably. "Without their weapons, of course."

If Durant's own officers were still remembering their indignity, they showed no signs of it in the pleasant dining room downstairs. Bishop and Edwards unbent enough to talk with Durant and Sadler almost agreeably. Grandon was full of jokes, most of them ribald. Keiser listened, sometimes grinned. The four Picked Guards might have been friendly soldiers without a care in the world, young and happy men in the mood for holiday. Dr. Dodge, assisted by a frightened young girl, served them an excellent dinner, which was accompanied by some of John Lincoln's fine wines and brandy.

It was Christmas Eve, but no one spoke of it. It was, to them, only the eve of Democracy Day. The colonel was toasted, and he toasted the Army and the Picked Guard. For only an instant, at the mention of the latter, did the Army men frown, and then it was only slightly. Edwards said that he supposed the Picked Guard "must do their job," and implied tolerantly that the Army sometimes had a good opinion of "the boys." Sadler smiled wryly, but his three young sergeants were delighted to the point of excruciation. Grandon suddenly became silent, and his buoyant face darkened momentarily.

"These kids are just out of training school," said Sadler, with indulgence. The explanation satisfied everyone except Grandon, who began to turn the stem of his brandy glass in his fingers, broodingly. Once, involuntarily, he glanced at Durant, and the latter was taken aback by that glance of pure hatred. So, Grandon was the one. He, Durant, had always known it, but it depressed him. Who had given Grandon the poison? The FBHS? He tried to remember if Beckett and Grandon had had any contact in the past, if only for an instant. Of course, it was very possible.

No one spoke of the dead man, whose body had been removed expeditiously. If Sadler were remembering, he showed no signs of it. He was talking to Bishop, while Dr. Dodge moved waveringly about the table and the girl refilled coffee cups.

All about the house lay the smothered silence of a country winter. Durant wanted to see the snow and the moon again, and he got up and began to draw a curtain which shrouded the window. He felt a touch on his arm, and Sadler was saying pleasantly: "No, Colonel." There was no change on his face, except for a warning signal in his eye. Durant's officers had stopped talking, and they watched him return to his chair curiously.

"Someone," said Sadler, "might want to be a martyr, by shooting at the colonel."

"Like Beckett, for instance?" asked Grandon, with that peculiar knife-flash of a smile running over his face. It was obvious that he was feeling the effects of what he had drunk; he lurched a little in his chair.

"Beckett?" asked Durant, puzzled. "Beckett committed suicide."

"So we heard," replied Grandon, and he giggled.

One of the Picked Guards was irritated. "Funny remark, Lieutenant, begging your pardon. We never heard that Lieutenant Beckett tried to kill the colonel. Did he? Do you know something about it, sir?"

Bishop and Edwards looked to Durant indignantly and in expectation that he would defend the honor of the Army. Durant said, with mildness: "Now, why should Grandon know anything about anything, especially something that didn't occur? I think it's just because he's an Army man, and doesn't particularly like—shall I say?—the Picked Guard. And Beckett was a Picked Guard." Durant smiled. "Sometimes our boys are willing to believe anything about your organization, you know."

"We are here to protect the colonel," said Tom Griffis, with dignity. "No Picked Guard would dream of trying to shoot him."

Grandon would not be quiet, in spite of the gesture of Captain Edwards. He smiled at Griffis unpleasantly. "But you think one of his own men might?"

Sadler looked about the table, and caught every eye. "One might," he said. He shrugged. "Who knows? We only have our orders to protect him."

"Now why," said Grandon, with exaggerated thoughtfulness, "would 'one' of us, his own men, want to kill our colonel?" He turned to his fellow officers. "Captain Edwards? Captain Bishop? And you, Keiser? Would you want to hurt a hair of our colonel's head?"

They were all deeply embarrassed, and angry. Durant said, with roughness: "Grandon, you're drunk."

Grandon went on, as if he hadn't heard. "It might have been one of the Lincolns, eh, and Beckett got shot protecting our colonel? By the way, sir—" and he turned his smile on Durant—"Bob Lincoln disappeared months ago."

Durant was silent. He regarded Grandon narrowly, remembering the secret conversation between Grandon and young Lincoln in the spring. Then he said: "Why wasn't I told?"

Grandon waved his hand airily. "Fact is, sir, I didn't know, myself, until a few days ago. Old Lincoln told me. Almost cried about it. I didn't think it important to mention it. If Bob wanted to run off, and starve somewhere, that was his own business."

Then, abruptly, he dropped his head and apparently fell into a drunken sleep.

Durant stood up, and the men rose with him. "Take Grandon to bed," he ordered, with a disgust he did not feel. He started to walk from the room, and the Picked Guard surrounded him. His old claustrophobia returned, and he felt he would choke if he went upstairs again. But he knew that he dared not walk stupidly in the snow as he had done the night before. Muttering, he climbed the stairs. The Army men did not immediately follow and their silence followed him portentously.

Once in his locked room, he sat down and smoked without speaking. His earlier exultation was gone. Fear crept into his flesh once more, a prickling fear that ran along his nerves and made sweat burst out on his forehead. Within a week, two weeks, a few days, it was very possible that he would be dead. There was no doubt in his mind that he would receive the signal very shortly, and when that signal came the world would be convulsed. He remembered the civilian clothes in his drawer. Murmuring something about what he would wear tomorrow, he got up and went to the chest. He opened it slowly; the faded clothing lay under his shirts. Something rustled on top of them. It was a thin gelatine slip of paper which was only too familiar to him, and on it was printed: "Campbell Road, Elton, Florida."

He looked down at it, dumbfounded, and his heart thudded. Wild thoughts ran through his head. Who had put that slip there? Who knew about him? Who knew of his family? His real name, his identity? Dr. Dodge? That was impossible. One of his own men? Impossible, too. No one had access to his room except Dr. Dodge and no one was permitted to enter it in his absence. Was this slip a gloating message that he was known, or had it come from a friend who had been able, mysteriously, to enter his room without being seen? He crumpled the slip in his damp hand and looked at the windows. Had someone, during the day, climbed through one of those windows and left the message, leaving as invisibly as he had come? He pushed the little ball into his mouth, his back to his Guards, and tried to control his trembling. "Campbell Road, Elton, Florida." A mockery, perhaps, or perhaps genuine. He tried to remember when he had last looked at the civilian clothes. A week ago? Two weeks? He could not remember, but he was sure it had not been more than two weeks.

"Is something wrong, Colonel?" asked Sadler.

Durant turned and tried to smile. Sadler commented: "You look sick again, sir. Better go to bed."

Durant nodded. "I'll take another sedative," he said abstractedly. He glanced at his watch. "Almost midnight," he remarked. He began to undress, and went to bed. He closed his eyes, but his consternation and fear made his heart beat too fast. He tried to turn his thoughts away from the onrushing violence of the immediate future. It was Christmas Eve. The bells should be calling now, echoing over the countryside. The churches should be lit with candles. There ought to be the smell of incense in the air, trees in quiet and happy homes, the radiant faces of children, and singing voices. A year from tonight? He thought again of the bells he had heard in his dream, and he told himself that he had been fully awake before the final echo of them had been drawn back into space.

He could not sleep, though he pretended to do so. He heard the changing of the Guard, their mutters. A brief wind rose about dawn. A dog barked mournfully. Gray light crept under the edges of the window shades. Someone was yawning.

It was Christmas Day. It was Democracy Day, and a whole world was waiting.

The President of The Democracy was to speak at three o'clock from New York, at the foot of the Statue of Liberty, and his speech would be broadcast over all the nation. In the Eastern and Northern Sections there would be prior celebrations, and in the Western and Southern Sections the public celebrations would follow. So Durant and his Guards and executive officers left the Lincoln farm at half-past one.

Before leaving, however, Durant ordered Dr. Dodge to send for John Lincoln. It had been a long time since he had talked with the farmer or any of his family; in fact, there were weeks when he hardly remembered that this was Lincoln's house in which he had quartered himself and his men. He had heard, without interest, that Lincoln and his wife had moved away entirely from the big farmhouse and had gone to live with their elder son in his own home on the farm. While waiting for Lincoln, Durant and his men sat in the living room and talked of the approaching celebrations. Grandon had quite forgotten his disagreeable remarks of the night before. He was exuberant and playful, goaded the Picked Guards with contemporary jokes about their organization, smoked incessantly. No one but Durant and Sadler ever glanced at the blood-stained pink sofa where Beckett had lain.

Bishop and Edwards were in a good mood, also, though they treated the Picked Guards with distant politeness. They began to tell Durant of the rumors they had heard in the city the day before. The Section which had once been Canada was reported to be in a turmoil; troops were being rushed by plane and train and vehicle to the border. Eight soldiers, including three sergeants, had been murdered in Philadelphia within the past twenty-four hours in spite of every precaution. Mr. Woolcott's new assistant, who had replaced Andreas Zimmer, had been wounded by some assassin who had fired at him while he was entering his home. The assassin had not been caught. The Section which had originally been named Mexico was in total revolt, it was said, and the troops of The Democracy had retreated ten miles north of the Rio Grande, with great casualties. Three vital bridges had been blown up in Section 18, city unnamed. Four thousand young recruits had deserted the Armed Forces during the past three weeks. There were many more rumors, and Durant listened acutely.

Then he said, with tolerance: "What rot. We'd have heard. Revolts! Murders! Retreats! Yes, I know about our eight men who were killed, but that's always happening."

He smiled at his men, but none smiled back. A sudden and profound tension filled the room. Grandon was holding his cigaret in his fingers, and he was examining Durant with a slight and inscrutable smile. He said: "Of course, the colonel is right."

"If those things are going on in other Sections, which I doubt, our own Section is quiet," said Durant.

Grandon contemplated his cigaret. "The colonel would know, of course, if it's true that two steel mills were blown sky-high in Pittsburgh last Tuesday? And that in Harrisburg, on Wednesday, a mob stormed the military prison there and released all the inmates, one hundred and fifty of them?"

Durant laughed, with ridicule. Grandon gave him a faint smile, and went on: "And that three subway trains, filled with troops, were wrecked in Brooklyn with a loss of two hundred lives—last Friday? Of course," added Grandon, "it couldn't have been sabotage, and probably didn't happen, anyway."

"Of course it didn't. None of it," said Durant. "By the way, where do you boys pick up these tidbits, when you're supposed to be working?"

"Remember, Colonel, we went to a party the other night?" said Edwards. "We heard from there. It was Mr. Judson's party, and he's a big MAST, you know. He was scared out of his pants. He had all these rumors on good authority, he said, and the other men, friends of his, just sat and drank and said nothing."

"What did Mr. Judson expect us to do about these rumors?" demanded Durant impatiently. "And what were you boys doing there, anyhow? I thought we were all persona non grata."

Edwards explained. "It's true they've not been inviting us very much since you came, Colonel." He grinned. "And I suppose they invited us the other night because they were frightened and wanted protection. They've always had a military escort, you know, until you took it away this summer, and they want it back."

"They'll not get it," scoffed Durant. "If they want to frighen themselves with ridiculous rumors, that is their affair, not ours." He let his eyes wander slowly from face to face. "You say

Judson and his friends were frightened? I thought, from reports, that they were being pretty arrogant lately."

"They have been," admitted Edwards. "It's just lately that they've been frightened. I don't know why, unless they've got reason to believe the rumors."

John Lincoln came into the room, dressed for his own excursion into the city. He carried a lighted cigar in his hand, and Durant stared at him in surprise. For Lincoln was no longer the farmer he had cowed and browbeaten, slinking away from the very sight of the hated Military. He wore a fur-lined overcoat over his suit of fine tweeds, and he did not remove his hat nor did he even touch it with his gloved fingers. Urbane, glinting of eye, distant, he said to Durant: "You sent for me, Colonel?"

"Yes." Durant added: "Take off your hat, Lincoln."

Lincoln smiled, his ruddy face amused. "Sorry, Colonel." And he removed his hat and held it negligently. "My wife and I are going into the city. I understand you are to speak, and we're very anxious to hear you." He smiled again. Something was indeed amusing him; he returned stare for stare with Durant, and he put his cigar between his lips very tranquilly, and puffed. "Heard someone tried to shoot you the other night," he remarked, as if unaware of the silence about him. "One of your Guards, Colonel?"

"No," replied Durant tightly. "One of my Guards committed suicide. Temperamental young fellow."

"Too bad," remarked Lincoln. He looked at his watch, coughed. "I hope the colonel has been take care of in my house." Now his cold eyes fixed themselves on Durant with secret triumph, and hate.

"Where's your son, Bob?" asked Durant absently. He had seen what he had desired to see, but it was hard not to get up and smash this fat rascal in the teeth.

"Bob?" Lincoln was all geniality. "Sorry, Colonel, I don't know. He, as you said, was temperamental, too." He sighed. "How he can get along without his ration cards and such is something I don't know, either. But I suppose he'll be back one of these days."

He set his hat on his head again, lifted a hand amiably, and left the room without permission. The officers and the Picked Guard gaped after him, then looked in outrage at Durant. But Durant laughed, and got to his feet. "You see, boys, you do your best with trash like that and they just bounce back in your face. Perhaps we've been too lenient with them lately."

They all went out into the brilliant snow of the winter day, and got into their cars. The roads had been well plowed, and the wheels of the cars hissed on the packed snow and blew up shining clouds. Durant sat in deep thought, trying to quell his nervousness and anxiety. He thought of Dean Burgess, head of the Confederated Association of Labor Unions, and Howard Regis, head of the national FBHS. What were they like, these sinister men? No photographs of officials in Washington were permitted in the newspapers, and had not been so permitted for years. And what were these very important men doing in Philadelphia today? National officials usually accompanied the President to New York on December twenty-fifth for the celebrations. One in Philadelphia would have been enough of an "honor" on Democracy Day, but two, and one of them the head of the FBHS, seemed ominous. It was quite in order for Burgess to address labor, at any time; however, Regis was another matter. Durant thought of the deadly Hugo Reynolds, and began to shake again.

The car rolled on, driven by Tom Griffis. All the Picked Guards were very quiet. They held their guns ready and looked alertly through the windows at the dazzling countryside. Each young face was hard in the pure light. When the car reached the suburbs the wariness of the Guards increased, and they sat on the edge of their seats.

"You make me nervous," remarked Durant. They did not reply, but their eyes darted everywhere.

Now Durant became aware, as the car rolled into the city proper, of an immense strange silence. The old houses stood huddled under their layers of snow, but the streets were empty. Of course, it was extremely cold, but not to see a single civilian was in some way alarming. Groups of soldiers clustered together at intersections, holding their rifles, their heads bent together, not patrolling as usual. Not a face appeared at any blank window, not a child's voice could be heard. The sun poured down its strong and colorless light on a city that had the aspect of death.

Durant's car slowed to permit the one carrying the executive officers to draw closer. The soldiers at the intersections looked up, staring blankly, and Durant saw fear in their eyes even while they made a gesture of salute. The men did not separate hurriedly and start to patrol at the sight of their officers; one or two of them aimlessly took a few steps away from their groups and then returned as if for protection. Durant looked back at them as he passed; they were glancing over their shoulders furtively, and clutching their rifles. There was no mistaking their terror.

However, as they approached the Philadelphia Sports Stadium, civilians appeared, first a few, then in groups, then in a dark and shabby wave moving in the direction of the Stadium. They were completely silent; the snow-covered walks and streets muffled their footsteps. They kept their heads bent as they flowed along under the sun. It was an eerie thing to see; it was like moving in a world from which all sound had been sucked away. The intense stillness made Durant's ears ring, and he experienced a shock of uncontrollable panic. He tried to see the faces of the people on the streets, but they were averted, caught in some somber dream of their own. He was immensely relieved when the bright cars of the privileged began to flash beside him and ahead of him. They might not make any noise on the snow but at least they broke the awful spell of the soundless city.

Now more and more official cars appeared and the streets near the Stadium took on a busy and reassuring air. The river of civilians poured across intersections, gathering tributaries from cross-streets. Soldiers patrolled here almost briskly, watching constantly. The people did not glance at them even for an instant. It was as if they were completely unaware of anything except their own thoughts, or as if they were deliberately ignoring the Military. Foreboding filled Durant. He saw no children at all. He understood that children were not permitted in the Stadium on Democracy Day, and that each industry sent chosen men and women to represent it during the celebrations. However, not all these people were going to the Stadium, which held about ten thousand seats. Most of them were going—where? If only there were a few kids around, thought Durant.

As they approached the Stadium, whose huge bulk loomed against the pale blue sky, he saw where the people were going. They were gathering themselves in utter silence about the Stadium; they were filling the adjacent streets. They stood in mute ranks, men and women both, not looking at a neighbor, their faces frozen and expressionless, bodies wrapped in worn and tattered garments, the women's heads covered by old kerchiefs. Durant remembered that the public address system was devised so that those outside the Stadium could hear the speeches of the President and others. But it was so bitterly cold, and there was no pressure on the people to gather for these speeches near the Stadium. They had their own meeting-places, provided by the State, where they could hear the broadcast.

They seemed to be gathering for a terrible reason of their own. Some signal had gone out to tens of thousands; an unheard voice had summoned them.

There they stood, banked together on the streets, motionless, staring inexorably before them. Here, at the Stadium, the soldiers patrolled very briskly, indeed. Some of them almost ran. They herded the people on the sidewalks; they kept an open place near the monster doors for the entry of the élite and those chosen to fill the seats. The people ignored the soldiers; if the soldiers pushed, they stepped back absently, then flowed outward again. New streams joined the massive ranks, stood shoulder to shoulder, obeying the ancient and compelling voice of the herd. The soldiers could not keep to the sidewalks; they had to patrol on the pavements below. They were pale and tense, and they moved together in squads. Their very activity gave an appearance of terror to the whole appalling scene, to the thousands of fixed eyes.

A sergeant recognized Durant's car, and the soldiers became even more active. Other cars had to wait while the commanding officer alighted. For the first time the people stirred. A malignant shadow, too gigantic for mere personal hatred, too enormous for mere rage, ran over the people's faces. It was a dreadful thing to see, if only for a moment, and Durant's flesh prickled. If they had shouted, if they had moved, if there had been one fierce fist upraised, if one curse had reached him, he would have felt less full of dread and mysterious apprehension.

The Picked Guard surrounded him, and he hurried into the Stadium through a special entrance. Soldiers were everywhere, lined up against the walls of the corridor, holding their rifles ready. They saluted mechanically as Durant passed, but they were watching the doorway. Durant's executive officers rushed in after him and his Guards; now more cars were arriving, and discharging their passengers. It was like a flight into the comparative safety of the great building.

The Stadium had been built for "sports," according to the State. But it had not been used very often. There was no time for trivialities these years; all energy, all life, all blood, every hand, every human creature, was engaged in the perpetual "war effort."

The building was a monster affair, of circular shape, with banks of seats raised on the left and the right, for the "important" people in The Democracy. The center was reserved for the thousands of the common people, and there was a large balcony above where the workers could also be accommodated. At the back loomed the tremendous stage on which speakers stood, and where public celebrations could take place. The building was well lighted and comparatively warm, in spite of the permanent "black-out" to save "fuel" for essential industry and the war effort. The seats allocated to the proletariat were only long benches, uncushioned and narrow, but those kept apart for the preferred and the privileged boasted leather upholstery and high backs and footrests, and the aisles were carpeted.

The flags of The Democracy smothered the bare walls, and rippled on the stage by the aid of strategically placed electric fans.

Durant had seen the Stadium before today, and also the fine large reception rooms where he was to greet the speakers for this occasion: Captain Alice Steffens, of the Department of Women's Welfare; Karl Schaeffer, of the local office of the FBHS; Walter Morrow, of the Grange; Dr. Joseph Healy, of the Public Psychiatry Department; and Mr. Woolcott, of the Department of Mobilized Labor. The heads of these Departments and Bureaus usually officiated in the huge work of "sustaining morale" among the people, and were confined to making the most of their grave opportunity in ten minutes of staccato talk, for, as Dr. Healy had informed them, the intelligence of the mob, and its attention, precluded long and serious addresses.

Surrounded by his Guards, and followed by his military officers,

Durant entered the reception rooms, which were all warm comfort, gold and brown curtans, gold-colored rugs, and fine ivory leather furniture. His speakers were waiting for him: Captain Steffens, pale and smiling and composed in her uniform, Dr. Healy, clothed in his renewed confident arrogance, Walter Morrow, stocky and gray and thoughtful, Karl Schaeffer, full of amiable jokes and ruddy of face, and Mr. Woolcott, drained and silent. They all stood up when Durant entered, and each gave him a brief handshake. Dr. Healy informed him importantly that the two distinguished guests, Mr. Howard Regis, of the FBHS, and his friend, Mr. Dean Burgess, had not as yet arrived.

"We are very anxious to know these wonderful people," said Dr. Healy, with enthusiasm, "for both have been comparatively newly appointed, that is, within the past six months. This is a great opportunity and privilege for all of us!"

"I hope they arrive before the President speaks," replied Durant, glancing at the gilt clock over the fireplace. He went to the good fire and rubbed his cold hands and studied each of his speakers minutely. His eyes lingered longest on Mr. Woolcott, his old friend, Ben Colburn. Ben appeared ill and too strained and very tired.

"I heard planes about ten minutes ago," said Schaeffer, smiling pleasantly. "They must be at the airport now, and ought to be here in less than half an hour. In the meantime, there is some entertainment going on in the Stadium, so the people won't be bored."

Durant listened absently. He could hear the faint and distant sound of music, raucous, bouncing, discordant music with a hysterical pitch. God knows, he thought, the old "popular" music of his boyhood had been bad enough, and cheap enough, and depraved enough, colored as it had been by perpetual adolescence and the raw rhythms of the African jungle. But the modern popular music was much worse. It had no form, no substance, and the old themes of juvenile "love" had been abolished in favor of themes concerning the nobility of unremitting work, patriotism and war. He reflected, again, on the differences among nations even when they had adopted absolutism in place of free and democratic government. Hitler had been vehemently partial to the heroic music of Wagner and other immortal German composers; Stalin had been favorably inclined to Russian symphonies. But absolutism in America had been reduced to imbecility, insofar as music was concerned. The ancient and noble composers, and their names, were practically unknown to this generation, and only the élite were permitted the consolations and pleasure of majestic music. Durant did not believe this was an accident. A nation can be debased very easily by "musical" mountebanks, subsidized by the State, and paid by the State. Proletarianism brought to its very lowest denominator, he reflected, in America.

The band shrieked to its final crescendo. Then there was utter silence. They all listened to it. They waited for the usual uproar of applause, and for the immense resumption of crowd noises and crowd laughter, in the Stadium. There was no laughter, there was no noise, and no applause.

Durant frowned. He turned to his speakers, and he saw grimness on every face, with the exception of Dr. Healy's. Dr. Healy merely looked bewildered.

"The Stadium's full," he remarked. "Crowded to the doors. Yet, there's no sound. I wonder what's wrong?"

"What!" exclaimed Durant, looking at him with his sparkling black eyes. "No 'group integration,' Doctor, no 'group dynamics,' today? Now, what could be the matter?"

The others smiled. Dr. Healy regarded Durant with dignity. "I beg the colonel's pardon, but our bureau has worked very hard for many years for group integration and group dynamics. After all, modern human society can't exist without them." He listened anxiously for any noise from the auditorium. None came. "Strange," murmured the Doctor. He turned to his fellow speakers. "Did you notice how silent the mob was outside? And what are they doing there? They have their own meeting-places set aside by the State for the celebrations."

"Perhaps," said Durant, with a slight smile, "they really have absorbed the teachings and guidance of your bureau, Doctor. Perhaps they really are 'group integrated' and just bursting with 'group dynamics.' Only, these are taking another form today. People are so unpredictable, aren't they?"

"Not to a psychiatrist!" cried Dr. Healy, stung by Durant's tone. "Their response to stimuli always takes a formalized pattern. We know, for instance, that masses are invariably conformists—"

"To what are they conforming now?" asked Durant, interested.

Dr. Healy flushed. He went to the door, applied his ear to it. He came back to the fire and stared at it, uneasy and visibly alarmed.

"Perhaps," Durant continued, "they've decided, in a mob, and through some unknown stimulus, to hold their tongues and to sit on their hands. Group dynamics, you know."

Even the exhausted Ben Colburn smiled at this. Durant shook a finger archly at Dr. Healy. "Letting down in your work, Doctor? None of your cheer-leaders out there today?"

Schaeffer said comfortably: "The members of our bureaus haven't arrived yet, Colonel. They usually come about five minutes before the President's speech."

Dr. Healy was relieved. "That's true! The masses must always be led, given a signal."

"Listen," said Durant.

The band, as if appalled at the lack of enthusiasm given to its earlier effort, swung into the national anthem: "All Hail to Democracy!" Durant opened the door, and heard the band's chorus roaring into the words of this idiot hymn:

"Raise your voices, men of labor,
Men who made the nation great!
Clasp the hand of fellow neighbor
'Gainst the hordes of foreign hate!
Rejoice, rejoice, in noble reedom!
Hold the sword at every door,
Guard with joy and hope each city,
Pledge your faith forevermore!"

This was the signal for the standing multitude to join in the exuberant chorus:

"Democracy! Oh, our Democracy!
Where no man dies for one man's gain!
Democracy, our Democracy!
Evermore, evermore!"

The banal, rapid and discordant anthem came to an end. And there was nothing but silence. Now all the others were crowded at the half-opened door, listening also. Durant closed the door after several long moments.

"Well," he said, "'group integration' and 'group dynamics' seem to have called a holiday today, don't they?"

Dr. Healy had turned white, and could say nothing. He wandered uncertainly back to the fire, accompanied by his fellow speakers. Durant's officers and Guards looked blankly at nothing.

Durant sat down and lit a cigaret, and appeared to be musing. The firelight rose and fell on all those silent faces around the hearth. Then there was a hard and fast knocking on the door. Sadler opened it, and a little, dark, fat man, perspiring and wild-eyed, rushed into the room, carrying a baton. He sought out Durant, and it was evident that all his wits were gone.

"Colonel, sir!" he stammered, in a shrill and incoherent voice. "I don't know what's the matter! Something's wrong! I—I'm afraid. The people—they didn't even stand up when we played the national anthem! They—they—they just sat there and stared at us—like dummies. They didn't sing. It's against the law, Colonel, not to stand up and salute the flag, and to—sing—when we play the anthem--" He snatched at his handkerchief and mopped his face, and gazed at Durant with bemused fright. "I don't know, Colonel—it was funny, playing, and our chorus singing—and the people just sitting as if they were deaf, or something. And, Colonel, you ought to see their faces!" He shuddered, spread out his hands despairingly.

Durant was calm. "Maybe that's how people in this city act," he said. "Staid, and such. Not emotional." He turned to Dr. Healy. "Would you say they're emotional, Doctor?"

Dr. Healy looked at him, opened his mouth, then closed it again. His lips were as white as his cheeks.

Durant waved his cigaret. "Well, maybe they're tired. After all, during the past six months, they've been working twelve hours a day, seven days a week, and their rations, never very abundant at any time, have been cut one-third. So, perhaps they're just too tired for anything, being so devotedly engaged in unity, duty, sac-ri-fice. Wouldn't you say that, Doctor?"

Dr. Healy could not take his eyes from Durant. The latter seemed to fascinate him in a dreadful kind of way. Then he said, in a faint voice: "The colonel has promised that he wouldn't become offended at anything one might suggest? He has asked for frankness—"

"Go ahead," invited Durant genially.

Dr. Healy hesitated. Then he took courage, and said with a kind of desperation: "The food rations—they haven't been sufficient. The people are inflamed. I told the colonel some of the other causes."

Durant was outraged. He sat up in his chair. "Are you implying that the people would put more food ahead of unity, duty, sacrifice? Are you implying that they might be questioning sacred Military orders? What have you been doing lately, Doctor? Neglectful of mass-indoctrination? Isn't that your job?"

Dr. Healy, stunned, could find no words. The little band leader gestured frantically: "Colonel! You ought to see their faces!"

"Their faces," repeated Durant thoughtfully, sitting back in his chair. "Yes. Their faces." He gestured to the man, and said: "Go back and play that fine, newest popular song. What's it called? Yes; 'Wake Up and Work, Now Don't You Shirk, the Bogey-Man Will Get You If You Don't Watch Out!' The people love it, I understand. They sing it everywhere. It's played everywhere. Go back and play it, and get the people to laughing."

The band leader groaned, threw hands and eyes toward the ceiling. "We've already played it, Colonel! And you ought to have—"

"I know," remarked Durant, smiling, "—seen their faces. Well, play something else. How about: 'Posy-Wosy, Rivetting Rosie'? An old favorite."

The other man dropped his hands, baton and all, and just stood there, shivering. He gazed at Durant and whispered: "Colonel, I'm scared. I'm just scared to death. I'm afraid to go back out there."

Durant had another thought, and he sat up. "The walls are lined with soldiers, aren't they? What were they doing during the singing? Aren't they supposed to join in?"

"They didn't," said the band leader simply.

"Well, well," mused Durant. "Well, well."

Dr. Healy slowly approached him, as if pushed by something he could not resist. He stood before Durant and his face was ghastly. He said, his voice thin with terror: "I think I'm beginning to understand."

"Understand what, Doctor?" asked Durant coldly. He looked into the other's eyes and let him see what there was to be seen. He could not help himself; his hatred and exultation were too powerful.

"Nothing," said Dr. Healy. There was a livid film on his forehead. He stumbled back to the fire. The others watched Durant gravely, and there were a few somber smiles.

The little band leader, with a yelp of shrill despair, ran from the room, clutching his baton. A moment later, noises in the corridor announced the arrival of the two distinguished guests from Washington. Durant rose and looked at Dr. Healy, and laughed a little. "Shall we discuss this again, some other time, Doctor?" he asked. "Somewhere, where it's very quiet?"

Sadler opened the door and everyone stood at attention near the fireplace. Mr. Regis and Mr. Burgess were entering the room.

"Good afternoon, Colonel," said the first gentleman who entered. "I am Dean Burgess of the Confederated Association of Labor Unions." He extended his hand and smiled cordially at Durant.

Durant's first impression of Mr. Burgess, to his own great astonishment and confusion, was that here was a man it was almost impossible not to like.

Mr. Burgess was a man in his late fifties, not tall but muscular and broad, with an air of powerful vitality and magnetism. He moved rapidly but surely and his handclasp was warm. His hair was a mass of springy gray curls high on the top of his round head and his features expressed a very sanguine personality, full of force and genial laughter. No weakness showed on his strong and smiling mouth; his nose was a wedge of firmness, and his eyes were frank and interested and alive with youthfulness.

Durant controlled an impulse of responsive warmth to this man, whose Bureau, vicious and oppressive, had been ostensibly formed some ten years ago to "protect" labor and labor's interests, but which in reality had merely absorbed all American unions in order to deliver workers in one huge tight slave organization to the absolute State. In this infamous work, thirty-two Communist-affiliated union leaders, and many more potent gangsters and criminals, had ably assisted. Remembering all this, and remembering, too, that he, Durant, had often met villains who could smile as kindly as Mr. Burgess, whose eyes were as candid, and who radiated similar integrity and masculine strength, Durant replied conservatively to Mr. Burgess' greeting. He had often been baffled by the fact that men who were truly good and honorable and sincere frequently did not reveal these virtues by feature or speech or manner, and sometimes were even possessed of repellent ways.

Durant turned abruptly to Mr. Howard Regis, Federal head of the most infamous Bureau in The Democracy, the FBHS. He extended his hand, began to make his set speech, then halted, puzzled and uncertain. Where had be seen this exceptionally tall thin man before, a man of sixty-odd, with a long narrow face and features distinguished and quiet, and who possessed such an air of quiet authority and control? He stared so intensely at Mr. Regis that it was some moments before he became aware that Mr. Regis had taken his hand. Embarrassed, but with growing alarm, he continued his greetings. He could not look away from Mr. Regis, who was smiling at him slightly.

Mr. Regis said: "I've often wanted to meet you since my appointment a short time ago, Colonel. I've heard a good deal of your fine administrative qualities and the work you have been doing in this Section for The Democracy."

That voice was much more familiar than the man's face. It was very quiet and yet had a stern, dominant quality. Durant had a strong if whirling impression of rain, firelight, pipesmoke, and the scent of a woman's sweet perfume—then he stood there, utterly shocked, utterly incredulous.

Mr. Regis continued to smile at him, and if he had noticed Durant's bulging eyes he gave no indication of it. He was holding Durant's hand, and it took a little time for Durant to notice that he had been expertly yet unobtrusively moved so that his face could not be seen by the others. "So," continued Mr. Regis, "I was delighted to come today, and to meet you." He dropped Durant's hand and turned his fine long head expectantly in the direction of the fireplace.

Durant steadied himself. He made a fumbling gesture toward Captain Alice Steffens, who came forward. The girl was paler than ever and her eyes were shining brightly as if suffused with tears. Her pretty mouth trembled even as it smiled; she shook hands with Mr. Regis and murmured something inaudible, and turned away. Durant caught the drift of her perfume, and now he was certain. A deliriously jubilant wave lifted his heart, and he was momentarily dizzy with joy.

"I believe you took poor Mr. Reynolds' place, after he was murdered," he said.

"Yes. Very sad, wasn't it?" replied Mr. Regis, with his slight cool smile. "I hear you've had your troubles, too, Colonel."

Durant smiled at him, a shade too vividly, then caught himself. He called the others to him, and introduced them to Mr. Regis. His voice was somewhat breathless in spite of all his efforts. He watched Karl Schaeffer as the latter was presented to his superior officer, and Schaeffer's face remained bland and smooth and noncommittal.

Walter Morrow was introduced to the visitors, as was Mr. Woolcott. Something had happened to Ben Colburn. His air of abstracted exhaustion had gone. His bent shoulders had lifted and his gray face had taken on color. Mr. Regis was courteous, but Mr. Burgess was very cordial to this Section head of the Bureau of Mobilized Labor, and Durant was sure that Burgess and Colburn knew each other well, and affectionately. Durant glanced at Walter Morrow of the Grange. Morrow's expression was serious, and if he knew either of the guests he did not betray the fact.

Dr. Joseph Healy was quivering with eagerness. He was in the presence of two of the most powerful men in The Democracy. Durant, grinning inwardly, could almost read the eminent doctor's thoughts: I'm among friends, now! I can tell them what I suspect about this ambiguous colonel, and they will deal with him and find out everything about him!

The doctor was very polite to Mr. Burgess of the Confederated Association of Labor Unions, but his real and passionate interest was in Mr. Regis, of the FBHS. Nothing could ever be concealed from the FBHS, which boasted the most skillful and intelligent spies in the whole country. Dr. Healy decided to concentrate on Mr. Regis, and tell him of his suspicions of Durant at the first convenient opportunity. His white face glowed with triumph; he could not refrain from shooting Durant a glance of elation.

Durant knew now, beyond any doubt, that the time of emancipation was here. It was no concern of his how General Steffens alias Howard Regis had secured his appointment to the cogent Federal Bureau of Home Security; he would never know, and was contented not to know. However, he suspected that the Chief Magistrate, so close to the President, so beloved of the President, had contrived this momentous appointment.

"We have about ten minutes before going into the auditorium, gentlemen," he said, indicating two comfortable seats near the fire. But Burgess and Regis ignored the gesture. They talked casually, and with the utmost kindness, with the others. They walked slowly about the pleasant room, complimenting Durant on the appointments. It was then that someone made a slight and choking sound, and everyone turned in surprise toward Durant's executive officers.

Young Grandon had apparently been taken suddenly ill, and Durant's first thought in his confusion was that his lieutenant must have eaten some of the poisoned ham. For Grandon had pressed his body against a wall for support, and his face was deadly white. Bishop and Edwards caught his arms as he began to slide toward the floor. His head had dropped to his chest and he was breathing stertorously.

Mr. Burgess and Mr. Regis looked at the young man with quiet curiosity. The officers had not been introduced to such eminent visitors, and it was apparent that this was the first time that the men had been called to their attention. They watched Grandon being lowered into a chair. Durant went to Grandon, perplexed and grim. "What's wrong?" he demanded.

Grandon did not lift his head, and Durant could not see his face.

"Stomach, or something, Grandon?" Durant continued. "If you're conscious, answer me at once."

Grandon, with an effort visible to everyone, raised his head. He was whiter than ever. He smiled forcedly. He said: "Too much party or something last night, Colonel. Excuse me." He kept his eyes on Durant as if he dared not look anywhere else. The Picked Guards, including Sadler, stolidly stared before them.

Durant was silent. Bishop said: "Perhaps if he could lie down, somewhere, sir?"

But Grandon shook his head; he passed his hands over his face slowly and almost firmly. "Just dizzy a minute," he muttered. "Sorry." He pushed himself to his feet, inch by inch, still looking nowhere.

"Did you eat anything at the house, that we didn't all eat?" asked Durant.

Grandon had attained the wall and was leaning against it, struggling against another collapse. He stiffened, then, at Durant's words. His pale lips tightened convulsively. He shook his head as if he could not speak, but his eyes fixed themselves on Durant with a kind of terror. Keiser had retrieved his hat and stood there, frowning thoughtfully at the young lieutenant.

So, thought Durant, it was you who tried to kill me and my Picked Guards. It is you who are the spy and traitor.

But something perplexed Durant. If Grandon were the enemy, with instructions to murder his superior officer, why, then, the disregard for the lives of the Picked Guard, the darlings of the President and the Joint Chiefs of Staff? A military officer's death, though deplored in Washington, did not arouse the spirit of vengeance as did the slightest attack on the Guard.

Mr. Burgess had approached and was now regarding Grandon with kind solicitude. "Your officer is ill, Colonel?" He smiled at Grandon, who looked at him with deep concentration. "Perhaps a little whisky might help him. What is your name, Lieutenant?"

Grandon could not answer for a moment. Then he muttered: "Grandon." And again: "Grandon."

"Grandon," repeated Mr. Burgess consideringly. He turned away and Durant wondered if, for a moment, Mr. Burgess' face had really expressed sadness. His bewilderment increased. Mr. Burgess said, as he approached the window: "I once knew some

Grandons. Very wonderful people. That was out West. I hear they're all dead now. I remember them best because they were brave and honorable men who always fought for their country, and who never betrayed it, voluntarily or involuntarily."

Grandon straightened and lifted his head. "Yes, Mr. Burgess," he said. Color was returning to his face, and his eyes sparkled. He said to Durant: "I'm all right, Colonel. Just too much party, as I told you."

Mr. Regis had joined Mr. Burgess at the windows, and Durant, frowning, joined them. They had parted the golden draperies and were looking down at the monster crowds below, so ominously silent, so ominously still. Mr. Burgess opened the window and he and Mr. Regis listened. Not a lip moved in all that vast congregation of humanity which filled the small square before the Stadium and flowed endlessly into the side streets. Yet, from their many thousands came a faint and sinister sound, a kind of throbbing.

"I don't like it, sir," said Durant uneasily, to Mr. Regis.

But Mr. Regis and Mr. Burgess did not answer him. To Durant's confusion, the two men exhanged a look of dark and secret exultation. They closed the window.

"A very orderly gathering," murmured Mr. Regis. Durant continued to look at that awful mass below, and then something struck him forcibly, something he should have seen before, and which had escaped him. The people, so dun-colored and faceless all these years, were wearing color! From some old hiding places, from some forgotten boxes, from corners and from lost drawers, they had retrieved bits of bright ribbon, brilliant headscarves, a little slash of blue or yellow or red or green silk, ties with gay hues. The amount each man and each woman was wearing was small, out of necessity, but Durant, dumbfounded, saw that the aggregate was impressive. The souls of the people had instinctively understood, and only after many years of grayness and despair, that color was their manifestation of revival and independence, their flag of rebellion, their insignia of individuality.

Now the mud-colored background of the people's clothing faded before Durant's eyes, and he saw the little flares of color merging together like a visible paean of defiance and strength. He thought of the glittering vivacity of color which had marked the Renaissance when it had emerged from the Dark Ages. He thought of the rainbowed brightness of the people of England, after Cromwell had died. All profound, noble and heroic emotions of a nation were expressed in sudden surges of color, just as oppressive, cruel and evil governments were invariably expressed in drabness.

This, then, is what the distinguished visitors from Washington had seen, Durant thought. But he was also certain that they had seen something else, besides, not known to him, something which had made them exchange that glance of exultation.

"Yes," said Mr. Regis, "a very orderly gathering. Masses are usually disorderly and undisciplined."

A soldier arrived to say that the seats of the privileged classes were now full, and that the President would speak in less than five minutes. Durant led his guests and the others into the vast auditorium where thousands awaited. They arrived on the stage, and the banks of people on the right and the left clapped feverishly. The sound of their clapping was like the sound of little children playing paddy-cake in a vacuum, so brittle was it, so feeble. The people below, in the center, and in the balconies, did not clap. They sat there in their great mass, in utter silence, and Durant saw again the little flares of color at neck, on heads and on thick and ugly coats.

Durant indicated the fine high-backed chairs for his guests and for his speakers. The privileged groups were standing, still clapping and feverishly grinning, but the people did not rise, and neither did they smile. The soldiers ranged along the walls and in the rear saluted. The band struck up a martial song complimentary to the Armed Forces. Yet, for all that every seat was occupied the music had a hollow echo, as if played in a deserted building. Drums thundered, cymbals clashed, trumpets blared, flutes shrilled. They exhorted to emptiness, to absence of spirit, to grim silence. The massed flags of The Democracy rippled as if in tune, as if stirred in a gale, and no eye glanced fervently at them.

Durant and his company sat down, and the orchestra beat on in a desperately accelerated rhythm. The leader looked up in panic from his pit; his bald head gleamed with sweat and his baton swung frantically. The musicians did their best, and the best resembled a demented funeral dirge.

In the meantime, Durant was studying the faces of the privileged groups to his right and left. Well dressed, fat, suave and ruddy-faced though most of them were—with the exception of the newspaper men—their smiles and their expressions indicated vengeful contentment. They looked at Durant and he saw their hatred. They might clap for him, but the clapping had been derisive. They, too, had their secret exultations, these farmers, these bureaucrats, these members of the MASTS.

There was an immense screen at the back of the stage, and suddenly it began to light up. The band stopped abruptly. From the public address system another band screamed out in the President's favorite anthem: "O Day of Liberty!" Now a life-size picture was forming on the screen, and all could see an enormous panorama of giant barges and floats bearing multitudes of people who had gathered around Bedloe's Island, where stood the Statue of Liberty. The barges and floats moved slowly up and down; between them flashed leaden glimpses of cold winter water. A stage had been erected on the island, and it was crowded with military officers and prominent officials against a background of flags. In the center stood the President of The Democracy, Mr. Slocum, a detachment of Picked Guards, and Arthur Carlson, Chief Magistrate.

The picture narrowed and centered itself exclusively on the stage, but not before Durant had seen that the multitude on the barges and boats was as still and somber as the multitude outside and inside the Stadium. The picture brightened, sharpened still more, until only the President and the Chief Magistrate could be viewed.

Mr. Carlson came forward, and his aristocratic face was grave and clear. He stood there, on the screen, in his uniform as Commander-in-Chief of the Picked Guard, and he was like an arrow in his straightness. He looked out at a listening nation, and began to speak. He praised the devotion of the nation in all matters, the loving obedience of the nation, and the accomplishments of the nation during the past year. He dedicated this Democracy Day of December twenty-fifth to "the workers of our country." His voice, full and yet quiet, filled the auditorium and his eyes seemed to be directed at every individual .

He moved back, and the privileged groups applauded. But the people did not applaud. Durant glanced at Mr. Burgess and Mr. Regis, and they were smiling slightly as they examined the congregation in the Stadium who sat there like a waiting and awful danger.

Then the President, the little rat-faced man with his tight grin and his dancing eyes, came foward importantly to the podium. He was waiting for applause. It came from those about him at the foot of the Statue of Liberty. He was listening; his raddled grin remained fixed. No applause came from the masses. He knew it, for the dancing eyes froze, visibly, and he paused, his speech in his hand. He turned his head from side to side, and though his grin stretched his mouth there was a look on his features of sudden outrage, bewilderment and fear. Behind him stood Arthur Carlson, remote and detached and courteously waiting.

The President stood there in a nationwide silence and emptiness, and he could not speak. He must have felt that silence and emptiness which flowed toward him from millions and tens of millions of people. He must have known. Now his grin faded, and the face turned back to the screen was a face cleaned of everything but stark terror. Millions must have seen it, must have seen him swallowing dryly, must have seen the trembling of his small hands.

Durant's heart began to beat furiously; he leaned forward in his seat the better to see. His pulses bounded in his temples and in his wrists and in his chest. It was almost here! It might be here at this very moment. His own throat and mouth dried, and he felt dizzy. He turned to look at Burgess and Regis. They sat there quietly, with only the calmest interest on their faces. He glanced at the people in the auditorium. They were watching the President impassively. He looked at the privileged groups. They were fascinated, and they were smiling, and it was an evil and triumphant smiling. Smile, thought Durant, malignantly, for you won't be smiling tomorrow!

He started violently, for the band before the President, as if aware that something most terrible was happening, struck up again in a thunderous frenzy, replaying once more the President's favorite anthem. Carlson was approaching the President; he was bending his head and murmuring something inaudible, as if with concern and encouragement. The President was looking up at him with abject fondness and agitation, clutching his papers. Carlson nodded, retreated. The band faded away, and now the screen concentrated on the President's strained face. He had begun to grin again. There was a shimmer on his forehead.

He spoke, his thin sharp voice emerging from the screen, breathless and without emphasis. He kept glancing down at the speech which Arthur Carlson had written for him. This was a momentous day, he read rapidly. All Democracy Days were momentous, but this was exceptionally so, for this was the Day dedicated in particular to the people. They had proved their devotion. Never before had they been so enthusiastic, so sacrificing. The nation could be glad that in their past they had lost no wars, though the enemy had sent his hordes against them time after time, year after year. The nation could be glad, today, that the new war was "moving into its final stages, and peace is about to dawn in all its splendor on this united people. Our enemy is staggering; his cities are in ruins. Our Armed Forces can congratulate themselves on brilliant achievements, in the air, on the land, and on the sea. The might of the people of The Democracy has been leagued behind them, with one purpose and one hope. Peace. Peace in all the world. Lasting Peace. Everlasting peace."

The discoveries of science should not be ignored on this occasion, because it was science which had invented those fantastic new weapons which had been directed against the enemy. And now that a true and democratic peace was almost at the threshold of the world, science would turn its great gifts to the uses of the people. No one could exaggerate the wonders that would come in the fields of health, prosperity, abundance and happiness. Science would bring all this about, and the people could praise themselves that their "Unity, Duty and Sacrifice," under the most pressing conditions of work and self-denial and austerity and devotion to the common good, had made all this possible for the future. The Democracy would vigorously engage in the restoration of order and peace all over the world. Its leadership had been ordained. Peoples everywhere were looking to The Democracy as to man's last hope on earth. The Democracy would not fail mankind. It would rise to its challenges against the forces of corruption, war and evil. It would bring forth the morning of a happy and glorious world. It would—

"Our people," said the President, in his high and rapid voice, "need to gird themselves for only one last effort. We know that reduced rations and new taxes and new directives and new disciplines are sometimes disheartening. I cannot promise immediate alleviation of these things. There must be renewed and firmer dedications to the principles of freedom and peace, before the day of fulfillment can arrive. I have faith in the people. They will not betray their children and their children's children. The world is looking to The Democracy as to the sunrise after a long night."

The President drew a deep breath. His eyes wandered from side to side, as if looking at the thousands congregated at the foot of the Statue. They were hunted eyes.

He shrilled, suddenly, lifting his head high: "Unity! Duty! Sacrifice!"

He stood there, that haunted and shaking little man, looking blankly before him, and his band clashed out into the strains of the national anthem. His face faded, and the gigantic flag of The Democracy, in color, streamed upon the screen. This was the signal for the rising of the people in the auditorium. They did not rise. Durant, bemused and stunned, got to his feet, and his company with him, and the banks of the privileged groups. But the people did not rise. They sat there, in their foreboding silence, and they stared implacably at the men on the stage.

However, Durant was not thinking of them now. For a code had been transmitted unknowingly by President Slocum to all Minute Men everywhere. All commanding officers of all Sections should remove themselves at once to a place of safety, and wait. They were needed, and must guard themselves, for upon their immediate survival depended the future of the country. Minute Men, other than commanding officers, should gather together quietly for final instructions which would be given them at six o'clock the next morning. Their duties would be defined individually, and they would obey without the slightest hesitation, and with as much speed as possible. Those Minute Men in the Armed Forces, who might be prevented from gathering as instructed, must await signals given to them by others, signals which must be acted upon immediately even at the risk of death. No man, anywhere, must move hastily or at his own decision and prompting. No man must move on his own. The instructions would be clear and unmistakable. The hour for striking had arrived.

From the shrill voice of the President came Arthur Carlson's last message to his friends and fellow-workers: "If I, your leader, see none of you again I shall be with you to the end. If I die, as perhaps many of you will die in the next few days, I die for my country, and I shall die anonymously. Do not mourn for me. Keep my secret. May God be with you."

Durant stood among his company and his eyes filled with tears. He was not exultant now; he was not filled with high courage and excitement. He was only sorrowful with a sorrow he had never known before. When he looked at the faces of his friends he saw that they, too, were pale and tense, and that they were as grief-stricken as he for a brave and heroic man whom they would probably never see again.

It was doubtful that any of the speakers, with the exception of Dr. Healy, cared or really knew what they were saying. Their voices droned lifelessly in their own ears, their faces were sad and withdrawn. To Durant, everything had lost meaning in this auditorium after the heroism of Carlson's message. He stared with stony indifference at the banked seats to the right and the left, and at the crouching multitude with their frightful eyes and their splatters of defiant color.

However, his sensibilities were heightened almost beyond bearing. In spite of his sorrow he found himself concentrating on the section which contained the Press. Half of the men were middle-aged or older, journalists, paid propagandists of of tyranny, and authors, and the other half were young men. He had often given out releases to these time-servers of evil and State slavery, and he knew many of them quite well.

Now a bitter and raging anger began to fill him. This group of men, perhaps more than any other single group, was responsible for the muddy horror which had choked the people for decades. The free and independent Press! The members of that profession had either supinely allowed themselves to be seduced into the betrayal of a nation, or had been voluntarily silenced out of cowardice or expediency. Many of them had been engaged for years in active and deliberate treachery, using the powerful means of communication to further the designs of wicked men. This latter half of the Press had deceived the people with lies and cunning and falsehood and synthetic rages against "the special interests" of the forties and fifties. They had denounced any man of spirit and courage who had dared speak against the foul servants of Communism and Socialism, whether that man were Senator or fellow-scribe, private citizen, ambassador, statesman or writer. Scores of them had hysterically upheld any politician who had attacked or evaded the Constitution of the United States of America; they had been the idolators of Communist Russia and had labored fervently, for hire or through the evil imaginings of their perverted minds, to thrustMarxism upon their nation. Nothing had been too debased for them, nothing too degraded. They had wielded their pens like poisoned darts to be hurled at the hearts of a free people. When the Washington bureaucrats had invaded private industry, had openly and ruthlessly seized private property in the fifties, "for reasons of defense," hundreds of newspaper men had applauded. The President's monstrous directives against the sovereignty of the people had inspired ecstasies in these creatures. They had greeted the terrible rising strength of the Military with inky enthusiasm. When traitors had conspired against the Republic, they had defended them at a signal from the President.

They had violently attacked other "reactionary" newsmen in the name of "progressive democracy" so that in the minds of the people the sacred name of democracy had become synonymous with oppression and slavery. Their squeezed, fanatic faces and their foul tongues had raised themselves everywhere like the heads of cobras in a jungle. For decades they had written so passionately of "Labor" and "The Masses" that these words, in the minds of the people, had become nouns of debasement. What had once possessed dignity and pride had become obscenities.

Perhaps some good will come out of their evil, thought Durant. If the people refused, forever, to be relegated to any class, to be designated as any "group" apart from the main body of the nation, it would be good. For the people would have learned that they were not mere plodding and mindless dwellers in the narrow confines of any class; they would know that they were men, individuals, proud and immortal souls, accountable only to fellow men for justice, accountable only to God for their lives and their rights.

Durant's eyes roved slowly over the faces of the betrayers of America. Then his interest quickened, and his bitterness. The young men's faces might be wizened and intense with their fanaticism, but the old men's faces were gray with hopelessness, exhausted and ghostly. Had they realized, now, what they had done to America when they, too, had been young, in the nineteen fifties and sixties, when they, out of greed or insanity or envy, had twisted the minds of a trusting and emotional public? Were they remembering the artificial frenzies of misguided "patriotism" which they had whipped up to serve tyrants and liars and thieves and murderers? Did they recall how they had shouted to the people that they were "exploited" and that only radicalism or Socialism or Communism would lead them to a brave new world? Did they remember how they had substituted "security" for self-respect and industry, planned economy for free enterprise, the power of the State for the power of the people? Did they remember their cries of Unity! Duty! Sacrifice! when any brave man had questioned the directives and commands of tyrants?

They were remembering. Of that, Durant was certain. Their eyes were too sunken, their lips too livid, their faces too somber, for anything else but remembrance of the treason they had committed against their fellowmen. They knew now, and they knew their guilt. The stench of slavery was in their nostrils; their victims sat before them in their awful silence and their condemnation.

It's too late for you, thought Durant. Whatever happens now, it will always be too late for you. You have too many memories. Once you had your opportunity, and you did not take it. You cannot come rejoicing in these latter days, when the people will be free. Never will you dare look on the banner of the Republic with joy in your hearts, for you will not have restored it.

Durant looked at them, and said to them silently: " 'Hang yourself, brave Crillon. We fought at Arques, and you were not there."

Mr. Burgess was extolling "the sleepless work of labor in this hour of our emergency." His voice, sonorous and full, echoed in the auditorium. The people only sat, staring at him with silent hatred. They did not move. The power of their silence permeated the air so that those in the banked and comfortable seats gazed at them with frozen uneasiness, their heads turned from the stage.

The travesty of celebration was over. The band struck up its pounding exhortation. Durant and his company rose, and the sitters in the banked seats rose courteously. The people just sat in their resistive ponderousness. Durant and the others left the auditorium with the officers and the Picked Guard, and returned to the reception rooms.

"Well," said Mr. Regis, "that's over for another year, isn't it?"

Dr. Healy gave him a significant glance, and said respectfully: "Did you notice, sir, how quiet the people were? I'm afraid they're not well adjusted any longer. Something has happened to them; someone has destroyed their group integration—"

"Oh, yes," interrupted Durant, smiling. " 'Group dynamics.' What's wrong with their group dynamics today, Doctor? I thought it was right on the job, eloquently."

Dr. Healy, in the presence of the Federal head of the FBHS, could face this hated man courageously. He said, with meaning: "Perhaps the colonel thinks so. Perhaps the colonel knows all about it."

"Yes?" asked Mr. Regis, with interest.

Dr. Healy hesitated, then plunged. "We psychiatrists had practically eliminated mass neurosis in the people over the past ten years, Mr. Regis. Our effort has been most impressive in the field of group integration. Without our work it would have been impossible for the State to secure the allegiance and mass-effort of the populace. Men and women, hag-ridden with complexes and hidden conflicts, harassed by ritualism and symbolism and emotional illnesses of many types, have been restored to health and have adjusted themselves to their environment. The colonel may laugh at group integration, sir, but that does not reduce its importance in national life."

Durant said indulgently: "Translated, Mr. Regis, all this means that Dr. Healy and his colleagues have secured mass conformity and have suppressed individualism, which was a menace to the State. When countless thousands refused to be 'cured,' as Dr. Healy would call it—well, then, they simply disappeared. That's so, isn't it, Doctor?"

The others laughed, and Mr. Regis smiled. Dr. Healy, aghast and incredulous, swung about to see that a ring had been drawn around him. His new color faded. His eyes filmed with fear. His hope was gone. He could only stand there under the mirthful ridicule and say nothing. Durant tapped him on the chest. "We'll have to see about 'integrating' you, Doctor. I think your personal 'group dynamics' have blown up in your face."

"Oh, come, come, Colonel," protested Mr. Regis gently. "Let's not quarrel. Captain Steffens, gentlemen: I have been asked by the Chief Magistrate to invite you all for dinner with me and Mr. Burgess at his country home. The Chief Magistrate believes that we need our own private celebration. Will you come?"

So, thought Durant, that is to be our "safe place" for the next twenty-four hours, until we receive our signal. The others understood, as Durant had understood, and agreed with pleasure. Dr. Healy, floundering in his despair, took hope again. He would find some way to speak of this obnoxious and dangerous military man to Mr. Regis, in private. He must convince Mr. Regis of the jeopardy into which Colonel Curtiss had thrown Section 7. He would hint solemnly of inefficiency, or worse. He looked up to see Mr. Regis nodding to him very slightly, and now he flamed with renewed elation.

He, Joseph Healy, had been temporarily reduced to childish hallucinations. His colleagues had not been laughing at him at all, with ridicule or derision. They had been laughing easily, and without any secret significance. His nerves had been shaken by that damnable silence of the people—He regarded Durant with hatred. He hoped he would be given the job of "adjusting" this man to his environment.

The cavalcade of cars rolled down Broad Street, whose craters were filled with ice on which the tires spun dangerously. And everywhere, on the downtown streets, the multitudes had gathered, impassive, silent and motionless. Durant, wtih his new understanding and awareness, knew that at last in this city, and in every other city throughout the nation, the people were presenting to their oppressors the evidence of their might, were demonstrating to their tyrants the massiveness and invincibility of their power, which could no longer be controlled or directed.

They made no overt gesture, they did not speak or shout. But they stood in all streets, everywhere, as immovable as mountains, as fixed as glaciers. Never did they become mobs, screaming, pushing, headlong. We, they seemed to be saying, are the People. We, who are the People, cannot be moved, cannot be shaken from our places. You can no longer disperse us into disintegrating and hysterical units. We stand together, and hell cannot overthrow us, neither by guns nor by propaganda, by emotion nor by lies. We are the Reality, and you are a delusion, because you are evil.

The soldiers who patrolled the streets were not molested. The uniformed boys had frightened and uneasy faces; sometimes they glanced at the massed multitudes with sheepish grins or childish wonder. They were confronted by no aggression, no excuse for violence. Even the most stupid and belligerent among them was restrained from any involuntary brutality by the very weight of these voiceless throngs who could very easily, in one wave, have flowed over and trampled any soldier who lost his head.

It was evident that the people were beginning to unnerve the Military, including the non-commissioned officers who directed them. Sometimes the boys would gather together in consultation, muttering among themselves, glancing over their shoulders at the people. Apparently they could come to no conclusion; bewildered, sometimes smiling boyishly and as if ashamed, sometimes even laughing a little, sometimes shouting a joke or a gibe at the voiceless multitudes, they patrolled with more and more briskness. And sometimes they would stop and light cigarets—a forbidden practice but now an indication of reckless comprehension—and try to strike up a conversation with men and women nearest them.

But the people ignored them. They might have been dark statues standing in solid ranks on the pavements. What are they waiting for? the soldiers asked each other. But many soldiers did not ask. They knew.

The streets were darkening, the faint lamps began to waver in the brownish air of a bitter winter twilight. But still the people did not move, did not disperse.

They are waiting for their signal, as we are waiting, thought Durant. Among them were thousands of Minute Men, their guides and their leaders, who had ordered this awful demonstration of the people's power.

Durant rode in a car with Mr. Burgess, Mr. Regis and Dr. Healy. Picked Guards on motorcycles accompanied them and the cars behind them. They might all have been ghosts insofar as the people were concerned. The people simply stood and waited. Only Dr. Healy was disturbed. He kept peeping out of the car windows, huddling himself in his expensive coat.

"What's the matter, do you think, Mr. Regis?" he asked, speaking across Durant as if the latter did not exist. "They should be celebrating as usual. They have whisky cards, and the State restaurants are open for them, with free meals and things they never get during the rest of the year."

"What do you think is the matter, Doctor?" replied Mr. Regis, with that kind interest of his. "This is something unusual, isn't it? Colonel, what do you think?"

Durant said, grinning: "I think they're demonstrating, sir."
"Demonstrating what?" demanded Dr. Healy.
Durant shrugged "Why, Doctor. You're the psychiatrist, aren't you? You know all about mob psychology. Mobs always reveal a 'pattern,' don't they? What's their pattern now, Doctor?"
Dr. Healy looked through the windows again, frowning and afraid. Then he had the solution. He said: "Passive resistance. An old contrivance. Infantilism. The reverting to the pattern of childhood—negativism. It occurs in children during the third or fourth year when they are just becoming aware of their own identity—" He stopped, abruptly, and fear sprang out starkly in his eyes.
"Yes?" said Durant. "Go on, Doctor. I think you've got something. I think the people are 'becoming aware of their own identity.' I agree with you. And now what, Doctor?"
Dr. Healy swallowed. He regarded Durant with wavering ferocity, but he was a man not without courage. "We—we ignore negativism in a child. We—we evade it by offering a child two or three other choices—he makes his own decision—"
"Good," said Durant. "The people are making their choice, their own decision. It's all very clear."
The presence of Mr. Regis and Mr. Burgess kept down the doctor's panic. He turned to Mr. Regis. "Mobs," he said contemptuously. "Why don't the soldiers fire on them and disperse them?"
Durant answered very quietly and slowly: "They have their orders not to, Doctor."
Dr. Healy was both aghast and incredulous. "Who gave them such orders?"
"I did," said Durant.
Dr. Healy shrank from him. His voice shook when he appealed to the other men: "Mr. Regis, Mr. Burgess! Did you hear that? The colonel has dispensed with discipline. He refuses to disperse that mob—!"
Mr. Regis looked at the multitudes again. In a gentle and reasonable voice he remarked. "I'd hardly call them a 'mob' or 'mobs,' Doctor. Very orderly and controlled. Not even talking among themselves. Why should they be fired upon, or dispersed? After all, this is Democracy Day. If they take this method of celebrating why should it be forbidden?"
Dr. Healy was stunned. He shivered even in the warmth of the car. He put out the delicate antennas of his mind to discover if any danger or enmity was about him. There was none. There was only amusement, secret amusement, even from the two powerful civilians.
"Let's just ignore it," said Durant. "That's what you do with 'negativism' in a child, don't you, Doctor? The people are just being negative; they like to be negative today. What do you sup-

pose they're being 'negative' about, Doctor?" He paused. "The Democracy, Doctor?" he suddenly demanded, with sharp menace.

Dr. Healy could only stare at Durant for several long moments. His heart fluttered with terror. He made a movement like one about to take flight. He said to himself, incoherently: I must get out of here. I must report—Report to whom? The majestic heads of the two most powerful bureaus in the country were in this car with him. He stammered: "Mr. Regis. Mr. Burgess. Did you hear what—what the colonel has said?"

"Yes," said Mr. Burgess, smiling.

Dr. Healy made another convulsive movement. He was no longer interested in "reporting" to anyone. He was a very clever man. The impulse for flight was a primordial one, and he instinctively reached across Durant for the handle of the car. No one moved, but Mr. Regis said kindly: "Don't, Doctor. You see, you are under arrest."

Dr. Healy's hand froze in mid-air. Durant nodded, without interest: "If you attempt that again, Joe, I'll shoot you."

Dr. Healy fell back. He looked from face to face as best he could in the dim light. He began to tremble. "What are you going to do with me? Is this a—a revolt? Are you—you all traitors, spies? I don't understand. Are you going to kill me?"

Mr. Regis' voice was very kind and considerate. "Yes, Doctor, this is a 'revolt.' The revolt of the people, prepared over the years by all of us. No, we are not traitors. We are not going to kill you, so set your mind at rest. We only kill, and will kill, the ones who are utterly evil, or fanatically convinced of the righteousness of this horrible and wicked State. These have no place in the bright air of freedom. As for you, Doctor, we can use you. You see, you are a cynic; you aren't an evil man, just an expedient one. You aren't convinced that The Democracy is good. In your heart, you know it is vile. We are letting you live, so you can serve us, and you'll serve us well. Men like you are for hire. Realists are always for hire, and I don't doubt at all that your services to us will be conscientious and thorough."

He smiled in a paternal fashion at the gaping doctor.

"So, Doctor, suppose you engage your excellent mind in ideas how you can help us condition the people for liberty and self-government. Let us know, later, what your conclusions are."

Dr. Healy was silent. He pulled out his scented handkerchief and wiped his face. He rubbed his palms on his handkerchief. At last he said: "Is this going on, everywhere, in the country?"

"It is," Mr. Burgess assured him. "You see, we have control of the country now. In a few days it will all be over. In the meantime, you are our prisoner, Doctor. Not that you can really do any harm to us and the new Republic. But you might—I say you possibly might—in a moment of impulsiveness, cause some trouble."

Dr. Healy drew a deep breath. He looked at Mr. Burgess with fear and respect. He said: "I'm not an impulsive man, sir."

Mr. Burgess nodded. "Good. I know you are not. But you might think that everything isn't lost for the evil men, and you could evoke violence, small but unnecessary. We aren't violent people, unless we have to be. We intend no violence toward you. We want your cooperation. You're a valuable man, Doctor. We might even make you Chief of Public Health. The people have been ill so long. You could help cure them." Now his eyes were no longer cold. They sparkled with geniality.

Visions of Washington, a magnificent suites of offices, hordes of underling psychiatrists and consultants, a mansion, position and immense importance, whirled through Dr. Healy's mind. A hospital. The Dr. Joseph Healy Psychiatric Hospital! Honors. Travel. A seat near the President of the Republic of the United States of America—! Dr. Healy could hardly breathe.

He said faintly: "Who is to be the President?"

"Why, I am," said Mr. Regis. "I was a four-star general at one time, Doctor. My name is John Graham. I have been nominated by the secret Conclave of Minute Men to be the candidate of the Constitution Party in the elections, which will take place within a month, or less. In the meantime, another party will be formed by the opposition. You see, we will have an opposition, but it won't win. However, in a free country we must have at least two parties. Some of us will actually help to form the other party. Whom they will nominate will be entirely their own affair. We have only one stipulation: that they conform to the Constitution of the United States."

Dr. Healy winced at that forbidden word. But his visions returned. The Constitution Party. He savored it. His mind became busy with many thoughts. Liberty. He was a cynic more than he was a psychiatrist. The people had always proved themselves incapable of liberty; in fact, they despised it in their hearts. They would have to be thoroughly indoctrinated in the uses of liberty, and shown how to manipulate it wisely. The children would have to be taught. The people would have to be taught. There would have to be great forums, presided over by competent psychiatrists under his own direction.

He became excited, and prickling thrills raced up and down his spine. He was seated next to the coming President of the United States! He was here in this car, because they considered him valuable. He had been chosen! They could have killed him, but they had chosen him, these powerful and determined men.

Mr. Regis said: "Colonel Curtiss has been sending highly secret and confidential reports of your talents and qualifications to the Chief Magistrate, Doctor. He wasn't inspired by any admiration." Mr. Regis laughed a little. "But he knew you could serve us. Incidentally, yours was only one of twenty names submitted for approval. The colonel was convinced, himself, and he convinced us, that you were the man we needed. You see, all the others were either completely evil men, or men who tried to assure themselves that they were working for the best interests of the people, or they were men of even greater danger to the people: men who were not evil, were not trying to delude themselves, but men who actually and fervently believed that this corrupt State was benign and perfect and that whatever it did was best for everyone. In short, they were zealots, fanatics." He paused a moment, then continued: "You didn't come into any of these classifications. You were merely clever and expedient, and being so, and a very intellectual man, you could be bought. We intend to offer you an excellent price, as I mentioned before."

The darkness, like a fog, settled down swiftly, and the car raced for the country. Dr. Healy pondered over Mr. Regis' words. He glanced sideways at Durant. But he was grateful. He said: "Thank you, Colonel. But how did you know—what I really thought?"

"Because," said Durant cheerfully, "you were so thorough in carrying out my orders against the children of the privileged groups. You seemed to take a sort of pleasure in it, a perverted pleasure. Have you analyzed yourself, Doctor? Or was it all subconscious?"

"If I did as you say, Colonel, it was subconscious," added the other, grudgingly.

Durant turned in his seat toward him, though every face was now merely a faint blur in the dusk. "Tell me, Doctor, what made the people, decades ago, turn away from freedom? And how can we turn them back to it so firmly that they'll never consent to be slaves again? I want the psychiatrist's viewpoint."

Dr. Healy, so shaken, began to feel immense importance. He thought for a few moments, then replied with serious honesty, a rare state for him: "They were afraid of responsibility. All men are. A small precentage of men react to that fear by aggression, that is, they use their fear of responsibility to face it, overcome it, and succeed in channeling it into what we used to call 'usefulness,' or personal success. Our outstanding men in the sciences and the arts and in business and industry are examples. A less virtuous segment of that percentage becomes famous, or infamous, criminals. Some, and these are even rarer, sublimate their fear of responsibility to a point where they assume universal responsibility. We used to call them saints, or martyrs.

"But outside these few live the hundreds of millions of ordinary folk who are hounded and distressed by a nebulous but no less frantic dread of responsibility. They instinctively try to evade it. The masses have always been so, but they never had a voice or a word until the last thirty or forty years. They got the voice through labor leaders and idealists. And they got the magic word. Security. In the name of the word they embraced slavery." He turned to Mr. Regis. "Mankind is always afraid. It is part of the nature of humanity, because humanity is a solitary species, not by instinct gregarious or communal. Man is afraid of man." Dr. Healy laughed lightly, but with some ruefulness. "With good reason, too. People know what they are, so they try to protect themselves against each other. Taking on responsibility exposes them to too many hazards; only a few men have the character, the vitality, the health, the courage and the intelligence, to challenge those hazards aggressively."

"Have you a solution to offer, then, for the coming generations?" asked Mr. Burgess.

Dr. Healy considered intently. "In a way, yes. Of course," and he mouthed the word with distaste, "there is always religion, or superstition, as we call it. It has a very useful purpose. It numbs man's natural fear of his environment and his fellowman, and sublimates his dependence on the objective world to the subjective. That, strange to say—and it's always been a mystery to some of us—brings peace and courage and fortitude to millions. So, for one thing, we should cultivate religion as strenuously as possible in the lives of the masses, not to debase them"—and he cleared his throat sheepishly—"but, I must admit, to strengthen them and give them a sense of personal dignity and value."

"I see," said Durant, thoughtfully. "And it's very clear now why evil men bent on enslaving their fellows destroy or weaken religion first. It's very necessary, for these men, to eliminate a 'sense of personal dignity and value' in the people, because men of dignity and value will never become slaves."

"You see," went on the doctor warmly, "when a nation threatens another nation the people of the latter forget their factionalism, their local antagonisms, their political differences, their suspicions of each other, their religious hostilities, and band together as one unit. Leaders know that, and that is why so many of them whip up wars during periods of national crisis, or when the people become discontented and angry. The leaders stigmatize the enemy with every vice they can think of, every evil and human depravity. They stimulate their people's natural fear of all other men by channeling it into a defined fear of just certain men, or nations. Attacking another nation, then, acts as a sort of catharsis, temporarily, on men's fear of their immediate neighbors. This is the explanation of all wars, all racial and religious hatreds, all massacres, and all attempts at genocide."

"In short," said Mr. Regis, "we must stimulate man's natural formless fear of his fellows by showing him that his fellowman will enslave him if he possibly can. Not the men of other nations, but his immediate neighbor. Every man, then, will be a vigilante for freedom. I can see that you were never an idealist."

Dr. Healy hesitated. But his excitement over his own ideas made him say quickly and positively: "There are never really any idealists, Mr. Regis. There are people who hate narrowly and murderously. They never hate ideas, in spite of what sentimentalists might believe. They hate definite groups of people, the successful, the proud, the independent, the strong. Scratch an idealist, and you'll find a desperately inadequate man consumed by envy. You'll also find that he has a very dominant characteristic: he is an egotist who believes that the world has not given him the honors he deserves, and that the world is deliberately, and malevolently, determined that he shall never be honored. So, for the purpose of hatred, he settles on some group in society who he is convinced is frustrating him, and despising him. I think that explains why certain personalities find absolutism or Communism or any kind of authoritarianism the answer to their inner conflicts. By embracing such ideas, these 'idealists' see a way by which they can revenge themselves on those they envy, who are 'frustrating' them. However, to accept this realistic explanation of their burning desire to 'improve' what they call 'conditions,' would further lacerate their egoes. It would be unbearable. So they explain to themselves, and very loudly to others, that they are moved by the prevailing 'injustice' of society in general against what the idealist calls 'groups,' or any other sharply defined segments of the population. The fact that they are eager and willing to use violence or aggression against the people they subconsciously envy is a dead giveaway."

Mr. Regis said gently: "You see why, Doctor, we called you a realist. And why you'll be so invaluable to us. Of course, the real credit for your discovery goes to Colonel Curtiss."

Durant, the incurable sentimentalist, said surlily: "Don't congratulate me. I'm not sure I like these realists. The good doctor served the State very ably, realist though he is. I don't like these people who can be bought, and be enthusiastic for anyone who buys them. There has to be some honor."

"There never was, really," replied Dr. Healy, who was smiling. "But some things are less dishonorable than others. Everything is relative, Colonel. Besides, I had to make a living, didn't I? But don't misunderstand me. I didn't make this State; I found myself in it. As a realist, and a psychiatrist, I had to accept my environment. A better environment, for everybody, will not displease me."

The black and white countryside flashed by, and the men in the car were silent. The farmhouses they passed had a curious air of abandonment. A moon, like a skull, peered from the sky. The cavalcade of cars gathered speed, accompanied by the Picked Guard on their motorcycles.

Now they turned in on the road which led to the Chief Magistrate's country residence. Mr. Regis said musingly: "I suppose it could all be refined down to this: we must teach the people to fear and hate slavery more than they fear and hate freedom, and responsibility. Man must come of age, or man must die."

But Dr. Healy was not listening. If he had any remaining doubts as to the magnitude of what was taking place in the nation tonight, he lost them now. For the road to the great country house of the Chief Magistrate was lined with hundreds of somber-faced soldiers with rifles ready. Detachments of Picked Guards stood in front of them, guns in hand. The landscape blazed with such enormous lights that full noon could not have been more revealing. They obliterated shadows, and the winter trees stood starkly on the white parklike land, which had an unearthly brilliance. Soldiers patrolled across it in a solid line, tramping through the snow, the skirts of their coats whipped behind them by the strong wind. The fierce and wolflike dogs Durant too well remembered raced beside them, watching everything with their phosphorescent and savage eyes.

As the cars approached nearer and nearer to the house, Durant saw that the ranks of the soldiers became more and more massive. There must have been thousands of these patrolling young men. They circled the house; they covered the snowy ground. Their rifles bristled like thickets. Durant was startled and amazed. Who had given orders that these soldiers be gathered here? As the commanding officer of this Section it was his duty, and his, alone, to direct the troops.

Then he knew. It was by order of the Chief Magistrate, who wished to guard his friends in the coming days of upheaval. These were soldiers he could trust; these were the Picked Guards he could trust. The Armed Forces, then, were also in revolt.

The house was as lofty and elegant as Durant remembered. Fires danced in every room, reflected themselves on the diamond-paned windows. The large bedrooms were warm, prepared for occupation. So, thought Durant, we are to remain here for a short, indefinite time. His own bedroom contained three beds, and he was informed by a man servant that this was so two of his Picked Guards would always be with him.

"Well, boys," said Durant to Sadler and young Griffis, "it seems that we're to have a little luxury, for a time at least." He was filled with high excitement and some apprehension. He told himself that a man in his position should be all sternness and preoccupation and heroism. It was somewhat deflating to admit that he was also considerably frightened. He reassured himself with the thought that this was infinitely better than waiting for the coming terror in the vulnerable precincts of the Lincoln farm. He went to the windows to satisfy himself again that the grounds were indeed swarming with soldiers.

Young Tom Griffis' eyes glistened with completely joyous anticipation. He sat on one of the beds and bounced happily.

Even Sadler's moroseness lessened. He said: "It's going to be a relief not to have to carry a gun in my hand every minute. I know some of the fellows down there, sir. I know who and what they are. You can even look out of the windows, Colonel, without expecting a shot." However, he pulled the curtains across the windows, for the lights outside, so blinding, so stunning in their wide intensity, penetrated into the room.

There was a quick knock on the white paneled door, and instinctively Sadler and Griffis put their hands on their guns. Then, laughing, Tom opened the door. A captain of the Picked Guard stood there, and Tom and Sadler saluted. "I have a message for the colonel," said the captain, and advanced into the room. Durant turned idly, then stiffened. For the captain was Bob Lincoln, hard-faced, black eyes cold and bitter, body strong and upright in his uniform.

Durant's hand fell on his gun, and he half withdrew it. Young Lincoln ignored the gesture. He saluted ceremoniously. "I have a confidential message for the colonel," he said.

"No!" cried Durant. "What the hell are you doing here, Lincoln?" He began to splutter in his anger and fright. He turned to Sadler and young Griffis, his blood ringing in his ears. "This is Bob Lincoln, son of our involuntary host, John Lincoln. I—I—arrest him at once, Sadler! He must be a spy, he must be—"

Sadler answered: "I know all about Captain Lincoln, sir. He isn't a spy. He was appointed captain of the Picked Guards by the Chief Magistrate, himself."

Captain Lincoln regarded Durant with a saturine smile. "Sorry, sir, that you didn't know."

Durant's fear and rage increased. He felt trapped. He could think of nothing to do but shout. He opened his mouth, but he had lost his voice. He would be murdered in this room! He recalled his doubts of Sadler, of all of them. If the Minute Men were desperate, then the others were desperate, too, and would stop at nothing. His wet hand fumbled for his gun, and withdrew it. He croaked: "I'm going to kill you, Lincoln. I know what you are."

The captain did not move. The saturnine quality of his smile lessened; it became amused and a little sad.

"I can only stay a few minutes, Colonel," he said. "If the colonel kills me he'll have to answer for it to the Chief Magistrate, and to Mr. Regis. I beg the colonel to listen to me."

Durant pointed the gun at Lincoln's belly. He backed away from Sadler and Griffis, who were frowning and alarmed.

Lincoln's mouth compressed itself impatiently. "I must speak to the colonel in private," he said. "The colonel may take my gun, if he wishes, if he doesn't trust me." He waited. Durant had reached a wall; his dark face was livid, and his gun remained pointed steadily at the captain.

"I overheard you and Grandon plotting together last spring," he said. Helplessness flooded him, and he put his hand on the trigger of his gun. If he died, at least another would die with him. His old claustrophobia clutched at his throat. "I know what you are. How you deceived the Chief Magistrate, I don't know, but you aren't deceiving me, Lincoln."

"But the colonel is deceiving himself," replied Lincoln, who had paled. He spoke earnestly. "I have been a Minute Man for at least three years. In spite of my father. Or, I should say, because of my father." He watched Durant apprehensively, then lifted his hand and made the signals of the Minute Men. Durant laughed a little, hysterically.

"Easy to come by." He glanced at young Griffis. "Go down at once and inform Mr. Regis that I have a spy here." He had no hope, now, that Tom would obey, but the boy, after an apologetic look at Lincoln, began to move toward the door. Lincoln watched him go, and shrugged. "It's foolish to warn Mr. Regis. He knows all about me. I've been one of his personal Guards for months, in Washington."

Tom Griffis paused at the door, and looked at Durant. The wildest thoughts were rushing through Durant's mind, incredulous and fantastic thoughts. But he said, as harshly as possible: "Wait, Tom. Let this man talk. What about you and Grandon, Lincoln?"

Lincoln was visibly relieved. He said quietly: "Grandon joined the Army for the reason you did, Colonel. But he's not a Minute Man. He was doing this by himself. Grandon, sir, is not Grandon. He is the nephew of Mr. Burgess. What their real name is, I don't know."

Durant suddenly remembered Grandon's fainting fit at the Stadium. He, himself, began to feel dazed, and the gun sagged in his hand.

"Grandon didn't know who Mr. Burgess was, until he saw him today," Lincoln was going on. "I understand it was a bad minute or two, according to Grandon, with whom I've just talked." He smiled. "Grandon's an impulsive feller. Colonel, what did you hear Grandon and me talking about last spring?"

"You were talking of me," said Durant. He straightened the gun again and his eyes raged at Lincoln. "I was a 'plotter,' you said. You had an idea I was a 'spy.' You said that the time would come when you'd kill me, for you suspected that I wasn't what I was supposed to be."

Lincoln concentrated on this. He scowled. He thought for a few moments. Then he said: "The colonel was mistaken. We weren't talking about you, sir. We were talking about one of your executive officers."

"Grandon tried to poison me and my guards," said Durant, with disbelief.

Lincoln smiled for the first time. "I know he did. He told me. You see, Colonel, we all have had to work in isolated cells, and it was rare when any of us recognized another. But the colonel knows this. Grandon and I, until today, had no idea of what you really were. We thought you were what you appeared to be, a military man and so our enemy. We discussed you once or twice, but not where you heard us first. You were marked off to be killed, by one of us, when this day came. It was a shock to us when we were told of your real identity. Grandon guessed it in the Stadium today, and he was terrified when he remembered he tried to kill you."

Durant pondered this in growing bewilderment. He scratched his left ear with his left index finger. Sadler and Griffis were smiling.

Lincoln went on: "I found Gracie, Colonel. She told me about you, and that night. I told Grandon today, and he's very happy about it. I began to suspect who you really were after I found Gracie. By that time I was a lieutenant in the Picked Guard. The poor girl was working under an assumed name in a factory. She didn't like it," added Lincoln, laughing a little.

Durant was not convinced. He said: "If you showed me a mountain of credentials, Lincoln, I wouldn't believe you. I remember the way you looked at me, on your father's farm."

"I thought you were just a military man, and not what you really are," repeated Lincoln, with impatience. "I didn't care what you did to my father. I've always despised him. I hated you for what you appeared to be, that's all. Colonel, I'm here now for just one purpose. Two of your men are FBHS spies. They know all about you they know all about everything. They're fanatics. They're planning on killing you almost immediately, even though they know they'll be killed, themselves, for it. They know they've lost. That won't stop them, though, from doing as much damage, themselves, before they're shot. The colonel knows all about the zealots."

"You mean two of my men, who are in this house, are FBHS men?" cried Durant incredulously.

"Yes," said Lincoln. "And we've got to find out who they are immediately. Even here, Colonel, your life is in danger. We can't risk it; the Chief Magistrate is holding me responsible for your survival." He eyed Durant gravely. "Grandon, we know, is not your enemy. But two of the other three men, Bishop, Edwards and Keiser, are spies They're authentic military men, in the bargain." He swung toward Sadler and Griffis so abruptly that Durant, in his agitation almost pulled the trigger of his gun. "Well?" demanded Lincoln. "Have you taken care of things?"

Griffis saluted He said: "Yes, Captain. They've all had blank cartridges in their guns the last few days."

"Good," said Lincoln. He went to the door and one of the Picked Guards on sentry duty there saluted. "Go and find the executive officers of Colonel Curtiss, and Sergeant Keiser, and tell them that the colonel invites them for a drink in his room," he commanded. He shut the door, and ignoring the trembling gun in Durant's hand, he went to the big wardrobes and closets and examined them. He beckoned to Sadler and Griffis. "We can hide in these," he said.

"Wait a minute!" exclaimed Durant. "You mean I'm to face them alone? What if one or two of them really have bullets in their guns? God damn it, I don't want to be shot!"

Lincoln hesitated, his hand on the door of a closet. "I think we can be almost sure they don't have real bullets. However, Colonel, it's a chance we must take. We can't have those men here, in this house. We can't let them loose, either. We believe that at least fifty percent of the Army is with us. However, there are the others. We can't overthrow The Democracy without some bloodshed, you know." He motioned to Sadler and Griffis to hide themselves in one of the closets.

Durant had had considerable to absorb today, and this was too much for him. He could believe nothing; he could believe everything. The one grim salient fact remained, however. It was apparent that someone was going to try to kill him. The idea appalled him, and he was almost overwhelmed. This is the time I should be brave and bold, or something, he told himself. Well, I'm not. I think I'm going to be sick.

Despairingly, he saw a closet door shut on Lincoln. He looked at his gun. Should he hold it, or not? If what Lincoln had told him was true, it was his duty to be very subtle indeed, and lead the spies to betray themselves, not only for his own sake but for the sake of his friends. I'm as subtle as a sore toe, he thought. Again, he had an impulse to shout frantically, to bring anybody, no matter what happened. He swallowed hard several times in a miserable attempt to lessen his panic. I'm trapped, anyway, he said to himself. There's no way of escaping. He heard soft music coming from downstairs. He was due to join the others in less than fifteen minutes. The music mocked him. In a few moments he would probably be dead, here, in this pleasant bedroom, here with thousands of soldiers and Picked Guards all about him, here with his friends about to go downstairs to eat a fine dinner in celebration of the day of deliverance! Mr. Regis, who was to be President, who might be killed unless the spies were discovered—He, himself, was expendable, it seemed.

He put his gun back into its holster. He sat down in a chair facing the door. Cold sweat ran down his back.

The door opened and Grandon, Keiser, Bishop and Edwards, all smiling cheerfully, entered, saluting. Durant glanced at Grandon, and saw how taut was the young lieutenant's smile, and how wary. Grandon knew this was to be a test. Or did he? Durant turned his attention swiftly to the others. Bishop, that granite and stupid Army man, with his unintelligent dull eyes? Not Bishop. There was nothing of the fanatic about him. Keiser, his sergeant? Not Sergeant Keiser, with his devotion to his colonel. Edwards, with the hard hazel eyes and the brutal arrogance and the insolent ways? Definitely, Edwards. Who was the other? Or was the whole thing a fabrication, a lie, which was to result in his death? He became dizzy. He forced himself to smile. He waved his hand.

"Well, we're alone for once, boys," he said, with false joviality. His voice sounded cracked in his own ears. "We'll have a drink together and celebrate—"

Grandon leaned nonchalantly against one of the posts of Durant's bed. "Celebrate what, Colonel?" he asked. Keiser and Bishop and Edwards grinned.

Grandon made a large and sweeping gesture. "Celebrate Democracy Day, or the insurrection of the Armed Forces, sir, and a general revolt? We all know what's going on, now. That's why we're here, isn't it?"

The other three men had stopped smiling. They were all watching Durant, and suddenly he knew death was in the room, that it was breathing in his face. God help me to be brave and bold for once, he prayed. Just once, God. What is my life, anyway? But his life was all he had. If he had to gamble with it there was nothing else to do, however much he regretted it.

He lit a cigaret very carefully. He had to look away from his men to do so, and the presence of death quickened. He said: "Yes, that's why we're here. It's all over, boys. You know it; I know it."

He stood up, now, and regarded them gravely. Then he went to a waiting tray of whisky and glasses, and filled them. His back was to his men, and he waited, tense, for the crash of a bullet in his flesh. All his muscles crawled, and his hand shook. There was such a silence in the room.

He turned around, his glass in his hand. He raised it, and in a louder and firmer voice than he had believed possible, he said: "To the Republic of the United States of America!"

Grandon still leaned negligently on the bedpost. But he was not looking at Durant now. He was staring at his fellow officers. They were all white and very still. Edwards' little hazel eyes had an expression of shocked incredulity in them. Keiser's face was blank and Bishop's face had become stony.

Then guns were in Keiser's and Bishop's hands, and their eyes brightened with rage.

"I guess, Colonel Whoever-you-are," said Bishop, "this is the end of the road."

"That's right," agreed Keiser. His whole face was transformed, and it was black with hatred.

"Get over there with our lovely little colonel, Grandon," said Bishop. "Right beside him, you son of a bitch. And you, too, Edwards."

Grandon lifted himself from the bedpost. Without hurry, he moved to a spot near Durant. He smiled at the other men. "So, it was you boys all the time," he remarked pleasantly. Edwards, still shocked and bemused, stood closer to Durant. He began to stammer: "I didn't know. I—I thought the colonel was—was a real colonel. A stinking—"

"He never was," said Keiser, with an ugly look at Edwards. "We've known about it for months. But we never had the chance to kill him, with you bastards around." He was no longer the stolid and respectful sergeant. "We're going to kill you and Grandon, too. We know who you are."

Grandon was still undisturbed, and even more amused. "Has it occurred to you nice little chaps that you'll never get out of this room alive?" he asked. "The corridors are full of our men, you know."

Bishop laughed raucously. "Who cares? If we die for The Democracy, we die for The Democracy!" He jerked his head at Keiser, who pointed his gun at Grandon and took careful aim. Grandon lifted his hand.

"I'm curious," he said. "How did you find out about me, and old Edwards, here?"

"Never mind," said Bishop. He was hardly recognizable, for he had become all competence. "—traitor," he added, with an obscene adjective, to Durant.

There was a blaze of light, a roar, the sudden acrid stench of powder. Durant involuntarily clutched at his stomach. Smoke filled the brightly lit room. Then the room began to gyrate in slow and sickening circles. A monstrous sharp agony assailed Durant's vitals. Dimly, he thought: There were real bullets, after all. He closed his eyes on unendurable pain, and his whole body went limp and numb, and there was nothing but darkness before him, and one little spiral of light in that darkness. An eternity shut down, pulsing like a thousand hearts.

The spiral began to enlarge, to brighten, to grow diffused. Voices crashed against Durant's ears. Something burning and biting was running into his mouth. Someone was saying in an unnaturally high voice: "That's what imagination can do to a man!" There was a shout of laughter, also high. "Look," said another voice, "he's coming around. More whisky, Sadler."

In the swirling light and darkness Durant told himself that he was not yet dead. He believed he could feel his blood oozing through his flesh, warm and sickly, and with it, his life. Why didn't they do something, besides forcing whisky on him? Blood transfusions, he thought vaguely. A doctor. His cold and feeble hands pressed themselves against his abdomen. "Jesus, Mary, Joseph," he muttered. A priest; he needed a priest. Then he was enraged; his guts were spilling through his hands, and they just kept pouring whisky into his closing throat. The laughter and the voices became clearer. He opened his eyes, and said simply: "Can't you bastards see anything? I'm shot." His voice was a croak. His dim eyes looked out on a chaos of blurring faces and lights.

Now the room came into focus, a crowded room. Sadler was there, and Grandon and Edwards, and half a dozen Picked Guards, and Mr. Regis and Mr. Burgess, and Bob Lincoln. They were all about him; his face was running with water; his mouth was drooling whisky. They were looking at him with laughter and concern and solicitude.

"I'm shot," he pleaded. "They've killed me."

Mr. Regis bent over him, smiling. "All right, Colonel? Of course, you aren't shot. But you're a man of very interesting imagination, which made you the man you are. There isn't a mark on you—Andy." The voice was gentle and understanding.

"Not a mark," agreed Grandon, with a laugh.

Durant was outraged. He took his hands away from his abdomen and looked at them. They might be shaking, but there was no blood. Starting violently, he examined his body. It was quite intact. For some obscure reason, he was further outraged. "I tell you I felt the bullets and the blood!" he cried.

"A brave man," said Mr. Burgess, in a moved tone. "The bravest of men. It always takes a brave man, with imagination, to face death valiantly." He patted Durant's shoulder. "But you were never in real danger, Colonel. Really you weren't. Do you think we'd risk your life unnecessarily?"

"Of course you would," replied Durant, still examining himself. He spit out the whisky still in his mouth. "Anybody would, under the circumstances. Your life, and Mr. Regis' life, were more important than mine."

He was still weak, and shivering. And he was ashamed. He had fainted, for no reason at all but that his imagination was too intense. His embarrassment flooded him.

"I think," said Mr. Regis anxiously, "that he had better be put to bed. He's had a shock."

Durant's reaction made him swear. His shame mounted. "A nice trick to play on me!" he shouted. "A hell of a nice trick!"

"But there was no one else who could help us find out who the spies were," said Mr. Regis. He wiped Durant's wet face with his own handkerchief. "I'm sorry, my boy," said Mr. Regis, with compunction. "Won't you let us help you to bed?"

Bed. A wonderful place. A nice, dark, restful place, after all this. Durant said: "No. Do you think I want to miss the celebration?" To go to bed would mark him as the weak and girlish poltroon, the man of cowardly imagination. He wiped his mouth with the back of his hand. Then he had a thought.

"What happened to Keiser and Bishop?"

"We killed them," replied Lincoln. "And they've been hauled away."

Keiser, with whom he had exchanged so many knowing looks, so much understanding. Bishop, the dull, eating, obedient military man. It was not possible. But he had seen their faces in this room, and their guns. He shook his head violently, and said: "If I had the imagination you all think I have, I would've known."

He was beginning to feel stronger, in spite of his shame. Now, if he had had a wound, just a small unimportant wound, he would not be so disgraced in his own eyes. Mortification made his pale dark face flush, and his anger return.

"I'm not going to miss the celebration," he said firmly.

Durant, still ashamedly unnerved by his ordeal, went downstairs with his friends to the magnificent dining room. A circular table had been set with the finest of silver and crystal, ablaze with candles. Another and smaller table waited for his executive officers, who were now only two.

It was this, more than anything else, which gave Durant a sick shock. He had neither liked nor disliked Bishop, but had enjoyed his jokes, his air of being a simple but jovial military man, his dependable manner. For Keiser, Durant had felt a reluctant kinship. It was impossible to believe that these men had attempted his life, had hated him for a long time, and had always been his enemies. I'm certainly naïve, he thought, as he sat down at the right hand of Mr. Regis. He was so wretched that for some time he could not be impressed by the fact that he was occupying the place of honor beside the future President of the United States.

Captain Steffens sat at her father's left hand. She smiled, but her eyes were distraught and full of suffering. Durant forgot some of his own misery when he glanced at her beautiful face and thought of her private grief. Ben Colburn, however, had recovered his old quiet buoyancy; joy and hope shone in his smiles and sounded in his voice. Dr. Healy was preoccupied with his own exciting thoughts. He was already head of his hospital in Washington; he had already outlined, in his mind, the entire course of reeducation of the citizenry. He proceeded from point to point: the schools for children, the schools for adults. Of course, there would be no compulsion for adults to attend these schools, but they could be made exciting. The press could be induced to publish propaganda in behalf of liberty, self-reliance, individuality, just as, for so many decades, hundreds of psychologists and psychiatrists had, at the command and behest of the State, perverted the people's minds to a belief that the State should be all-powerful, and should be obeyed implicity under pain of being designated as "abnormal." We'll have to abandon the dangerous "father-image" concept, Dr. Healy thought, not because it is not true in individual cases but because it was used to betray the people.

Dr. Healy was much excited. He had served The Democracy

well, if cynically. He confessed to himself that it was a relief to be able to abandon cynicism and "work constructively." He, himself, would be a free man! This thought excited him even more. It had not given him particular satisfaction to deliver "recalcitrants and psychopaths" over to the loathsome FBHS. He had had to produce scar tissue and callouses over a certain area of his mind. To deliver the young from mindless death and spiritual enslavement would be very good indeed. He began to entertain the idea of God, tentatively.

Walter Morrow talked with Karl Schaeffer, and Durant, who still did not know who or what Morrow was, remained in perplexity. However, he knew that his directives against the farmers had been carried out with strong precision by Morrow, and that Morrow had delivered many inciting speeches to the farmers of Section 7. Durant was annoyed; Schaeffer and Morrow appeared to be old and excellent friends. The fact that Morrow had never confided in him hurt Durant.

An atmosphere of tenseness and happy anticipation pervaded the dining room, with its lofty beamed ceilings, its subdued candlelight, its fire. Only Picked Guards were present, and they lined the walls, shoulder to shoulder, their green uniforms almost black in the low light, their brass buttons twinkling in the reflections of the fire, their faces impassive. They were trustworthy men, and many of them were probably Minute Men, but Durant could not look at their uniforms without the old powerful aversion.

The curtains of the dining room had not yet been drawn, and it hurt the eye to glance at the windows which glared glassily in the floodlights outside. Durant wished that these floodlights could be shut out before the dinner started. But it seemed that this company was waiting anxiously for something to happen. At the end of the room a huge screen glimmered, and the big dining room table was occupied in a manner to give every diner a view of that screen. Now Durant sensed most keenly the tenseness of his fellow-diners.

A sudden grinding roar sounded outside. Mr. Regis nodded at Mr. Burgess, and everyone rose and went to the windows. In the fierce illumination of the floodlights tanks were being wheeled into position at some distance from the house; they ground and turned like heavy, prehistoric monsters, guns lifted. Army vehicles, loaded with soldiers or anti-aircraft guns, moved into place within the circle of the tanks. Now fresh lines of soldiers appeared, hurrying to join the others. Durant uttered an exclamation.

"We hope—nothing—will be necessary," Mr. Regis explained. "But we can't take any chances. We believe that over fifty percent of the Armed Forces are with us, in this Section. However, the forces still have a large quota of fanatics and others who believe we are traitors and rebels, and must be destroyed. Our own men are working even more frantically than ever, tonight, at convincing the unconvinced, or the stupid, or those mistakenly 'loyal' to the evil men of The Democracy."

He lifted his hand, and someone outside caught the signal. Immediately the floodlights went out. It was some moments before Durant could adjust his eyes to the blinding darkness. Eventually the dimmed whiteness of the snow returned, and the still and silent moon. The soldiers, thousands of them now, patrolled in dark and orderly ranks. The guns pointed in every direction, including the purple sky. It was an ominous sight, and Durant was dismayed. He had only casually thought that the State would resist. Bombs! He strained his ear for the sound of aircraft, and was unhappily rewarded. The roar of a whole fleet of planes sounded overhead, great twelve-engined planes which could carry six hundred men and their equipment, armored planes with guns. All listened, as Durant listened, and he saw the clenching of fists, the strained whiteness of faces. Even the soldiers were looking up, in a mass.

The planes circled, and they all waited. Lower and lower they circled, like nightmare birds of prey. What if the bastards drop an atom bomb on us? though Durant. Mr. Regis and Mr. Burgess were pressed against the windows, looking upward as the flocks of iron buzzards went over the house, wheeled, and returned, in precision formation.

Then Mr. Regis and Mr. Burgess cried out exultantly. The bellies of the planes had become alight with flashes of blue and red and white, in perfect patterns. A deafening roar of joy went up from the soldiers outside. It was impossible for their officers to control them. They shouted and laughed and embraced each other hysterically. Then, as if at a signal, they began to sing, and Durant's emotional heart turned over and his eyes filled with tears. For the soldiers, turning now to the house, were singing the old and forbidden anthem of the Republic: The Star-Spangled Banner. The anthem welled, rose, swelled into a very thunder of joy and deliverance; the sound made the big house vibrate. The sky, with its iron pulsing of aircraft engines, seemed to quiver.

How wonderful was the song of those thousands of young men outside, who sang as they had never sung before, waving their caps, faces illuminated by the moon, drowning out, by their voices, the throbbing pulses of the planes! The song of freedom.

There was a flagpole outside, and though it was night a huge banner began to climb its stem, flowing out into the winter wind. The song of soldiers rose to a majestic pitch:

"Whose broad stripes and bright stars!"

There were tears on Durant's face, and tears on the faces of the others. Their eyes rose as the flag mounted, and a single spotlight followed its course. The Picked Guard in the room were singing also. Dr. Healy, who had heard the melody in his boyhood, but did not remember the words, began to hum.

"—gave proof through the night
That our flag was still there!"

It had always been there, thought Durant, openly weeping; always, in the hearts of the debased and enslaved people, it had been there. We could have worked forever, but without the people we could have done nothing. They remembered the words; they remembered the song.

"—the land of the free, and the home of the brave!"

Now the streaming and blowing flag hung unchallenged between earth and sky, proudly aloft over the massed faces of those who hailed it with reverence and passion. Then, all at once, there was a thunder of guns and a vivid explosion in the winter air, the salute of men made free. Twenty-one guns, shattering the night, echoing back from the whole white countryside, echoing back from the sky. The soldiers saluted the flag, standing at attention, their thousands of eyes fixed upon it sternly and with exaltation, while the red lightning of the guns lit up the snowy landscape, and the earth trembled.

No more hiding now, no more fear! Tyranny, like hell, might not be easily conquered. But it could be conquered by brave and devoted men. It had been conquered tonight.

The last gun sounded in the salute. The floodlights rushed out again, blindingly. The flag soared and the soldiers re-formed into the patrol. Mr. Regis dropped the curtains over the windows, and smiled at his friends.

"We haven't quite won, yet," he said. "But we have thrown down our challenge."

They went back to their table, smiling at each other. Morrow said. "But surely no one can resist us now."

Mr. Burgess replied: "All the commanding officers of all the Sections are with us, except two, and those two are ugly and determined men. They are under the President's command, and they control their soldiers. If those soldiers revolt, on their own initiative, if they hear of the revolt of the other Sections, then we can be sure we have won. In the meantime, we have to wait."

"But what can these commanders, and their men, do with a whole nation in a state of passive rebellion?" asked Durant. "The bureaucrats are revolting, the MASTS are revolting, the farmers are revolting. It's true that they have been working for the restoration of the Republic, but they've been working for their own ends, believing that the overthrow of The Democracy would return their power to them. They'll eventually learn that they've been deceived, by themselves, of course. However, they've helped to stimulate this revolt. How can a few overpower the many?"

"The few have always done that," said Mr. Regis sadly. "It's a fact we must never forget." He added: "And the people are not without guilt, as you know."

The dinner was excellent, but no one was aware of it. In the middle of the meat course there was a sudden crackling in the direction of the screen, and the screen glimmered, an image shifted and rippled over it, and finally the life-size face of a news commentator appeared, full of excitement.

"The President of The Democracy has just issued a statement!" he shouted. "It is no longer a rumor that a few traitors among the Military have dared to declare that the old Republic of the United States has been restored! However, the President has made this statement: 'I am confident that the people of The Democracy will remain calm, and loyal to their free Government, and will not respond to the appeal of the traitors. The People's Government is not alarmed, here in Washington. We know that the people will not endure this insane assault on their liberties and their dignities, this wild insurrection of a minority of the Military and certain other groups who wish to enslave and control our free and mighty Nation, for their own evil ends. On this Democracy Day, dedicated to the people, we are firm in our determination that right and justice and liberty will prevail, the traitors be routed and punished, and our enemies be overcome.'"

Durant thought of the hundreds of thousands of implacable and silent faces which had filled all the streets that day in Philadelphia. He thought of the immobilizing of the people in every city in the country. Millions were listening to the President's statement now. Millions were thinking. Would they be deceived again, to their death?

No one was eating in the dining room, now. All attention was fixed on the screen. Another commentator from the nation's capital appeared. Behind him were ranks of furiously writing men, and men listening at telephones.

The Section formerly called Canada was in full revolt. An hour ago an unknown spokesman in Ottawa had declared Canada free from The Democracy, a nation in its own right. The armies of The Democracy had suddenly and mysteriously disappeared from the ancient border, and were reported in complete and disorderly retreat. The people of Canada, armed and revengeful though they were, had not pursued the soldiers. It was rumored that the soldiers of The Democracy, in certain sections along the old border, had saluted the flag of Canada as it had ascended on quickly improvised flagpoles, and had cheered it. It was only a rumor, of course, said the commentator, who was stammering in his excitement, his face gleaming with sweat, his shirt open. The people were implored by President Slocum to understand it was only a rumor, conjured up to confuse the nation.

Another commentator appeared; there were five others lining up behind him.

The Section once called Mexico was in bloody mutiny: "Thousands" of The Democracy's troops had been slaughtered. But it was only a rumor, only a rumor! cried the commentator hysterically, as he wiped his sweating face. Wait a moment, please! The commentator scanned, feverishly, a dispatch which had been given him. Now he faced his audience and screamed: "Mexico has declared herself free from The Democracy only an hour ago, according to rumor! The bridges over the Rio Grande swarm with the retreating armies of The Democracy. The armies are not firing as they retreat, nor are they blowing up the bridges. The flag of Mexico has been raised—but it is all only a rumor—a rumor—the people are not to believe, they are to remain calm—"

Mr. Regis and his company looked at each other in profound but silent emotion. They sat in their chairs and waited.

The people were begged to remain in their homes or official meeting-places for the next few hours. "News of momentous importance would be broadcast from time to time, to acquaint the people with the full treachery of 'a few' and to dispel dangerous rumor." The screen became blank again.

"They've called off the other commentators, temporarily, at least," said Mr. Regis: "Something is happening, somewhere—"

A voice blurted from the darkened screen, and no image appeared: "The President has just informed this station that the Chief Magistrate, disturbed and annoyed by the persistent, unfounded and malicious rumors, has hastened to the White House for a consultation with the President as to the means to be employed in overcoming these rumors, and to assure the President of the devotion of the Armed Forces and their loyalty. In the meantime, wait for further announcements."

"All good men," said Mr. Regis, of the commentators. "It's taken two years to pick them."

He rose, a glass of wine in his hand, and the others rose with him. He smiled at them all, one by one. He lifted his glass.

"To the Republic of the United States of America!"

They drank the toast solemnly, the glasses trembling in their hands. Mr. Regis said: "I'm not one to raise too many hopes. This will not end without violence. The two 'loyal' commanders of those 'loyal' Sections have large detachments of troops. They could do much damage—"

The screen came to light in a blaze. The broadcasting room was shown again. Another commentator was raising his right hand for attention, and was looking down at a sheaf of papers in his left hand.

"More rumors, I'm afraid," he said mournfully. "In Sections 1 and 6 the people, who have been massing on the streets of various cities in those Sections, refused to go home. Or, rather, they passively and silently disobeyed the commands of the Military. On orders of the two loyal commanding officers, the troops fired on sections of the crowds. It is rumored that at least five thousand civilians were killed during the past hour. But here's another rumor: mobs swarmed over the soldiers and inflicted many casualties on them, seizing their arms and trampling their bodies in the gutters. However, the mob seemed to be well disciplined and commanded, and after this rumored assault on the Military, they resumed their places on the streets. The President, hearing this rumor, regretted the hasty action of the Military in firing, unprovoked, on peacefully assembled citizens, and promises that the guilty shall be punished."

The commentator moved aside, and another young man took his place. He regarded his audience of millions with sparkling eyes. He began to speak, in a distinctly Southern drawl.

"It is rumored—and remember, friends, it is only a rumor!—that the Southern Sections have revolted as a body. Traitors, allegedly speaking in the name of the Southern people, have declared that the South is free of The Democracy as of this hour, and that unless a Constitutional government is restored in Washington within the next three days the South will announce to the world that it is a nation distinct and apart—Friends, one must never believe in rumors. The President implores you not to believe in all these wild rumors! He is calm, he is firm, he is eating his dinner, and when questioned five minutes ago he denied he will speak to the country at midnight because he is confident that all these rumors are lies, and the people loyal to their Government. The President laughed heartily—"

Again, the screen went blank.

Mr. Regis exchanged a long look with Mr. Burgess, and glanced at his watch.

The meats and fish and salads and wines stood on the table, but no one ate or drank, now. Alice Steffens sat with her head bent and tears on her cheeks. All the men were pale and grim, playing absently with their table silver and their wine glasses. The Picked Guards stood motionless. The young soldiers outside were singing again as they marched, the happy songs of youth and joy. The candlelight and the firelight flickered over the great warm room. Somewhere a clock struck ten loud and booming notes. Somewhere, outside, there was laughter, and the people in the dining room listened. Laughter! The people were laughing again in America; the young were laughing!

Durant thought of his family, and he said to himself that all his labor and all his suffering had been nothing compared with this free light laughter of liberty. All the work his fellows had done, all that they had endured, all the many deaths they had encountered, all the pain and the tears and the prayers and the bitterness, were a small price to pay.

Mr. Regis was speaking. "I often remember what Goethe said on the subject of truth and error: 'The chief thing is to have a soul that loves the truth and harbors it where it finds it. And another thing: the truth requires constant repetition, because error is being preached about us all the time, and not only by isolated individuals but by the masses. In newspapers and encyclopedias, in schools and universities, everywhere error rides high and basks in the consciousness of having the majority on its side.' "

He regarded his friends with deep gravity. "Let us remember that. Let us remember that it is the few who love liberty and guard it and overthrow tyranny when it appears, and who teach the people what it means to be free, and who rescue them from slavery.

"This is the most fateful day in the history of America. It is a day which must never be forgotten. There must always be vigilant Minute Men, like sentries guarding a vulnerable border. Never again must we be complacent, conceding this small liberty and that small law, in the name of 'security' and 'national welfare.' Security and national welfare depend upon the most exact adherence to law, and no false or artificial 'emergency' should ever be permitted to abrogate the least of our laws, or to shackle them, or to modify them. Even wars, if they ever again arise to degrade us, should not be an excuse for an attack upon the Constitution. When one law of a nation is broken with impunity the rest are rendered ineffectual. A spot of disease on the body of a nation makes the whole body sick."

Dr. Healy said respectfully: "I have been outlining, in my mind, a course of instruction which should be mandatory in all schools, public or private. The children, above all else, should be taught to be jealous of their liberty and to recognize the enemy when he appears." He paused, and the delicate skin of his face flushed with enthusiasm. "I'm not merely speaking of American history. I mean that the children should be taught the meaning of liberty and self-reliance and dignity, and this course should be the most important in the curriculum. I've come to the conclusion," he added, as he saw how the others were concentrating on his words, "that without liberty there can be no real arts and sciences, for the proletarian spirit inhibits them. The twentieth century produced no giants in any of the classic arts, for the aristocratic spirit declined as industrialism captured the minds of the people. Industrialism is not evil in itself; it is necessary. But its values are crude and materialistic, and these values must be changed."

Ben Colburn spoke in his soft and hesitating voice. "The masses, as a mass, have no spirit, no heroic emotion, no creative passion, no dignity or splendor. It is only when the mass is broken up into its distinct individual units, acutely independent, and acting alone, that variety emerges, and with variety, the true arts and sciences."

"It seems to me," said Walter Morrow, "that one of the best safeguards of the country would be to stimulate pride, and, yes, factionalism. A man should be proud if he is a mechanic or tool-maker, and he should believe his work the most important. The farmer should believe his acres are sacred, and he should act in accordance with that belief. The teacher, the doctor, the lawyer, the grocer, the plumber, the weaver and the miller—they should all cultivate an intense pride in their work, convinced that the country could not exist without them. Pride is the enemy of the mass-mind—"

"A nation without honor and self-respect must fall," said Mr. Burgess, nodding.

The screen blazed and crackled again. A huge head floated into view, with enormous excited eyes. "It is rumored that the people are still standing in their hundreds of thousands—in their millions—on the streets of all the cities throughout The Democracy! Rain, snow, tropical downpours, hurricane winds, and sleet and ice, can't dispel them! Friends, this is impossible! A nation stands and cannot be moved either by guns or persuasion. It is nearing the hour for the midnight shifts in our great warplants; the workers do not move. The farms and ranches and plantations have been deserted, and all have gathered in the villages, the towns and the cities. This is a most impressive and most awful demonstration! What are the people demonstrating? Why this appalling silence and motionlessness all over the country? They have apparently no leaders, no inciters. They just gather, the people, and remain where they have gathered.

"The ships stand dark and deserted in the harbors. The longshoremen have gone. War materials are piled up on the docks. No one guards them. Where are the soldiers who should be there? Where are the watchmen? Where are the sailors on the battleships in port? Why are the airfields abandoned? Why are the trains pulled off onto sidings?"

The voice cracked. Then the commentator spoke again.

"I am again warned to tell you that all these things are rumors—only rumors. It is only a rumor that the miners will not return to the mines, and the farmers to their farms. Surely the people have not lost their minds and their devotion to those noble words of our President: 'Unity! Duty! Sacrifice!' Surely the people are not betraying their country in this desperate hour of war with the enemy! But it is all rumors! There is no revolt! All is calm; all is quiet. The President is entertaining his friends—"

Mr. Regis looked at his friends, and they all smiled with quiet savagery. "If I know Slocum, and I know him well," said Mr. Regis, "he is being fortified with whisky in large quantities, and someone is bathing his head. He is a very stupid man. Earlier tyrants of this century always left one country intact into which they could flee when matters got too hot for them. But Mr. Slocum has no place to go."

The clock boomed eleven. "At dawn, I shall leave to join our President," Mr. Regis continued. "I think he'd like my advice."

The voice was shrieking: "Where are the civil service workers tonight? The offices of the bureaus all over the country should be filling now. But the buildings stand dark. There are no fires in the furnaces. Ah, another dispatch! A skeleton force of workers is appearing at the railroad yards, moving silently to their work. Trains containing food, and food only, are on their way again. The same small skeleton force is arriving to keep public utilities in restricted use. Another dispatch! All political prisoners are being freed by their jailers; the prisons have been opened! It's rumored that word went out from the people that unless this was done mobs would descend on the places of incarceration and would attack prison officials, and would have no mercy. Anarchy! Mob violence! Will the Armed Forces permit this? But where are the Armed Forces?"

Another face swam into view on the screen. There was a flourish of recorded trumpet calls, a flutter of drums. The President would speak at midnight.

At midnight, precisely, the screen swam with jagged lightnings of color, very agitated and blinding. Apparently the engineers of the broadcasting station at the White House were extremely nervous, for they had difficulty with transmission.

Then there was a jolt of color, and the President's face, three times life-size, rushed into view. Another flourish of trumpets, another rifle of drums, a strain or two of the President's favorite anthem, and an apprehensive voice, too shrill: "Ladies and gentlemen! The President of The Democracy!"

"They're all out of sequence and proper order," remarked Durant, watching Mr. Slocum's confused expression, his attempts to speak, while the trumpets lagged, the drums stammered and the anthem became a jumble. Mr. Slocum made a distraught gesture, and everything became profoundly silent.

The silence evidently confounded the President even more than the ill-advised flourishes and music had done, for now that he held the floor alone he could not speak at all. His wide rodent's mouth moved impotently; his cunning little eyes darted about frantically; his nose twitched. His face was pale and drawn, and a muscle jerked violently in his right cheek. He put the palms of his hands to his head and smoothed down his meager gray hair. It could be seen that he was breathing too fast, that he was trembling. He tried to smirk, as he dropped his hands, and then he stood there, the very image of terror and distraction, visibly quaking, swallowing spasmodically.

The silence grew longer. The musicians tried to fill it with tentative strains of the anthem. The President swung his head about on its narrow neck and apparently uttered an expletive. The music died abruptly.

There was no dignity in him, no courage, no fortitude, no pride. His voice when it came at last, was a womanish squawk, the voice of utter dread and fear. He grinned, and his haggard flesh pulled into folds.

"Fellow citizens. I addressed you before today, a few hours ago. On this our heroic Democracy Day, dedicated to the People and the People's Government. I felt it fitting that it should so be dedicated, because without the enthusiasm and support and devotion of all of you, The Democracy could never have established and we should, in these days, be the slaves of reaction and reactionary Government."

He paused, and gulped. "Ah," murmured Mr. Burgess, softly, "he knows not how well he speaks."

"—slaves of reactionary Constitutionalism," the President went on, his voice tight and squeaking with its terror. "Our country is now enjoying the greatest freedom in its long history, its greatest productivity, its widest triumphs. Poverty has been abolished; a few do not exploit the many. Because of our long wars with the Enemy, there has, of necessity, been forced upon us a state of slight austerity. The People have understood this, and have voluntarily agreed to rationing and other restrictions, for the greater Good, for the Welfare of the State. Selfishness, as a way of life, has been abandoned. We work together collectively, sharing our hardships equally, our labor equally, our accomplishments equally. I repeat: without the People of this democracy your Government could not have established itself so firmly and have attained the leadership of the world."

His hands were apparently sweating. He took out his natty handkerchief and wiped them convulsively. He did not replace the piece of linen; he kept it in his hands and twisted it in the revealing gesture of panic.

"Labor has been dignified as never before in the history of our country. I might even say that Labor rules us, and Labor's welfare and Labor's necessities. Until the advent of The Democracy, Labor occupied the meanest stratum in our national existence. Labor made our State; Labor supports our State. Labor will lead us to even higher peaks. Labor crushed reaction, and is responsible for us."

His voice trailed away. He stared from the screen in impotent fear. It was some moments before he could speak again. He seemed to be feeling the enormous hatred and shame and rage he was exciting in the hearts of millions, and it terrified him.

"You made this Government, my dear friends. You made me your leader. Because you wished a State more in accordance with your desires and your dreams. Together, we abolished the old

Constitution, which we had decided inhibited us all. I salute you, every man and woman of Labor, and all others who have made this nation what it is."

He gulped. His eyes darted as if in pleading challenge.

The soldiers outside were singing and laughing. The flag soared over them in glorious pride, flung its stars at the higher stars, spread its brilliant stripes under the moon.

"It has been brought to my attention." squealed the President, "that the people are so enthusiastic over this Day which has been dedicated to them. that they are standing in all the cities, as if reluctant to let the Day end. I wish, dear friends, that I could be standing with you tonight, enjoying your victory and your happiness. But, there is a war on! There is a job to be done! Essential industry must not be stopped even for a moment, even for a prolonged celebration of Democracy Day! There are millions of you due at this very minute, in your own war plants, your railroad yards, your electrical factories, your many other areas of war effort. There are other millions who will not be recalled to duty until six o'clock in the morning. I know that all of you, after my humble address to you, will return to your homes for well-deserved rest. or to your battle stations.

"An intimate advisor has told me that you insist that I speak to you now, and that you are waiting to hear me, otherwise I should not be taking up your time which is so valuable to our war effort. I am touched, dear friends, by your devotion. But I am also alarmed by some treacherous rumors which have come to my ears tonight, rumors issued by mongers of hate and disruption and lies. These very few enemies of The Democracy have been issuing falsehoods to our various broadcasting stations. In your name, therefore, I shall demand that more rigorous censorship prevail after tonight so that you'll never again be diverted from your labors in the common cause by any falsehoods and confusion, by any attempts on our national unity.

"Sabotage! Rebellion! Disobedience! Revolt of a large section of our wonderful Armed Forces! Revolt of the farmers, the workers, the leaders of industry! This is what you have been hearing for the past few hours. Believe me, dear friends, they are lies. Never has the nation been so united. Are you incredulous at these reports of the enemies of The Democracy? I am not incredulous, for I know how the Enemy works, and what he wishes to do. He wishes to make you slaves of selfish interests and reactionary government again! He wishes to deprive you of your liberties and your national honor. But we shall not permit this! We shall be firm and strong, one together under one flag!"

The President's wizened face turned scarlet on the screen, and drops burst out on his forehead. Someone handed him a glass, and he gulped it. It had a suspiciously amber color. Then a hand thrust a paper at him and he took it eagerly. His face lighted up with jubilation.

"Friends! I have just been handed a message by the Secretary of Protection! Our brave troops have just announced that the flag of The Democracy now stands everywhere on the spine of the Andes Mountains! We have not yet completely conquered all the nations of South America, but I prophesy that within a few months our enemies on that continent will beg for peace. Your sons have done this, my friends! They have given their blood and their lives in order that we, their parents and their wives and their children, will enjoy everlasting peace in this world, everlasting progress and civilization and prosperity. We shall soon have at our complete disposal the nitrates and copper of Chile, the rich fruits and rubber of Brazil, the raw materials and industrial organizations of Argentina, the minerals of Peru, and the willing laboring hands of millions of oppressed South American citizens! Rejoice with me in this triumph, or, rather, let me rejoice with you, for you have made this possible!

"And now, dear sisters and brothers, return to your homes and to your plants, which are your battle stations. Do not let the enemies of national unity disturb you, or beguile you into passive resistance to your country. Do not listen to them; it is treason to yourselves. Our enemies are very few, and we feel that the country and all its protective organizations are disciplined enough to overcome any emergency. We know who the enemy is. We shall keep our eyes upon them and before long, with your help, and the help of your Bureaus, they will be rounded up and dealt with according to their crimes."

He had become hypnotized by his own voice, which had a stronger note and a less hysterical one. He could grin more naturally, now. He lifted his hand and shouted: "Unity! Duty! Sacrifice!"

Music clashed, the President's face faded, and the flag of The Democracy sailed into view. The strains of the national anthem roared from the screen.

Mr. Regis and his friends laughed aloud. But Dr. Healy was very serious and excited. "I've just discovered something," he said, looking at them eagerly. "Slocum isn't an evil man. He's just a fool. Of course, fools are more dangerous than bad men, but fools can be frightened in a pinch. Evil men can't be frightened, because evil is their nature."

He asked: "Mr. Regis, what tinge of political faith will the new Republic wear? A little of Fascism, or of Communism, or a touch of Socialism?"

Mr. Regis regarded him with sad surprise. "You are quite a young man, aren't you, Doctor? That is the tragedy, that all the millions of your contemporaries, and millions younger, have never known what it is to live under a free system of government. There must always be an 'ism,' with you. You don't know any better, so you can't be blamed. But let me tell you this: there will just be the old American Government, under the restored Constitution."

The dim screen billowed with light again, and there was another commentator, shouting: "The President has delivered his most moving speech tonight, to the People. But the People are not returning to their 'battle areas,' as the President called them. They are just quietly going home! The factories and the plants remain empty. The streets are emptying. The houses are dark. The People, to make it short are just doing nothing!

"But it's another story about Section 1 and 6. The two heroic commanders of these Sections are rumored to have invaded their neighboring disloyal Sections tonight in order to put down the rumored insurrections of the Armed Forces and to restore order among the people. It is rumored that both of these loyal commanders have just been murdered, and by their own officers! The troops, after a bloody sortie or two, are retreating behind the borders of Sections 1 and 6. It is only a rumor that thousands of them have joined the mutinous ranks of their neighbors! As the President has said, all this is only rumor, fabricated to confuse and frighten the people. Only rumor, friends!"

Another face appeared, looking shocked and incredulous, but the eyes danced. "It is rumored that three members of the Joint Chiefs of Staff have fled Washington, including five Bureau heads. If this is so, it is possible that they are merely gathering for consultation about the floods of rumors—"

The voice paused, then shouted: "The -treets of Washington are full of official cars leaving the city! Their headlights are not on. Where are these cars going, at one o'clock in the morning? For 'consultations'? Why are no Picked Guards with them, or other escorts? Why is the White House blacked out, as if expecting an air raid? Why are no lights shining on the Capitol? It's rumored that hundreds of Senators are fleeing the city, too. But where will they go?"

The voice stopped. The young man's face on the screen became dark and somber. The eyes looked out sternly. "Yes, where will they go? Back to their native Sections? Back to the rumored insurrection of the populace? Dare they go back? Where will they go, these men Where will they hide?"

Yes, thought Durant, grimly, where will they hide, these traitors and liars, these murderers and oppressors of the people? Where can evil ever hide, that it can never be found?

The face was replaced by another. "Such rumors! It is said that the old flag of the Republic is appearing everywhere, paper flags furtively pasted onto shop windows, on doors, on telegraph poles. Crudely handpainted flags! If this is so, how long have the people been preparing these flags. Who directed them? Who is controlling them, now, so that they are not attacking public buildings or blowing up war plants tonight and other key industries? Who ordered them to turn quietly to their homes, and wait there? Wait for what? If this is revolution, then never was a revolution so disciplined, and so without bloodshed. Unless, of course, it is just a rumor!"

The screen abruptly dimmed.

"There will be more, all night, all day tomorrow," said Mr. Regis. "I won't go to bed. If any of you, however, wish to sleep, you are at liberty to return to your bedrooms."

But it was impossible for anyone to think of sleep, or any kind of rest. When the screen was blank, they talked with excitement, or were soberly quiet, thinking. More news came at intervals, all prefaced by the exhortation to remember that it was only "rumor." Durant, watching the smiling, vehement or mercurial faces of the various young commentators, marveled at the silent and patient work which must have been done by anonymous Minute Men over the past year or two. There had been no violent or explosive "seizing of public communications," which had marked changes of government in other countries. The Minute Men were simply there, infiltrated in the broadcasting stations, waiting for their own particular signals. When they had arrived, they had moved into action, with no hindrance, no bloodshed, no spectacular gestures, giving the people news of their fellows in all the other Sections, and, by their smiles, the pursings of their lips, the glancing of their eyes, inciting the emotions of their listeners. As they spoke in the name of the State, and were deferential when they mentioned the President, and repeated that all was rumor, no effort could be made to silence them.

Thinking of this, Durant went to Lieutenant Grandon, and said: "You weren't a Minute Man, George. What did you think you could do by entering the Armed Forces?"

"Stir up disaffection, sir," replied the young man, smiling. "Do you remember all those parties I used to attend? Most of them were parties for officers like myself, and I just talked. Very subtle, if I admit it, myself. And then there were thousands of young fellows who were only drafted or enlisted, and they were Minute Men, right in there, working. That's how it happened that we now have over fifty percent of all the troops. Nobody knew what anyone else was doing. It only mattered that it was being done." He inclined his head courteously at Durant. "But, of course, things couldn't have moved with such order and precision without the Minute Men, and with such a chance of succeeding."

He was sitting beside his uncle, and Mr. Burgess looked at him affectionately. "I thought I was the only one in the family left alive," he said. "No, don't ask me how I got to my present position. It's too long a story. The country is so full of stories that writers will have material for at least a century."

The screen brightened for another face. It was "rumored" that all commanding officers of all the Sections had "deserted" their posts! They were nowhere to be found. Their men were in a state of "anarchy," abandoned by those who should be guiding them and protecting The Democracy. In Chicago, the people had not been able to contain themselves. They had been armed with many weapons, and they had attacked the military barracks in that city. Before they had been "calmed," over two hundred soldiers had been killed, but less than fifty civilians. The people had then taken over the barracks and the soldiers were fraternizing with them.

"You see," said Mr. Regis, "you had forgotten the fanatics and those who were convinced of the righteousness of The Democracy. You had forgotten that those soldiers who were killed had been simple military youths whose minds had been so regimented that they had no thoughts of their own. This will happen everywhere before the end."

More and more reports flooded in. The food warehouses in all the cities and towns and villages had been attacked by the populace, which, however, had not been disorderly. They were being "led." The food had been distributed by men and women evidently trained for this contingency. Trucks, confiscated from the Military, had been expertly and completely loaded, and carted off for further distribution.

The Armed Forces, at dawn, were offering only "token resistance," under their immediate officers. At dawn, the people were not returning to their "battle stations" in industry, though a competent skeleton force of workers was operating essential utilities, and trucks, loaded with milk, were entering the cities. In New York, hundreds of men, wearing white armbands, were directing operations and maintaining order. The white armbands were also appearing in great numbers in the other large cities throughout the nation. Banners were mysteriously being produced, banners made in secret and bearing the Stars and Stripes of the Republic. City halls everywhere were flying them. The flags of The Democracy were being burned openly on the streets amid general rejoicing. However, here and there, civil war had broken out among the troops in all Sections, and there had been some bloody fighting. But the people had surged to the assistance of the mutineers, and the others were quickly overcome.

In Cleveland, a detachment of troops had invaded many homes and had dragged out men and women who refused to return to "essential industry." In full sight of their families, these victims had been shot, in an attempt to intimidate others. But the people had rushed from their homes and had murdered the murderers, and had retrieved their dead and wounded. "As of this hour," said the commentator, "Cleveland is quiet."

"The courage of the people," said Karl Schaeffer. "At the last, tyrants always have to reckon with that."

The reports came in faster and faster, of similar incidents. But the people were holding together, in the face of threats, in the face of death. They had been assured of their own might; they were confident of their strength and they knew what they did not wish to do they could not be compelled to do. It had taken them decades of suffering to learn that simple and inexorable fact. It has always taken them decades, and even centuries, to learn it, thought Durant. A people need never accept tyranny or oppression. If they accept it, they are guilty of their own death. A people always deserve their government.

Farms were being taken over by the conscripted labor, in disciplined fashion. Where there was no resistance, no attempt at intimidation, there were no bloody incidents. The people moved to take their government, in their strength and their power, and nothing could withstand them, neither fanatic nor zealot, neither evil men nor force. A mass of over two hundred million people was integrated as one.

At seven o'clock a huge helicopter descended with slow majesty on the grounds near the house, and a young man, a general of the Army with three stars, descended. He was brought immediately to Mr. Regis, who received him with affection. "General Freeman, of the Joint Chiefs of Staff," he said to his friends. "He has come to take me to Washington."

Durant was amazed. A Minute Man among the Joint Chiefs of Staff! There he stood, this young, fresh-faced man with the strenuous blue eyes, smiling at them, shaking their hands, congratulating them. His voice was controlled, but had undertones of excitement. He had a great deal of news for them. Washington was in complete disorder and lay under a fog of terror. The bureaucrats were barricading themselves in their homes. Most of the Senators had fled the city. Nothing moved there at all, except the patrolling soldiers. President Slocum was drinking himself blind. He alternately called for his friends, or cursed them. He wept and ranted and raged; and he carried a gun in his hand. He trembled when a door opened. The Joint Chiefs of Staff were with him, and the Chief Magistrate. The Chiefs of Staff could only sit, staring before them in dread, and drinking. The Chief Magistrate, said General Freeman with gravity, was very calm.

And the people were doing nothing at all, unless briefly provoked. They simply stayed in their houses, ponderous in their might, unshakable in their silence.

The first white rays of the cold morning sun fell on the white earth. The flag met the sun with a billow of pride. The company went out with Mr. Regis to watch him take off. Long after the helicopter was only a speck in the frozen blue of the sky they waved to it in their excitement and relief. Alice Steffens cried unashamedly, and smiled and laughed, though her eyes remained haunted.

They ate breakfast in front of the screen, and listened intently. An officer came in, somewhat disturbed. Thousands of people from the city were congregating beyond the line of Army tanks and vehicles. They were shouting and pointing at the distant flag near the house. They were singing and calling and gesticulating. None of them attempted to rush the Military. They were content to stand in the snow, feasting their eyes on the banner.

"Perhaps I should go out to them and tell them that they are free," suggested Durant, the actor in him clamoring for drama.

"No, sir," replied Sadler seriously. "Remember? You are the hated officer who added to their miseries for nearly a year. You are their enemy. They'd kill you on sight, in spite of the soldiers."

"Yes, I remember," said Durant, crestfallen, and newly alarmed. How was he going to escape death, after all? He had no doubt that, in a case of necessity, he and his fellow commanding officers would be tossed to the implacable mob, honorable sacrifices to freedom.

"They don't even know you are here, and for that we ought to be grateful," Ben Colburn reminded him. "They don't know who is here, in fact, or we'd probably all be killed."

Durant thought passionately of the civilian clothes in his drawer at the farm. Very soon, he would be needed no longer, if he were needed even now. He might be able to escape anonymously, if his luck held. He had escaped death three times lately. Fate could be tempted too far, however.

After twelve o'clock, an abrupt announcement came from the screen. There would be no more news until six o'clock that night. At this, the guests decided that they should rest until that hour. Durant lingered until he could be alone with Alice Steffens, who was sitting by the fire in an attitude of profound loneliness and abandon, forgetful of everything. Her pretty face was strained and lost, and her lips were white. Durant said gently: "Perhaps it will be all right, Alice. Perhaps your father will persuade him—"

She shook her head, without looking at him. "No, he'll never come back to me. He believes he must do what he must do." She glanced up now and tried to smile. "It's 'Andrew' isn't it? Thank you, Andrew. Arthur admired you so much, and trusted you always. You see," she added, "we can't think of him as an ordinary man, but as a man who was willing to be reviled forever, if it would save his country. He thought of nothing else. Except once." Her eyes filled with tears. "We were married the day you met my father, by an old clergyman we always knew. And I'm going to have Arthur's child. It is something for me."

She turned away, then, and Durant left the room, deeply moved. When he reached his bedroom he looked through the windows. Far off, beyond the line of tanks and Army vehicles, he could see the multitude which had gathered to look at the flag. They had been drawn by some mass instinct to this place. There they stood, swarming black ants on the white snow. Durant thought of Carlson, and all the many countless thousands of Minute Men who had worked and had died and had suffered for these people, and he was bitter. Were they worth it, these millions who had eagerly embraced slavery in the name of "security," who had delivered up their freedom literally for thirty pieces of silver? Durant said to himself with as much firmness as possible: "I have compassion on the multitude." But he was ill and weary and he could not feel the words.

Washington was the least orderly of all the cities. The wet streets seethed with mobs, both white and Negro, going nowhere aimlessly, but shouting and filled with violence. This was the infernal city of the beetle-bureaucrats, who had sucked away the juices of a nation for four decades, and had grown fat and sluggish with the juices. Here was the heart of corruption and all evil, a white parasitic city which had never produced anything, which had contributed nothing to the nation but oppression and disease and dishonor. Little wonder, then, thought Mr. Regis, that here there could be no order, no self-restraint, no dignity, no purpose. He thought of the malformed swarms of bureaucrats hiding and shivering in their homes, barricaded behind their doors or quivering in their cellars, while the mobs shouted and ran through the city, smashing windows and hurling stones with random wantonness at everything. General Freeman told him that the mob had invaded the empty Capitol, had overturned statues, had slashed paintings, had befouled the Senate Chamber, had even attempted to fire the majestic building.

"I've ordered the troops not to fire on them," said General Freeman, with disgust. "They aren't armed, this mob, so the troops just try to keep them moving and attempt to protect public buildings. If they had their way they'd sack Washington—for their own crimes. You should see the White House! They've pushed through the gates and are milling all over. But there are five lines of soldiers farther in, and it's only here that we've given orders to restrain violence by shooting, if necessary."

The car waiting at the deserted airport for Mr. Regis and the general flew the flag of the Republic. Four Picked Guards sat in the car with the two men, and Guards in cars and on motorcycles accompanied them. The banner flew high and free on every vehicle, and as the cars raced into the city the hot-faced mobs parted, stared, and burst into wild and thunderous cheers. They did not know who these men were; it was enough for them that they flew the Stars and Stripes.

"The accolades of mobs are as reliable as the temper of tigers," said Mr. Regis. "If we were to lose, they'd cheer the flag of The Democracy with just as much frenzy. This isn't true of the rest of the nation, but it is true of Washington."

Pennsylvania Avenue ran with a flood of humanity, surging, beating back on itself, sending out disorderly waves into the side streets, littering the walks. The roar that came from it was the roar of a monster jungle, savage, bloodthirsty and mindless. The cars had to slow down in this river, and the Picked Guards showed their guns. But the flag was their passport, and the river divided like the Red Sea to admit the cavalcade. Hundreds of shabby men and women ran behind them on the grounds of the White House, shrieking, screaming and cheering. The lines of soldiers parted, and closed after the cars, and Mr. Regis, with relief, saw that behind the soldiers everything was quiet.

They were taken at once to the President's private chambers, where he waited alone with the Chief Magistrate and the magistrate's father, old Mr. Carlson. The Chiefs of Staff had fled; the servants had fled. The huge building resounded with echoes. Silent rows of Picked Guards lined the walls like statues.

The President was drinking steadily, and weeping and cursing and threatening and imploring. When Mr. Regis and General Freeman entered, he jumped to his feet and burst into fresh tears. "My dear friends!" he sobbed. "I'm not deserted after all. Dear Howard, dear Pete! I knew you'd come back to me! What would I do without you and Arthur and old Bill? Did you see the mobs? It's only Washington, isn't it? You've got everything under control elsewhere, haven't you?" He became frenzied, and clenched his fists. "What happened? Why can't we arrest the traitors? Why can't we *do* something!"

Mr. Regis shook hands with Arthur Carlson, who smiled at him gravely, and with old Mr. Carlson, who was too tired to speak. The President bounced around frantically at these formalities, and burst out: "Where are the Chiefs of Staff? Where are the officers? Where are the men of my Cabinet? Have they gone, the rats? Why have they left me here? Where are the Senators, and all my friends? Do you think those bastards and sons of bitches out there will break into the White House? I hear they're hanging me in effigy." He began to whimper. "What have I done, except work for the people? I've given up my life to the —— dogs! Everything for the people. And here I am now— D'ya think they'll break in?"

"I don't know," said Mr. Regis seriously. "It all depends on you. They're in a vicious temper."

The President stared, whisky glass in hand. "Depends on me?

What d'ya mean? They'd kill me if I showed my face. That's what they've been yelling: 'Kill Slocum!' "

The others said nothing. The President examined each face with rising panic. "Freeman!" he shouted, finally. "You're the general in charge now. Why don't you give orders, all over the country, for the soldiers to massacre the bastards? Shoot them down, everywhere. Turn guns and bayonets on them. Herd them into the war plants. Burn up their homes. Kill their kids in front of them. Why don't you do something?"

General Freeman spoke quietly: "We have three million soldiers in the country now, your Excellency. All the others are fighting in South America. We have two hundred million people here. At least fifty percent of the Armed Forces are revolting. That leaves one and a half million soldiers. Do you think that they can subdue this whole nation and fight a civil war with their own troops? They could try, but they wouldn't succeed. It would only result in anarchy; all order would go. Do you want the streets of the cities to run with blood, in a useless cause?"

"Yes!" shouted the President. He banged his whisky glass so violently on the gilt table near him that it shattered in his hand. "I want to see that—I want millions of them to die, and lie slaughtered in the gutters! Why not? Haven't they raised themselves against me? Haven't they revolted? Shouldn't they be punished? Damn it, even if I die, myself, it'll be worth it, thinking of what's happening to the rats that dared to—" He sobbed again, his meager face scarlet with insane rage. He looked at his bleeding hand, and wept in self-pity. "What about the atom bomb on the cities?" he added.

Then old Mr. Carlson spoke tranquilly: "There'll be no more death than necessary, Slocum. You see, I was supposed to kill you today. But my son persuaded me to his point of view. If we killed you, we'd be giving our assent to anarchy and chaos and probably to civil war. What we must do we must do lawfully and with restraint and dignity, so as to impress the people with the necessity for order and justice."

The President regarded him incredulously. "You—Bill?"

No one answered him. Aghast, he looked at the Chief Magistrate. "You—Arthur?" When Carlson did not reply, the President turned in anguish to General Freeman. "You—Pete?"

He saw their faces, and he cowered.

Old Mr. Carlson, slight, gray and haggard, raised himself in his chair, and his voice was soft: "Slocum, you must know by now that you can do nothing. The people have risen in passive rebellion. You can't subdue them. And I'm afraid that unless you follow our advice the people will rise in active rebellion, and you'll die. Cities will be burned to the ground. Neighbor will kill neighbor. The people will lose their minds. We've controlled them so far. I can't promise that we can hold them much longer. And whe that happens, you'll have to die."

The President moaned and wrung his hands. "I thought I ha three friends, at least—you, and Arthur and Pete, here. But I'v been betrayed. Enemies surround me. I did my best for the cou try. We're fighting a war—"

"You never had any friends," said the Chief Magistrate sternl "Even your fellow-criminals were never your friends. The fawned on you while you had power, and they ran when the found themselves in danger. As for us, we've always been yo enemies. Mr. Slocum, make up your mind. Shall we issue a stat ment that you are resigning, or shall we just wait here until th mobs rush into the White House and kill you?"

The President had turned a dull gray. He looked at Arthu Carlson, and said: "I loved you as my own son. I did everythin for you."

"And what I have done has been done for my country," replie Carlson.

Slocum looked at all the somber faces. The windows of th beautiful room were shrouded in pale silk. Suddenly, a sound lik savage thunder shook those windows, and Slocum shrank, fell int his chair. "Listen to them," he muttered, forgetting all else in hi terror. "They're coming nearer." He quailed, and cried like woman.

"They've been coming nearer for a long time," said Carlson.

The President ignored him, in his dazed agony. He said to Ge eral Freeman: "I'm your Commander-in-Chief. I order you t dispel the mob. I—"

"I never recognized you as my Commander-in-Chief," replie General Freeman bitterly. "I worked, as thousands worked wit me, for this day."

Mr. Regis approached the President, slowly, and looked dow at him with a terrible face. "Do you know me, Slocum?" he sai and his voice was relentless with hatred.

The President shrank from him. He stammered, incoherently "You—you are Howard Regis. You are head of the FBHS—"

"Look at me more closely," said Mr. Regis. "You haven't see me for fifteen years. You were a captain, then, and I was you general. You rarely saw me, and you do not remember me. M name is John Graham, and I am supposed to be dead. You issue orders for my assassination many years ago, when I retired be cause I could not endure you, because I knew what you were. didn't die, Slocum. I worked, as we all worked, for this day."

The President glared at him in his mad fear. He stuttered "John—Graham. Traitor—resigned after a speech about me, whe I was elected—said I would enslave the country—campaigne for my impeachment—" He sat up, and yelled: "Why, you dirt yellow dog! You traitor! I'll put you under arrest—shot—!

"You'll do nothing," said the Chief Magistrate, rising and standing with Mr. Regis. "You'll do nothing at all, ever again. Are you so stupid that you don't realize what has happened in this country? Don't you know that I could kill you this very moment and would be honored for it?"

His huge loathing made him tremble. "I will give you one minute to issue your statement of resignation, and the appointment of General John Graham as Acting President until due elections can take place. If, after one minute, you do not issue that statement, I shall kill you."

The President thrust the fingers of his right hand into his mouth and whined like a dying animal. He was afraid to look away from Carlson. "You can't do this to me; I'm the President of The Democracy. The People's Democracy. You can't kill me!" The whine rose to a shriek of uncontrollable terror. "Where shall I go? What shall I do?"

"I promise you that you will leave this building in safety, and go into hiding," replied Carlson.

Another roar shook the windows, and now there was a volley of shots. Carlson turned pale. He seized the President with both his hands and shook him strongly. "They're getting nearer. The soldiers have been forced to shoot. At any moment now, you dog and rascal, the mobs will overpower the soldiers, and they will roar into the White House, looking for you. And when they find you, you'll be torn to shreds."

The President pushed him away and sprang to his feet. His voice was hoarse and shrill with dread. "I'll issue! I—I'll give— Protect me! Don't let them get me, Arthur! I promise you—" He babbled on and on, clutching the Chief Magistrate with frantic hands, affrighted and shocked beyond all control and all human dignity.

Carlson pushed the creature from him, and turned to Mr. Regis, and saluted.

"Speak to them, sir," he said. He looked at his father, and smiled.

At five o'clock that night a whole nation was alerted. The people poured from their wretched homes to places of public meeting where broadcasting equipment was installed. Millions raced and walked and hurried through the broken streets where they could hear the public address systems; they swarmed into their halls and into what were, formerly, their churches. Women carried children; young men assisted legless veterans of many wars; old men were supported by their sons. Girls and youths ran side by side, shouting, eager, laughing. Soldiers hurried with them, clumsily. The cities lit up as they had not been lighted for years; buses roared over the battered pavements; cars flashed, loaded with humanity. Every house flared with lights, where private broadcasts could be heard, and these houses admitted every passerby who desired to enter. As one, the nation came to hear and millions of faces grew brilliant with hope.

At six o'clock, on every small and every great screen in the country, lights flashed and the face of a young man appeared, strained with excitement. Behind him sat batteries of newsmen, scribbling frantically. Beyond them stretched the gold and white walls of the broadcasting room in the White House.

The commentator said simply: "Ladies and gentlemen, Mr. John Graham, retired General of the Army of the United States of America!"

From millions of mouths a deep cry went up, and millions of eyes dimmed for a moment. "Did you hear?" voices called to each other. "The United States of America!"

Then John Graham stood before them, gently smiling, full of authority, and he looked out at the nation with affection and quiet passion.

"My dear people," he said, "I have, today, been appointed as Acting President of the United States of America by former President Slocum, who has resigned. It was you who forced his resignation. Without you, this could not have happened. It was your revived spirit, your final rebellion against slavery, the end of your long meek patience, which has terminated the decades of your enslavement and your degradation."

"Yes, yes!" exclaimed tens of thousands of voices jubilantly. "We did it!" And eyes flashed with pride and heads, once bent so humbly, lifted themselves.

John Graham's face darkened with somber sternness. "But you, my people, were not guiltless, not guiltless of your own ruin.

"Freedom, once so imbedded in the hearts of all Americans, was surrendered by Americans who believed the sinister men who were determined to enslave them. It was to be for a limited time only, we were assured. But tyrants never relinquish the powers they have gained; they incorporate them into perpetual law. It was done so quietly, so skillfully. A nation will fight when its full liberty is threatened, and the full plot exposed. But if liberties are subdued, little by little, no provocation for a nationwide revolt is given. Like thieves in the night, who move stealthily and without sound, so did the evil men move in your former free government, robbing away the heart and the body of your liberty, denuding your homes of its treasures, slowly stifling your tongues, imperceptibly silencing your press. They invaded the schoolrooms of your children, poisoning and debasing their minds, twisting them to their purposes so that future generations would know nothing of honor and pride and the might of free men. But you were not guiltless.

"Do not believe that this was just a plot in America. It started far back in history, in 1917, with the Bolshevik revolution. Like the black plague of the soul, it seeped into Germany, into Scandinavia, into Britain, into France, into South America and Asia and Africa. It was a nightmare and deathly disease with many names. It was called Fascism and Communism, People's Democracies and Socialism, the Welfare State and totalitarianism and authoritarianism. In America, is was called Progressive Democracy. But it was the same foul disease that blinded and sickened a whole world, and made the whole world slave. It was the same abominable illness of the spirit, the same madness, that plunged an entire planet into endless wars and degradation and despair. It had for its object the unlimited power of a few men, working together in every nation even while they were ostensibly enemies, and even while their respective nations were engaged in combat against each other.

"There was no quarrel among these arch-devils of death and ruin; there was only complete understanding. They knew that man cannot be enslaved in a peaceful society, prosperous and full of ambition and hope. So they plotted wars with each other; they taxed the fullness of their nations to finance those wars, and in so doing reduced their nations to poverty and starvation. They blew away the natural resources of the earth, for their wars, which were not against each other, but against their own people. They outlawed God, for a people staunch in their faith will not renounce their liberties and they will not engage in wars. But you, the people of America, were not guiltless of all this."

He paused, full of emotion and anger, and his quiet eyes blazed from the screen with mounting passion. He lifted his hand and pointed at the listening millions.

"We, in America, were not guiltless. For decades, we saw the disease spreading in Europe and Asia, and many of us knew when the infection had reached our own country. But too many of us were greedy; we saw opportunities for individual gain and profit if we supported the emerging tyrants in Washington. Tyrants are so full of pleasant promises; they are so skillful in arraying one section of a people against another, in stimulating false suspicions, false hatreds, false envies, and natural human greed. When we Americans should have stood together, defying with our votes and our voices and our anger each tyrant as he appeared, we turned our innate and instinctive jealousies and dislikes upon our neighbors. We betrayed each other. The disease entered our souls, and we sold our honor for a handful of silver, whether we were workingmen or capitalists, farmers or bankers, bureaucrats or clerks, industrialists or shopkeepers.

"We could not have so betrayed ourselves and each other up to the year 1914. In the first years of this century Americans were free and prideful and independent. We were an ambitious people, and any social injustices were being slowly but steadily eliminated. We were a kind and generous people, guardful of our liberties. But, after 1917, the black plague spread over Europe, and we were infected long before 1939, when a new and deliberately plotted war broke out. We were infected in the very halls of Congress, in the very inmost chambers of Washington. The disease was already in our flesh, and its foul breath was already in the mouths of our children, and its cries were ringing in every schoolroom, every college, decades before we were plunged into this series of wars which have lasted over twenty years. We were a diseased nation long before we were slaves. We were impotent before we knew we were impotent."

An enormous and incredible silence lay over America, as the people listened. John Graham looked at them in that silence, and he felt it. He lifted his hands, and said, with a shaking voice:

"God has had mercy upon us, though we have committed monstrous sins against each other as well as against the world. God has brought us to this day, though we are not worthy of it. For many years, He has stimulated the hearts and the souls of a few free and just men, who have worked among you, unknown to you. He gave them a lash with which to arouse you. He gave them words to awaken you. He gave them courage to deliver up their lives for you, though you were not worthy of it. You betrayed them to your oppressors and your tyrants, but still they loved you. You called them 'traitors' and 'subversives,' when they cried out to you that the walls of your nation were tumbling into the seas of tyranny and death. When they warned you on the day religion was turned against religion, and race against race, in America, you laughed at them and denounced them as 'dividers of the country.' When they cried to you that States Rights were being abrogated, you shouted 'Unity!' at them, and beat them down, and silenced them. When they exposed the causes of wars to you, and the plot against you in those wars, you jeered at them with such epithets as 'isolationists' or 'pacifists.' While you still had a measure of liberty and could vote vile tyrants and corrupt men out of office, you listened, instead, to the promises of those men, and you voted honorable and decent men out of office.

"But still, God had mercy on you, and did not abandon you. He gave you the Minute Men of the United States of America. They were your neighbors, and you did not know it. They spoke to you furtively, and you did not know who they were. You lifted yourselves in your chains, and heard the words of life and liberty, and saw the glimmer of the sun again. You did not know who called to you in your despair and your agony. And you would not have listened had you not been reduced to hopeless slaves."

He paused again, and his eyes kindled on tens of thousands of screens, large and small, and to every man and woman it was as if he spoke to each individually, rousing shame in them, and sorrow, and bitter grief.

"These heroic men infiltrated every branch of this despotic State, the Armed Forces, the Picked Guards, the industries, the farms, the schools, and what remains of our churches. They used the weapons of the tyrants, which had wounded you almost to death, to save you. They knew that you could not be aroused out of your deathful despair and apathy until driven to your last fortress, the instinct for self-preservation. So, to deliver you, they oppressed you; to bring you liberty, they took away what little liberty remained with you. They carried, to the last mad excess, the directives of your tyrants, and so overcame your tyrants. Under their rods, you revolted. But under their voices and with their guidance, you did not hurl yourselves into anarchy, as Europe and Asia have hurled themselves. You controlled your desire for vengeance, and you waited for deliverance, as a people have never controlled themselves and waited before."

Multitudes of eyes looked at other eyes, and millions thought: Were you one of the men who saved us? Was it you? Or you? Or you? And thousands, standing anonymously among their fellows, glanced away serenely and blankly and gave no answer. To the last they would be nameless, and it was of no importance to them.

John Graham was speaking very gravely and slowly now, and the people brought their attention back to him.

"I would not have you deceive yourselves. The battle is not entirely won. At least half of the Armed Forces are with us, and a portion of the Picked Guards. But the others will resist you. 'Tyranny, like hell, is not easily conquered.' Your courage and your faith must sustain you for many months. Attempts will be made to delude you, to lead you again into slavery, to confuse and divide you. Your enemies are still alive, and still full of hate for you. They have been momentarily silenced, at your command. They will speak again.

"We are a free nation, tonight, and in the name of our freedom we cannot silence our enemies. The very opportunity we are giving them will damn them in your own ears. They will betray themselves to you with their own voices. Or, if they choose not to speak in this hour of peril for themselves, they will withdraw to plot against you again. But you are armed. You know who your enemies are.

"Working together, we can restore this nation, and restore the peace and the liberties of all other nations. A whole world listens to us tonight. With patience and with justice, with mercy and with knowledge, we must work slowly and with enlightenment, for there is so much to be done.

"Tonight was born a new political party in America—the Constitution party. Tonight there will be issued by me a directive to the commanders of our Armed Forces on all battlefields to call an immediate truce, and to negotiate an armistice. Within a few hours all fighting will stop, and the guns will be silenced, and the war planes will retire. Your sons shall be returned to you as speedily as possible, and there shall be no more war.

"As of tonight, all work on war orders shall cease. Plans will be made to convert all war plants to the making of civilian goods. All conscripted labor laws are abrogated at once. During the period of reconversion from war to peace your former employers will pay you full wages. When work is resumed, hours of labor shall not exceed forty hours a week, under any circumstances, unless by consent of the employed. All rationing ceases as of midnight. You men and women employed on the farms may remain there, if you desire, at decent wages to be fixed tomorrow, or you may leave. It would be better, however, for all of us, if you continued to work on those farms for the time being, in order that the nation may be fed.

"All confiscated private property shall be restored to the former owners, and those who confiscated that property, with or without the consent of the State, shall pay back rentals for the periods the property has been at their disposal.

"All labor camps shall be disbanded tomorrow, the inmates furnished with food and with transportation to their former homes. All children shall be returned to their parents. All political prisoners everywhere shall be freed.

"Orders are being prepared at this moment to wrest power from the Military and return it to civilian authority. The Military, at midnight, shall be recalled from private homes where they have been quartered, and payments shall be later adjudicated to those who gave the Military involuntary hospitality.

"As of tonight, the Military has no authority whatsoever, no powers, no directives except as given by me, your Acting President of the United States. Any officer or soldier attempting violence against the people of America shall be judged insubordinate, and shall be punished by death after court-martial. I, the Commander-in-Chief of all the Armed Forces, now call upon all officers and all soldiers and all military men of any designation to retire to their barracks and lay down their arms. I call upon all our ships at sea, in any port, to wait for further orders from me, under pain of death."

He looked out from the screen with stern command, and the people smiled at each other with joy and laughed aloud, and embraced each other.

"We have so much work to do, my dear friends, my dear

fellow-countrymen," he continued. "The ruin of decades cannot be cleared away in a day, a month, a year, or years. It will be a long and slow and sometimes bitter progress, and sometimes disheartening. But, we can do it. We can rebuild our cities and restore our streets and prepare good homes for all of us. This will take much time, and we shall need all the patience and faith we can summon up.

"Within two months there will be general elections. You will elect a free Congress again. I shall be the Presidential candidate of the Constitution Party. Those who differ with me—and there are free men, too, who might differ—may form their own party.

"You, the people of the United States of America are in command of your nation. Take that command. Restore your cities and your churches. Speak of God again, freely, and teach your children, and your children's children, of His mercy. Never let them forget this day of their deliverance, and never let them forget the men who died and worked that they might be free, that peace might live with them again, and the promise of the centuries might be fulfilled in them.

"Teach your children to be brave. This century of ours has been marked most conspicuously by cowardice of the people everywhere. It was by our cowardice that we were betrayed into the hands of corrupt men who promised to make life 'safe' for us and devoid of hazard, and robbed of the adventurousness by which the spirits of men are strengthened. It was by our poltroonery that we lost our liberties. It was by our fears that we almost died. A brave people never become slaves."

He lifted his hand in somber warning. "If we, the people of the United States of America, again lose our freedom it will be by our own lack of courage and faith and manhood.

"Tonight States' Rights are restored. Guard those Rights as you would guard your lives. They were intended for just that purpose. A centralized government is a centralized evil.

"On the day when you again allow abominable men to confiscate your freedom, your money, your lives, your private property, your manhood and your sacred honor, in the name of 'security' or 'national emergency,' you will die, and never again shall you be free. If plotters again destroy your Republic, they will do it by your greedy and ignorant assent, by your disregard of your neighbors' rights, by your apathy and your stupidity. We were brought to the brink of universal death and darkness because we had become that most contemptible of people—an angerless one. Keep alive and vivid all your righteous anger against traitors, against those who would abrogate your Constitution, against those who would lead you to wars with false slogans and cunning appeals to your patriotism.

"For, remember, if you die in prison, you will have built that prison. If your sons are again conscripted, you will have penned the writ. If a company of malignant men again assures control of your lives, you will have given them that control. When you hang your enemies you will be hanging yourselves.

"Always, the peoples are responsible for wicked lawmakers, oppressors, exploiters, criminals in government, tyrants in power, thieves, liars, malefactors and murders in the capitals of the world. You, the man in the street, the man in the factory and in the shop, the man on the farm, the man in the office, you, the man everywhere, are guilty of the creatures whose crimes against you have been so monstruous, and will be again, by your own consent—if you give it.

"Do not cry to God if you repeat your frightful errors: 'Deliver us, Lord, from this Evil!' Pray, rather: 'Forgive us, Father, for we have sinned.'

"A wise man distrusts his neighbor. A wiser man distrusts both his neighbor and himself. The wisest man of all distrusts his government. Therefore, be watchful and sleepless; be brave, be strong; be without fear. This is not the end. Villains will try again and again and again, to enslave you, until the end of time. It is in your hands to defeat them and to destroy them, whenever or however they appear.

"If you do not, then may God have mercy on your souls!"

His face slowly faded, but to the last his warning and urgent eyes remained, commanding and exhorting the nation. Even when the Stars and Stripes appeared, swelling into brightness and starry glory, his eyes seemed to pierce through the flag. The majestic chorus of the Star Spangled Banner once more sounded from border to border and rang through every city and struck upon the air with its thunder, setting a nation to weeping for joy. But even as they wept the people vowed to themselves that never again would they be slaves, and never would they permit their children to forget this day.

At dawn the bells began to ring, everywhere, the jubilant bells of victory, of freedom, set spontaneously into sound and motion by tens of thousands of hands. Durant went out with his friends onto the bright snowy earth to listen to them as they rejoiced from the city and the countryside, and they listened as the brilliant air caught up the clamor and whirled it to the smiling sky and threw it on the winds of the world.

It was not all to be fully accomplished for three more days, for the privileged groups, recognizing now that they had betrayed themselves into the cause of liberty, gathered together for resistance. Thousands of their confused and stupid slaves joined them, at the command of the fanatics and the zealots and other madmen, who would not be reconciled to the fact that their fellows were free. Military officers banded together and called themselves "loyalists" and herded their troops for revolt. The young soldiers, bewildered and frightened and completely ignorant, obeyed their orders and took up arms against their government.

Public buildings were burned, populations harassed by guerilla warfare, individuals terrorized, troops fired upon by troops. Up and down the land raced the opposing armies, engaging in short but bloody fratricidal combats, sometimes in villages or towns or cities, and sometimes in forests or in open fields.

But the people stood strong and invulnerable, filled with fortitude and faith. They resorted to no violence, themselves. Their very weight overcame the resistance, and at the end the rebels laid down their arms and begged for official clemency. The three days of death and destruction ended, and everywhere the banner of the Republic flew high and unthreatened beneath a free sky.

They had waited three days in the country house of the Chief Magistrate. On the third day had come his simple coded message: "All is quiet. All is successful. Those Minute Men in the Armed Forces and the Picked Guards may disband at once, and go their ways. The others will be needed for a time to keep order before relinquishing their offices."

There was no word of praise from the Chief Magistrate for what had been accomplished by these devoted men, no farewell message. They did not feel the need for these: they had done their duty as Americans. That was sufficient. It was enough for them, that at the end of his message, Arthur Carlson quoted from the Bible: "—I, like my brethren, offer up my life and my body for the laws of our fathers: calling upon God to be speedily merciful to our nation."

They had been deeply moved by this. It was not for some hours that they detected that there had been something else expressed in that quotation besides its more obvious meaning. The men in that house looked at each other with frantic grief, assured, now, that Carlson had been speaking of the future also, and himself in particular. All their hopes for his survival were swept away.

They dared not speak of this to Alice Steffens, but they knew that she had understood. There was a quiet white dignity about her which fended off sympathy and even kindness. She told them that she would join her father, the President of the United States of America, in Washington, and she made her few preparations to leave them. When her hour of departure came, she smiled at them gently, shook hands with them, and then left in silence.

Durant wondered if they should remain in the house. But when he saw that the others were leaving rapidly, to go their unknown and anonymous ways, he prepared to leave also. Most of the Picked Guard had melted away, and then there came a morning when only Durant, Grandon and Edwards were left in the empty and echoing house. The soldiers had gone, and the dogs. The flag flew in a brilliant snowy stillness, but no one moved in or near the grounds.

For days these three had watched the television screens with a hope that was rapidly dying. There was no mention of the Chief Magistrate at any time. The news commentators merely reported incidents of joy and courage and resolution occurring in the nation, and of the orderly establishing of European governments. In the ruined cities of London, Moscow, Paris, Berlin, Rome, Oslo, Stockholm and Copenhagen and Brussels and Vienna, and many more capitals, the peoples were electing their new free rulers. It was apparent that a furious and resolute activity was prevailing everywhere. The news from Asia was somewhat vague, in comparison, but there were reports that similar activity was under way there, also. The sweet quiet of peace lay over the world while men worked together to restore their earth.

There is no use staying here any longer, thought Durant. He was confident that the message pertaining to the whereabouts of his family was authentic. Now a wild haste and anticipation came to him. He needed only to return to the Lincoln house for his few belongings, and the civilian clothes which had been secreted for him. However, it was still somewhat dangerous for a commanding military man to appear openly on the streets of the cities. He, like the others, would have to move at night. So, on the last evening, he called Grandon and Edwards to him and told them of his plans.

Grandon and Edwards were dismayed. "But, Colonel, you have to wait for orders, don't you? You have to be mustered out—"

Durant laughed. He pointed at himself. "Remember me? I'm not a real soldier. I did not enlist, as you did. I have no commander at all. My chief was Arthur Carlson, and my oath was to the Minute Men." He hesitated, and became sad. "We don't know where the Chief Magistrate is, but my orders were to disband, and to disappear. My work is done. In due time, you will be released from the Army; there's no obligation on me, your fake colonel, to wait for official notification."

Grandon said: "It was confusing to me, and to Edwards, here. We knew you must have had some military training, at one time, but you didn't act like an officer." He grinned affectionately at Durant. "You didn't know the words; you didn't know what to do, some of the time. That's what confused us. If we hadn't been confused you'd have been dead a long time ago—Colonel."

"We used to talk about you," added Edwards laughing. "Were you, or were you not, what you were supposed to be? We'd watch you, and you muddled us up. Once we had it all fixed to shoot you in the back, one dark night, and then you'd do something, or say something, that made us suspicious that you were one of us, in your own way. There was that time in your office when you were talking with Mr. Schaeffer. I knew one or two of the signals of the Minute Men; we'd been taught them so we could catch them. We saw you exchange the signals; but even then, we weren't sure. It could have been an accident."

"I'm sorry about the ham," said young Grandon. "That was my own idea. The captain, here, had told me to wait. But I was thinking of Gracie. By the way, Bob Lincoln told me she has come home, and I want to see her."

"So, we'll leave tonight, and I'll get my civilian clothes and go home," said Durant.

He was tired and drained and full of a strange lassitude. He was free to go, and he would find his family. The future was uncertain. No reward would come to him in the way of money, he was convinced. He did not want the money. However, it would be hard to begin again, even in a free country, with nothing at all. In his listless state, the result of too much past strain, he felt that he was old and without vitality. He sometimes wondered how it would be to have nothing but the independence and self-responsibility of a free man. He began to sympathize with the millions of his fellow citizens in their thirties and forties and fifties—men who had never known self-reliance before. It would be much easier for the very young, who were resilient, and adaptable. They could accept the rigors of liberty and maturity with no effort at all. But men who had been guided, channeled and directed all of their lives would have some hours of bewilderment and dejection. Like invalids, they would have to learn to walk on their own legs. The winds of freedom would be very harsh for a time, thought Durant. To make one's own decision would require much courage, and much remembrance. The young were striding strongly throughout the nation; but a great part of the population was crippled, their crutches taken away. One painful step at a time, Durant told himself. We'll walk, but it will hurt.

He was finished with law. He could never again live in a great city. He wanted the land. But how to live on the land? How to make adjustments?

That night he left for the Lincoln farm with Grandon and Edwards. He knew that Sadler was already on the farm, with his father, preparing to take the old man away. He hoped that he was not too late to see these two again, before the final parting. He was encouraged, in his thoughts, that Bob Lincoln would be on the farm to greet him. That would obviate any awkwardness. It was not pleasant to think of Bob's parents. He had no doubt that they would hate him more than ever now knowing his real identity.

The three men drove off into the country, avoiding the city. Grandon said: "By the way, Colonel, what is your name? As you know, mine is really Burgess, and Edwards' is Dahl. You've never told us yours."

"Durant. Andrew Durant. Does it matter?"

Nothing mattered, all at once, but getting out of this uniform, and leaving this territory. He had two hundred paper dollars. Would that take him to Florida? He would have nothing in the way of clothing but those poor thin rags in his drawer at the Lincoln farm. Yes, freedom had its own peculiar stringencies.

The farm looked the same. Men were moving about it, working vigorously, free men with a wage. They held up lanterns, as they came from the barns, to inspect the newcomers. They smiled at Durant, and came forward eagerly to shake his hand. But Dr. Dodge was not in sight, nor Sadler. Durant leaned out of the window of the car and said: "George, are Sadler and old Dr. Dodge still here? I want to say goodbye to them."

The man, workworn and gaunt from past suffering, became grave. "I'm sorry—Colonel. Dr. Dodge shot himself the day after —Christmas. We tried to stop him. But he told us he couldn't live any longer. He said he was too tired." George hesitated. "He said he had lived long enough, and now that we were free he wanted to go."

Durant was profoundly shaken and distressed. With a pang, he remembered that he, himself, had given Dr. Dodge a gun. The old man must have been preparing for his own death all the time, and not the death of anyone else. Yes, he had been tired. He remembered too much, had suffered too much, and had been too guilty.

"And Sadler?" Durant asked, after some miserable reflection.

"He's gone away, Colonel."

They went to the door of the house. It was locked. Grandon banged on it, and in a few moments it opened. John Lincoln stood there, gray and shrunken. He stared at the three officers with detestation and hatred. "What do you want?" he demanded. "You've no right to come here. The Military's been ordered out of private homes."

Durant regarded the older man with his own hatred and detestation. "We only want our property. We'll stay just a couple of minutes."

A sly look crept over Lincoln's haggard face. "No, you don't get into this house. You've done enough damage." He shouted over them: "Hey, you, George, Henry! Get over here right away and find these—these men's rubbish, and throw it at them!"

George and Henry came up without hurry, smiling somberly. John Lincoln had momentarily forgotten that they were free men now, and his shout had had in it all his old arrogance and bullying. "Don't yell at us, Mr. Lincoln," said George, with considerable pleasure. "Or you'll find yourself without any help tomorrow morning. Bad for the cows and other stock."

Lincoln immediately remembered, and became placating. "Now, then, boys, I was just kind of mad at these—" He glanced at the officers with loathing. "These bastards," he added. "Coming here like they owned the place, or something. Please get their stuff, boys."

"No," said Durant. He eyed Lincoln coldly. "I want to be sure that nothing's been stolen. De we have to go back to the city and get a warrant or something?"

"Stolen!" shouted Lincoln, turning crimson. "I want you to know I'm an honest man—"

"Since when?" asked Durant, contemptuously. "Reformed lately, Lincoln?"

Grandon smiling, took a step forward and pushed Lincoln out of the doorway. At that moment Bob Lincoln appeared, and he exclaimed with pleasure at seeing the visitors. He held out his hands, roaring happily, and pulled them into the house, ignoring his father who had fallen back. "Come in! Come in!" he cried. "Wondered when you'd be coming. How are you, Colonel? How are you, boys? Come right in. Had your dinner? How about a drink, or something?"

He led them into the fine living room where a red fire spluttered. His father stood in the doorway, furiously silent. They pretended he was not there. Bob brought out whisky and glasses. He was no longer either the sullen farmer or the stern Picked Guard. He was a young man again, happy at the appearance of friends, and full of laughter. It was as if all the years of his misery and rebellion had been forgotten, and Durant thought again of the easy and joyful adaptability of the young.

Mrs. Lincoln joined her husband in the doorway, glowering. The two stood there like stout images of hate and resentment, arms akimbo, hands clutched into fists at their hips.

Bob smiled at Grandon. "By the way, Gracie wants to see you." He suddenly lifted his voice, and shouted for his sister. At this, Lincoln started. "She can't come here!" he protested. "I won't have her seein' this rabble, Bob. I'm warnin' you."

But there was a rush of steps on the stairs, and Grace Lincoln peered over her parents' shoulders. When she saw Grandon standing near the fire with his glass in his hand, she squealed for joy. She pushed her mother aside, brushed off the restraining hands of her father and ran into the room. She fell into Grandon's arms and they hugged each other passionately.

"That settles that," said Bob Lincoln, with satisfaction. "Understand you're a farming feller yourself, George. How about staying and helping us out?"

"No!" whimpered John Lincoln. "He ain't comin' here. Gracie's not going to marry any goddamn Army bastard."

George Grandon gave Gracie a loving and resounding smack.

"No, thanks, Bob. I've got a big ranch in Wyoming. We'll go there, after we're married."

"A ranch?" repeated John Lincoln. "In Wyoming." His face changed. He came into the room. "Goin' to get it back?"

Grandon stared at him. "It's already 'back.' Taken away from the sons of bitches who stole it from my family. It was stolen, Lincoln, just as you stole the farms of your neighbors."

Lincoln winced. He stammered: "Well, sir, it was legal—then. We didn't do nothin' that wasn't legal. The other farmers were subver—" He stopped as he saw Grandon's cold and bitter eyes. Helplessly, he glanced at his wife for support, and she came to his side. She was no longer sulking. She said: "Well, it's all over. And maybe it's for the best. How many acres, Lieutenant?"

"About four thousand or so. Don't remember, exactly." Grandon replied, kissing Grace again. "Maybe five thousand. Haven't seen it in years." He fondled Grace's pretty hair. "A real ranch, honey, not just a farm. Room for half a dozen kids."

Grace, in Grandon's arms, held out her hand to Durant, shyly. "I haven't forgotten you, Colonel Curtiss. You were so good to me. I've been telling Daddy and Mom all about it. They ought to be grateful," she added severely, glancing at her parents.

"We are, we are!" exclaimed Lincoln, all effusiveness and bland hospitality again. "Bob, give us a glass, too. Want to celebrate. What do you know! A ranch! Thought you knew too much about farmin', Lieutenant."

Grandon winked at Durant. Yes, thought Durant, heavily, it's easy for the young to forgive. Grandon would, in time, forget the murder of his father and his brothers. He would live on his land with Grace, and all the ugly and terrible past would have no more reality for them. The Lincolns would visit their daughter in the West, and there would be much exchange and argument about cattle, and there would be grandchildren. And Grandon would forget. For the young, there was always the future. For the middle-aged and the old, there would always be the past, and the pain, and the grief.

Lincoln was prepared to accept everyone now, and with affection. He was even cordial to Durant, who could not force himself to be affable. Finally, discomfited, Lincoln turned his cordiality on Edwards. He settled himself comfortably in a chair by the side of his beaming wife, who was blinking with sentimental tenderness at the two young lovers. Sometimes she patted Grandon's shoulder maternally, and sighed. Durant sat alone, looking into the fire.

Finally, he got up and went to his old room. There it was, as he had left it so hastily. He tore off his uniform, and replaced it with the worn and shabby clothing which Dr. Dodge had hidden for him. Now his grief for the old man, and for Sadler, returned.

He wondered if Sadler had indeed gone back to marry Beckett's sister. He fervently hoped so.

The clothing was a poor fit, and thin, He hesitated, then stripped the insignia from his Army overcoat. He would have to wear it over his civilian clothing, for the weather was so cold. Sighing, he threw aside his uniform, then kicked it. He counted his money again, and thought of his wife and children,

Then, for the first time, he noticed a small square wooden box on the table near the bed. He examined it without curiosity. It was very heavy, and his name was neatly printed on it. It grew heavier in his hands, and now he began to wonder. He pried open the nailed wooden lid, then gasped. It was full of golden coins.

He sat down, weak and trembling, the weighty box on his knees. He had never seen golden money before, though yesterday the President had announced a return of the gold standard in the Republic. These were old coins; bemused and dazed, Durant saw the date on some of them. So long ago: 1929, 1930, 1931. He held a few in his hands, balancing them. They glittered in the light of the lamps. They were his. They were his new life, with his family. He began to laugh, shakily, and did not know there were tears on his cheeks. The Chief Magistrate had not forgotten him. This was not a payment for services; the money had been given him, not in gratitude, but in understanding.

But where was the Chief Magistrate? The broadcasts never mentioned him. It was as if he had never lived. The coins clinked in Durant's hands. His joy and relief were like a haze of light in his mind, but now it was pierced with sorrow and anxiety.

He pounded the lid on the box again, tucked it under his arm. He went downstairs in a sort of mist.

The celebration in the living room had become quite uproarious. Mrs. Lincoln had gone off to prepare a supper for her guests. Grace was sitting on young Grandon's knee. Bob Lincoln and Edwards were frankly drunk, and so was the old man. They shouted when they saw Durant in the doorway. He smiled at them, but refused to join them. He was obsessed with a desire to hurry.

"Will someone drive me to the railroad station?" he asked.

The cold winds and the snow had been gone for twenty-four hours. The train moved slowly, for there was still some confusion on the railroads, and all trains were loaded to uncomfortable capacity with men and women and children returning to their homes and long-lost families. The shabby coaches, however, rang with laughter and singing and the excited roar of voices and the screams of infants. There was much drinking, too, and quantities of dust and dirt, and many packages of food, as the American refugees moved from city to city in their flight to liberty. What little new equipment had been built for the railroads during the past three decades had been assigned to the Military, and so it was that Durant lived and slept on a narrow coach-seat he shared with an old woman. He was dirty and exhausted, and as grimy as all the others in the crowded car, but like them, too, he smiled and laughed and talked in the fraternity of freedom. For two nights, he had shivered with them in the unheated coach, and had gotten off, with them, at way stations to purchase sandwiches and coffee.

He was still anonymous. He listened to dozens of harrowing tales of past slavery, suffering and abuse. He marveled, with the others, that America was now free. With the others, he good-naturedly insulted any young soldier who entered the coaches on his own way home. The common soldier was safe, but there were still incidents of bloody attacks on officers of the regular army. He told his new friends that he had been a worker in a factory in a Northern city, and that he was looking for his wife and children. They smiled at him sympathetically, assured him that he would find his family, and shared their oranges and sandwiches with him. They could not get used to the oranges, or the butter, or the white bread or the hot thick meat. They would devour them, wonderingly. They were full of exuberant plans, naïve, touching and pathetic. But many of them, when asleep, cried out in strangled anguish and had to be shaken awake. This was particularly true of the older people, and of women who had lost their children forever.

Never must it happen again, so help us God, Durant would think, with terror.

Each hour the winds were warmer and the sun brighter. People got off the train, were replaced by others. When Durant stood outside while the train halted it was a marvelous thing to him that now, in January, there were flowers blooming in the fields. He was in Georgia, and eager for his first sight of a palm. Back in the train, he would rub the filthy window and stare out, blinking in the warm sun, opening the neck of his shirt collar. The land was white and green; he rolled past shining blue water and shacks where Negro children played.

Then he saw the first live oak with its hoary gray beard waving in the gentle wind. His eyes feasted on it, and his excitement grew. He saw trees strange to him, and flowers whose names he did not know. He saw red earth as well as white, and ancient houses at a distance. And there—there was a palm! A scrubby palm, somewhat wilted and brown, but a palm. Now he was filled with an emotion he had forgotten he had ever felt; exultation. More and more palms were appearing. Windows were being opened in the train, and no one minded the billows of soot and grit which blew in. The voices had changed hour by hour, as people came and went. These voices were soft and lingering, and Durant listened to them with eager pleasure.

The train stopped at a small station, and Durant, forgetting that he had ever been tired or hopeless or driven, ran out onto the platform. He lifted his pale face to the hot sunshine. He breathed in the silken air. Why, I've come home, he thought joyously. He smelled the tang of salt, and he turned to two men who were standing on the platform. "Are we near the sea?" he asked.

They were about to board the train, ragged men carrying parcels wrapped in newspapers. They were young, and as pale as he. They smiled, and one of them answered: "Yes, sir, we sure are. And this here is Florida. Where you from, sir?"

Durant had his answer ready. "From Chicago," he answered. "I'm going to buy a farm down here."

They smiled at him again, with sympathy. They, too, were on their way home, one from Cleveland, the other from Louisville. They had been conscripted labor, working in the war industries. One of them had been traveling for several days, due to the confusion on the railroads. They offered Durant cigarets. One of them sighed. "Sure is fine to see home again, away from that goddamned snow," said the man who had worked in Cleveland. "Thought I'd never get out. Well, sir, it's all over, and we Americans are free again. We've got a new world to make." He glanced at some Negroes who were working on a track, and said sheepishly: "Reckon we'll understand about the colored folks, now. We know all about it, ourselves."

"That's right," said the other young man. "Sometimes you got to die, almost, 'fore you know what it's like to live. Well, like you said, Jack, it's over. Won't be any more sons of bitches ridin' us." He turned to Durant. "I see by the papers this morning they got that bastard up in New York. That Chief Magistrate, Carlson. He was sure a bastard, wasn't he?"

The sun was no longer hot, the air no longer like silk. There were no flowers and no palms, no live oaks, no light. Durant's throat had thickened. He said, very faintly and slowly: "The Chief Magistrate? What happened to him?"

The young men laughed delightedly, and shifted their parcels. "Why, sir, didn't you hear? It happened yesterday afternoon. Reckon you didn't get no papers on this train. He was in New York, disbanding that lousy Picked Guard, and he walked out of the City Hall, and was just going down the steps, and someone shot him. Never rightly found out who. Saw a photograph of it in the papers. There he was a-lyin' on the steps, with his head shot away. Served the son of a bitch right, didn't it, after all he had done—"

After all he had done.

The train whistled. The young men jumped aboard, and Durant, feeling broken and sick, and with a fluttering darkness before his eyes, followed them. He stumbled back to his seat, automatically felt under it for his coat and his box of gold. Then he sat there, immobile and stricken to the heart, as the train began to move.

The two young men were sitting across from him. They were talking of Arthur Carlson, and Durant listened. "Reckon we'll never forget that dog," one was saying. "We don't never dare forget. He was worse than the others. Thought up all kinds of bitchy things—Yes, sir, worse than all them others put together. I'll be a-tellin' about him to my kids, when I have 'em, and they'll tell it to theirs, too. We'll never forget."

After all he had done.

Anathema. A symbol of terror and slavery and death, which America would always remember. She would remember that symbol at every election; she would listen for Carlson's accents in the voice of any ambitious politician. If there were, ever again, any rumors of wars, of "emergencies," of "crises," America would remember Arthur Carlson, and there would be a swift end to mountebanks and hysterical screechers in the night. Anathema, forever.

More and more palms were darting by the windows. There were hedges of hibiscus, but Durant did not see them. There were turquoise lakes and avenues of live oaks and flashing glimpses of aquamarine seas, but he did not see them. There were white beaches, and beyond them, the dark purple ribbon of the Gulf Stream, but still he did not see them. He saw Arthur Carlson on the steps of the City Hall, a dead and bleeding and shattered symbol of all that was most horrible in the memory of America.

Now a wave of the bitterest hatred swept over Durant. They aren't worthy of him! he thought. They never deserved him. He clenched his fists; it was not until he tasted blood in his mouth that he became aware that he had been biting his lips savagely. There was salt on his cheek and a red mist in his eyes, and a hard lump in his throat.

There would be paintings of that shameful death on the stony steps. There would be novel written about Arthur Carlson, and biographies, and there would be moving pictures featuring the monstrousness of his regime. He would be in all the history books in the schoolrooms. He would be the Horror from which America had escaped. He would be a symbol to all the world of what could happen to men if they became, once again, lethargic and indifferent, careless of their liberties, greedy, envious and stupid.

Those who had known what he was would never dare speak. They would never dare, in exonerating him, lift the blackness and fury of that symbol from the minds of the people. They would keep silent when he was cursed and reviled. They would only listen when his crimes were recited. In themselves, they would honor him, and remember, but they would hold their tongues forever. For the sake of America, for the sake of him who had delivered America. He had willed it, in his love for his country, and in his courage.

Durant could again hear Carlson's voice, grave and strong: "I, like my brethren, offer up my life and my body for the laws of our fathers: calling upon God to be speedily merciful to our nation."